SEMPITERNAL
THE NINTH LEGION

A Vampire Saga By
S. GOSHEA

Sempiternal- The Ninth Legion

Published by CreateSpace Publishing Platform

Cover Art: Ravenborn, at SelfPubBookCover
Editor: Becca Bates Editing

ACKNOWLEDGEMENTS

Caitlin Prouty Lund: To my best friend. Thank you for always being here for me to bounce ideas off of. Talking things out with you is how the stories in my head begin to unfold.

Selena Folkard: To another one of my best friends. Thank you for the time and effort you put in as my personal editor. Without you, I don't think I would have had the confidence to put this book out. Book two here we come.

Pamala Conrad: Thank you for taking the time to read the very first uber rough draft of Sempiternal. All your input and time was greatly appreciated.

Kevin and Chance Goshea: Without your constant love and support, I don't think I would have made it this far.

I'd like to thank my parents for always supporting every little crazy think I do.

Anika Willmanns – Beautiful cover work as always. Can't wait to work on book two cover with you.

Becca Bates: Thank you for the great suggestions and overall awesome editing job. Editors really do help bring it all together.

SEMPITERNAL
THE NINTH LEGION

Prologue

Michael and his brother Riley came to the states over a century ago. Brother's by blood, they joined up with a group of nine males of the Ninth Legion led by a warrior named Justin. He has reached out across Europe and to other legions recruiting for the states. He's a master of swords as well as computers, and a pureblood from old royal bloodlines.

Derek, Cash, Brian, Riley and Michael are headed out on a raid tonight. Michael feels Riley getting restless and dangerous again. He knows he will need to keep a close eye on his brother in the coming days. The last time Riley got out of control, he had a hard time cleaning up the mess his brother left behind. Moartea and humans alike don't stand a chance when Riley goes dark. Maybe darker is more appropriate, because his brother is pretty damn terrifying most of the time.

They get ready, head up the stairs, and come out of the bunker ready to take off on their next mission.

"I need to hit the club first," Cash says.

"Me too," Brian adds.

"I could use blood." Riley smiles.

"Alright, we'll hit Distortion but we're out in twenty," Derek says.

They appear in the alley a couple of blocks from the club. They walk down the street and enter through the back door of the club. The five of them sit in the VIP section. Michael and Derek order drinks, while Cash and Brian have already spotted females and head off to feed.

Michael looks over and sees Riley scanning the crowd. Most females won't come anywhere near him. His brother may be good looking, but the only females that seem willing to approach him are the prostitutes. Speaking of, Riley's spotted one and she's met his gaze. She flashes him a huge smile as she walks towards them.

"Looking to party handsome?" the red head asks.

Riley nods and gets up.

He watches as Riley heads out back to the alley with her. He finishes his drink, rubs his face, and then gets up.

"He's riding that edge again. Isn't he, Mike?" Derek looks up at him.

Michael takes a deep breath. "Yeah."

Derek shakes his head and goes for another shot.

He isn't the only one that's going to be watching Riley closely. He comes out the back door only to find the onslaught is already underway, and that female has figured out quickly she's in way over her head.

Riley has her pinned to the wall and her mouth covered. She's stuck until he's finished with her. As Riley finishes up, he flips her around and runs his hands around her throat.

"Leave her," Michael yells out as he starts towards them.

Riley turns around growling.

Met with his brother's red glare. *Great.* At least his eyes aren't black. If they were, she'd already be dead. He shoves Riley away from her. "I said, leave her."

Riley stalks off.

Michael shakes his head. *Killing where we feed, what the fuck is wrong with him?*

He pulls the girl up, seals her throat, and then locks his gaze onto hers so he can wipe her memory. "You came out to meet with a trick but he didn't follow you. You're tired so you're going home."

Humans are so weak. He sends her on her way and heads back into the club. He looks over at their table and sees Riley sitting with Derek pounding shots.

Great. Let's add alcohol to the mix of crazy he's already got going on in his head tonight. "This outta be fun," he mumbles as he slides back into the booth.

They finally get to the warehouse they're hitting. The Moartea count has been ten to fifteen varying.

"Michael, Riley, you two take the back. The three of us will take the front," Derek says.

Riley hasn't said two words to him since the club. No doubt he's pissed he couldn't finish that female off. Michael knows it's because of what that female did to him in the past, but he's tired of cleaning that shit up.

The two of them come in the back and are met with three Moartea. The brother's draw their swords. Michael faces off with one that isn't armed and takes it down quickly. As he takes its head off and it turns to ash, he looks to Riley who has already taken out the two others.

They continue to move through the warehouse towards the commotion coming from around the corner. Derek, Cash, and Brian are facing off with eight Moartea. Riley runs in, joining the mess, and he's right behind him.

When the last one is dusted, Michael realizes they're staring past him. He turns around only to find Riley dripping with the blood of two new human recruits he's just torn to pieces. He has a sadistic smile across his face as he materializes out. The others shake their heads and start searching the warehouse for any intel they can find.

Moartea are demon descendants of Cain that corrupt human souls. Once the demon inhabits the human's body it eventually burns out the humanity within. When they're struck through the heart with silver and their head is taken off, they turn to ash—returning them to hell. Sort of a natural supernatural clean up.

The human recruits are another story entirely. Their bodies will be left behind and a murder investigation will be started. This is another place they'll need to torch to cover up what happened.

Maybe if he can focus Riley's energy elsewhere, it will help him control the beast within.

Chapter 1

I'm standing outside in the Gas Lamp District of downtown San Diego waiting for Mary and Danielle to get out of the Rubio's bathroom. I really want a cigarette but I keep telling myself I've quit. Turning thirty five, getting divorced, and trying to start my life over again is playing hell on me. Maybe this wasn't the best time to decide to quit smoking.

Looking around, I'm still amazed at how I ended up standing here today. Me, Skylar Coppola, newest member of the single elite, out on the town looking for who the hell knows what.

Ran into the ex about a month ago. He was with some twenty something he's messing around with. Our divorce finalized six months ago and he's already on chick number four, I think. I say more power to him. He's probably making up for lost time, but personally I think he's lonely and looking for something he's never going to find.

Right before I started the divorce papers I reconnected with my best friend from high school, Danielle. She was in an abusive relationship and looking for an opportunity to leave. She just needed a roommate so she could afford to move out and still be in the city.

Luckily for us, a doctor she works with was looking to rent out his penthouse while he's doing work overseas. It's a beautiful 2500sq' condo right in the heart of downtown San Diego. It's a two bedroom master suite on the sixth floor of an exclusive condo complex. There's also a great view of the city from the floor to ceiling windows.

Everything had seemed to come together like it was fated to be. He didn't even end up charging us rent. We only pay HOA dues and the utilities. I figure it must be because he feels sorry for the two thirty five year olds starting their lives over from scratch, and I think he may be interested in starting something with Danielle when he comes back.

As soon as I had myself all set up, I handed my husband divorce papers, packed up my things, and moved out all in the same day. He was shocked, but didn't put up any kind of fight. He had more of a….whatever, about time kind of attitude. But that pretty much sums up my entire marriage in a nutshell.

Once my things were all moved into the condo I felt free in a sense, but also bogged down by the past at the same time. I got my bed all put together and then took off to roam the neighborhood. Running through the past in my mind I felt like a complete failure trying not to sink into a depressive state, wondering what was coming next and hoping that it could only get better.

I walked for hours that first night on my own. As it got later and later I began to notice how the types of people on the streets changed. They went from older yuppie types, to the punks, homeless, drug dealers, and overall hard asses. Then I started to notice even more. Late at night is when the streets really seem to come alive.

This would be that harder edge crowd around me. Well….that, and the clueless club kids.

About a week in, on one of my nightly mind clearing walks, I came across an alley entrance and noticed a couple near a dumpster. The guy was buttoning up his pants and the woman he had against the brick wall was bleeding from the neck. He leaned into her, and then when he stepped away her neck was no longer bleeding. He spoke a few words to her, and then she stumbled off down the alley.

When he turned and looked over at me, he had bright golden eyes and blood on his lips. I was a good twenty feet from him and realized I was way too close, but I couldn't get my feet to move in any direction. Away would have been good, but instead I just froze and stood there like an idiot. In my head I heard *vampire,* just as if someone had actually spoken it to me.

The guy came at me fast, pushing me up against the building. His pupils dilated until all I could see was a thin yellow ring around them. In a calm tone, he told me I had come out to get dinner and then decided I wasn't hungry any longer. He said I was going to go home and go to bed.

The voice came to me again. *Look into his eyes, don't move.* So I froze. Then the guy just stalked off. I wasn't sure what the hell happened exactly, but I ended up with the worst headache I've ever had.

After that night, I knew other things existed in the world which may be hard to explain in most people's sense of reality. But I will definitely be keeping everything I've seen up until now to myself. I don't need to end up in a mental institution.

I haven't stopped my late night walks, and for whatever reason, I sense when vampires are close. If that's in fact what they are. Whenever I sense them I go in the opposite direction. I tend to feel drawn to them in a way, my gut tells me to go towards them while my head has my feet taking me in the opposite direction. I've always been a fan of vampire books, TV, and movies, but it's a different story when you finally see one standing before you. Yet seeing is still far from actually believing.

Now and then I still see them. It's the yellow eyes—they all seem to have them. There was only one other time I interrupted one. To this day, it makes me smile when I think about it. Terrifying, but intensely hot at the same time.

This vampire was in the middle of tearing something apart. He was larger than any of the others I had seen before. He had some serious knife skills and was using them on this….thing is all I can describe it as. Once again I just stood and watched in awe of what I was witnessing.

He was beautiful, but deadly at the same time. The thing disappeared as soon as he cut its head off. As he stood up, his eyes met mine and he came at me fast. Covered in blood and smelling of the thing he had just ended, he towered over me. Muscular build, tattoos on his neck, and his head was shaved.

I wasn't scared of him exactly, he seemed familiar in some bazaar way. Admittedly, I was attracted to him.

Pushing my back up against the wall, he paused for a moment, smiled, and then leaned in. Fangs came across my neck and he growled. My body warmed at the thought of him biting into me.

He pulled back to look into my eyes, and then kissed me hard. It took me a second to process I was kissing him back, but I put my hand on his chest and slowly pushed him away. That got me a strange little smile.

A hand was placed against my cheek causing me to gaze into his beautiful eyes. His thumb slowly came across my bottom lip, and then leaned back in kissing me softly this time. That kiss took my breath away. When I looked back up at him, he dropped his brow and slightly shook his head.

Next thing I knew, he was trying to get into my head like the other one had before. Once again all I ended up with was a headache.

Maybe I wish it would have worked on me, then I could have forgotten about everything I've seen and felt up to this point. But the thing is, those first couple of months on my own, taking the late night walks helped me concentrate on the world around me instead of dwelling on my past. Being able to watch this other world that exists alongside of ours has kind of saved me from myself.

"Damn they're taking forever in there," I mutter to myself.

As I glance down the sidewalk, the crowd seems to be parting the way for something. Then I see what looks like three Chargers linebackers coming towards me. All three tower over the crowd. Gym six times a week easy. Two in jeans, combat boots, and leather jackets, while the other one is in black cargo pants, combat boots, and a Dickies jacket.

The guy furthest away from me has blond spiked hair. Cute with soft facial features. Less menacing then the other two.

The one in the middle is the largest. Short black hair, a little longer on top, spiked into a short fauxhawk. Very handsome and giving off a dark sexy vibe. The whole punk look is definitely working for him, black plugs in his ears and a lip ring included.

Then there's the one closest to me. The edgiest looking of the three. His dark brown hair is brushed back from his face. A few pieces of his bangs have fallen forward, resting against his cheek. It looks like he hasn't shaved in a couple of days. And despite the fact he looks like he wants to kill something, he's model gorgeous. Chiseled jawline, hard muscled body, and he walks with such confidence.

Out of the three of them, the homicidal looking one is the most attractive. I can't take my eyes off him. Figures. I seem to like the assholes.

Women on the street are staring at them, while the men can't seem to get out of the way quick enough. It's comical watching them try to avoid eye contact at all costs, even if they just stare straight up into the sky like complete idiots.

I can't make myself look away or even move out of their way. The closer they get I see their yellow eyes and I feel what they are. These vampires are huge and dangerous like the one I kissed months ago in the alley. I know I need to move out of the way and stop starring at the one coming right at me, but I just can't make myself move from his path.

Mr. Homicidal comes so close to me his hand brushes against mine. I get a jolt of electricity that begins to course through my entire body. I stare down at my hand, and then turn around just as I swear I hear him hiss.

The glare shot back at me is intense. Kind of look that says he wants to kill me where I stand. Charming.

"Well excuse me for touching you," I bark as I hold his glare. It's probably not a good idea to start something with the huge angry vampire, but damn he pisses me off. "Try moving out of the way next time asshole. I was actually standing here first." I rub my hand. "And try shaving, goatees are stupid," I mumble.

Yeah, real smooth.

Now I'm all irritated, thanks a lot jerk-face. I try to relax and remember that tonight is all about having fun, and these brats better hurry up or I'm walking back home. We're supposed to be at Club Distortion before Mary's bouncer friend gets off or the only way in is going to be through a huge line.

Think it and they will appear. I'll have to remember that. "Damn, finally you two emerge."

We start walking towards the club.

"Sorry Sky, D ran into her ex and the two wouldn't shut up." Mary rolls her eyes and shakes her head.

I look over at Danielle and raise my brow.

"Not Tim, it was Daniel," Danielle blurts out. "I just wanted to make sure he's doing alright. His girlfriend just broke up with him."

"Ah, Daniel. He'd be fine if he'd quit pining away for you and actually try to move on with somebody else." I take a deep breath. "We really need some new guys."

"Ha. Does this mean you're actually going to be looking for someone tonight?" Danielle asks.

"Sure, why not?"

They laugh.

"I'll believe it when I see it," Mary says.

"Ditto," Danielle adds.

We're almost there. I hope we aren't too late, I really need a couple drinks. We come around the corner and the line at Distortion wraps around the side of the building. Luckily for us, Mary's bouncer friend is still at the door. She waves to him and he motions her over.

"Hey Roger." Mary walks up and hugs him.

"I'm off in thirty, then I'll come find you," he says.

"I'll be waiting." She kisses his cheek. Then she loops her arms around us and pulls us inside.

Mary and Danielle are both dressed sexy. Short skirts, barely there tanks, and thigh high boots. Whereas, I'm sporting black cargo pants, a black t-shirt showing minimal cleavage, and my burgundy skate shoes that almost match my hair. Meh….whatever, I'm just here to drink anyways. I'm on my way to become a bona fide alcoholic.

As we come to the end of the hall, the large expanse of the club is laid out before us. Bar to the left, VIP lounge in the back on the right, and then straight ahead and down three stairs is the dance floor. It's dim in here with colored lights everywhere.

"Hey D, I'm going to hit the bar. I need a drink," I yell out over the music and I point at the bar.

I'm still irritated about the guy and his attitude about being touched by a measly human girl. Whatever, maybe vampires don't like to be touched, or….maybe that vampire doesn't like to be touched. Because the one that kissed me in the alley sure didn't seem to mind it. Hmmm, thinking about him makes me want to revisit that alley in the near future.

"Come on Sky, you said you were going to have fun tonight," Danielle says as she tugs on my arm.

"I am. I just need to loosen up first if I'm going to be expected to go down there with you two."

"Alright. You better or we're coming back up here and dragging your ass down there," Mary says.

They hit the dance floor while I head to the bar, making minimal eye contact with everyone as I weave my way through the crowd. I lean up against the bar and sigh. The bartender's eyes meet mine. A smile spreads across his face as he bypasses quite a few impatient patrons on his way over.

Nice. "Shot of Jack and a Guinness if you have one."

"Sure, comin' up."

He's cute. Now him….maybe. I pay him, down the shot, and then grab my beer. I walk over to the railing and look out over the dance floor—taking in the scene. I guess it's more of a dance pit. The club is running metal tonight and the crowd is eating it up.

I watch as Mary and Danielle dance with each other and a couple of guys around them, smiling and laughing. I wish I could be like that for a change and just let all my shit go. But the last time I let go….yeah, so not going there again anytime soon.

Picturing myself with any of these guys makes me cringe. They all look so damn pathetic. Ha, maybe that's what I look like and why it's all I seem to attract.

As I scan the crowd, my eyes lock on the three huge vampires from earlier. They're sitting back in the VIP section. A girl with a micro mini, ten pounds of makeup, and a sway in her hips that says she's seen a lot of action, is trying to pick up the blond one. She's dismissed as the waitress serves them drinks.

They're all business, I don't know why they even bother coming in here. Well, probably because it's loud, not to mention the hookers and other willing slutty girls around.

I've spent the last thirty minutes staring in their direction. My eyes meet the douche bag vampire's eyes. Man, if he glares any harder his eyes are going to fall right out of his head. I finish my beer and toss it in the trash.

"Once again, excuse me for touching you asshole." I shake my head.

Thankfully I still have my cigarettes with me. Looks like tonight's going to break my three months of being smoke free. I'm almost to the back door when my back is pushed up against the wall. A heavy arm come across my chest, making it hard to breathe. I look up and meet the cold black stare of Mr. Homicidal.

I close my eyes as I take in an intoxicating blend of pine and leather. His body is huge and pretty much engulfing mine within it.

As he leans in, his gaze narrows. "See something you like, female?" he says in a deep voice.

There's a glimmer of something else behind that hard, "I'm going to fuck you up" look. Maybe desire?

Oh no, that's so not happening. I struggle to push him off, but I'm not gaining any ground. "Uh, not interested. Get off me," I glare tying to be as menacing as he is.

"I've seen you looking at me. Why don't we take this outside?" He growls as he presses himself into me.

Crap.

The hard length of him is slowly moving against me. His breath is warm and smells of alcohol. My lips part and I begin breathing deeply. God I need this, need him.

What! Get a grip here, Sky.

What I need, is to get it together. No way am I going to be another one of this guy's whores. Unlike the others he uses, I'll get to remember everything he does to me. And this one seems like he likes it rough.

"Get….off me now." I continue to struggle but I'm not making any more headroom. I sigh and relax my body. I'm not going anywhere until he wants me to.

The warmth of his breath comes against my neck. My body tenses up as his tongue slowly makes its way up to my ear. This should gross me out, but instead a strange fluid current begins to flow through me everywhere his flesh meets mine. My hands find their way to his belt loops, drawing him into me, desiring so much more. Yep, I want him.

What the hell is that about? I must be going crazy. How freakin' much did I drink? Like one shot and a beer, that's nothing....seriously.

In a deep sultry voice almost on a purr he says, "You smell and taste so sweet. I want all of you, female."

Damn, he's killing me here.

As he slowly pulls away from me, his cheek softly brushes mine. I turn towards him just as his lips pass mine. Passion and longing are gripping at the core of me, drawing me to him.

He lingers, barely letting our lips touch. He takes a slight breath and his arm drops from my chest. Arms snake around my waist pulling me in even tighter.

I close my eyes and press my lips against his. My mind is swimming. All I can think about is having his lips on mine and being completely with him. I place my hand on his cheek and softly kiss him.

A tightness spreads across his whole body like a wave.

Meeting his intense gaze, I try to pull away again, but hands are still tightly gripping my waist. I bring my finger up millimeters from him and give him the meanest face and glare I have.

"Listen up, vampire, I have no desire to be taken out to some dirty alley and used like a common whore. You may be hot, but that shit isn't going to happen. You feel me? And you will let me go now."

He looks down, brow raised.

Not sure which part struck him stupid exactly. The evil look in his eyes has faded for the moment, and the side of his lip begins to curl up to a smile. As soon as his grip loosens I push him off of me.

We're still close as we stare into each other's eyes. Neither one of us seem willing to move. All I want him to do is grab me up and kiss me hard. I'm completely delusional at this point, and need to get the hell away from him as quickly as I can before I do something stupid, or stupider than….whatever the hell all of that was.

"And don't bother trying to mess with my head, because for whatever reason, that shit doesn't work on me." I turn around and head back to the bar.

All I want to do is go back over to him. It's this crazy pull in the center of my chest. I rub my face and try to get the bartender's attention. "I need three shots of Jack and another Guinness please."

"Rough night?" Bartender cutie drops his brow.

"Meh, I'm good. Thanks."

"Hey baby," some guy says next to me.

I roll my eyes and don't even bother looking over. He gets a talk to the hand as I start pounding shots.

"Ooookay," the guy mutters and walks away.

****

Riley watches as that female sits down at the bar. His whole body tenses up and he about loses it the second a male approaches her.

"Thought you found a female?" Derek asks.

"Nah, just a toy that got boring real quick," he says still glaring at the male standing next to her.

But she hadn't been boring, had she? She was fearless, demanding, and so beautiful. He could feel her desire and longing, but she refused to let him have her. Never in his life has he felt a female longing to be with him. She knows what he is, but how is that even possible?

He likes his females terrified it makes the sex so much better. Only thing that gets him up really. Yeah, he's an asshole. Not like they'll remember how rough it was anyways. They would just be a little sore in the morning….if they lived through it. Sometimes the feel of their lust begins to tug at his soul, dragging him to a dark place he can't be, and then he snaps—or rather they do. Taking them from behind seems to work out best, that way there's no touching or kissing. He can't stand anyone's hands on him.

Did I really just let that human female kiss me?

Trying to distract his mind from that female, he rubs his face and looks over at Derek. "I take it Cash found something?" He's still trying to distract his mind from that female.

"Yeah, he's out back with a blonde."

Nobody talks to him like that, not even his own flesh and blood brother. They all know better. He wants to talk to her more, look into her beautiful blue eyes, run his hands through her long burgundy hair, feel her lips on his, and he wants to take all of her.

Damn, there goes my cock again. I need some fucking release before I lose it.

The red head from earlier strolls up.

Yep, she'll do.

He nods and they head to the bathrooms. He takes one last look at the female at the bar. He meets her gaze just before he rounds the corner to the bathrooms.

"It's a hundred for sex, handsome." She goes for his cock.

With a quick motion he catches her by wrist. "No touching on your end, got it?" Money exchanges hands. He fights the alcohol clawing its way back up his throat as this human's lust begins seeping into him. Just one of the many reasons why he can't stand them touching him.

"Sure, whatever you want baby."

"And no talking," Riley growls.

Turning her around, he unbuttons his pants, shoves her skirt up, and drives into her all at once—fast and hard. She cries out, trying to pull away from him. Tightening his grip around her waist, his other hand makes its way to her mouth.

Fangs are sunk deep into her neck and he finds himself leveling out as he takes his fill. He seals her up and continues thrusting his hips into her, but he just can't get there with this female.

Letting his mind go right where it longs to be, he pictures the female from earlier. Her beautiful face, the way her lips felt against his, the softness in her touch, the longing in her eyes, the feel of her in his arms, and her desire to have him burning through his whole body.

Finally, his release comes. He pulls himself together, wipes the female's memory, and then leaves as her body crumples to the bathroom floor.

Shoving the door open, he heads back to the table.

She knew what he was, even feared him at first. But then she flipped some switch inside of anger and aggression as she spat her words at him. That surge of passion and desire threw him right out of his boots, onto his ass.

Riley's still all tied up inside. He's never wanted any female as much as he has to have that one. Humans are for feeding and release. Other than that, humans are weak. Useless. Cattle. But that female, he will see her again.

Good thing she dismissed the male that came up to her. If he had gotten any closer, he would have found himself ripped to pieces out back. He must be going absolutely bat-shit crazy.

Fuck. I need something to do before I walk right over there and make and ass out of myself in front of everyone. Not that he really gives a shit what anyone thinks.

"Justin called, there's been some activity up north of Bryce Canyon. Were supposed to check it out," Derek says.

"Let's get Cash and go. I need to fucking kill something," he says.

That female's eyes stay with his until the moment he goes out the back. It takes everything inside of him to leave her there. But he'll check on that female later since he lifted her I.D. from her back pocket. Skylar Coppola, 5th Avenue.

Chapter 2

I wake up with a crazy headache. I look over at the nightstand and see two aspirin, a glass of water, and my ID.

I take a deep breath. "D you're an angel."

I wonder where she found my ID. I pop the aspirin and then head into the shower. All I can think about is that guy from last night with his hands all over me, the almost kiss, and his huge erection. I wanted him. Still do.

Screw it. I should have just went into the alley with him. Maybe he could have made me feel something, because right now I'm numb and life is just passing me by. Yep, I'm totally thinking crazy again.

I get dressed and head into the kitchen. Danielle is already at work. The note of the fridge says they want to go out again tonight. Why not but maybe this time I'll hold off on all of the alcohol.

Fridge is empty, good time to hit the grocery store and distract my mine from all of that craziness. No such luck. The entire time I'm shopping all I can think about is that guy. But he wasn't a guy, was he, and all he wanted to do was use me. Whatever, new experience I guess.

Once back home, I put everything away, and then go to my room and pick up a book. At this point, I'm trying to do anything to get his face out of my head.

Danielle finally walks in the door around seven. I'm already dressed and ready to go. I haven't said anything to her about the guy/vampire I met at the club, or that I want him to use me like some whore. I'll just keep all that craziness to myself for now.

"You're going with us, yay." She comes over and hugs me, jumping up and down.

I laugh. "Yep, I'm going to keep going out until I remember how to have fun again. What do you think of that?"

"Excellent. I'll be right back." She heads to her room.

We meet up with Mary at the club. We hang out for a while just talking and drinking. They eventually head out to dance while I continue drinking and staring into the VIP section.

He never shows up. None of them do.

Back at home, I look up and see it's just after midnight. I set my keys down and go for a glass of water.

"What's up with you tonight Sky? You were so happy earlier," Danielle asks.

"It's nothing. I just hoped to see this guy I met the night before."

"What guy? There was a guy?" she says smiling.

"Yeah, this definitely-too-hot-for-me kind of guy."

"Shut up, you're hot."

I laugh. "He's like one of those guys off HBO's Spartacus if you get what I'm trying to say."

"Why didn't you say anything?"

"Meh, maybe I was drunk and imagined the whole thing. He wasn't there tonight so who knows."

"What happened exactly?" She sits down at the table, puts her elbows up, and holds he head in her hands.

I smile, "You look beat. We can talk about it when you get home tomorrow."

She yawns, "Okay, but you're only getting away with this because I'm tired." She gets up to hug me and then heads off to bed.

"Night, D."

"Night, Sky."

Man did he miss out. I was ready to go right up to him and grab him if I had to. Then I would have led him out back and hoped he took over from there. I think I would have actually let him have me right there too. Rough, raw, and overall intense is how I picture the sex with him being. I slide into bed as my mind continues to run in circles until I finally pass out.

****

Riley finds himself irritated. He's supposed to have the night off, but Justin has them out checking another spot for Moartea. They took out five on the last job, but even that hasn't cleared his mind of that human female.

He longs to see her again. Skylar. He watched her sleep for hours. She almost woke up when he couldn't take it any longer and pressed his lips against hers. He groans. Soft lips, and the smell of her hair and skin make him long to taste her.

There's this strange urge inside of him to take care of her. He left her aspirin and water next to her bed. He also returned her ID even though he would have preferred to keep it so he could at least look at her whenever he wanted.

She was pretty drunk from what he could tell. It took everything he had not to climb into bed with her and wrap her up in his arms. The longing he has for this female is so foreign.

"Hey, where's your head?" Michael asks as they appear outside the bunker.

Riley glares at his brother. "Here."

He heads to his room. Talking to any of these males about the shit that's going on in his head isn't going to happen. Infatuated with a human female of all things. He'd never hear the end of it. He showers, suits back up, and is hoping he can make it out of the bunker without getting any shit.

"You coming to dinner?" Michael says.

"Nope, busy." He gets by Michael, and is almost to the stairs….Damn.

"Hey, food's ready, where you going?" Derek asks.

"Out," he snaps.

Riley can't get out of here fast enough. He nearly knocks into Derek on his way by. He hardly ever eats with them, yet they always ask him to join them. He feels suffocated by it all. Probably childhood shit, but he just prefers to be on his own.

It's two in the morning and he wonders if she's still awake. He materializes to her bathroom, closes his eyes and listens. Everything's quiet, and as he steps out he can see she's asleep.

He kneels down at her side. She has beautiful ivory skin and is fit like she could be a warrior, sure is tough enough to be one. He wants to sit by her bed all night and protect her while she sleeps. He's patrolled the four block radius around her condo making sure there are no Moartea in the area.

It would be so much easier if he could just bring her back to the bunker. She'd be safer with him. He rubs his face as his brain goes into an over drive of crazy. As he brushes the hair back from her face he leans in to softly kiss her lips.

"You weren't there tonight. I waited for you," she says quietly.

Shit....buuusted. He freezes, and then smiles when he realizes she's still asleep. "Where?" he whispers.

"The club, you weren't there....I came to tell you."

"Tell me what?" He leans in closer.

"That I dream of you, that I want you."

Arms wrap around his neck and he finds his lips back on hers. Her tongue finds its way into his mouth. It all feels strange, but good. He meets her tongue with his and their kiss deepens. As the hunger begins to consume him, she stops abruptly.

When he realizes she's woken up, he materializes out quickly. He just about tore all his clothes off and jumped into bed with her, to finally be completely connected to her. He longs to take that female with everything inside of him.

What the fuck is wrong with him? More crazy shit. How would that have worked out if she opened her eyes and he was in her bed bare and at her neck? He needs to keep his distance from her. He needs more raids, more missions, more killing.

Fuck. I'm losing it.

He needs more shit to occupy his mind. Not that he thinks it's going to help fade this obsession with her, because that's what she's becoming….an obsession.

****

The three of us are headed out to Distortion tonight. It's been a week ago today since I encountered the vampire that has me all wound up inside. I've been fighting the urge to go there every night to look for him. He's all I think about all day, every day. It's totally crazy.

One dream was so vivid: I swear I could feel him on my lips, and actually taste him. When I woke up I saw a brief shadow and then it was gone. Basically, I'm hallucinating about him as well.

When they asked me to come out tonight I jumped at the chance. It threw Danielle for a minute, but she quickly guessed what was going on in my head. She knows how preoccupied I've been all week thinking about the hot guy I met.

We walk into Distortion and it's packed. Music's great and loud as always. Unfortunately, that also means the bar's packed. As soon as I look over I see I'm right. It's going to take forever to get a drink. Danielle and Mary start towards the dance floor and I stop.

"Is he here?" Mary stops and looks around.

I look over at the VIP section. "Nope, not holding my breath either."

"Well if he shows up, make sure you let us know so we can check him out," Danielle says.

"Yeah, you better. No over drinking either. You're turning into an alcoholic," Mary says.

I laugh. "Okay mom. Go dance already. I'm fine." I wave them off as I start towards the bar.

The bartender looks up and smiles at me. He walks right over, ignoring everybody else. "Hey you, you're back."

I smile. "I am, can I get a Jack and……."

"Guinness….I got it." He gets my drinks and sets them down in front of me.

"Thanks." I pull out ten bucks.

He takes my hand in his and closes it around the money. "Nah, it's on me tonight." He winks. "My name's Bret, I'm a friend of Roger's. I get off at midnight. If you're still around would you mind if I came and found you?"

I shrug. "Sure. I'll probably still be here, and thanks again for this." I hold up the shot.

He grabs my other hand and runs his fingers around mine. "It's my ploy to get you to come see me again." He pulls me closer and leans forward. "Is it too forward to ask you for a kiss?"

"Knock yourself out."

"Bret, move your ass," the other bartender barks.

He smiles as he rolls his eyes. He kisses my lips softly and then goes back to work.

Well that was sweet. He is really cute. Anger is shot through the core of me and my body tenses up. *Weird.* I down the shot and grab my beer. I turn around and see that he's here at their table in the back. As usual he's wearing his "Don't fuck with me face."

The goatee is gone. I was right, he looks so much better without it. I long to kiss him and run my hands down his bare chest all the way to his….holy crap. *Shhhh, head.* This time there's another guy with him and the same two from before.

His eyes are on me. All of this is so ridiculous, because I know what he is, and what he wants from me. But maybe that's part of this burning desire I have for him.

I down the rest of my liquid courage and my eyes lock back on his. Yep, still watching me.

"You have no idea the things I want you to do to me vampire," I mutter.

Damn. Am I really going to do this?

Nerves have my stomach twisting up on me. I walk to the back of the club and break eye contact with him as I step out into the alley. I take a deep breath of the cool night air trying to calm my nerves.

The door creaks open and then closes. I turn around and he's already to me. His hands come down on my hips and he licks his lips as his gaze falls to mine.

He walks us to the building on the other side of the alley. We come to a stop as my back hits the wall. He takes my face in his hands and brushes his thumb softly across my lips. I slide my arms around his waist and get a slight smile as he slowly presses his lips to mine.

We begin kissing deeper and deeper.

He wraps me up in his arms, drawing me in as close as he can get me. I feel him throbbing against me. My whole body is tingling and I have butterflies in my stomach. Stuff like this doesn't happen to me….like ever.

He pulls back slightly and puts his forehead to mine.

Wow, I want him, all of him. To feel his skin on mine. He puts his hand on my face again softly caressing my cheek. He seems a little freaked—that can't be a good sign. His hard features have softened, and he seems different tonight.

"You're really beautiful, you know that?" Wow. Can I sound anymore ridiculous?

He smiles. "Since I first met you I've thought of nothing else but feeling you in my arms again."

"Well, that makes this a whole lot easier to say. I've thought about you every day since I met you. I want you, but not here." I shake my head and cringe at the thought of just becoming another one of his whores he screws in an alley. But am I really going to take him back to my place?

Oh yeah. "My place is just a couple blocks up the street." I point.

"I know where you live."

"Okay, weird. But whatever."

"I've watched you sleep," he says as his gaze burns into mine.

I smile. "Well, if you don't want to freak a girl out, you should keep that kind of stuff to yourself, vampire."

"Riley."

"What?"

"My name….is Riley."

"Ah, my name is…."

"Skylar, I know." He leans in and kisses me again.

Good thing he already knows my name, because I've completely forgotten who the hell I am.

I pull away slightly. "I think we need to go now or we won't make it back to my place. Will you walk home with me?"

He nods.

I text both girls on the walk home. I let them know I'm turning my phone off so they can't bug the crap out of me, and that I'll be needing a little privacy for an hour or so.

He gets on his phone. "Hey, business has come up….Yeah, before dawn."

Hmmm, business. I guess I get it. But what the hell did he mean when he said he's watched me sleep. The walk to the condo is quiet. He keeps his distance and looks like he's searching the streets for something. There aren't many people on the street right now.

We come to the front of my building and the doorman nods as he holds the door open. The ride up the elevator is just as quiet, and as we come inside it gets even more awkward.

I set my keys down, look over at him, and he's staring right at me. Right….vampire. Sex. Blood. He probably just wants to get this over with and split. I'm just business, right? I take a deep breath, my nerves are getting the better of me.

He narrows his gaze. "You're scared of me now, here in your home?"

It seems to be more of a statement then an actual question. "No, more of….well, what if I'm not….you know, good I guess." Good God. I did not just say that out loud.

He doesn't say anything, he crosses the distance between us and pulls me into his arms. As soon as our lips meet, all rational thoughts are gone except for being with him. I'm instantly ready for him; Thank God his body seems to be screaming the same thing.

Large arms swoop me up like I weigh nothing and he brings me to my bedroom. Once there his hands roam my body. His hands come up my sides pulling off my shirt, then my bra comes off next. He runs his thumbs across my breasts as his hands come back down my sides.

"You're so soft and beautiful, I want to feel more of you," he says on my lips.

I take his jacket off of him and find he's fully armed. Interesting. He begins pulling off his weapons and setting them down on the dresser, never breaking eye contact.

I pull his shirt off and then run my hands down his chest. He growls and a smile spreads across my face. He begins kissing my neck, and as soon as I grip him I feel him tense up as his fangs glide across my neck.

A deep growl vibrates though my whole body.

I move my hand back up and begin to unbutton his jeans. The feeling of his skin against mine is sensation overload. I still feel this crazy current and warmth that follows everywhere our flesh meets.

The rest of our clothing is shed and he walks me backwards to the bed. I climb up, with him crawling up after me. The hunger in his eyes is making me a little nervous. Not enough to stop what is about to be all kinds of good, I'm sure.

Riley comes all the way up and hovers over me, stopping just as the warm hard length of him begins pressing against me. I run my hands across his back feeling every muscles on the way down.

He kisses down my neck, cups my breast in his hand, and then moves down to swirl his tongue around my nipple. Soft kisses begin moving up my body back to my lips.

"Can I go here now?" Riley says as his hand slides down between my legs.

"Yes," I gasp.

The kiss become hard and then he comes inside with one sharp thrust. He arches up moaning as I dig my nails into his back.

I tense up and cry out.

Everything stops as he looks down at me. "Are you okay? Did I hurt you?" he rambles out.

He's about to pull out when I wrap my legs around him and just try to breathe through the pain. It's all a good pain but....yeah, he's pretty large and I need a minute.

Taking a minute to catch my breath, I smile up at him. "No, everything is fine. I just need a minute."

Riley comes back down on my lips softly. Then he begins moving in me slowly while kissing me deeply. I figure it's because he's worried about hurting me again. But I feel him making love to me….and yeah, really can't be there in my head right now.

I gently push up on him and urge him onto his back. He looks at me confused for a second, until I climb up on top of him. Then he smiles up at me with the sexiest smile I've ever seen, I melt.

Dang it. What the hell is he doing to me?

I feel so many emotions swimming around inside of me, and I swear they're coming from him, because there's no way I'd ever admit that it's me with these crazy feelings. Love? Really?

I move my hand down and grab ahold of him. Then I come down on him hard. I grab onto his chest as he thrusts his hips up into me.

He runs his hands up my thighs as I begin to move on him, riding him hard. I'm met with a sexy smile as he pulls me down to his lips.

We kiss as he continues to move under me. I sit back up as his rhythm begins to quicken, his whole body tightens up and we lose ourselves together. He's so loud I swear the entire sixth floor can hear him. I tense up cursing myself when I feel him warm inside of me.

Oh crap. Can vampires get humans pregnant? Guess that's a conversation a smart girl has before the sex. Yeah….sex with a vampire, because there's anything normal about any of this.

He runs his hands slowly from my thighs, up my back, until he reaches my face, and he pulls me down to his lips.

I kiss him, then I pull up to look into his eyes. I see something, or rather feel something, a warm grip around my heart that fills my entire chest. Love….I feel love, I swear I do. More crazy thoughts coming from the girl that just had sex with a huge, obviously dangerous, but very gorgeous vampire.

I slide off of him and he pulls me into his side. His arms wrap around me tightly, and I feel warm and safe. I rest my head on his chest and run my fingers over his stomach tracing his muscles.

"I didn't know it could be like that," Riley says shaking his head.

"Um, like what?" I will admit it was pretty damn great.

"Perfect, the way we fit together. I feel….I don't know, I can't find the words." He squeezes me tighter.

I know these guys have women all the time. I saw him take a prostitute into the bathrooms the night I met him. "Riley?"

"Yeah?" He runs his fingers up and down my arm.

"Don't you have women….like all the time?"

Turning his head towards me and pulling my chin up with his finger, he waits until my gaze meets his. "You are the first female I have ever been with like this, and….."

He stops talking, probably due to the look I'm currently sporting on my face. He turns his head and looks up at the ceiling.

Is this super badass guy getting all shy on me? I sit up on my elbow so I can look down at him. Damn, he's pretty. I place my hand on his face and pull him back towards me. He finally looks at me.

I smile. "And what Riley?"

He sighs and breaks eye contact again. "You are the first female I have ever kissed."

I try to hide the shock on my face this time. I lean in and kiss his lips softly. I like that nobody else has been here before, like his lips are mine.

What the hell am I thinking now? How could any of this even be possible?

He kisses me deeper and wraps me up tightly in his arms, I fall back pulling him on me. This time I let him make love to me, and boy does he. The feelings I have when I'm with him make me want to let go of all the crap in my past and just be here with him now. I've never felt this much love and passion with anybody in my entire life.

I look over at the clock. It's two in the morning and we've had sex for three hours straight. So crazy. It seems like he could literally go all night if he wanted to.

I run my hand across his cheek. "I'm glad you shaved. I didn't like that scrubby look you had going on."

He smiles. "I know. I shaved for you." He rubs his nose on mine and kisses me again.

I lower my brow. "What? How did you know I didn't like it?"

"I heard you on the street. You told me I looked stupid." He grimaces.

"Not that you look stupid, that it was stupid. You have really good hearing don't you?" I bite the side of my lip.

He laughs. "Yeah."

"I better watch what I say then."

He leans in closer. "I like kissing you."

"It's hard to believe you've never kissed anybody before tonight, because you're really good at it." I smile on his lips. "I could kiss you forever."

"I might hold you to that, and I never said I hadn't kissed anybody before tonight."

I pull back slightly and narrow my gaze. "I don't get it."

"I said you were the first female I ever kissed. Tonight is not the first time I've kissed you."

"Well, we didn't really kiss at the clu…." I remember what he said on the street about watching me sleep, and the dream I had about us kissing that woke me up. "You were here before weren't you? In my room?"

"Yes."

"You kissed me while I was sleeping?" I raise my brow.

"Yes." He runs his hand across my cheek and then hangs his head. "I couldn't stop myself after you told me you wanted me."

My face drops. I bring my arm across my eyes and take a deep breath. What the hell else have I said to him while I was sleeping? Because I've had some pretty crazy vivid dreams about what I want to do to him.

He pulls my arm down. "Sorry."

"Sorry?"

"I know I shouldn't have been here, but I wanted to see you again."

"I'm just worried about what kind of crazy things I might have said to you in my sleep."

His smiles wide. "Why? What kind of crazy things do you think about me in your sleep?"

I laugh. "So not going there with you, vampire."

"We've already come this far, how much crazier can it get?"

"Hmmm, not sure how to answer that exactly." I yawn. "I'm so tired," I admit reluctantly. I'm not ready for him to leave yet.

He slides off next to me pulling me back into his arms.

"Can you stay until I fall asleep?" I run my arm around him and squeeze him to me.

"Yes." He pulls me in tighter. "I love the feeling of you in my arms."

"And I love being in them." I snuggle into him.

Even throwing the L word out there at all is scary as hell. Weird how it feels so comfortable to be with him. It's going to be sad when it's over, but how much time can a human and a vampire have really?

****

Riley feels dawn approaching. He has less than an hour to get back to the bunker. He just can't bring himself to move her from his arms. Her warm bare flesh against his is driving him mad. He wants to take her again so badly, but she's exhausted. Unable to stop himself, he's already woken her up twice to take her again.

No idea why the hell he'd admitted all that shit to her. This human is driving him over the edge, of what….he has no idea. It's so easy to talk to her. He smiles. Maybe it's because he wants to sit gazing into her beautiful face as he listens to the sound of her voice.

He gently eases her off his chest and instantly feels cold and empty. What the hell? Being close to her makes him feel calm, whole.

He gets dressed and materializes near a florist four blocks over. He walks down the block and looks in the florist's window. Good, nobody's inside. He goes around to the alley and appears inside to find her the perfect white rose.

Appearing back in her room he finds a sheet of paper, writes a note, and leaves the rose. He softly kisses her lips one more time before leaving. He runs his hand down her face and is still having a hard time leaving her.

Nothing will ever keep him from her, except maybe the sun. Nature's fucked up way of masking the supernatural. He appears back at the bunker.

Brandon catches sight of him first. "Where ya been, Riley?"

"Nowhere," he says coldly as he walks towards his room.

"Alrighty then."

This is all going to have to end as quickly as it started. But the way he feels now, and with how much he wants her, he knows it's only going to get worse the more he sees her. He's already running through his mind how many nights he's going to be able to go to her, and how the hell he's going to shake his brother from following him.

A smart male would end things now, but that's not something he's ever been accused of, now is it?

****

I wake up tucked tightly in my bed, and my whole body is sore. Wow. I really did do that didn't I? I sit up and look to where he was. A white rose is sitting on the pillow with a piece of paper underneath it. I pick it up and read the note.

Luv,

Sorry I had to leave you, I wanted
to stay with you curled up in my
arms. Can I see you again tonight?
555-869-5156

Yours, Riley

Interesting. Well, I really could use one more night of whatever the hell all that was. As I pass the bathroom mirror, no bite marks. Wasn't that the whole point for him? I think he wanted to.

"Okay, now I'm offended the vampire didn't bite me?" I shake my head. "I'm totally losing my grip on reality."

I shower and then get ready for work. I'd love to talk to Mary about all of this. But she'll think I'm crazy for bringing a stranger into the house, not even counting the part where I had sex with him all night. Unprotected sex at that. And let's not forget about the vampire part.

It's nine in the morning. I figure I can just send him a text since he's probably sleeping.

Me: Hey its Sky from last nite, anyway I'm off at 9

My phone rings a minute later.

Crap. "Hi."

"Tonight at nine I'll be at your door waiting for you."

"Sounds good. Is it weird I really missed you this morning?"

"I smell you all over me. I want to take you again right now."

I laugh. "Shouldn't you be sleeping?"

"Yes, and now that I've heard your voice I can. Also, now that I have your number, I can call you anytime I want to hear your voice."

"Okay….well good night, or morning. Whatever I'm supposed to say."

He laughs. "Have a good day, Luv."

"Riley?"

"Yeah?"

"Last night was….yeah, um great. Really freaking great."

"Tonight Luv, tonight," he growls.

That deep raspy sultry voice and growl shoots right to my core. If he was here right now, I'd jump on the poor guy again even though I can barely walk as it is.

Chapter 3

"Are you going to spill about what happened last night with that guy from the club or what? Where did you go?" Mary asks as she comes to the register to clock in.

"Don't yell at me okay, but I took him back to my place."

"Oh my God. Are you insane? What if he was some sort of rapist or serial killer?" she groans.

"Well....if you saw him, you wouldn't mind if he was a rapist. Seriously though, this guy would never have to take it. Women throw themselves at guys like him." I smile.

"Sky that's so not funny. Spill, I want details my friend."

"Alright, he's like six-three and cut. I couldn't stop myself from running my hands all over his body, feeling every muscle."

"You totally slept with him, didn't you?" She shakes her head and smiles.

"What we did last night, you can't call sleeping."

She laughs. "How was he?"

"I cannot tell you how many orgasms that guy gave me. We went at it for three hours straight. He would come, then be ready to go again. It was crazy, like he couldn't get enough. He woke me up twice to make love to me."

Her jaw drops. "Make love? He stayed the night with you?"

"I told you, the whole thing was crazy. He became so gentle and loving. It kind of freaked me out. He was gone when I woke up this morning, but he left me a rose with a note. I called him and we're supposed to meet up when I get off."

"Wow. When do I get to meet him?"

"Let's see where all this is going first. I'm not sure what he's thinking or looking for. He's way out of my league Mary, you have no idea."

"I better get to meet him soon. And maybe the guy has been burned by so many Barbie dolls, it's made him look for a real girl. Not to mention you're hot. I've seen how Bret from the club looks at you. Roger says he really likes you."

We finish cleaning up. This whole day just seems to be dragging on and on. I think I've made a million mistakes. I can't think about anything else but seeing Riley again. These eleven hour shifts are brutal but I need the money.

Danielle left a note this morning saying she would be pulling another double, so we'll have the condo to ourselves tonight. I pull in the garage at a quarter till nine. Good, I have fifteen minutes to clean up and try to make myself look presentable.

I get off the elevator, round the corner, and he's already at my door. There's a red rose in his hand. I smile as our eyes meet. I feel a warm wave run through my entire body as he looks me over.

"Hi." I smile.

I walk down the hall and then lean in to kiss him. He closes his eyes and touches my face as his tongue lingers on mine. I feel a warmth flooding all throughout my chest, giving me goose bumps.

We come inside and I walk over to the dining table to put my stuff down.

He doesn't close the door, and he suddenly seems cold and tense. "Do you want to go get dinner somewhere?" he asks as his eyes dart around the room.

Uh oh, light of the next day and I'm not what he thought. He's as far away from me as possible, and the door is still wide open for a quick escape.

I take a deep breath. "Nah, I'm okay. Is everything okay with you?" Well this sucks. It's my fault for thinking he would actually like me.

"You haven't eaten."

"Riley, if you don't want to be here I totally understand."

"What?" He lowers his brow.

"I get it. Next day, you're all sobered up, and people don't look as good as the night before."

"You think I don't want you?" His gaze narrows as he slowly closes the door. He flips the lock and starts towards me.

"Well yeah. I'm not stupid. I'm not the beautiful model type I'm sure you're used to. I'm just an average girl." I shrug.

He gets to me quickly and pushes me up against the wall pressing himself into me. "Sky, tell me what you feel. Does it feel like I want you?"

I close my eyes trying not to totally lose it as he kisses my neck and runs his hands down to my ass.

He pulls me into his body tighter. "Answer me Sky, does it feel like I want you?" he says in my ear.

"Yes," I choke out.

"Do you want me inside of you? Because I couldn't sleep, or think about anything else except being inside of you again and kissing your lips. I'm barely holding my shit together here. I want you bare and underneath me now," he growls.

"So take me."

He's on my mouth hard. He has us both bare and in bed so fast that time is lost. He enters me just as quickly and as hard as he kisses me. I swear he growls as he comes inside me.

When he clamps down so hard on his lip that his fangs pierce it, I pull his face to me and lick the blood from his lips. I have this strange desire to taste him.

He pulls back brow raised.

"It's so warm and sweet." I lick my lips. "I want more of you."

The kisses becomes even harder, hungrier. I take his lip in my mouth and take more of him in. It's so thick and tastes crazy good. He kisses down my neck, running his fangs and tongue across it, but he still doesn't bite into me.

I stop moving.

He looks down at me. "What's wrong, are you okay?"

I sigh, "No."

"What is it?" He pushes himself up.

"Why don't you want me?"

He drops his brow and swirls his hips. Then he comes back in hard. "I do, I'm right here."

I gasp. "No, here." I bare my neck and feel a wave run through my whole body. "To take from me."

"You would want me to?" he says softly.

"Yes, I want you to. Am I not good for that?"

"I just didn't want to hurt you. I couldn't bear to ever hurt you. But if I take from you, you will be mine."

I'll be his? That sounds really good in this moment. "I want you to, and I know you want all of me."

"I always want all of you female," he growls.

He begins to move in me again. This time it's deep, and intense. He kisses me as he caresses my cheek. Then he looks down into my eyes as his fangs elongate. They're huge and he looks fierce, which scares the crap out of me for a second, until he bites into me and it drives me over the edge instantly. I ride it for what seems like an eternity. Best orgasm ever, even with him. He comes just after me, moaning loudly with an 'I love you' at the end. He moves next to me and pulls me into him tightly.

Well, I won't hold him to that slip of the tongue, but when he said it my heart practically leaped from my chest. My stomach growls and cramps up on me. It's eleven and I haven't eaten since breakfast. I feel like I'm going to pass out or throw up.

He pulls away from me and jumps up. He glares down at me. "Female, I knew you needed to eat."

I can't seem to come up with anything. I'm too awestruck staring at him as he pulls his boxers on and then storms out of the bedroom. I hear him rustling around in the kitchen.

That's why he wanted to take me to eat earlier, he knew I was hungry. That so creepy, but maybe a little sweet too. I can't believe I misunderstood all of this. But for whatever reason, this vampire wants me.

I wonder if vampires have regulars they keep and feed from for a while. Maybe they have several girls. Even thinking that he may have others makes me sick to my stomach.

Five minutes later he returns with a sandwich. Damn. If I had said I wanted a sandwich to my ex, he would have said, "You know where the kitchen is." This guy senses I'm hungry and brings me food. He's really amazing.

"You don't like it?" He's staring at me.

Crap. I realize I'm just sitting here staring at the plate like a complete idiot. "No, sorry it's great. I'm not used to somebody caring how I feel, let alone doing things for me. It's just different." I shrug. "Thank you."

He sits across from me smiling as he watches me eat. As soon as I finish he takes the plate to the kitchen. Then he comes in with a glass of juice.

"If I didn't know better, I'd think you were getting me all carbed up so you can have your way with me all night."

A devilish smile spreads across his face. "Maybe."

I laugh. "How about we hit the shower first?"

"I make no promises to keep my hands to myself."

I finish the juice and get up. "Good, because I was hoping you'd maybe want to soap me up." I raise my brow and smile.

Flying off the bed fast, he has the shower running, and soap in hand by the time I get in there. "Get in here."

He's barely keeping himself together as he washes me. Body tense and an arousal that keeps bumping into me. I rinse off and turn around to face him. I soap him up, have him rinse off, and then I pull his lips to mine kissing him deeply.

I run my hands down his body and begin to stroke the length of him. His whole body jerks forward as he moans on my lips. As I slide down to my knees in front of him he stops moving and tenses up. I see confusion in his expression.

I smile.

He steps back from me.

I grab the back of his legs to stop any further retreat. I look up at him. "Trust me." I pull him towards me. "Just relax, okay?"

Before he can protest any further I take the length of him in. He moans and plants his hands on the shower stall above me. I use one hand to help with his shaft, because let's face it, there's no way I'm getting more than half of him down my throat. With my other hand, I work the rest of him.

I feel him about to explode. I use both hands and my mouth to bring him to the edge twice. I gaze up at him and his eyes beg me to finish him. Finally, his release comes and his body shudders. No idea how this guy has anything left inside of him. He is an amazing creature to watch.

As he recovers I kiss my way back up his body. I run my teeth across his neck and lightly bite him. His hand comes up my back pulling me into him as he brings his mouth to mine.

I turn around to wash up. When I turn back around he's hard again. His desire burns through my whole body. With a growl he flips me around, shoves me against the wall, and then takes me from behind.

Riley's hands move slowly up my body. The feeling of warmth and desire that follows his touch make me come the second his fingers slide I in between my legs. He pulls my lips to him, kissing me while he continues to work me.

As I moan on his lips he growls, then he moves down to my neck and bites into me, drawing me in. He drives into me with more urgency and sheer power until he loses himself.

A heavy head drops to my shoulder. He pants as I sag forward against the wall, completely exhausted. He straightens up abruptly, spins me around, looks me over, and then brings me into his arms. I feel like he's always checking to see if I'm still alright.

This sense of really being a part of one another is insane. It feels like I've known him my whole life. His feelings flood my mind and heart. We finally end up in bed completely spent. I know he's as exhausted as I am, yet he always pulls me into his arms.

I look up at him and he smiles. "Was that another first for you….you know, my mouth on….you?"

"Yes." Riley runs his fingers across my lips.

"Was I okay?"

"Yeah." His smile widens. "Sky?"

"Yeah?"

A hand finds its way down between my legs. "I want to kiss you here." He looks like he means business. Then he leans down to kiss me.

****

No female has ever made him feel like this human does. He's tired but still can't get enough of her, and he wants to taste all of her. He has heard males talk about going down on a female's core, but he's never had the desire to have a female this way—that is….until her.

As soon as he penetrates her with his finger she moans on his lips. He kisses his way down her body stopping to give each of her beautiful breasts some attention. Flicking her tight nipples with the tip of his tongue. She arches up into him and moans. Damn she's beautiful, more than he deserves for sure.

"Do you like me kissing you?" he says on a growl.

"Yes," she gasps.

He comes down on her running his tongue up her soft flesh. As he kisses into her, she rocks her hips and breathes deeply.

"I want more of you," he groans.

Spending all day here pleasuring her seems like a great game plan. He comes back down on her and kisses her deeply, penetrating her with his tongue. He must be doing something right, because she gasps and runs her fingers through his hair, pulling him in deeper.

He figures out pretty quickly that as he goes faster around the top she shudders beneath him. He keeps it up until her whole body tenses up and she's crying out his name.

His cock has answered the call and is begging to be inside of her again. *Damn, I'm going to wear this female out. But I have to be inside of her again.* He kisses his way back up her body.

He comes down on her lips. "I'm going to take you again, my female." He kisses her deeply. "Do you want me as much as I want you?"

"Yes, always."

As he moves up and dives into her again, he knows in this moment he will never leave this female's side. She belongs to him and he belongs to her. He's going to get a whole lot of shit for it as well. Females in their world have a hard enough time, but a human female? He has no idea how this is going to work, but he loves her. How is that even possible? With everything he is, he truly loves her. He has completely bonded to a human female, and this bond is some crazy shit.

He lies with her as she falls asleep. It's four in the morning and he isn't ready to leave her yet. He isn't sure he's ever going to be able to leave her again. He pulls her into him tighter and closes his eyes.

****

I look over at the alarm clock and see it's seven in the morning. I figured I'd wake up alone but Riley's still in my bed sound asleep. A slice of yellow light is coming in through a slit in the curtains. I get up, grab a blanket, and then pull the curtains closed.

Do vampires actually burn in the sunlight? The earlier conversation he had was about being in before dawn. Makes me wonder about all these vampire myths. Which ones are truths, if any?

A phone goes off. He jumps up and grabs it out of his jacket. "Yeah...I know. Shit...I got tied up and lost track of time....Yeah, I'm safe. See you tonight."

I'm so glad I have a night light in the bathroom. I stand here and take in the sight before me. A completely bare and perfect specimen, and boy do I want him again. It's like I can't stay close enough to him. He's making me a very needy girl.

He sits on the bed and rubs his head.

"I guess you didn't mean to spend the night with me. It's alright, I won't read anything into it."

He looks up and grimaces.

Great now he looks annoyed with me, and by the sound of his conversation he's stuck here.

He sighs. "Come here." He lays his hand on the bed next to him.

I walk over and sit down.

"If I told you exactly what I was thinking about you, about us, you may decide to throw me out into the sun."

"Hardly." I roll my eyes. "So the sun is bad?"

"Yes, unless I wish to become ash."

"Sorry you're stuck here with me all day."

He grabs my face in his hands. "Can't you see it's more? Can't you feel that it's more?"

I shake my head. "I don't trust people anymore. When I think things seem one way, they aren't that way at all. Normally, it's the complete opposite of whatever I think." I take a deep breath. "I know I don't make any sense. It's just that everybody always ends up letting me down or hurting me in the end."

He puts his forehead to mine and sighs. "I love you, I'd die for you, and I'd never let anyone hurt you."

"Why? How?" I gasp at the confession as my stomach does somersaults on me. The little butterflies that are fluttering around in there are threatening to make me throw up on him.

"It's just the way it works. When I first touched you something happened inside of me. Then I saw you again and I had to know you, had to have you. When I first laid with you, I knew you were mine and always would be. Our souls bonded the instant we touched on the street. I will always be with you, if you'll have me."

I start shaking my head. "My head tells me how crazy all of this is, but my heart bleeds at the thought of you ever leaving me. When I first touched you, it felt like electricity running though my whole body, it woke me up from a state of being numb to the world."

With that, he pulls me into his lap. I run my arms around his neck tightly. No idea how any of this is possible, but I ache for him. "Riley, I don't know how….but I do love you."

He squeezes me so tight I can't breathe.

****

Did he really just hear her right? She loves him. At that confession, his throat tightens up and he knows he's holding back tears of joy. Sissy shit, this bonded shit is just getting crazier and crazier.

"This isn't going to be easy is it?" she asks.

"No."

"They will know I know about them?"

"Yes, and there will be consequences."

"For both of us?" She tenses up.

"No, only me." He holds her tightly.

When they find out he's bonded to a human, shit's going to get real. But law will prevent them from harming her because of their bond. Thank God, because he'd kill anything or anyone that tried to harm her, even his own brothers.

"Guess we'll figure it out. Too bad you couldn't have wiped my memory that first night." She shrugs.

"It wouldn't have kept me from you. The bond was already there."

"I can't even think about somebody hurting you. It makes me want to kill anyone that tries." She laughs. "I can get a little violent if I need to you know, and maybe a little possessive where you're concerned."

If he didn't know better he'd swear this human is bonding to him. But humans don't bond. He can't get into her head to scrub her either, and her blood….Oh God, her blood gives him so much strength and power, and taste like nothing he's ever had before. She's something else, something more.

"Are you hungry? I could make us breakfast. I guess I should ask you if you eat food," she asks.

He laughs. "Yes, I eat food, but I'll cook for you."

"Come on." She gets up, puts her hand out, and pulls him to her. "We should at least try to cover up though. I have a roommate." She puts a long shirt on.

He put his jeans on and then holds her underwear up in his hand. "You'll need these, or I make no promises I won't take you out there on that dining table."

She smiles.

As they come out into the hall he has her by the waist and her back is firmly pressed into him. They can barely walk, but he doesn't care as long as she's close to him. He pulls her face around to kiss her perfect lips.

"Holy shit," a girl says smiling at them.

They stop dead in their tracks.

"Hey D, this would be Riley. Riley this is my roommate and best friend Danielle."

"Hi." He feels lust pouring off of that female for him. He smiles and holds Sky even tighter to him. He has no desire for that female at all—he belongs to Sky. The realization that he truly belongs to her doesn't scare him. It makes him feel well. "Sit, I'll make breakfast." He points down at the chair.

****

Danielle comes over to the table. She tries to whisper, but I know there's no way she's going to be quiet enough. "Oh my God Sky. He's gorgeous. This is the guy from the club?"

I look up as he glances back and smiles. "Yep, he's the one. I told you he's too good for me."

"Shut up. He would be lucky to have you."

"I agree. I like your friend, she's very smart." He turns around smiling at her.

She puts her hand to her mouth.

"He has like….really good hearing." I laugh.

Twenty minutes later I have eggs, bacon, and hash browns in front of me.

"Danielle do you want some?" he asks.

"Uh, sure."

He sets a plate down in front of her.

"Thanks."

She looks like her eyes may pop out of her head at any moment. But looking at him standing in the kitchen in just jeans, as his muscles move and flex while he cooks, it's hard not to stare. He brings his plate to the table and smiles as he scoots his chair closer to mine.

He leans into me. "We can always eat later and head back in there now." He brings my face to his and kisses me softly.

"Wow, just freaking wow," Danielle says as she shakes her head. "Do you have a brother?"

He looks at her very seriously. "I do."

I laugh.

"Hook me up you two, seriously." She laughs.

After breakfast, Danielle heads off to work. I have to force him to stay sitting while I clean up. He gave me some crap about me not touching dirty dishes. Whatever, it's killing him to sit there on the barstool and watch me do it. I have to admit though, it's pretty entertaining watching him squirm.

"You like to torture me don't you?" He glares with a smile.

I smirk. "If I recall, you didn't seem to mind in the shower."

Man I love that deep growl. I finish up and then slink up right in between his legs. I run my hands up his thighs to his chest.

Wrapping my arms around his neck, I get right into his face. "How is it that I just can't seem to get enough of you?" I lean in to kiss him.

He slides down and picks me up by the butt. I wrap my legs around his waist and he brings us back into the bedroom. We make love for another two hours. Afterwards, I can't move I'm so tired.

We wake up together at half past four. Surprisingly, we're still in each other's arms.

"I don't want you to go." I pout and hold him tighter.

"And I don't want to leave Luv, but I have to."

"Maybe next time we can talk more so that I can actually get to know you."

He tenses up. "There's some things I want to protect you from." He frowns. "I don't always do the right thing. I hurt others."

"You're like a warrior or soldier right?"

He looks up at me brow dropped.

"Well the dagger, knife, and guns suggest you protect yourself from something, and since you're really strong, I assume it's not from humans."

"No, not humans."

"Riley?"

"Yeah?"

"Something else is kind of bugging me. Actually it's making me sick to my stomach thinking about it."

"What?"

"Will you still feed from other women…and, you know, have them?" I drop his gaze. I know he's not mine, but I can't help that I feel like he is. "Sorry, I know I have no right to claim you, and it's not my business what you do. But I don't think I can be the kind of girl that shares you."

"Sky, look at me."

As my eyes lift, I'm met with a huge smile.

"For as long as you'll have me, I'll only be with you. I belong to you."

"I have a hard time with you actually wanting to be with me."

"I love you. To me you're beautiful, more beautiful than any female I've ever seen, and you are mine."

"Damn, I love you." I kiss him quick. He's probably completely crazy, but whatever.

"I have to get dressed. They will come after me if I don't get back by sun down."

"They can find you?"

"Yes, through my blood. We can all find each other, but I'm not ready for them to find you yet." He kisses me again.

He gets up and has his pants in hand, backside to me. Hell, one more quickie won't kill me. I slowly slide the covers off of me and I spread my legs.

"Riley, I'm not ready for you to leave yet."

****

Riley knows he has less than thirty minutes to get back to the bunker before his brother comes looking for him. But as he looks down at that beautiful soft pink flesh she bares him, instinct takes over.

It's like it's his life mission to please this female. As soon as he takes her vein, her orgasm causes her to shudder beneath him. She feels so good under him. As her orgasms runs the length of his shaft, gripping and stroking him, his own climax slams into him. Her flesh grips every inch of him tightly. He could lie here all day and just be inside of her.

She wishes to claim him as her own. He knows she has no idea what that truly means, but when he heard it, something told him they would always only belong to each other. Only a king can lay claim to a female. Consequences of another male laying a hand on that female is death. A king may also lay claim to as many females as he wishes.

It makes him sick to even think about. No way could any truly bonded male take more than one female.

Focus idiot.

He has five minutes to get out of here before Michael will be standing in front of them. He gets up and grabs his phone just in case. "I'm on my way….Yep, still fine…. I will be, relax….Yeah, I know it's important. Shit. I said I'm coming. Back the fuck off," he yells.

He hangs up. His brother can be a real pain in the ass. He looks back at Sky. Shit. She looks freaked. His fangs are elongated, brow tight, and his eyes are probably red.

"Man, I never want to be on your bad side."

He turns away from her and gets his jeans on, trying to calm himself. But he doesn't sense fear from her. He looks over and sure as shit she's smiling up at him.

"Hey Riley….I really fucking love you."

"Listen female, I have to go. If you keep looking at me like that, and saying shit like that to me, I'm never getting out of here."

She pouts.

He laughs, shaking his head. He pulls his shirt on and then sits next to her. "Hey Sky?"

"Yeah?"

"I really fucking love you too."

She laughs hard.

Hearing her happy warms his heart. He brings his hand to her cheek and kisses her one more time before he leaves. He doesn't want to leave from this spot. Thinking about her in the city alone has him about to snap. He wants to bring her back to his room and lock her in there where she'll be safe.

"I have three days of recon and....well other shit. If I can't make it back to you, I'll call you." He sighs, "It's dusk, Luv, I have to go. Please be careful."

She nods.

He appears in front of the bunker. One minute he's looking into her beautiful blue eyes, and the next he's looking right at his brother.

"See, I'm here. All in one fucking piece." He goes to walk by him but his brother steps with him.

"Where were you?" Michael glares.

"Not your business."

"Riley, What the fuck? We have orders, and since when are you late when you're on?"

"I'm here, right? Give me five and I'll be suited up."

****

Michael's so tired of covering up for his brother's bullshit. Last time it was drugs and alcohol, and he got crazy with the females. Killed a few. He's not sure if he has it in him to bring his brother back from that shit again. He killed humans for sport and tore Moartea to pieces before ending them in the name of fun.

He didn't tell anyone his brother was out all night. They would no doubt be wondering the same shit he is now. What kind of damage was that male out doing for twenty four hours straight? Plus he's strong, very strong and recently fed. No telling how many humans he killed or the mess that was left behind.

Tonight they're checking out a possible Moartea safe house. Five will be on point. He thought about talking to Justin about substituting Riley out, but no doubt that would have brought up questions he didn't want to answer. No doubt, it would have also gotten him a beating from Riley.

The team tonight is Derek, Brandon, Markus, Riley, and himself. They're supposed to confirm the house as Moartea and then clear it out. They head out in the SUV. Riley looks freakishly happy, and Michael isn't the only one that's noticed. Not a look any of them is used to seeing on Riley, but definitely a look that says he's going to have a good ole time ripping shit apart tonight.

They pull up at the end of a long road. It leads up to three houses. They're here to check out the house on the far right to confirm it as a Moartea safe house or not, but first they will make sure the other two houses are clear.

As they materialize to the windows of the first house they see a family inside. Human. House in the middle is also clear-- nobody's home. When they check out the house on the right they find what they're looking for.

"I count seven," Brandon says.

Derek's getting ready to give everyone their assignment when Riley takes off.

"What the fuck are we waiting for?" Riley calls out as he runs for the front door.

"Fuck." Michael takes off after him.

"Shit, he's off again." Derek starts after them. "Take the back," he yells out to the others.

Derek would be the only other male besides Justin his brother respects. Somehow Derek and Riley have become best friends over the last century. Derek tolerates a lot of shit from Riley just like he does.

Michael comes in the front door and his brother has already taken out two Moartea. Another one tackles him from behind. Riley loses his blade and the Moartea jumps on top of him. Before Michael can get to Riley, he has one square off in front of him. It lunges for him but he punches it in the face and it drops.

Before he can strike, another one hits him from behind and he's knocked backwards into the couch. He draws his gun, but Riley's already on the Moartea with a blade through its heart and his next swing takes off its head. Black ash is all that's left behind.

His brother's pummeled face appears before him smiling ear to ear and holding out his hand. He looks up at Riley, who's covered in blood and ash. He sees that Riley's been stabbed in the side and most of the blood on the front of him is his own.

"Your hit." He takes his brother's out stretched hand.

"Nah, I'm fine." Riley pulls him up.

"The fuck you are. Look at all the blood."

"Just a scratch, look," Riley says as he pulls his shirt up.

It's almost completely healed.

"What the fuck?" He drops his brow.

Riley shrugs him off and walks away.

They torch the house and then materialize back to the car. Not one of them speaks the entire way back to the bunker. That's what they do when Riley's so far on the edge he could possibly snap at any moment and take one of them out with him.

When they pull in, Riley's the first one out of the car and headed inside. The rest of them look at each other shaking their heads. He will need to keep a close eye on his brother if he's to try and save him from himself again.

They come into the great hall only to find Justin stepping out of his office brow raised. "That was fast?" Justin says.

"Went in and took it down quickly. Not much intel, and there were only seven Moartea on site," Derek reports.

"Is everything alright?" Justin presses.

Derek looks back at Michael. "I hope so."

Justin also makes eye contact with him. "Riley?"

He nods. "I'll keep an eye on him." No doubt it's what they all want to hear. It's always been his job to keep his brother in check, probably because he's the only one that can.

Chapter 4

Watching the clock and counting down the minutes until I'm off work. Riley promised me he has a break tonight and that he's going to stay with me for a couple of days. It's been three days since we've seen each other. Even though he calls every morning before he goes to sleep, I still miss him. It's almost a comfort that he's a vampire, because in any other scenario this relationship would be completely ridiculous.

There are two women and an older couple left in here shopping. I grab a box of scarves and start to fill them. I look up and see Mary waving me towards her. I mouth what, but she just keeps beckoning me towards her.

I finally walk over. "What, freak?"

"Look at the guy coming in here," she says under her breath.

I look up as he opens the door. His eyes have locked on mine and a smiles spreads across my face. It's so good to finally see him, like I don't feel right inside being away from him.

He looks different tonight. His hair is wet like he just got out of the shower. His bangs are falling forward on his cheeks. He's also cleanly shaven. I think he likes the goatee, but he doesn't have it because I don't like it.

Minus the combat boots and leather jacket concealing weapons, he would almost look like your average guy. I smile. Well, minus the yellow eyes and the fact he looks like a gladiator.

The two women have spotted him and have stopped to stare.

"Good evening sir. Is there something I can help you with tonight?" I say as his gaze burns into mine.

Taking my face in his hands he kisses me deeply, then he pulls me into him tightly. "I missed you Luv. Figured I'd come here and take you to dinner."

He brushes the hair back behind my ear. The longing and desire in his touch has my body warming all over. There's so much love.

"I'm off in five minutes. Do you want my keys so you can wait in the car?"

"I'd rather stay here and watch you." He smiles.

I grab a hold of his jacket and pull his lips back to mine. "I'd never finish if you stayed in here. Plus, you're distracting the customers."

He takes the keys from me and kisses me again before he leaves. He walks with such confidence. I really admire that about him. But I guess when you can kill anything, you can be pretty confident.

"Damn, that's Riley? You weren't kidding were you?" Mary says. Her elbows are on the counter with her face in her hands as she stares out at him.

"Yeah." I laugh. "I know, crazy right?"

She nods.

The two women finally make it up after the couple leaves.

"Your husband?" one asks.

"No, actually….well, it's my boyfriend I guess. Sorry, he gets pretty intense. I'll have to talk to him about the PDA while I'm at work. I apologize again."

"Awe honey, never apologize for that," the other woman says.

"Yeah if I had that, I don't think I'd ever let him out of my sight."

We finally get everyone out. I set the alarm and lock up.

"Have a good night, Sky." Mary looks at Riley again, shakes her head, and then goes to her car.

"You too."

I look over and see Riley leaning against the front of my car. There are two pretty girls coming out of the massage place next door. He doesn't look over at them, but they've noticed him and look like they're going to approach him.

"Ready to go?" I call out.

He points in front of himself. "Come here, female."

The girls stop their approach and look at me wide eyed. *Yeah, yeah, I know he's too good for me.* I stop five feet from him next to a concrete pillar and smile. "No, you come here." I point in front of myself.

Narrowing his gaze, he walks over and then grabs me up in his arms. "I see you've already figured out that I'm completely under your spell."

Gotta love the public displays of attention. I move my body against his as I run my hands down to his ass and bring him in tighter.

I take a breath. "How about we pick up something to eat, and then go back to my place? I don't think I can wait for all of this."

"Agreed." He takes my face in his hands. "One of these nights, female, I will take you to dinner." He kisses me quick. "I love you, and I've missed you."

"I love you too." I look around and we have a little bit of an audience watching us. "Enough with the PDA for one night, let's go."

We pick up dinner and then he drives us home. He holds my hand the whole way. Everything about him screams dangerous and maybe a little crazy, but he's so damn sweet to me.

The making out starts up again in the elevator all the way to the door. I drop the keys, he picks them up and opens the door. We drop the food by the door and continue to make out. I take his jacket off, then he removes his weapons and drops them to the floor. I pull off his shirt and then run my hands up his bare chest. He takes my shirt off and then runs his hands around my back to undo my bra.

Somebody clears their throat.

I look over and find Danielle standing in the kitchen smiling.

"Just let me get my drink and sandwich, and I'll go to my room so you two can carry on."

"Sorry." I laugh.

Riley picks up our stuff and heads to the bedroom.

I bring the burgers to the counter. "I haven't seen him for three days."

Danielle giggles. "No explanation needed." She grabs her food. "By the way, I'm totally jealous."

I head to my room and close the door behind me. What I look over at is a very large, very hot, and very naked vampire male on my bed looking at me like he's going to tear me apart.

My clothing is shed quickly and then I come up between his legs, lingering for a moment. He licks his lips and I know exactly what he desires from me.

As I take him into my mouth he arches up and moans. I play around a little, then I climb on top of him and take him all in. As we slowly move together he runs his hands up to my hips. He flips me onto my back and continues to move inside of me slowly. His gaze intensifies as his fangs elongate.

I smile, and turn my head to expose my neck. Totally satisfying knowing I'm the only one that keeps him fed.

Riley strikes fast.

My body responds, immediately driving me over the edge. The feeling of him taking from me while he's inside of me is intense, like we're one. He seals me up as he begins to drive into me with more urgently, and then he loses himself.

He comes down on my mouth and kisses me softly as he runs his thumb across my cheek. "I love you so much, female."

"I love you too, and I've missed you as well." I kiss him quickly and then get out from under him. "I'm going to get the food, I'm starving." It takes a lot of carbs to keep up with him.

****

Michael avoids the great room. Riley didn't come in again this morning and he's turned his phone off. He had followed his brother's blood to a large condo in downtown San Diego. Riley was still inside as dawn approached, and he assumes he's still there now.

There's a knock at his door. He sighs and opens the door to find Derek standing in front of him.

"He didn't come in before dawn?"

"No, he didn't."

"Do you know where he is?" Derek crosses his arms over his chest.

"Yeah. I followed him into downtown. He was inside a large condo complex."

"With humans?" Derek raises his brow.

"I didn't sense any vampires there, so yeah….humans. It's a real nice upscale place too."

Derek shakes his head. "Let's hope it's not what I know we're both thinking it is." Derek rubs his face and walks off.

Yeah, like his brother going apartment to apartment killing everyone inside for fun. He's already begun thinking about the clean-up job that's going to be. There's no way he'd be able to clean it up and dump all the bodies by himself.

****

We sleep until five the next evening. He kept me up until six in the morning switching off between talking and making love. He got a little crazy a couple of times and seemed to feel the need to apologize afterwards. I think we're going to need to have a little talk about how rough is not necessarily a bad thing, for me anyways.

"You awake?" He runs his fingers across my back.

"I am."

"I'm taking you out tonight."

"Oh yeah, where are you taking me?"

"Anywhere you want. We could go someplace nice."

I look up at him. "I don't know where to go other than around here. I've never been anywhere nice."

He smiles. "Then I guess it will be up to me to change that."

I pull myself up on his chest and kiss his lips. I smile wide as I look down at him. I run my hand down his stomach and stop just below his belly button.

He laughs. "Here I thought it was me that was going to wear you out. Maybe it's the other way around."

"I need to tell you something, but I'm not sure how to start the conversation." I'm already having a hard time maintaining eye contact and I haven't even started yet.

His face gets serious. "You can tell me anything."

I rub my face and then flop back on my pillow. I put my arm across his chest. "Just stay there. I can't have you looking at me when I say this."

"Alright," he says slowly almost laughing.

I take a deep breath. "Sometimes I feel you holding back during sex. The couple of times you apologized afterwards, you should know that for me….the rougher times have been some of the best with you." I barely get the last part out. I'm so embarrassed, I can't stop smiling. Just not a conversation I ever thought I would have with somebody.

He isn't saying anything, and it seems like maybe he's stopped breathing.

I put my hands over my face. "I know, I'm weird. Sorry. Feels even weirder to admit to somebody that you like it rough with them. I like when we make love too if that helps." Now I really do feel like a total weirdo.

He rolls to his side and then pulls my hands away from my face.

I look up and see him smiling.

"I hold back so that I don't hurt you. If I was to let myself go with you….I'm afraid it could end badly." He touches my face. "I don't ever want to hurt you."

"Have you ever heard me tell you to stop?"

He shakes his head.

"You've never hurt me in a bad way. The power I feel when you let yourself go as you drive into me, is amazing. Like I can't get you close enough, deep enough. I want so much more of you. I want to taste you again, and for you to make me yours."

"You are mine," he growls.

His eyes go black with a thin ring of yellow around them. He sits up on his knees and puts his hands on my waist to pull me towards him, then he holds me in place and looks down at me.

"You will tell me to stop if I hurt you?" a deep crazy voice asks.

I nod.

The anticipation is killing me. With the emotions I feel coming off of him right now, this is going to be crazy good. Looking up at his beautiful cut body is only driving up my own desire.

"Are you ready for me, female?"

I bite my lip and nod.

He comes in quick and drives into me hard, possession begin struck like that of a branding iron.

I gasp, but I don't have time to think about the pain as it rages on. He never breaks eye contact with me as he pounds into me. I watch as his body glistens with sweat, and his muscles flex with every thrust.

I moan as the waves run through my whole body. And the only thing that comes to mind is—"More."

Riley drives in harder until his whole body tenses up and he comes in a roar. His hips pump into me for over five minutes, giving me everything inside of him. The throbbing drives me over the edge again. With my hips still tightly in his grasp he begins to slow his rhythm.

He pauses and looks down at me. Which I'm sure is to make sure I'm still alive. I smile as I try to catch my breath.

While shaking his head, a smile begins to spread across his face. He comes down settling back on me, then he softly kisses my lips. "That was…."

I laugh. "Awesome."

"Yes. I didn't hurt you, did I?" He brushes the hair back from my face.

"No, not at all. Riley, I promise I would tell you. I love when you make love to me, but all of that….was really great."

"I swear you were made for me."

"I think I was born to love you." I reach up and touch his face. I pull him back to my lips. "Because I can't imagine ever loving somebody as much as I love you."

"It's the same way I feel about you, Luv." He kisses me deeply and comes back inside of me again.

When he makes love to me, it's filled with so much passion and warmth. I feel love with every touch, every kiss, in everything we do together. This is fairy tale shit--you aren't supposed to get to find this in real life....are you?

As I lie in his arms, I run my fingers back and forth across his chest. "I've noticed when you're angry your eyes are red."

"Our eyes tell others our mood." He looks away from me. "If mine are ever all black you need to get away from me, alright?"

"What does it mean if they're black? Because when two others tried to scrub my memory their eyes were black, but they still had a thin yellow ring around them. Just now before all of the crazy hot sex, yours were like that."

"It means we're so closed off that we've become completely irrational and out of control. I....I'm like that sometimes. More than others are." He takes a deep breath. "Sky, I'm dangerous. I'm not this male you see before you."

"I'm not scared of you." I take his face in my hand.

"Promise me, if you ever see me like that you'll get away from me."

I can't ever imagine him hurting me. "I'll be careful if I feel I need to be, alright?" I kiss him to shut him up.

"Come on. I know where I want to take you."

"Should I be worried?" I laugh.

Riley grimaces.

We get dressed and take off in the car to Seaport Village. He groans as he drives around looking for a parking space, completely human like. It's times like this when I forget what he truly is. He finally gives up and lets the valet park it.

"Would have been so much easier to just materialize here."

"Could you have brought me with you?"

"Yes."

I laugh. "Then why did we take the car?"

He looks over at me and frowns.

I shrug. "Meh, next time."

We walk hand in hand on the boardwalk. It's interesting being with him here like this. Like we're a normal couple. I look in a shop window and see a two carat square diamond necklace on a white gold chain. One can dream.

"Which one are you looking at?"

I laugh. "I'm so not going to tell you that."

"Why not?" He smiles.

"Alright, answer me this first, are you poor or well off?"

Riley shrugs. "I have enough."

"Yep, sticking with….I'm not telling you." I take his hand in mine and try to pull him away. With a quick tug, I'm back in front of the window. Arms come around and hold me tightly against his chest.

"If I had to guess, I would say…that one." He points to the necklace.

I hold my breath. "Nope, you're totally wrong." I pull him away.

Riley laughs and comes right next to my ear. "You gave it away the moment you tensed up and stopped breathing."

I shake my head laugh as I pull away from him. "Is it weird to say I actually feel like you're my boyfriend out here like this?"

Riley pulls me back into his arms. "I told you, I'm yours."

Met with a soft kiss, I melt into him.

Dinner on the pier is perfect. He wants so badly to take me to some fancy restaurant, but I like it better when it's just me and him. We finish up and then walk towards the carousel.

"Do you want to ride it?"

"No, I just like watching it."

He takes a breath and looks relived.

"The whole going around in circles thing….not really my thing."

"Mine either." He shakes his head.

"Then why did you offer?"

"Don't you know yet, female? I would do anything for you."

"Damn, I love you."

"Not as much as I love you." He hugs me tightly.

His body tense up. I feel anger coming from him. I still think it's strange that I can feel what he's feeling. It does help with my whole insecurity issues though. Now I just need to trust my own feelings.

I pull back slightly. "What's wrong?"

Riley glares behind me, pulling me to his side tightly. I look around and then I see a large guy coming towards us.

"Vampire?" I look up at him. He has to be a soldier like Riley. "Do you know him?"

"Yes. It's my brother, Michael."

"Hmmm, the whole follow you by your blood thing?"

"Yes." He looks down at me.

"This should be fun, huh?"

"Not the way I would have put it, Luv."

Michael comes before us and looks perplexed as he looks at me, then back to Riley. "Human?" He raises his brow.

"Yes, vampire, I'm human. Is that a problem for you?"

Michael narrows his gaze at me, and then looks back to Riley. "You've been with this girl the whole time?"

Riley pushes me behind him and then goes nose to nose with his brother. "I told you this was none of your business," he growls.

"Your reckless behavior is my business when it puts us all in danger," Michael's voice begins to escalate.

"You will back off from this."

"As soon as you explain to me, what exactly it is you think you're doing here." Michael crosses his arms over his chest.

Crap. This is getting loud and people are starting to stare. I move in between the two of them, extending my arms to push them apart. His brother is completely relaxed, but Riley's body is tense.

"We're in a very public place." I look at Michael and then back to Riley. "You need to calm down and lower your voices."

I hadn't noticed that Michael moved his arm around my waist at some point. I look down at the same time Riley does.

Riley growls deeper and his eyes go completely black. "You will remove your hand from her now," he yells.

"You need to be careful," Michael says quietly. He slowly tries to pull me away from Riley.

I see fear behind his eyes. I push Michael's hand off of me and glare. I look up at Riley and push him back a few steps. "Look at me."

Riley looks down at me, glaring with those crazy black eyes of his. I'll admit he does scare me a little like this. I feel a darkness and anger coming from inside of him. He's definitely different, and I don't feel him like I normally do.

I put my hands on his face and talk softly, "Calm down. I'm going to go get something to drink. You two obviously need to talk, but remember where you are. People are watching this."

He nods and his eyes begin to lighten until they turn back to yellow. I wrap my arms around his waist and hug him tightly. He tilts my chin up and comes down on my lips. "Don't go too far."

I smile. "You worry too much."

"Only for you, Luv."

I look back at Michael. "And you, I go by Sky, not human. Okay, vampire? I'll give you two a minute to work out whatever this is. Just please don't draw any more attention to yourselves. I think we all know that wouldn't be a good thing, right?"

They nod.

Well that was fun. I wonder if he has parents and the whole thing. His brother doesn't seem too happy about me, I can only imagine how his parents will take the news. Man I have got to get him to talk more about himself. I really don't know anything about him except the basics. He wasn't kidding about the whole crazy black eyes thing either. I couldn't feel him like I normally do. But what I did still feel, was his love for me.

****

Michael shakes his head as his brother watches that girl until the moment she disappears into the store.

Riley turns back and glares. "Why did you follow me?"

"I wanted to make sure you weren't, I don't know….being you I guess. I didn't expect to find her."

Riley narrows his gaze.

"Are you bonded to her?" Michael can barely get the words to come out of his mouth. He can't believe he's actually asking his brother, of all the males, such a thing.

"I told you, this is none of your business."

"You need to be careful. A human knowing what she knows is dangerous for us all."

Riley gets right into his face again. "You will stay out of this, and you will stay away from her," he growls.

Michael throws his hands up and steps back. If he presses this any further, Riley's likely to flip out on him, he can sense it. He's protecting this girl. With what he felt between the two of them when they were together, he's positive Riley's bonded to her. He can feel their connection like a wave through his whole body.

Watching her tame the dark side of Riley was amazing—scared the shit out of him—but amazing just the same. She has power over him like no other, and he seems different. This could be dangerous for them all.

"I will leave you, for now. But this here is not a good idea."

"Because I don't know that?" Riley rubs his face.

"Yet….here you are, brother." Michael shakes his head.

"Nothing I can change now. You will leave this alone?"

"For now." Michael walks a ways out and then turns back to watch as Riley meets that girl, Sky, outside the store. He pulls her into his arms and kisses her.

Michael never could have imagined this is what he would find when he went looking for Riley this evening. He looks like a human male out with his female. They look like they're in love, which is exactly what he felt when they were in each other's arms.

He appears back at the bunker and comes downstairs.

"You find him," Derek asks.

"Yeah."

"Is it bad?"

"No idea how the hell to answer that yet. When I figure it out I'll let you know." Michael shakes his head.

"Anything we're going to have to clean up?"

"I hope not. I'll keep a close eye on what's going on with him. It's nothing to worry about for now." Michael heads to his room. Nothing to worry about? Right. Only the human female that clearly knows about them all.

He can't decide if finding Riley with a female was a better scenario than what he thought he was going to find. But his brother felt different to him tonight.

Chapter 5

Riley and I have spent the whole weekend together. It's been great, and the more we're together, the more right we feel together. Even though I have no idea where it is exactly that we fit. After seeing his brother's reaction last night, I'm not sure I would be very accepted in his world. I wonder where he lives and what his world is like. He can only be in mine for half the day.

"I hate this part." I squeeze him harder.

He runs his hand through my hair. "What part?"

"The part where you leave me. I want you to stay here with me." I look up and pout.

Smiling, he says, "I would like to bring you home with me where I know you'd be safe, and I'd love to be able to come home to you in my bed."

I drop my head on his chest. "This is so damn complicated, and it's only getting worse. Will your brother tell them about me?"

"No. But I'm sure I'm going to get a lot of shit for it."

"I take it you're supposed to be with a girl vampire right, not a human?"

He shakes his head. "Warriors don't take a mate at all. A female living among warriors would be unheard of."

"Oh. So this is like double bad in his eyes. What about yours?"

"I wouldn't change anything that's happened. I love you, and I will figure out how to make this work." He squeezes me tighter. "You need to get to work and I need to go before dawn."

I groan, "I hate the sun."

He laughs.

"Do you have a mom and dad? Or more family?"

"No. Michael and I were orphans."

"Oh, sorry."

"It's okay, Luv. That was over two hundred years ago."

Holy Shit. "You're two hundred years old?"

He smiles wide. "No, I'm two hundred thirty one."

"Huh." Not sure where to go with that information.

He laughs and grabs me up. "What? Am I too old for you?"

"I don't care how old you are, the only thing that matters is that you're mine."

"Yes I am." He leans down to kisses me.

He leaves before I start getting ready for work. I wonder a lot of things about him I've never asked. Like how long do they live? We're completely in love with each other and my own mortality is beginning to scream at me. Can he turn me into what he is? Do I want to be what he is? Where does he live? What will they do when they find out about me?

We never talk about those kind of things. Mainly we make love, eat, and he asks me a lot of question about myself.

****

As Riley comes into the bunker, he figures Michael is going to be waiting for him. But instead he's met with Derek, glaring, arms crossed over his chest.

"So where is it you keep disappearing to?"

"You're going to get the same answer every time you ask me that."

"You've fed a lot, and you're very strong." Derek narrows his gaze.

"I am, so why the fuck do you want to pick a fight with me right now?"

"Maybe next time I'll be the one to follow you. Michael can't protect you forever."

Without thinking he grabs Derek and slams him up against the wall. "You will back off of this."

"Don't give me a reason to question you," Derek says dryly.

He growls, "What I do is none of your business."

Derek throws his hands up.

"Riley, chill out brother." Brandon comes over and pulls them apart.

"What's going on here?" Markus asks.

Riley lets him go and then walks to his room.

Making a big deal out of any of it will just make everyone more curious, and he isn't ready for them to know about Sky yet. It's bad enough Michael knows. But Michael hasn't said anything yet or he'd be getting a lot more shit from Derek than he just did.

She's his, and he will protect her from all of this shit as long as he can. Not sure how all of this is supposed to work. But damn does he want her here where he can keep her safe. It makes him sick to his stomach to think about her anywhere in that city alone.

He's bonded to her, and any vampire or Moartea that gets near her will be able to sense him all over her. Just by being with her he has put her in danger. He's going to go mad thinking about all of this shit. He needs to come up with a solution fast.

****

Michael is restless tonight. The thirst is growing, and since Riley's preoccupied with recon, he heads downtown to find someone to take.

Everything on the street is so mundane. He continues to walk until he comes upon a group of three human females. They look him over.

The blonde with the expensive jewelry and designer clothes. Yep, that's the one. "Hi, will you take a walk with me?"

She smiles wide and looks at the other girls, then back to him. "Totally."

Lust is pouring off of her and seeping under his skin. He takes her hand and brings her out of view of the other two.

"So I'm Trina, what's your name?"

"Michael," he says coldly. He leads her down an alley and she begins to slow up. He turns to her, taking her face in his hands. "Tonight, I'm going to take all of you Trina. Are going to let me have you?"

She nods slowly as she smiles up at him.

He knew he wouldn't have to mess with her mind to take her. They come around to a small dock on the backside of the building. He pushes her up against the wall and runs his hands up her skirt. He pulls off her underwear and tosses them aside.

He looks into her eyes. "Do you want me, Trina?"

"Oh yeah, you're so hot."

Taking a step back, he unbuttons his pants. "Get on your knees."

Met with a confused stare, he puts his hands on her shoulders—forcing her to her knees. She gets a clue and begins to work him. His hunger grows as he watches her try to take in as much of him as she can. He puts his hand on the back of her head and makes her choke as she takes him even deeper.

Every once in a while she looks up behind black tear streaked cheeks to smile at him.

He pulls her up, turns her around, and comes up against her. He lets his shaft stroke her in between the folds of her soft flesh and thighs.

She moans.

"Do you want more of me?" He thrust in and out.

"Yes," she gasps as he pinches her nipples.

"Do you want me to fuck you?"

"Yes, please," she groans louder.

Grasping her hip in one hand, he shoves her forward with the other and begins pounding into her hard. After a few minutes he pulls out and turns her around before she climaxes. "You still want more don't you?"

"Yes," she says breathless.

Sliding into her again, he lifts her leg up and drives in until she's about to come—then he stops. She cries out and tries to pull him closer to her.

He growls. "You want me to finish you, don't you? Ask me to finish you, I want to hear you beg me for it," he says in her ear.

"Please, I'm so close. I want more."

Thrusting in again, he fucks her harder and faster until she's crying out his name. He bites into her and takes as much as he can. Her body begins to sage in his arms. He seals her up and continues until his own release comes.

He pulls out, puts himself away, and then stares into her eyes. "You and I had nothing in common. So all I did was fuck you like the whore you are, and then I left. That's all that happened here, now go back to your friends."

Humans are so pathetic.

Not wanting to go back to the bunker, Michael ends up wandering around downtown. He has no idea where else he wants to be. Maybe the club, alcohol could work. He heads that direction.

When he looks down an alley and thinks he sees a familiar face, it brings him to a halt. A human female with a male.

"I told you to leave me the hell alone vampire," she says.

"I sense a male all over you. Are you going to let me have a taste of you too?"

"No. Now get off of me." She shoves the male away.

He finally sees her face clearly. It's Riley's human. *Shit.*

That male comes back at her and shoves her against the wall. He comes down on her neck and she cries out. Michael gets to them fast, throwing the male across the ally. The male flies back up growling.

He draws his sword. "We really going to do this?" He narrows his gaze.

"You're Legion and drawing against me, protecting her ….a Human?" he spits out.

"This human, yes I am." He moves closer to the male.

The male takes a few steps back. "She knows we exist, she needs to be silenced."

"That isn't going to be something I'll allow." He glares. "You will leave, or I'll have your head."

"It's you she belongs to isn't it? Maybe the council should hear about this. A warrior with feelings for a human."

Michael slams him up against the wall hard, biting into his neck as the male struggles in his grasp. Then gets right in his face. "If the council hears of this, you'll be the first one I come looking for. Got it?" He shoves the male towards the end of the alley. "Leave."

The male takes off.

He turns to his brother's female. *Oh man, that's so weird to even say in my head.* "What are you doing out here?" He smells blood and sees where that male has bitten into her. She needs to be sealed.

"I was going to get some dinner when that guy got all grabby," she says, annoyed. "I can take care of myself you know."

He groans. *Figures my pain in the ass brother would find a pain in the ass female.* "I need to seal that." He points at her neck.

Her hand goes to her neck. Bloody finger tips are brought back in front of her. She looks up at him and nods.

He walks up to her and closes his eyes as he leans in to seal her neck. This feels so wrong for so many reasons right now, especially since he finds himself lapping up every bit of the blood on her neck before he seals her. That male was right, Riley all over her.

He steps back. "I'll walk you home."

"You're his brother right? Michael?"

"Yes."

"What did he mean by silencing me?"

"He meant to have you, then kill you." He starts towards her home, which he assumes is in the condo complex. He turns and she isn't following him. He takes a deep breath. "Please?"

"Look vampire….I'm starving, and there's no food at home. So go do whatever it is you were doing, and I'll go get some food on my own like a big girl."

He sighs, "I can't do that."

"What?" She crosses her arms over her chest and glares.

"Where do you want to eat?"

She points down the alley. "There's a Chinese place right around the corner. That's where I'm going."

"Alright, let's go." He smiles at her.

She shakes her head, clearly annoyed with him. It just makes him smile wider. They don't speak as they come down the alley. He stops and then pulls her back when he smells them.

"What?"

"Shhhh." He pushes her next to a trash can.

They come around the corner and there's four of them.

Shit. Fucking Moartea. This is what his brother's female would have run into by herself, not to mention the male that wanted to kill her. She should be back at the bunker where they can keep her safe. Holy shit. A human female in the bunker, because that could ever work.

Michael steps forward drawing his blade. They draw and come at him. One gets around him. He knocks the one in front of him down, takes out the other two, and turns as the other one has a blade at his back.

Next thing he knows it's on its back as that female sweeps its legs out from under it. The one he knocked down is coming at him again, while the other one heads right towards her.

"Run," he yells out.

After finishing off the one in front of him he turns and sees she's facing off with the one that almost took him down. Crazy ass female.

He takes it out before she gets herself killed.

Riley's female is holding her arm tightly and staring off.

"Let me see that." He holds his hand out.

Sky doesn't move.

Fuck, she's probably in shock or some shit. He takes a deep breath and then gently takes her face in his hand. "You're losing a lot of blood. Will you let me see the wound?"

She finally focuses on his eyes and takes her hand away.

"Shit. That's deep." He brings her arm up to his lips. "I'm going to help you, alright?"

Sky narrows her gaze but nods.

Michael runs his tongue along the cut. Her blood is so strong. Somewhere along the way he forgets what the hell he's doing and ends up biting into her—taking more. He seals the wound quickly and steps away shaking his head trying to clear his thoughts.

"You can take more if you need to."

Looking up into her beautiful face as she smiles back at him has his mind running in circles. He wants to bite into her neck and take more so badly, but instead he comes up with, "I'm fine."

"Thank you for helping me. What the hell were those things?"

"Demons." He holds his hand out to her. "Come on, let's get you something to eat."

She takes his hand and he pulls her into him. He tucks her into his left side and keeps his right hand near his blade. He heads towards the restaurant.

"I told you to run. Why did you stay?"

She shrugs. "I was worried."

"Worried?" He looks down at her.

"Yeah, there were four of them. What if something happened to you?"

"You worried for me?" He drops his brow. "I can take care of myself female."

"As can I, vampire." Her smile widens. "But if something happened to you, and I had to tell him I ran away….well I couldn't live with that. I'd rather die fighting by your side."

Michael's never had anyone but Riley worry for him, but she did. This female is tough and loyal, and he's beginning to understand why Riley chose her. She isn't like any other human female he's ever come across. He just can't figure out what the hell made her go anywhere near Riley.

"Just so you know, he would have killed me if anything happened to you." He shakes his head.

They come to the restaurant and he holds the door open for her. They walk inside and it's pretty busy but the line to order is free. He looks up at a board that has pictures of different teriyaki dishes on it.

She looks up and orders a couple of items, then she turns to him. "Are you hungry?"

Michael thinks about it and yeah he could eat. He shrugs.

Two more items are ordered. She turns back to look him up and down, her gaze narrows, and then she orders two more.

Michael laughs. As she goes to pay, he pushes her hand away and hands the guy his card. "Here."

"What? I just figured you probably eat as much as he does."

He grabs the food and they head to the condo complex he was at before. They come up the elevator riding it to the top floor. A penthouse girl, that makes this even more confusing. They come inside and he sets the food on the table.

Sky goes to the kitchen and grabs silverware. He heads over to the window and looks out. Great view of the city, and they have floor to ceiling black out curtains. Well that's convenient for Riley isn't it?

She comes back to the table. "My roommate and I usually just eat some then pass the containers around. Do you want a plate?"

"No that's fine." He comes back to the table and sits down. "You're well off?" He grabs one of the containers.

"No. This place doesn't belong to me. My roommate and I are renting from a friend. So why were you downtown?"

He tenses up and takes a deep breath. "I had some business to take care of."

"Hmmm…feeding, huh? At the club?"

"No, not at the club. How did you know?"

"Business." She laughs. "That's what Riley said the night he met me. He called me business."

He smiles. "I think you know way too much."

"I can't be….scrubbed, that's what he calls it. It doesn't work on me."

"So he tried to scrub you?"

"No, I told him it wouldn't work on me. I had one guy try to and it didn't work. I wasn't exactly sure that's what he was doing at the time. But then I watched this huge vampire with a shaved head killed one of those things like we saw tonight, and then afterwards he kissed me."

"Shaved head?" He narrows his gaze.

"Yeah, he was cute and had tattoos on his neck. But I wasn't into the whole sex in an alley thing, so I stopped him. He was cool about it, then he tried to erase my memory and left. I've never met one before that wanted to kill me."

He takes a deep breath. *Markus.* "It's because you know what we are, and they sense vampire on you. They sense Riley. When did you see the guy with the shaved head?"

"It was a few months ago."

Not sure how Riley would feel about Markus with her at all. Doesn't matter how long ago it was. He's just glad that he didn't have her. Although that in itself is interesting, because if Markus kissed her, he wanted her. Yet he didn't try to scrub her so he could take her. Which is when he would have figured out that she couldn't be scrubbed. He's never known Markus to walk away from a female he wanted. Maybe it wasn't Markus.

They finish eating and she gets up to put everything away.

Sky comes back to the table, smiling. "So, how long are we hanging out?"

He gets up. "Sorry, I'll go."

She laughs. "I'm not telling you to leave. Where is he tonight?"

"Recon."

"Would you like to watch a movie?"

"What movie?"

"Come with me." She takes him to a huge cabinet of movies. "D has a ton of them, so pick whatever you want."

Michael looks them over, and then looks back at her. "I don't watch movies, so I'm not sure what to choose."

"You've never watched a movie?" She says brow raised.

He grimaces. "Not in a very long time."

"Then I better pick a good one. Do you want something funny, action, or romance?"

He pauses. "Action?"

She smiles and chooses a movie called Underworld. "I find this more funny now....well because of knowing Riley and everything, but it's all action."

The movie comes to an end. It was fine, absurd, but fine.

"There's actually four movies in this series, but I'm beat. I need to go to sleep, he calls me at like six in the morning," she says.

"He talks to you every morning?"

"Yeah. Thanks for dinner....and well everything else."

"Says the human that saved my life."

"I was just paying you back. I don't like to owe anybody anything."

He nods and heads home.

Leaving her in the city is not sitting well with him. It's dangerous, but a human female in a bunker full of males, Riley would kill them all. He takes a deep breath. He will keep what happened tonight to himself. He just wonders if that female is smart enough to do the same.

****

Riley comes into the bunker bypassing everyone. He gets in the shower and then grabs his phone on the way to bed. He hasn't made it back to Sky in four days, and he needs to hear her voice right now or he's going to fucking snap.

Damn I hate that female in the city alone.

He dials her and as soon as she answers the phone his whole body relaxes.

He takes a deep breath. "Morning Luv."

"Hi," she clears her throat. "Wow, it's really early."

He looks at the clock and sees it's five in the morning. *Shit.* "Sorry, I just really needed to hear your voice."

"S'ok. Is everything okay with you?"

No, I've become this crazy pathetic male who falls apart without hearing his female's voice. "Yeah, I just miss you."

"I miss you too. Are you in bed?"

"Yeah."

There's a long pause. "What are you wearing?"

He pauses. "Um….nothing."

She takes a deep breath. "That's so depressing."

"Depressing?"

"Yeah, the things I would do to you if I was next to you."

He growls.

She laughs. "Riley?"

"Yeah?"

"Are you hard right now?"

He looks down and yep, he was the moment he heard her voice. "Yes."

She groans. "Can you take a hold of yourself for me?"

Hmmm. As she talks to him he takes a hold of himself and moans. Yep it could work, but all he can think about is her hand on him.

"I'm lying here completely bare thinking about you inside me right now," she moans.

He stops and looks over at the clock. He has a matter of minutes to make up his mind. "Luv, I have to go."

"Wha…."

He hangs up, gets dressed, throws his shoes on, and runs up the stairs to the garage. He comes out the door and his skin tingles. Dawn is approaching fast. He closes his eyes and focuses on Sky.

****

Huh? Thought that could be fun, but I guess he isn't into the whole phone sex thing. I sigh. I'm totally amped up now, in between finishing myself off and being irritated. Then he appears before me. Wow, he's on edge and the clothes are coming off fast.

"Hi." That's all I get out before…. "Oh God," I gasp. Oh yeah, so much better than phone sex.

Two hours later I look over at the clock and groan. "I have to go to work. I assume you'll be sleeping here today?"

He has me wrapped up in his arms and begins kissing my face softly all over. "Can you call in sick and stay with me?"

They will be so pissed if I do, but I haven't seen him in four days. "I can do that. Then I can watch over you while you sleep."

Riley growls, "There won't be much sleeping going on here today, female."

That makes me laugh.

He was right, there isn't much sleeping until eleven, and only five hours at that. I wake up first and look up at him. I love looking at him. I keep the curtains pulled back in the corner now so I can see around the room. He said as long as the sun isn't shining right on him he's fine.

I look up into a beautiful smiling face. "You're awake."

"I am." He pulls me closer. He kisses me softly as he runs his hand across my body and down between my legs.

I laugh on his lips. "Not tired of me after all of that huh?"

"Never." He pulls me on top of him. He looks up at me smiling as he begins to move underneath me.

He ends up leaving at six. I didn't mention all the stuff with his brother, the vampire, and demons. He's already worried enough about me here alone, and I don't want to make it worse.

Chapter 6

I get home after eight in the evening. Riley said he would come by tonight, but I'm not holding my breath. He's been busy the last four nights with business. Whatever that means. At least I was able to see him yesterday morning. Not that I can afford to keep missing work and losing sleep.

The phone vibrates. This is normally the time of night he tells me he's sorry and can't make it. If he was human I'd figure myself the other woman. But since he's a vampire that goes 'hunting' in the evenings, I'll have to deal.

> Riley: Can't meet till late. Shit is going down. Sorry Luv
> Me: Ok I understand. Hope I see you later but ok if
>   you're busy
> Riley: Nothing short of death will keep me from you tonite
> Me: =) K
> Riley: Can I stay with you tomorrow?
> Me: Of course
> Riley: Tonight Luv, tonight

Well I like how that sounds. I can't believe how badly I want him all the time. It's ridiculous how this vampire bond stuff works. I met him eighteen days ago and you'd think we've been together for years. Plus, he's model gorgeous and wants me, which is still hard to wrap my brain around.

Pulling open the refrigerator door, I sigh—bare again. Danielle's been working doubles at the hospital and my head hasn't really been here lately. I feel bad, I know she works hard and it must suck when she goes to look for food and there isn't any.

Well then, Jimmy John's it is. I'll pick her up one so she can take it to work with her tomorrow. I start off down the street and soon realize it's freezing and I should have grabbed my jacket.

Oh well.

One block down, I get ready to cut through the alley when something stops me dead in my tracks. It feels wrong somehow, like death. Everything inside of me is telling me to go around, but I'm starving and not about to walk an extra three blocks. I sense a vampire as well. Even after all of the crap that happened two nights ago, I continue on.

Cautiously entering the alley, I figure I'm just being paranoid. About a quarter of the way down I hear noises. Crying, struggling and gasping.

Crap, maybe it's a prostitute and a john.

I keep walking and see something slumped against the wall a few feet from me. As I get closer, I put my hand over my mouth trying to hold back a scream or maybe throw up when I see it's the body of a woman. Her eyes are open, throat's been cut, and there's blood everywhere.

She was vampire.

What the hell have I just walked into? Maybe it's more of those demon things. Crap. Crap. Crap.

The gasping gets louder the farther I go down the alley. I round the other side of a large trash bin and smell raw wet putrid earth. The sense of death is thick in the air.

A huge man with a black glow around him, has another vampire girl by the throat—she looks terrified. Wide-eyed, she makes eye contact with me and begins shaking her head.

If I go for help, he'd be gone and she'd be dead before I could get back here.

"Run," she chokes out.

I stumble over a bag of trash.

Shit.

His body straightens up and turns around, keeping his grasp on the girl. There's black holes where his eyes should be and a distorted black mouth. Nope, not a john, and I must be out of my mind thinking of doing what I'm about to do. But I can't leave her here to die.

Michael took out the four from the other night pretty quickly, but he had a sword and all I have is my bare hands. Not that I could use a sword anyways. Looking around, there's nothing here to use as a weapon.

I'll bum rush him and maybe it will knock the girl free. Then hopefully the two of us together can beat him off. I run at him full force, but before I can hit him he swings his arm around catching me in the side with a knife. Sharp pain causes me to double over, gasping for breath. Then he swings his arm again, backhanding me so hard I hit the building wall ten feet away on the other side of the alley.

Damn. Epic fail.

I pull the knife out and throw it down. I'm trying not to pass out as I struggle to breathe. Nausea washing over me. Great, probably a concussion along with whatever is going on with the stab wound.

The woman begins choking as that thing laughs. Pressing my hand to my side, I know there's too much blood. I'm fading and finding it harder to breath. On the plus side, with as cold as it is I won't bleed out as quickly. My mind falls to Riley, and my heart breaks.

****

Riley's in the club with Michael, Derek and Cash. They have another job tonight, then he's going to Sky's no matter what. He puts his phone away and knows he needs to focus on the task at hand. Not focusing gets people killed. Interesting, not something he much cared about before. But now he has a reason to live, so he can hold his female again.

They will be raiding another Moartea safe house. But she's all he can think about. The feel of her body against his, kissing her, holding her in his arms. He will have to talk to them about her soon.

He has a feeling of dread wash over him. Death, dirt, Moartea. As his eyes scan the club, he can't figure out where it's coming from.

"What's up Riley?" Michael asks.

A sharp pain nails him in the side of his stomach. He doubles over grabbing at his chest, gasping for breath.

"You okay?" Derek's hand grasps his shoulder.

It begins to pass. "Fuck. I guess."

Then his heart feels like it's being ripped from his chest. He gasps again. It's her. She's hurt, and badly. He gets up and flies out the back door. She's close. He closes his eyes trying to get a lock on her.

Derek's right on his ass. "Yo. What the fuck's going on?"

"She's hurt," he rambles out. He needs to get to her quickly.

"Who's hurt?" Derek looks around.

"Riley, what's going on?" His brother's voice barely comes through his head.

He sets off at a slow jog. Something invisible is pulling him towards her, but it's faint. Of course, she took his blood in, but barely. When he gets to her he's going to make sure she drinks a gallon of it so he can find her wherever she is.

As the pull gets stronger, he takes off running. Derek and Michael are flanking him. They come to the mouth of an alley.

Moartea.

All three draw their weapons.

One female dead, another female slipping away in the grasp of a Moartea, and one human dying. *My human.* Internally freaking out, his worst nightmare has come true before his eyes.

As he gets closer, she moves her hand and a knife is brought from the ground to the base of the Moartea's skull. She never actually touches it. It's a clean shot as the Moartea falls to his ass, spinal cord severed.

He looks over at Sky as she slumps over and he can feel her fading. He lets out a roar as he takes off towards the Moartea. He will rip it to pieces for what it's done to his female.

He picks it up off the ground and runs his blade through its heart. In a rage, he begins slicing it across its entire body before cutting off its head. Nothing's left but ash.

Derek stands over Sky's body with his blade at her heart. "This one's human and almost gone," Derek calls out.

"Derek no," Michael yells.

But Riley's already knocked the blade away and placed himself between Sky and Derek, fangs bared and crouching into a fighting stance.

"What the fuck, Riley?" Derek says.

"I will kill anyone that fucking touches her," he growls.

Michael steps forward and pulls Derek back. "Nobody's going to hurt her Riley," Michael says calmly.

Sky cries out in pain. He feels her slipping away from him. The wound is mortal. Sliding down the wall to his ass, he sits beside her. He pulls her into his lap, holding her tightly in his arms. The crushing pain in his chest is consuming him.

This can't be happening. I can't lose her.

His world is crashing before his eyes and it takes everything he has to hold back the tears and sorrow.

"Riley?" Sky looks up at him.

"Yes, Luv, I'm here. Why are you here?"

"He was hurting her. I had to try and help her. He wasn't human." She coughs up blood.

Fuck. It's probably her lung.

She doesn't have long. He looks up and sees Cash get out of the van and slowly walk towards them. He looks back down and knows what he has to do.

"She's alive Luv, you saved her. I can help you if you will stay with me."

Tears run down her cheeks. "I can't leave you, it wasn't enough time. I love you," she cries.

"Do you want me to try to save you? It will hurt, and it may not work."

"Then I can stay with you?" She grips his arm tightly.

He leans down to her lips. "Forever." He softly kisses her.

"Help me stay," she whispers as she reaches up and touches his face. Her hand begins to slide down as she fades.

Capturing her hand in his, he holds it to his cheek trying hard not to completely lose it. There isn't much time. All three males staring down at him like he's a fucking circus attraction. Mouths hanging open, and Michael shaking his head slowly. He grabs her up in his arms and stands before them.

"Are you fucking kidding me with this shit, Riley? What gives you the right to make a half-breed?" Derek yells.

"I love her," he barely chokes out.

"Shiiiit." Derek rubs his face.

"You are bonded to this female?" Michael asks.

"Yes, sure as shit. Whole fucking mind, body, and soul shit." He sighs. "If she dies, Michael, I die."

"Fuck," Derek yells. "We have to get the females out of here. Riley, deal with your female. But you'll have a lot of explaining to do brother."

He materializes with her in his arms back to her place. He lays her in her bed and puts pressure on the wound.

****

Michael watches his brother disappear with that female in his arms. Figures she decided to help that female instead of run. It's just her nature, and she's as dangerous as Riley is. After what he just saw, he's sure his brother is completely bonded to her.

God help them all if they can't save her. His brother is ruthless and dangerous. If Riley loses that girl, Michael can't imagine what his brother would be like with a broken heart. Riley's cruelty has known no bounds when he's dealt with Moartea or humans. Even the rest of the males in the house watch themselves around him.

What the hell was she doing out walking these streets alone again? Apparently, she didn't learn her lesson after the other night.

"Did you know about all of that shit, Mike?" Derek demands.

Michael nods. "I saw them on the boardwalk together a few nights back."

"How long do you think it's been going on with this human?"

"Sky," Michael says staring off, barely paying attention.

"What?"

"Her name is Sky."

"So how long?"

He looks over at Derek. "He's been off for a couple of weeks, so I'm not exactly sure. Remember a week ago when he didn't make it in before dawn? I assume it's because he was with her. Then he was gone all last weekend, and I know he was with her."

"Damn." He rubs his face. "She knows about us."

"Yeah. Did you see her throw that knife without ever touching it?"

"I don't want to think about any of this shit right now," Derek growls. "Cash, get them loaded. We'll drop them off to their families." Derek looks back at him. "What?"

"I need to go to him, he needs help."

"You asking me or telling me?" Derek glares.

"He's bonded. We have to try. You know she needs more than he can give her." He isn't ready to let go of this female that saved his life, as well as Riley's.

"Pray that human lives through the change, or that edge you brother's been riding this past century is libel to claim him right off it." Derek sighs. "Call as soon as you know something. I'm sure you're the only one he'll let anywhere near her."

"Got it."

He appears outside in the alley of the multi residential building Sky lives in. He texts his location to Derek and Justin. Then he appears close to his brother. He's standing in the living room. He feels his brother's pain as he enters the room they're in.

****

Riley's knows the likelihood of changing her is slim, but he also knows he has to at least try, he can't lose her….not now. He scores his wrist and puts it to her lips. He won't survive the pain if she dies. She's become his entire world.

She's very still and barely breathing. He feels her slipping away even further from him. Maybe he's already too late. Her mouth is full of blood but she isn't swallowing. Panic washes over him and his own darkness is creeping in. Then he senses Michael in the room.

"I will not let you kill her."

"I'm not here for that. She needs more than you can provide. I'm here to help you." Michael grips his shoulder.

Riley looks up as the panic shifts to worry. Turning a human is forbidden without just cause and permission from the entire house, let alone the council. He won't let his brother pay the price for his decisions.

"I can't let you get caught up in all of this, Mike. She can drain me dry. I don't care as long as she lives."

"They know I'm here. But I would have come no matter the orders." Michael smiles. "I'm not ready to see this female meet her end. Especially after she saved my life."

"Saved your life?"

"I was in the city two nights ago. A male had her in his grasp and was going to kill her. I stepped in and then walked her to a restaurant so she could get dinner. We came upon four Moartea on the way and one almost stabbed me. She saved my life brother."

He takes a deep breath. "You saved hers, thank you. Why didn't you tell me?"

"I ate dinner and just spent some time with her. I knew then you were bonded. I didn't want you to worry for her." Michael shakes his head. "But by being with her, you've put her in danger. She's no longer safe out here."

Riley hangs his head. "I know." He knows Michael would do anything for him, even if it means standing against all others to protect him. Maybe together it will be enough to save her. "Thank you," he coughs as tears well up in his eyes.

****

Looking out the window as the city streaks by him, Derek begins shaking his head, thinking about the night's events. They drop the females off and then head back to the bunker.

"So that was some crazy shit back there, right?" Cash blurts out in the silence.

"Yeah."

"What I saw back in that alley was….hell, I'm not sure what the fuck I saw. But I know I felt some crazy shit when I saw them together."

"Their bonded," he says.

"Seriously? I've never felt anything like that before," Cash says. "What happens now?"

"No idea. If she makes it, we have an unsanctioned half-breed on our hands. If she doesn't…."

"We'll have a crazy ass homicidal vampire on our hands." Cash says. "Looks like I'll be praying for that female to make it."

"You and me both, brother."

Derek rubs his face as they pull into the garage. They head downstairs and through the hallway to the great room. He sees Justin in the office.

"How did it go?" Justin says as he sorts through blueprints.

"We never made it," he says.

Justin looks up. "What?"

"We made it as far as the club before Riley took off to help his female."

Justin pauses and raises his brow. "His….female? Riley has a female?"

"Oh yeah. She was mortally wounded this evening. He's trying to turn her with Michael's help."

"Making her a half-breed?" Justin barely chokes out. "You allowed that?"

"He told me he loves her, brother. I wasn't given a choice. He's bonded to her."

"Riley?" Justin raises his brow. "We are taking about Riley here right?"

He laughs at the face Justin's sporting. "Yeah, you can feel that shit. Did you know that?"

"If the bond is strong enough….yeah, others around them can feel it." Justin rubs the back of his neck. "Shit."

"Yeah, pretty much where I was at about an hour ago."

"He's bonded to her, so I understand why he has to try. The council is going to flip out. They haven't sanctioned a turn in over half a century."

"How can we help protect them from this shit storm?"

Justin smiles. "So you're for this turn? This mating?"

He shrugs. "I guess I am. He's my friend, and he was different tonight. You should have seen the way he held that female in his arms. Not sure I know the male I saw before me tonight."

"How was she hurt?"

"She faced off with a Moartea that killed one female, and was about to kill another. She tried to help the female and was stabbed. When we came upon her she was dying. She threw a knife and hit the Moartea in the back of the skull. She did it with better precision than anyone here could have, except maybe Markus."

"I can tell the council that the house voted in favor of the half-breed before the turn, and we were prepared to come to them when this tragedy happened. She proved herself when she came upon our enemy and made it her own. Which resulted in saving one of our own." Justin turns and pulls papers out of the filing cabinet. "I can back date these forms, but everyone in the house will have to vote in favor of her."

"Let's hope it works. If they don't accept her, I'm not sure how he'll handle it." Derek sits down. "And I'm not sure I could stand behind the council if they don't accept her."

"If they're bonded, the council will be bound, she will be untouchable. I need to notify them right away. Gather everyone up and explain what's going on."

****

"She isn't drinking Michael," Riley says.

Michael feels his brother's panic. "Here, let me help." He checks and she's still breathing, but barely.

She needs to be nearly drained in order for Riley's blood to flood her system and do its job. He holds her nose and puts his hand over her mouth. She struggles then swallows. They wait a few minutes, then her breathing finally becomes stronger. Riley puts his wrist back to her lips and this time she's swallowing. Her arms slowly come up and lock around Riley's arm.

Michael sighs in relief. This female has to make it. He would still like to know how this female was able to tame his brother, after so many others have fallen at his hands.

Their bond is so strong. Michael feels their love for each other. He feels the bond from her as well. He never knew humans could bond, but he felt it the night they were together as she talked about Riley.

"It's only the beginning, brother. Hell awaits her very soon." He lays his hand on his brother's shoulder. "We need something for her to bite down on so she doesn't break her teeth."

"It has to work. I can't be without her."

"She must walk through hell and back. I hear it's when most pass. They can't fight their way back from the darkness through the pain."

"She's strong enough. I know she is," he whispers. "You'll see Michael, she's amazing."

"That….I already know brother." If he knew nothing else about this female, he'd know that just by looking at the male before him.

She brakes her hold on Riley's wrist and lays back down. She's shivering. Riley seals his wrist, drops his weapons to the floor, and then curls up next to her. The tenderness this male is showing for his female is so out of character for him. Just like when he saw them together on the boardwalk.

"I love you. I know you can come back to me. Just fight," Riley says quietly.

Riley is thrown from the bed as she arches up and kicks her feet. She grips the bedding in her hands so tight her knuckles turn white as she writhes in pain. She screams out and he gets to her and shoves a thin book into her mouth.

"Riley, get her legs now," he yells.

"She has to make it," Riley says shaking his head.

"Her body must die as your blood floods her system. If she wakes, you'll have to watch or she will drain me as the thirst takes her over."

Riley nods.

She thrashes for twenty minutes then goes completely still. He holds his breath as he waits for her to take her first. She's so still, he finds himself trying to will her to breathe. He leans down and listens. She's breathing, but it's shallow. His brother's mate has made it.

Riley is still talking to her and caressing her face.

For the next eight hours they watch her. Michael knows she'll need to feed again soon or she will die. They will have to get her through the next twenty four hours before the change is complete.

****

Oh God, the pain.

It felt like I was on fire. Now I'm in a tunnel and with voices echoing around me. One is familiar and filling me with love—and worry. As I follow the voices, my body begins to burn again. The pain is intense, but I have to get to the voice. I try to force my eyes open, but I can't.

Riley.

He's here with me. He brought me home very fast. One minute we were in the alley and the next I was in my bed. I had been hurt badly—I was dying.

Oh no. Did I die?

I hear another male's voice.

Michael. His brother is here.

"She isn't waking up. She has to wake up," Riley pleads.

"She's alive, give her time."

"Luv, open your eyes for me. Please come back to me."

"Forever remember," I whisper.

He swoops me up in his arms and holds me tightly. I'm back to barely breathing again, and every inch of my body hurts. He's softly kissing me all over my face.

"She needs to feed," Michael says.

"Luv, Michael's going to give you something to help you. You must take it for me, alright?"

I nod.

A wrist is placed on my lips and I feel something warm slide down my throat.

Blood, they're giving me blood.

Before conscious thought can take over I bite down and begin to draw it in. It's so good, and it's putting the fire out inside of me. I want more. I'm lost in my head for a moment when suddenly I'm slammed back into reality.

I bit down into his wrist with fangs. I have fangs?

I release him immediately and then push myself away from them. I sit up against the headboard drawing my knees up to my chest. My eyes shoot between the two of them. I begin blinking rapidly, trying to focus my eyes.

They are vampires. I was dying. No, I did die.

As the room and its occupants come into focus, I reach up to my mouth just as two fangs begin to retreat. I look back up at Riley and his brother.

Both stare at me wide eyed.

"Riley, her eyes," Michael chokes out. "They're so blue."

"I don't understand?" Riley shakes his head.

It's dark and I'm having a hard time focusing. If I had more light I could see them better. Five candles in the room light.

Michael jumps up from the bed looking around. "I knew she didn't throw that knife, she willed it." Michael narrows his gaze. "She has powers." He rubs his eyes like maybe he can make me disappear. "It's almost dawn, I need sleep. I'll give you two some time alone. She will need to feed again soon. I'll be in the living room when you need me." Michael leaves the room.

Riley reaches his hand out towards me. He looks like hell. I take his hand and let him pull me into his lap. I wrap my arms around his neck and hold him tightly.

"I thought I lost you," he says in my ear.

"You did." I shudder. "What am I?"

"You're half vampire, a half-breed."

"You came for me. You found me."

"I will always find you, Luv. Forever."

Pulling back slightly, I take his shirt off and run my hands up his chest to feel his warmth. Stripping of my shirt and bra, I lean back into him and run my arms around his neck.

Riley wraps me up in his arms tightly.

"Will you lie with me? I'm so cold," I say as my teeth chatter.

He stands up with me still in his arms and then pulls back the covers. Setting me on the bed, he undresses us both, come in next to me, and then wraps me up in his body completely. Safe, warm, and completely exhausted, I fall asleep quickly.

I wake up two hours later clenching my stomach. It's like the worst hunger pains ever, times ten. My fangs elongate and I can only assume it's my body telling me I need blood. My body is being pulled up on Riley's chest.

He touches my face and pulls me to his lips.

The desire is intoxicating and a little distracting at the moment.

He guides me to his neck. "Take from me."

I lean in so hungry for him. I want his blood, but I also want all of him. I reach down and guide him into me.

He moans and locks his hands onto my hips.

I slowly lean down and gently bite into his neck. As soon as my fangs pierce his flesh, his hips arch up, he digs his hands into my thighs, and climaxes in a deep throaty moan. I take him in until the pain leaves me. I lick the wound to seal him up and kiss my way back to his mouth.

"I love you," I say.

He turns us over and runs his thumb across my cheek. "You are a dream I never want to wake up from."

He makes love to me again and then we both fall asleep.

I wake him up a couple more times to feed. Each time he takes the opportunity to make love to me again. He is so sweet and gentle with me, but I'll never forget how fierce I saw him become in that alley. He's also dangerous and lethal. Maybe I forgot somewhere along the way that Riley is not human, he's a vampire.

****

The thirst starts again. I've taken from Riley three times already and I feel how weak he is. He needs rest. Maybe food will help. I get up, pull my robe on, and go to the kitchen. I pull open the fridge and sigh. I really need to go grocery shopping. I open a drawer and get excited over a small package of lunch meat. I pull it out and close the fridge. Vampire, blood, meat maybe?

I open the package and get one piece down before I double over in pain. I spit out the little bit that comes back up, but I'm on my way to the ground when I'm caught and supported in large arms. I look up and remember Michael's here.

"Thank you," I choke out.

"You can't have food right now. You need to feed."

"I can't take from him again he's exhausted."

"Come here." He walks me to the couch and sits beside me. He lays his arm across my lap, wrist up. "Take from me."

My fangs elongate at the thought of having his blood.

"This is why I came. You need more than one male can give you right now."

I take his wrist in my hand and bite into him. He's different than Riley, but somehow still the same. The pain passes, and I seal him up. "Thank you for helping me….again."

"Will you stay and talk with me?"

"About what?"

"My brother."

"Sure." I sit in the recliner across from him. "Why didn't you ask me before?"

Michael shrugs. "I guess I was trying to get to know you and figure it out for myself. How did he come to know you?"

"Hmmm….well, I guess from the club. We first talked in Distortion."

He gets a look of confusion across his face. His eyes get all squinty like he's trying to process something he doesn't understand.

"I get it, this is all very sudden. I'm living it and I still don't believe it."

"You are one of the prostitutes he has sex with?"

"No," I snap as I shake my head. Then I find myself laughing. We did eventually have sex without knowing each other. "The first time I met him at the club he was very pushy. He tried to take me out back to the alley, but I told him to leave me alone." I smile. "You can see that didn't really stick"

"I don't understand?"

"After that first night, I couldn't stop thinking about him. He was on my mind night and day. A week later I saw him at the club and there was just this overwhelming draw to be with him. Something was pulling me to him. I knew I had to see him again. I think back now and I'm pretty sure I already loved him. I know that sounds crazy, but I wanted him. I felt he was meant to be mine."

Michael looks up.

Riley's behind me, I feel him. I'm even more connected to him, and now I feel Michael as well. And wow, are that guys emotions all over the place.

****

"It was the same for me." Riley comes around the front of the chair to pull Sky up into his arms. She looks up at him and he softly kisses her.

"She's beautiful. And you were right, she's also very strong," Michael says.

"I keep trying to tell her that."

Michael narrows his gaze and smiles. "You're different brother."

"And you will keep that shit to yourself."

Michael laughs. "Of course, but I think the others will notice the moment you walk in the door. The look I see on your face now as you gaze upon your female, says it all."

He glares.

"What does he mean?" Sky asks.

"Nothing." He kisses her neck.

Michael smiles.

"Are you all dark, broody, mean, and dangerous to all those poor males you live with?" she says with a smirk.

"Ah, and she's very smart too."

"You two going to be ganging up on me now?"

****

Riley pulls away from me clearly annoyed at his brother and me for picking on him.

I grab his hand. "Riley."

He turns his back to me and starts to walk away.

"I love you." I'm smiling as he turns around to look at me.

His facial expression begins to soften. I pull him back towards me and stand on my tip toes to kiss his lips.

Riley sighs and kisses me back. "I don't think I could ever stay mad at you."

I nod towards the bedroom. "What do you say we head back in there?" This poor male, I can't get enough of him. I think it's actually worse now.

He picks me up in his arms and heads back into the bedroom.

"Hey," I say as he sets me down on the bed. "I'm not stupid you know."

He looks down at me brow tightened.

"I may not know your past, but I know you. They're scared of you aren't they? I've seen the way they look at you. You brother loves you, but even he's careful around you. What I saw you do to that demon thing in the alley, was savage."

Leaning up against the wall, he crosses his arms over his chest, and that dark mean side of his stares back at me.

"You're dangerous and deadly." I get up and put my hands on his arms and lean into him. "But I also know I love you. That strength and power doesn't scare me, it makes me feel safe. I love you even more for the way you are with me. Know that I too would die to protect you."

He's still staring at me, but his body begins to relax.

****

As Riley hears the words pass her lips he can't stop himself from what's about to come out of his mouth. "Will you be my mate?" The smile she gives him goes right to his heart and fills him with so much love. *What could I have ever done in my whole life to have deserved her?* The answer is nothing.

Her eyes dart around. "Is that like me marrying you?"

Ah, the human way. Maybe he should have said it that way. "Yes, will you marry me?"

Tears begin to stream down her face. Which confuses the shit out of him because he senses her happiness.

She pulls his face to hers. "Yes Riley, I will be your mate."

Bringing his arms around her, he kisses her deeply. He never would have thought in a million years she could be with him forever. The internal struggle began the moment he realized they were bonded. How long would he have with her? Could he bear trying to turn her? Would she eventually see through to the male he really is inside? If he was going to ever try to turn her, it wouldn't have been for many years. There's no way he would have risked losing her on purpose.

Things seem to be finally working out for him after all these years. Now all he has to do is deal with the council, and if he has to run with her, he will. No one will ever take her from him.

****

Did I just agree to get married? I've only known him for three weeks, but I love him fiercely….and I'm a vampire. What the hell.

He pulls away and seems instantly anxious.

"What is it?"

"Tonight I'll have to face what I've done. Falling in love with a human, and turning you without permission isn't going to go over too well."

"How bad can it get?"

"Together we will go before the council. But I won't let anything happen you, I will always protect you."

"I know. Together we pretty much break all the rules of what is considered normal and rational. Who's to say this will be any different?"

He smiles, shaking his head. "Michael said you saved his life."

I shrug. "I'm not sure I was anything more than a distraction. He was so worried about keeping me safe, that he wasn't paying attention to those things. But he saved my life first."

That tight brow and glare was across his face. "Yes, the male in the alley that threatened your life. He better pray I never find him."

"Your brother is pretty cool. Different from you."

"I heard you spent the evening with him?"

"We had dinner and watched a movie. It was nice to get to know another part of you." I drop my robe and slide into bed. "You coming….or are you going to brood some more?"

He strips down and then in after me.

I laugh. I've never felt anything as intense as this. It's like our souls are all tangled up in each other.

"I could lie in your arms forever." I run my hands across his chest. There's a knock at the door

"Yeah," Riley calls out.

Michael comes in. "I'm going home first to try and explain a few things. You both should be right behind me. They will demand to know about everything before you head to the council."

He rubs his head. "Uh….Sky?"

"Yeah?"

"Are you a witch?"

He's probably asking me because of the knife in the alley and the candles earlier. "I don't think so, but…." I close my eyes and wish the candles in the room lit. By the gasps I hear I know it worked. I open my eyes. "So….well yeah, I have no idea what any of that is."

"No longer than an hour Riley, or they will come here."

"I got it, don't worry so much."

"Remember what I said before, nothing has changed." Michael disappears before my eyes.

****

Michael appears at the bunker, takes a deep breath, and then heads inside. All nine members of the Ninth are seated at one half of the large dining table.

Derek gets up and approaches him. "Where is he Mike?"

"He's coming. I wanted to talk to everybody first."

"Has the human made it through the change?" Justin asks.

"Yes."

"Is he bringing her here?" Justin presses.

"Yes, he understands the laws. They're both coming, but she wasn't human. She has powers."

That statement is met with narrowed eyes, and he hears a few growls. Witches are not very popular among vampires.

"He's turned a witch?" Brandon chokes out.

"I'm not exactly sure what she is, but she is amazing. You'll see. She had no idea about the powers she possesses," Michael says.

"Are they bonded?" Justin asks.

"Oh yeah, trust me. You'll all be able to see and feel it. Give them a chance to explain everything."

"The council has already been informed of the half-breed. They are requesting an immediate audience. Derek and I will go with them on their behalf before the council."

"I request to come along as well," Michael says.

"No," Derek says coldly.

"I will not allow any harm to come to my brother or his mate."

"Shit Mike, you think I would let that happen?" Justin says. "Not for this. They will have to deal."

"Swear to me no harm will come to either of them."

"On my honor, brother." Justin puts his hand on Michael's shoulder. "And on my life."

"You'll see, then you will understand so much more." Michael shakes his head somewhat relieved. "She saved my life two nights ago." Michael runs through that nights events.

"So she's as crazy as he is, great," Derek says. "Take a seat and hope they show up very soon."

Michael takes a seat next to Cash.

Cash leans over to him. "I've already felt that shit, it was crazy. I could feel their love through my whole body."

Michael takes a deep breath. He had hoped that they'd be able to feel what he has felt. But when they see Riley....that in itself will mean much more than words.

Chapter 7

I slide up on Riley's chest, smiling as I reach back and grab ahold of him. He pulls me to his lips. As he lifts me up, I gasp as he enters me in one quick thrust.

"You have fifteen minutes tops, I need time to get ready."

He swirls his hips under me and growls. "I will take as much time as I want, female. Remember, you are mine."

I'm finally able to get out of his grasp and ready. I stare at myself in the mirror. My eyes have turned a bright cobalt blue color. Not yellow like theirs. "So why are my eyes just bluer and not yellow like yours?"

He comes up behind me. "We're not sure, something to do with the power maybe. You were not exactly human before. I was stabbed when I was out a couple nights back. Your blood healed me almost instantly."

"So what the heck am I?"

"Half vampire, and half something else." He wraps me up in his arms. "You're beautiful." He smiles. "I love the color of your eyes."

"Hey, remember you and me against the world." I turn in his arms. "Stop worrying. I can feel all of that in there." I point at his head.

"I don't know how it is I found you, but I can't ever imagine my life without you now.'

"Ha. Here I am wondering how it is you would even want me in the first place. You could have had anybody you wanted."

He shakes his head. "I never wanted anybody, especially a female. Then I met you and crazy shit happened."

I laugh.

"You ready to go?"

I take a deep breath. "About as ready as I'm going to be." One minute I'm in my bathroom, and the next minute I'm standing in front of a metal door in a forest. "Whoa." I grab my stomach with one hand and my mouth with the other.

He laughs. "Take a deep breath, it will pass."

"The spinning and nausea?"

"Yeah." He holds on to me tightly.

I try to get my bearings, but I still feel his worry and it's not over me. He's worried about what we're walking into. Wow, the flood of his emotions doesn't help all of the nausea.

"Riley, it will be fine. I feel it. I don't know how, but it will be okay."

He takes a deep breath and grabs my hand.

We come through the door and we're on a large metal platform with stairs leading down. It gets dark as the door closes and locks behind us. As we start down the stairs, I see a bright light coming from below.

I tug on his hand to get him to slow down. At this point I have all his emotions of dread, wrapped up with my fear. I pull him back up on the step right below mine making us almost the same height.

Reaching out, I take his face in my hands and talk as quietly as I can, "Please relax. I can feel everything you're feeling and it's overwhelming me." I smile. "I love you, we'll be fine."

Riley wraps his arms around me and squeezes me. "I just want to keep you safe."

"And you will. Do you really think any of these guys would hurt me?" I narrow my gaze.

"No, because they know I'd kill them," he says fiercely.

He's prepared to take on the world for me. But I'd fight right by his side if I needed to. He had it right when he said this bond is some crazy shit. I kiss him deeply and feel him relax in my arms.

"So….you have a bedroom here right?" I look deeply into his eyes and smile.

He smile begins to slowly spread across his face and then nods.

"I plan on you having me every which way on that bed of yours."

Fangs are drug across my neck, as his hands make their way up my shirt and across my back. Oh yeah, I feel so much better now. All that's left is the love and burning desire we have for each other. I take his hand and try to head down the stairs.

Shaking his head, he looks down, adjusts himself, and then stares at the ceiling.

I laugh and run my arms around his neck squeezing him tightly.

He shakes his head and laughs into me. Then he pulls me down next to him and we walk hand and hand towards the light. Eventually, I see twenty pairs of eyes on us from across the room. I don't make eye contact with any of them. I realize how dumb I must look staring at the floor. I can tell all of them are as large as Riley, or larger.

One of the guys with Riley the first night I saw him, stands up. He has short black spiked hair, golden eyes, and a large chest.

"Come forward, brother, and introduce your female," the guy says.

Riley wraps his arm around me tightly, pulling me into his left side. His right hand is on his weapon as he begins clenching his jaw. Once again he seems to be rethinking coming here. I'm losing part of him inside again.

I turn and stand right in front of him. Damn. There's the dark ruthless side of him I saw in the alley, and when his brother confronted us in the village. He's tense and ready to snap.

"Shit, this isn't good," the guy that walked toward us says.

"Derek, get the female," one yells out, while two others stand.

"No, just watch her with him," Michael says calmly.

Placing my right hand on his chest, I use my left to pull his hand off the handle of his blade, and take it in mine. He looks into my eyes. I remember that he can feel all of my emotions mixed with his. I need to relax and just be at ease. I feel how calm Michael is, and I don't feel threatened here.

I take a deep breath. I smile up at him and talk as quietly as I can. "Hey, it's me and you against the world remember? It will be fine."

He begins to relax and his yellow eyes are coming back.

When I see that he actually sees me, I slide my arms around his waist. "I love you." That I let them hear.

He wraps his arm around me, tilts my chin up with his finger, and kisses me softly. "And I you, Luv."

Five of them blurt out in unison.

"Holy shit."

"What the fuck?"

"Did you see that shit?"

"Dude."

"Crazy."

"I told you," Michael says.

I look into his eyes and smile. "They're all staring at us aren't they?"

He looks up. "Yeah."

"Can I talk to them?"

He smiles. "Fuck, can't really hurt can it." He brushes his thumb across my cheek and kisses me softly.

I turn around to meet the gaze of those in front of me. I walk the twenty feet or so to the center of the table. There are a few gasps. Damn, it's my eyes, I keep forgetting. Not like I can see myself.

"So hi, I'm Skylar." I half wave. "You can call me Sky. I know you have a lot of questions for me. I'll answer almost anything you ask me. I will be respectful of you as long as you're respectful of me. And if anyone tries to hurt Riley or Michael, I will die trying to protect them."

Michael smiles at me.

"Seriously, I'm already in love with her," this really gorgeous guy with short brown wavy hair says as he gets up smiling at me. He extends his hand. "I'm Brandon. Nice to meet you."

"Anybody that can do that to him,"--another one points to Riley--"has my vote. I'm Cash. I saw you in the alley, but you were....well, pretty out of it."

"Vote?" I ask.

"Yes. Every brother here must approve of a half-breed before they can be made. But this has been done a bit out of order. To protect Riley, I told the council we already approved it before he did it. If anyone at this table vote's nay, I will suffer the same fate as the two of you." He takes a breath. "I'm Justin, by the way."

Riley steps forward and put his hand out to Justin. "Thank you, but you didn't have to do that for me. I understood the consequences when I chose to turn her."

"Do you love her?" Justin asks.

"Yes, I wish to mate her."

A few curses and whistles come out of the bunch.

"That's why I had to," Justin says.

Riley grabs him up in a hug. The guy tenses up, then just pats Riley on the back. As he steps away he's smiling and shaking his head.

"Dude, am I fucking dreaming right now or does Riley have a twin we didn't know about?" says a male with long black hair.

Another male stands up. He has dark blond medium length hair, about six two, and pretty cute. He walks up to me. "That bastard over there is Chris,"--he points to the long haired guy that just spoke--"and I'm Chaz. Nice to meet you. Your eyes are beautiful by the way."

Riley leans down to my ear. "Told you." He laces his fingers in mine.

Justin begins to introduce me to the rest of the guys. "That's Derek, Brian, Trevor, Markus, you already know Michael and everybody else."

Each of them give me a wave as he introduces them, except for Trevor. He's barely looked in my direction. He looks kind of scary looking too, so of course I have this urge to want to talk to him.

"Alright, I need a vote," Justin says.

There's three yay's. As Riley pulls me in closer to him I wrap my arms around his waist. We get six more yay's, and then Justin steps forward.

"Yay, from me as well. So it's unanimous. Welcome to the Ninth Legion, Skylar."

"We meet with the council in two hours," Derek interrupts.

"Riley can I talk to you for a few minutes?" Justin asks.

Riley looks down at me

"I'll be fine." I see a knife on the table. I move my hand from the knife to the wall. It flies across the room landing in the wood mantel. "So yeah, I'll entertain them with this crazy shit."

A couple of them jumped back from the table as I did it. Riley shakes his head. He comes up and kisses me before he follows Justin to a room off to the right of the stairs.

"What else can you do?" Brian asks me.

"Well…." I close my eyes and concentrate on the candles around the fireplace. When I open my eyes the candles are lit.

"Crazy, anything else?" he asks.

"It's all kind of new, so I actually have no idea what I can do or why I can do it."

I look next to me and Michael is glued to my side, hand near his blade. I loop my arms around his arm and look up at him smiling.

Michael looks down at me shaking his head and smiling. "You are a very interesting female."

"And you two don't know the meaning of relax do you? Why are they so surprised?"

Michael takes a breath. "He's been lost and angry at the world for….well, everything I guess. He can be reckless and dangerous."

"Why, what happened to you guys?"

"Another time maybe."

Ah, he clammed up quick. "Are you the older or younger brother?"

"Younger."

I narrow my gaze. "But you've had to be like the older brother haven't you?"

Michael smiles. "And definitely too smart for your own good."

I laugh. "Are we going to finish our movie marathon?"

He laughs. "The crazy vampire werewolf one?"

I nod.

"I could do that."

"Riley looks happy. In the last century I've known him I've never seen that look on him," Markus says.

"That's sad. It's the only way I've known him." I grimace. "You look familiar. Yeah….I remember, it was you. I saw you in an alley tearing up one of those demon things. Then it turned to ash. You tried to wipe my memory but all I ended up with was a headache. Thanks for that by the way." I look up at Michael only to find him glaring at Markus. I think he just remembered our conversation and realized who kissed me in the alley.

"Holy shit, that was you," Markus chokes out.

"Good job covering your tracks there Markus," Chris barks.

I wonder what Riley would think about Markus being the first vampire I ever kissed.

"She was so calm, I thought it worked." He shrugs. He gets closer to me and Michael tenses up. "Can we maybe keep that night to ourselves?"

I nod, trying not to laugh. "I think all of that should just stay between us."

"I, too, think that's something that should never pass anyone's lips, unless Markus wishes to be picking himself up off the floor. And I see that as the best case scenario."

Markus nods as he meets Michael's glare.

Michael lowers his voice, "Maybe someday you can tell me what made you walk away from a female you so clearly wanted to take."

"When will the two of you be mated?" Brian interrupts.

"I don't know, Riley just asked me on the way here. We haven't really talked about it."

As Riley comes back into the room, they move away from me quickly. He takes me by the waist and kisses me deeply. So

PDA in front of all of these guys is apparently not a problem. Good to know.

"We'll be in my room," Riley says never breaking eye contact with me.

That gaze always makes me smile, and the little talk on the stairs is starting to come back to me. He leads me down a long hallway. We stop nine doors down to the right and he opens the door.

"Wow." I look around. "This place is huge."

There's a small kitchen with a sink, microwave, and frig in the corner. In the main part of the room is a dining room table, desk, chair and sofa. I can see a bedroom through a doorway. This place has nine foot ceilings so you don't even realize you're underground. This is basically a large two bedroom apartment.

Crazy. I notice it's completely spotless as well. "You're a neat freak aren't you?"

He smiles. "Maybe."

"I can be messy ya know."

"I do know. I guess I'll be cleaning up after you."

I walk to one of the bedroom doorways and will the light on. "Talk about weird. I don't know if I'll ever get used to that." I see a large bed and a bathroom off to the left. I can tell this is the room he stays in.

He comes up behind me wrapping his arms around my waist, and lays his chin on my shoulder. "I love that you're in my room." He pulls my hair aside and kisses down my neck.

I turn around and look up at him, "I think I…." I look down and bite my lip. It feels really weird to ask him for blood, but my stomach is cramping up on me again and I feel weak.

"Sky?"

I sigh. "I need blood."

He smiles. He takes my hand and leads me to the bed. "I love you. Never think you can't ask me. I want you to be well." He sits on the bed and pulls me into his lap. He kisses me and then bares his neck.

My fangs elongate as I lean in to him. He's instantly hard under me, and as his blood moves throughout my body the desire becomes insane. Sharing blood makes us so much more connected to each other.

Riley caresses my back and runs his hands down my sides brushing my breasts with his thumbs. I seal him up and move to his mouth. He lays me on the pillow, comes up between my legs, and then slides his hand up my shirt. I feel his hunger. Not just for sex, but for blood.

"I'm stronger now, take from me."

"No." He continues to kiss me.

"I want you to."

He ignores me, and then tries to kiss me again. I turn away from him causing him to just kiss down my neck. I bite into my wrist and draw blood into my mouth. I push him off of me and then climb up on his chest. He smiles as I run my hand down to grip him.

I lean down to kiss him and as his lips part I let the blood fill his mouth. He kisses me harder and I feel his fangs elongate. I pull back and put my wrist to his mouth.

"Stop being stubborn and drink." I glare.

He slowly bites into my wrist never breaking eye contact with me. When he finishes I know he's going to take me.

"You should know I always plan on winning," I smile.

"I could have waited one more day. I want to make sure you're strong the next couple of days."

"When will we be mated?"

"When you say we are to be."

"Ha. What if I say tonight?"

"I would say no. You need to be stronger first."

I must look confused just staring at him. But stronger to be married. "I don't get it."

"When we are to be mated you will be taken in by every member. It's so that they may always carry you with them to protect you. You will also take in each one of them so that they will be able to find you as I did."

I gasp. "That's how you found me, but I barely had any of your blood."

"It was enough. I think it's because of the bond. This bonded shit is all new to me. Well, to all of us. Not one warrior here has ever bonded to a female. Warriors don't ever take a mate because of the danger we are constantly in."

I laugh. I can't control myself. "Sorry."

"Why is that funny?"

"Because it explains a lot. They've never been bonded but they see the meanest asshole here acting completely different and being kind to a girl."

He shoves me down on the bed and gets right into my face. "Oh yeah, you think that's funny huh?" He pins my arms above my head and grinds the hard length of himself into me.

I want these clothes off now. Am I ever going to be able to control myself around him? "You going to take me or what." I glare with a slight smile.

The clothes come off quickly. I pray that either the door is locked or they know better than to just waltz on in here. He drives into me hard. I can feel his vitality and the strength of my blood running through him. I bare my neck and he takes my vein again. As soon as he sinks his fangs in, we climax together. As we finish up the baby thing flashes through my head again.

He pulls me into his side. "I shouldn't have taken from you again. I just desire all of you all the time."

"It's fine, I wanted you to."

"We need to make sure you stay strong for the next twenty four hours, until the change is complete."

I grab his face in my hands. I lean in kissing him slowly and deeply. I pull back and look at him. "I've never had this before. So much love for someone, and for that person to feel the same for me." I shake my head completely amazed at the turn my life has taken. "Come on, we need to get ready."

We get dressed.

I go into his bathroom to try and fix myself up. He has the basics of everything. This is definitely a guy's bathroom. Toilet, sink, shower, and a mirror. He comes up behind me running his arms around my waist.

"Now I look like crap. Nice rats nest on the back of my head. Do you have a brush somewhere?"

He opens a drawer and then hands me a comb. "I think you're always beautiful."

"Riley?"

"Yeah?"

"Can vampires get pregnant?"

"Yes."

I whip around. "What?"

He smiles. "Relax, it's rare and only when you are….well you know."

"When I'm what?" I raise my brow.

He hangs his head on my shoulder. He's so cute when he's embarrassed. "When you're in heat."

My face drops. "Like a friggin' cat."

He laughs. "No. Once a year there will be three days when you become fertile. It's then when you will be able to conceive a young."

I sigh in relief.

"You don't want my young?"

"It's not that exactly. I don't want any child right now. But if I had gotten pregnant with yours, I would have been okay with it, because I love you, and it would be part of you."

"You're not saying never?"

"No, just not now." I wrap my arms around him. "I want you all to myself for a little while longer. I'm selfish that way."

He laughs and holds me tighter. "Before you, I would have never thought I wanted a young. But to see your beautiful face in our young, I long for that day." There's a knock on the bedroom door. "Come in, Michael."

"Is it weird I knew it was him too?"

"Justin wants me to tell you it's time," Michael says.

"I never thanked you for taking care of her, brother."

"I will protect her as I do you, always." Michael smiles.

I smile and walk to him. "Thank you for everything." I throw my arms around him. He gets very stiff, I hold him tighter. "This is the part where you put your arms around me and hug me back."

Michael slowly brings his arms around me and finally relaxes a bit. He smiles and shakes his head. I go back into Riley's waiting arms.

"She's very pushy isn't she?" Riley says.

"She's very special, and you are very lucky."

"That I know." Riley pulls my chin up and kisses me.

"I feel like you two are my family now," I say.

"That we are, Luv."

"I feel sorry for any male that tries to harm you again." Michael smiles.

****

Back in the office, Justin sits down and reads a fax that was just sent over from the council. They've gone from spitting out punishments for turning a human without asking, to a lot of questions about Riley and especially Skylar. It has to be her blue eyes and power that have them all riled up.

Justin gasps as he continues to read. Is it possible after all this time? Now he understands why the council is demanding Riley and Skylar be brought to the castle immediately.

He gets up and hangs his head out of the office. "Derek, can you come in here for a minute?"

Derek gets up and heads over to the office. "Yeah, what's up?"

"Close the door," Justin says.

Derek closes the office door. "What is it?"

"Read this fax the council just sent over here and tell me what the hell you make of it."

Derek takes the paper from Justin's hand and reads it.

The one will come, the Queen,
with the blood and power of an angel.
She with the bluest of eyes, so blue the Sky weeps,
shall lead and protect them.
At her side is the true King.
Eldest of two brothers born of noble blood
once thought dead, but only lost.
He is the most dangerous and savage of them all.
Only she can tame and heal his soul.
Together they fight side by side against the enemy
as a new war and era dawns.

"What the fuck. They think this is about Riley and Sky?" Derek blurts out.

"I don't know. They seem to want to see them pretty badly though."

"What do you think?"

"I think when I look at her, I want to drop to my knees before her. And I know I would protect her to the death. Crazy right?" Justin admits.

"I know exactly what you mean," Derek says.

"Let's just go and see what they have to say." He holds up the fax. "We keep this to ourselves for now."

"I already felt I needed to be fully suited when we go in there with them. Looks like that's exactly how I'm going in now," Derek confesses.

****

As Riley and I come into the great room everyone gets quiet. They look worried. "Okay, you can't all be worried like this or you're going to freak me out. We'll be fine, I feel it."

Derek and Justin come out behind us and are fully decked out in leather and weapons.

"Did I miss something?" Riley asks.

"Come on, let's go," Justin says.

Riley grabs Justin's shoulder. "You know you can't enter the council room with weapons."

Something is definitely up. Justin won't even look Riley in the eyes.

Derek speaks first. "Look, there's no way we're letting the two of you face whatever this is unarmed. End of discussion. They don't like it, we all leave."

"Justin?" Riley tries again.

"End of discussion," Justin says.

"Justin, if she's in danger we're not fucking going," Riley says.

Justin turns around and puts his right arm over his chest. "On my life brother, no harm will come to you or your female."

Derek and Justin head upstairs. I look at everyone else and they seem as confused as Riley is. Riley is internally freaking out again. He stands before me rubbing his face and not moving in any direction.

"Ugh. Just go get them already so you'll feel better."

Riley looks down at me.

"Your weapons, your stuff, whatever….go." I shove his towards the hall.

Two minutes later he emerges with his sword across his back and dagger at his side. Finally, we head outside.

"Derek and I will go first. You two come in right behind us."

They disappear.

"Something's up with those two. They're off aren't they?"

"Yes. For whatever reason they're breaking a serious law. Stay close to me."

I nod as I curl up against his chest.

We appear in the most beautiful room I've ever seen. I take a few minutes to let the nausea subside. We're in a sunk in circular area surrounded by pillars and golden arches. The ceiling has angels and clouds painted on it and the walls are cream colored. Very Victorian looking.

Derek and Justin fall in right behind Riley and me as we start down one of the hallways. We get to a large set of doors and are ushered in. Riley seems surprised we were allowed to pass.

There are seven people sitting up on a raised platform. Reminds me of city council meetings I've seen on TV. I don't make eye contact with anyone since my eyes just seem to freak them out. I want them to give us a pass on the whole changing me thing so we can leave. Not that looking at the floor like an idiot shows any kind of respect or confidence at all. Riley has me tucked closely at his side.

"Warriors, you presume it acceptable to come before the council armed?" the man in the center says.

"I stand here before you this day only as a guard for the two before you now," Justin says.

"Would you lay your life down for them?"

"I would."

"So say you warrior?" He turns to Derek.

"I too would lay down my life for theirs."

"Interesting." He looks to the others and they nod at each other.

Now he looks to Riley. "And you warrior, who breaks laws to turn a human for your own amusement. What do you have to say for yourself?"

"I saved my mate from a certain death, and I'd do it again if I had to."

"You love her?"

"I do."

"Would you die for her? If you were asked to save her life by giving up your own on this day, what say you?"

"Yes, I would give my life for hers."

"What! You most certainly will not." I grab the knife at his side and then turn around glaring at the council members. They look wide-eyed upon me. I step forward. "I would kill every last one of you before you ever got near him. You will not threaten his life again." Hate and anger are boiling up inside of me.

They look at each other and then in unison they get up and step down towards me. Riley's at my side fast and trying to pull me behind him as the council's guard steps forward with them.

I push Riley back. "Stop."

They stop five feet from of me. Then the council and the guard drop to their knees bowing their heads. "Forgive us your grace, for we were not certain it was you."

I turn to Riley, throwing my hands up. "What the hell is all of this?" I wave my hands over the council and guard.

By the look on Riley's face, he too has no idea what's going on. I take a deep breath trying to calm myself down.

"Um, can you guys like….please stand up or something?"

They stand.

I hand Riley back his knife. Like I have any idea how to use it anyways. "What's your name?" I ask the guy that's been doing all the talking.

"It is Leon, your grace," he says.

"Explain what's going on here fast, and why you keep calling me that."

"It's who you are, your grace, the Queen," Leon says. "Torbin, bring the parchment."

I shake my head and then look back at Riley. "Seriously, what the hell is going on?"

"I have no idea." He narrows his gaze as he turns to Justin and Derek who have flanked him every step he's made. "What is this?"

Neither one answer him.

I'm handed a very old looking piece of paper. I look down at it but I can't read it. "Riley, can you read this?" I hand it to him.

"It's the old language," Riley says.

"She must be the one to read it sire," Leon says as he takes it from Riley's hands. "Just try your grace." He hands it back to me.

"I don't know what it says, it's just swirly lines." I stare at it for a little bit. I concentrate and take a deep breath. I see the script begin to change, and somehow I can read it now. I read it out loud.

"Riley?" I look up at him.

He takes the paper from me. He rubs his face, then turns to face Justin and Derek who take knees in front of him. "You knew of this?" he asks.

"We did sire," Justin says as he looks up at him.

"I am nothing. I'm an orphan that grew up starving on the streets with my brother," Riley rambles.

"Sire, may I ask your brother's name?" Leon asks

"Michael," Riley snaps.

"Who named you and your brother?"

"The nuns at the orphanage. We had a blanket with RM monogramed on it, so that's how we were named."

"Sire."

"Quit calling me that," Riley yells.

"You are the son of Richard Magnusson. You are the eldest of the sons once thought dead. The nuns did not name you, your mother did. Your name is Ryland Richard Magnuson, and you are the rightful King."

Riley draws his sword and points it at Leon. His eyes are black and I see a tear escaping down his cheek. The darkness in him is growing and I feel it starting to run through me.

Putting myself between Leon and the end of the blade, I lean forward so it's at my heart. "Love, please put the sword down. You don't want to hurt anybody here."

His eyes lock onto mine.

I smile as he begins to drop the sword to his side. I walk to him and wrap my arms around his waist. He leans forward, dropping his forehead to mine as he looks into my eyes with clear eyes.

"Whatever this is, we'll figure it out together," I say.

"Always," he says on my lips.

The anger lifts. I turn around and look at the crazy people around us. "Listen up, we need more information about these sons and the King. We will be back at the…,"--I throw my hands up-- "whatever the place we live is called, and we'll get back to you when we're ready to."

"Yes, your grace." Leon bows.

I take a deep breath and look at Derek, Justin, and Riley. "Let's go."

We're in that golden room and then back outside their home. Justin and Derek stand staring at us. Riley's mind is somewhere else. I can feel his emotions all over the place.

"We need a minute," I say.

They look at each other. "We should stay," Derek says.

"Really?" I glare. *Queen huh? It's worth a try.* "Leave us now," I yell out. Let's see how that works.

They both hesitate for a moment and then head for the door.

"Nobody says anything until Riley says it's alright." I collapse on the ground as soon as the door closes. I bet they're just inside the door and will stay there until we come in. I'm so overwhelmed with everything that's going on. "Is all of this possible?" I look up at Riley.

He's still staring out at nothing.

"Riley," I blurt out.

Still nothing. "Fine, I'm out of here, wherever here is. I will hitch hike home." I take off walking.

I expect him to stop me, but he doesn't. The farther I get, the more I'm starting to feel like a selfish brat. He learns he's potentially the King of his entire race and I throw a tantrum.

I've been walking for at least an hour, and at this point I don't even know why I took off. I keep rambling to myself, and I'm still heading away from their place. I'm not paying attention to where I'm walking and my foot slips into a hole. My ankle twists and I hear a crack as I fall to the ground. I scream, then I just sit here and cry. Not sure where I thought I was going in the darkness.

Great. I am utterly ridiculous.

After a little while Michael appears before me. He kneels down and gently takes my ankle in his hand. "Deep breath."

As I do, he yanks my ankle back into place and I cry out.

"You heal quickly now. Broken bones have to be fixed right away or they must be broken again and reset." He smiles up at me as he rubs my ankle.

"Thank you, I think."

He picks me up and we're instantly back outside the front of their place.

"Where's Riley?"

"He never came back to the bunker." He sets me down.

"Can you take me to him?"

"I don't know if that's a good idea. When he disappears he wishes to stay that way. He tends to lash out when he doesn't want to be found."

"Please, just take me to him."

He sighs rubbing his head. "Come here."

I go back into his arms.

He appears in front of an old abandoned church. He drops his brow and shakes his head.

"What?" I try to stuff down the nausea. He appeared two places before this one. Materializing three times is way too many times at this point. I'm so dizzy.

"This is where we came in the beginning. Why is he here?"

"Crap, you don't know do you?"

"Know what?"

"There are prophecies about how you and your brother are the lost sons of Richard Magnusson."

"They told him that?" he chokes out.

"Yes. As the eldest son he is to be King. He kind of freaked out and had the same….look on his face as you do right now. Please don't freak out and leave me here," I whine.

"I won't leave you."

"Damn, I'm so dizzy. Why did we materialize three times?"

"We're in Vermont. I can't just appear here, it's too far."

More things for me to learn I guess. "Stay here. I'm going to go see if he's here." I start to limp towards the stairs.

"Let me help--you're still healing." He tries to help me up the stairs.

"I'm fine. I should go alone." I squeeze his arm and smile.

I hop up the stairs and then enter the church. I see Riley sitting in the pews looking up at a large angel statue.

"Hi, love." I stop as my ankle begins to throb.

Riley drops his brow. He looks around the church, down at my leg, and then walks over to me. His arm comes around me and he helps me to the bench.

"You're hurt. How did you get here?"

"Michael brought me." I curl up against him and lay my head on his chest.

He holds me tightly.

"Are you alright?" I ask.

"Not sure." He shakes his head.

"Can we go home? Mine or yours, I don't care as long as we're together."

"You're amazing and strong. I could never be like that."

"Are you crazy? That's the only way I've known you."

"You truly are a queen."

"Okay, if you say that shit to me again, I will punch you in the face, then I will leave you for good. I've been a half-breed vampire for a day. I'm nobody's queen."

"I fear the more we try to run from this, the faster it will catch up to us. You read what I read."

"For tonight, I just want to be with you. Then tomorrow, I would like to be mated."

He smiles and hugs me. I pull him up and as soon as I get one hop in he swoops me up into his arms. As we come outside Michael is waiting for us.

"You should tell him everything before we go back," I say.

He looks over at Michael. "Thank you."

"Always, brother."

After they talk we go back to the bunker. We come down stairs and every male is standing in the great room, swords drawn and on the floor in front of them. As we step all the way into the great room and come before them, they kneel and bow their heads.

"Catch up faster than we can out run it huh," I sigh.

"This shit stops now. We are all brothers and here we are equals. If anybody acts any differently than that, Sky and I will leave."

I know the nods he gets is because essentially their King just gave them an order. "Come on. Let's go to your room. I'm tired and my ankle still hurts."

Riley picks me up and takes me to his room. "Are you hungry?"

"Yeah. I would kill for an In and Out burger, but any burger is good."

"I'll be right back with food." He kisses my cheek.

"I love you."

"And I you, my Queen." He smirks and walks off.

"I know you can still hear me. I'm punching you in the face as soon as you come back," I call out.

Twenty minutes later he has a plate with a burger and fries on it. "You just got me In and Out didn't you? You have been given a temporary reprieve, but I make no promises for the torture you will suffer tomorrow."

"I need to go out for a little while with Derek and Michael. I'll be back as soon as I can."

He's acting weird and not moving. "Riley, what's the problem?"

He rubs his face. "There's shit I wanted to protect you from, and instead you've been thrown into the middle of it."

I walk over and open his closet. "Wow. That's a lot of crazy weapons. You're going out tonight, to fight?"

"Yes." He looks everywhere but at me.

"When you're armed, you become so powerful to me. I feel safe, and it's damn sexy too."

He meets my gaze. "You're amazing, you know that?"

I smile. As I watch him get dressed I'm having a hard time keeping my desire for him to myself. I want to rip it all off of him and mount him.

"If you keep looking at me like that it's all going to end up on the floor." He frowns.

"Sorry." I pout.

He finishes suiting up. "Come here." He puts his hand out and pulls me to him. "I will always come back to you." He kisses me deeply. "I'm so glad you're finally here with me." He steps away to leave.

"I hate watching you leave. I already miss you."

He smiles wide. "Not as much as I hate leaving you."

"Be careful tonight."

Chapter 8

Not too long after Riley left there's a knock at the door. I open it and see Justin with a box of papers.

"Hi….Justin right?"

"Yes. The council sent these documents over for you."

"Yay me. He gets to go out and kill things, while I get homework." I frown and take the box.

Justin stands in the doorway looking at me.

Hmmm. Wonder what this is about. "Would you like to come inside?"

"Yes."

"Do you want to talk?"

"Yes."

I laugh. "Alright. Well you're going to have to give me more to work with then that."

He comes in and walks over to the table. "How are you just fine with all of this?"

"Well my mom died when I was five, and I've been shuffled around my whole life. When I finally got married, that didn't work out much better for me. So you see, this is just another stop on the revolving door that is my life. I'm a thirty five year old divorcee that's now engaged to a vampire, and living in an underground bunker." I look over into huge eyes. I laugh hard. "So which part got you?"

"Not sure. I was actually going to ask you about Riley and you."

"What is it you would like to know exactly?"

"How did you meet him, and how did he bond to you?"

"Well, I met him at the club. But before you ask, no I'm not one of the whores he takes."

"See, that's what I'm talking about. You knew what he was. You've seen what we do, and yet you got close to….him?" he says.

I smile. He looks so confused. I run through the night I met Riley, and everything that lead up to us being together. "But it's so much more than I can even tell you in words."

"The bond," Justin says quietly as he nods.

"Not something you guys do often?"

"A vampire only bonds once in their life. It's rare and a warrior almost never bonds. But he's the King, so for him….finding a mate is important."

"Can I request nobody call me 'queen' or 'your grace'? 'Sky' works just fine. The other stuff is really freaking me out."

Justin smiles. "Yes, your grace. We will call you whatever you wish."

I punch him in the arm.

Justin raises his brow and laughs. "I know why he fell in love with you. It's your spirit, and the fact he couldn't control you. Riley likes to control his entire world, so it makes sense he would be our long lost King. You weren't ever scared of him?"

"No. But don't get me wrong, Justin. I am well aware of how dangerous Riley is."

He shakes his head. "Come on. Come out here with everyone else. I know they'd all like to spend some time with you."

"Spend time with the half-breed huh?" My brow raised.

"Half-breed Queen, changes things a bit don't you think?"

"I don't know….does it?" I smile.

"You're going to be a handful aren't you?"

"Yeah, but you'll learn to love me."

Justin reminds me of that actor that plays Thor in that Marvel movie. He's the biggest one here and a giant teddy bear.

We come out into the great room. Everyone stops what they're doing to stare at me.

I sigh. "Can you just keep doing what you were doing please, and do you have any Jack in this place? How about music? I'd settle for Disturbed, Korn, Social D, Pennywise, anything?"

"Told you she was awesome." Brandon gets up, heads over to the bar, pours me a glass of Jack, and sets it on the bar.

I walk over and grab the bottle from his hand. "Drink with me?" He takes the glass and drinks it as I take in about four shots from the bottle.

"Hey, I'll get in on that action." Cash holds out a large glass.

"You have Riley so wrapped," Brandon says.

"It was crazy the first time I saw him with her in the alley. Riley was a wreak looking over his female as she lie dying. I didn't recognize that male at all," Cash says.

"Watching him with you is crazy, I mean he really loves you. I feel it," Chaz says.

I smile.

"How the hell did you do it? You weren't scared of him? I've never seen females around him. Only the prostitutes go anywhere near him," Brandon says.

"Dude." Cash smacks Brandon's arm.

"Sorry," Brandon says.

I cringe thinking of Riley with all those prostitutes. "No I wasn't scared of him, he pissed me off. I knew what he was the first time I saw him. The eyes give it away, and I could feel vampires as a human."

"You knew we existed?" Brandon asks.

"Yeah, you don't really blend you know. I think some people just choose what they actually see. I've had a few run in's with vampires. As Markus found out, I can't be scrubbed. I got used to vampires around, I just never made it a habit to be alone with one." I throw my hands up and smile as I look around the room. "Yet here I sit now in a room full of them."

They laugh.

"The first time I saw him he was with Derek and Cash at Distortion. Riley caught me watching them, uh and you," I point to Cash, "and he came on to me in that bull-in-a-china-shop-Riley way. I ended up telling him off, and I think I kind of threw him off his game. But I'm not a whore to be taken out back in an alley."

"But at that point they were both already bonded," Justin interrupts.

"Seriously? Just like that?" Chaz asks.

"This thing, the bond, is so intense. The pull in your heart, in your very soul, it's like you know this person is meant to be yours, and you are theirs."

"Fucking crazy," Cash says. He elbows me. "Too bad I didn't meet you first."

"I would watch saying shit like that to her around Riley," Brandon says.

"Man, I would kill for a comfy pair of sweats right now. I really need to get some of my things from my place," I say.

We talk and joke around for over an hour.

Next thing I know, I look up and see Chaz walking in carrying a bag that says GAP on the side. I didn't even realize that he left.

He hands me the bag.

"What's this?"

"What you asked for," Chaz says.

I look inside the bag. "Oh my gosh. I love you." I hug him and kiss his cheek.

"No problem," Chaz says smiling.

I take the bag and head back to Riley's room.

****

"Lucky," Cash says.

Chaz laughs. "Anybody else notice she smells like candy, like sweet or something? Interesting."

They watch her bound away down the hall. Brandon knows why they're all mesmerized by her, because he too can't stop looking at that female. She's strong and beautiful, and wishes to just be around her more. She must really be something to get through to find this strange even-tempered side of Riley none of them have ever seen before.

"I, too, find myself trying not to just stare at her. Why the hell is that?" Markus asks.

Brandon smiles to himself and mutters, "Because she's perfect and beautiful."

Justin comes to the doorway of the office. "Brandon. Markus. Cash. I need you three to go check out another site across town. Nothing big, just need to see if the intel is right. We may have another training facility about to open up."

"Cool," Cash says.

"On it." Brandon heads down the hall.

"Need to hit the club first," Markus says right behind him.

Brandon gets suited up. As he heads back out to the great room he can't help but stop at Riley's door. He stands here for a minute, then decides to knock.

Sky opens the door. "Oh, hey Brandon."

She's in the clothes Chaz got her, and her hair is wet like she just got out of the shower. "I'm headed out with Cash and Markus. I wanted to see if you needed anything. I could stop on the way back."

"I can't think of anything. Really I just need to go to my apartment and pick up my things, like make-up and a hair dryer to try and look half way decent. But thanks for asking."

"No problem. And, Sky?"

"Yeah?"

"I think you look pretty great just how you are." He smiles and then walks down the hall to the great room.

Brandon knows he should have kept that to himself. She belongs to another male, and a crazy male at that. But thinking about the mating ceremony coming up has him smiling ear to ear. Sky will be the first female to ever take from him.

"What's up with you?" Cash asks.

"Nothing."

"Maybe we should see if she needs anything. We could bring it back after."

Brandon laughs. "I already did, and she said she doesn't need anything."

"Seems like maybe you should take your own advice where that female's concerned brother," Markus pipes up.

"I was just asking the Queen if she needed anything from us."

Markus nods. "Yeah, yeah, just be careful."

****

That Brandon guy is hot. He must have all kinds of women all over him. It's strange how they seem to be waiting for me to ask them for things. I don't know how I feel about this queen thing. It's not me, and I don't want to be a part of it. But how does that work if Riley's the King, and I choose to be with him?

Taking a deep breath, I look over at the bed where the box of papers from the council sits. Maybe starting there would be a smart thing to do.

There is so many books and parchments in this box. I still don't understand how at first glance I can't read them, then all of a sudden it changes so that I can. I'm an angel? My mother was a Fallen Angel? How is any of this possible? Can I really say I still don't believe in Heaven and angels anymore when I'm now staying in a house full of vampires and I've seen demons?

One prophecy is eating away at me. I want Riley here now so he can read it. He's been gone for over four hours. Is this going to be my life now, sitting around waiting for him to come home like I'm just some ornament in his apartment?

I wish I had somebody to talk to about all of this stuff. I really need Danielle right now. As soon as the thought enters my head I have a pain in my chest. It's been Danielle and me again like old times, always there for each other. Maybe she could come here.

I hear the living room door open.

"Sky?" Riley calls out.

"In here."

Riley comes into the room and looks around. "What's all this?" He points to the mess of papers on the bed.

I notice a large box in his arms and narrow my gaze at him. "Papers and texts from the council. Justin brought them to me after you left." I'm still staring at the box in his hands. "Where did you go?"

He smiles and holds it out to me. "I made a little stop on the way back."

"So what's in the box?" I raise my brow.

"Open it."

The nerves I feel from him make me smile. I climb off of the bed to take it from him. I remove the lid and run my fingers over the soft white fabric. I set the box on the bed and then pull it out. It's the most beautiful long white flowing gown I've ever seen, like something you would see an angel pictured in.

I gasp. "This is way too beautiful for me." I'm staring at it shaking my head.

"You are more beautiful than that dress is."

"For the ceremony?"

"Yes, do you like it?"

"I love it. Thank you." I put it back into the box and then turn around to hug him.

He takes the opportunity to kiss me.

"I could kiss you forever," I say against his lips.

"I'm going to hold you to that just so you know. I'm never going to let you go." He looks down at my clothes. "Where did you get these?"

"Yeah….so, weird. I said I would kill for some comfy sweats and then Chaz shows up with these."

He growls. "Seems they're falling all over themselves to please you."

The fierceness in his eyes makes me laugh. "They're just being nice, but from what I hear it's not something you have much experience with."

"They're being nice because they know I'd kill them otherwise."

"That's what I'm talking about. You really need to lighten up." I point to all of the papers on the bed. "About all of this, it's pretty specific about your obligations as King."

His glare intensifies.

I throw my hands up. "Hey, I'm just telling you what those creepy council members expect from you. Say the word and I'll disappear with you tomorrow. And Riley? I'm not sure all of this royal stuff is something I want at all."

"I need some answers, and I still need to talk to my brother about all of this."

"You mean Prince Michael?" I smirk.

That makes him smile.

"Oh yeah, and he's like the diplomat between the council and you and your general. Which I assume would be Justin, because, well, he seems to coordinate things. I guess it would also make Derek the Lieutenant, second in command to Justin?"

"That should work out well for Michael. He hates the council as much as I do."

"Your soldiers are your warriors in here." I point to one of the texts. "From what I've read so far, you guys pretty much follow most of the old traditions and customs."

"The King died over two hundred years ago, and with him the throne. I will not be King."

That actually makes me a little relieved, but I don't know if they will ever leave him alone, or if he will truly turn his back on his family's legacy.

"I also found more about me in all these papers. I want you to read it so I know I read it right."

He takes the paper from me and reads it out loud.

The quiet tortured warrior with no past
will be the one to teach the Queen to fight.
Eyes as gold as the sun, surrounded
by the blue of the bluest sky.
It is he, the Queen's blooded brother
that can help her control her power
as he learns of his own.
Twins born of the Fallen Lahash
One Vampire sired, both born of angels,
Separated in their fifth year, after the angel's death.

"Do you know who this is talking about?" I ask.

"Yes."

"It's Trevor isn't it?"

He lowers his brow, "How do you know that?"

I don't answer him, he has only confirmed what I've already felt. I leave the room and head towards the great room. Riley is on my heels.

Trevor is reading in a large chair near the fireplace. I stand motionless for a second and just look at him.

"I feel it--somehow I know it's him."

Same thing I felt earlier when I was watching him, just this crazy invisible pull to go to him. I make a b-line towards him when someone grabs my arm.

Whoa.

My eyes fall to the hand on my arm and then to Derek's eyes. I feel warmth run up my arm from him. He's stares at his hand, and then his eyes lock on mine.

"Uh, Sky, he doesn't like to be bothered. He's right up here with this one. Well, maybe even worse at times."

"I need to see him." Pulling away from him, I go towards Trevor a little more cautiously.

"Fuck," Derek says under his breath.

"It's fine. Just be ready in case he goes off," Riley says.

The room has gotten really quiet. Trevor hasn't moved or even noticed what's going on around him. I walk right up and kneel before him.

He looks up from his book slowly, looks at me, and then looks around a little freaked.

I take the book out of his hands and set it on the table next to him. I look back into his eyes. He's so tense. The range of emotions pouring off of him is crazy. But mostly he's feeling trapped by me, and it's scaring the crap out of him. This male isn't mean or violent, he's terrified. But we are connected, I feel it, stronger than Riley's bond.

"Your eyes are so beautiful." I try to touch his face, but he flinches away from me and his eyes get wide.

He has some of my features in his face. I know he's my brother. He's a part of me, my family. I take his hands in mine quickly so that he can't pull away from me. As soon as I touch him, our bond run through my whole body.

I smile.

Trevo looks at our hands confused and then back into my eyes. His body begins to relax.

"Warmth, love, and a feeling of finding the other half of one's self. We're family, you're my brother." I throw my arms around his neck and hug him.

He hugs me back so tightly I can barely breathe. I flash back to the two of us as children around five years old. I had fallen off my bike and cut my leg badly. He healed me. He was already vampire.

He pulls back and looks at me. He takes my face in his hands wiping the tears from my cheeks. "We are blood?"

"Yes, I'm your twin sister." I climb into his lap to hug him more tightly.

"What the fuck did I miss now?" Brandon blurts out.

Riley hands the prophecy to Derek. Derek reads it out loud.

"So Sky and Trevor are twins?" Cash says.

As I hold Trevor I finally feel like I'm home, part of a real family, and whole. I pull the sweats up my leg to reveal the scar on my knee. "You healed me."

He quietly answers, "I thought you were just a little girl in a dream." He brushes the hair back from my eyes. "I will always protect you, and I will always be with you."

"And I you." I hug him again. I can't believe all of this is working out this way. Finding Riley and almost dying has led me back to my brother.

Riley walks over to us. "Trevor, can I have my mate back?"

"Can I come talk to you later?" I ask.

"Yes," Trevor nods.

"Good." I hug him tightly one more time and kiss his cheek.

Riley holds his hand out to me. "Looks like we are to become family, brother."

"We always have been." Trevor smiles.

"Seriously, Sky's working some serious mojo around here," Chris says. "So, she's not a witch. They were born of angels and have powers."

"Seems so," Justin says. "Things are changing."

"Come on, we still have some things to talk about for tomorrow," Riley says.

"Riley, custom states when the king has his mating ceremony it must be observed by the council," Justin cringes.

"As far as the council is concerned, the mating ceremony took place yesterday before she was turned."

"Yes sire," Justin replies.

"Riley, it's just…Riley. What's our next target? Why don't you get working on that, alright?"

"Yes….Riley." Justin sighs, "This sucks."

"Nothing has changed," Riley blurts out.

"Everything has changed, brother. Whether or not you want to accept it."

I look over and see Trevor look up at me. His gaze has narrowed. He tosses the book aside and is coming towards me fast. I get a crushing pain in my stomach when everything goes black.

As I come to, I'm on the floor and in Trevor's arms. He scores his wrist and then puts it to my lips. His blood is electric. As it fills my body to the tips of my toes I feel instantly stronger. I feel everything he's feeling as well, like it has sealed our bond. It's amazing. It feels like he's an extension of myself, and at this moment he's worried.

> *Me: I'm fine.*
> *Trevor: I felt your pain as if it was my own, I*
> *knew you were sick.*
> *Me: I think I just needed to feed again, but I*
> *feel much better now. More like myself.*
> *Thank you.*
> *Trevor: I just got you back. You need to rest.*
> *Me: This is so weird, I can hear you irritated*
> *at me in my head.*

"Is she alright? All of this has been too much, she hasn't finished the change," Riley says.

> *Trevor: He will be a good mate, he's a very*
> *strong male.*

Trevor looks up at Riley. "She's better now, and fully healed. I feel it."

I seal his wrist. He helps me up and then hands me off to Riley. Riley pulls me into his side.

"She needs to rest," Trevor says.

Riley picks me up and starts to walk towards the hallway. "Trevor, can I see you in my room for a minute?"

I feel Trevor's relief. He wants to make sure I'm really okay, or so I hear him rambling in his head.

Me: I said I'm fine, relax.
Trevor: I know.
Me: This is so strange how I can talk to you like this.
Trevor: Yes, very strange.
Me: I want to talk to you more.
Trevor: As do I, but your mate decides who you
        can talk to and when.
Me: I decide who I talk to, and you're my brother,
        you will always come first above anyone else.

Trevor shakes his head and smiles.

Riley lays me on the bed. "I need to do a couple more things tonight for tomorrow's ceremony. Will you sit with her while I'm gone?"

"Of course," Trevor says.

"I will never tell you that you can't see her. She's your blood, you can come to her whenever you want." Riley smiles and claps him on the shoulder.

"They're right, she has changed you," Trevor says.

"And you as well. You look at ease."

"I've found my other half, my sister."

I smile at them. I feel sorry for anybody that tries to hurt me. These two would tear them into so many little pieces it would be unrecognizable. Remembering Riley killing that demon in the alley makes me shudder, but it also makes me feel protected. I see Trevor look up at Riley and smile.

Riley leans over and kisses me. "I'll be back soon, Luv." He gets up and then walks out.

I try to get up, but Trevor pushes me back down.

"I swear I'm fine."

"For me, just stay in bed," Trevor pleads.

I sigh. He's too far away from me. I have this need to be touching him. I'm so afraid I'm going to wake up and this was all a dream. I want to talk to him and just be close to him.

Trevor sighs.

I look up as he pulls his shoes off. He climbs in bed next to me and then wraps his arms around me. I scoot as close to him as I can get and curl up into his chest.

> *Trevor: You are going to be a pain in my ass*
>> *I just know it.*
> *Me: Hey, I can hear you ya know.*
> *Trevor: I know.*

He holds me tighter. "Sleep sister, you will need your strength for tomorrow."

"Trevor?"

"Yeah?"

"I love you." If he holds me any tighter I really might actually stop breathing.

He comes to my ear and whispers, "I love you too."

I fall asleep.

****

"Guess I'm on the couch tonight," Riley says to Michael.

"Why?"

"Trevor and Sky are wrapped up together and sleeping so soundly I didn't want to wake them."

"Trevor's sleeping?" Derek asks brow raised.

"Yeah, out cold," Riley answers.

"That brother never sleeps. Twins are an interesting oddity for any world. Human, vampire, and angel, I suspect we're going to see a lot more from those two. They are deeply connected."

"You could see it awaken that male as soon as she touched his hands," Michael says.

Riley nods.

"Definitely. It's like a light went on inside of him." Justin comes over and sits down. "And he's to teach her to fight?"

"I don't want her fighting. I want to keep her from all of that."

"Brother, your female almost died because she felt the need to fight instead of run. She's strong, and she could learn to protect herself using her power," Derek says.

"I told her to run when we came upon Moartea. She not only stayed, she tried to help," Michael says.

"I'd like to see the power they have together," Justin adds.

"Let's just get her through the change and the ceremony. The other shit comes later," Riley says.

"I like this new version of my brother with that female. She truly is your other half. I think great things are coming," Michael smiles.

"You think so, Prince Michael? Why don't you tell us all about these great things?" Riley smirks.

"What?" Michael looks over brow lowered.

"Oh yeah. She has been reading all of that shit the council sent over. You're the Prince, Derek's the Lieutenant, and Justin here is my General," Riley laughs as they stare wide-eyed. "Yep, shit's changing. Guess we're going to see how far all of this takes us."

"That female told me she was never scared of you. It's like she was meant for you. She was definitely meant to find you, and Trevor," Justin says.

"How is it possible that female came to love you?" Derek asks.

"When I figure that out brother, I'll let you know." Riley shakes his head.

"You're different. You seem well," Justin adds.

"It's what she does to me when I'm near her. She fills me with so much love that there's no room for the rest of the shit." Riley rubs his face. "It's been a very long few weeks. I'll see you all in the evening."

Riley comes back into his room and hits the couch. He wants to be with Sky so badly, but he knows what it is to have family, and he won't take this bonding time away from them.

Chapter 9

Today is going to be a good day. I feel healthy and strong. I'm a little confused at first, until I remember where I am. I'm in my brother's arms. I turn to face him.

Trevor is still asleep. As I lie here looking at him, I can sense a weakness in him. He needs to feed. I softly run my hand down his cheek.

He opens his eyes and smiles.

Trevor: How do you feel?
Me: Strong, it's amazing. Can you feel it?
Trevor: Yes.

"Trevor?"
"Yeah?"
I put my wrist to his lips. "Take from me."
"No, you need to be strong."
"Oh my God. You and Riley are like a broken record. I know you need to feed. I will not talk to you for a week if you do not take from me."
He glares.

Me: Please, I need you to be strong for me.

He sighs, takes my wrist, and bites into me as he looks into my eyes. I can actually feel him getting stronger. He seals me up and then lays his head back. "I feel…"

"Stronger, and whole." I smile. "It's the same thing I felt when you gave to me."

"Yes." He turns and looks at me.

His eyes are as blue as mine are now.

Me: Whoa.
Trevor: What?

"Your eyes are the same color as mine now."

Trevor jumps up and goes to the bathroom mirror.

I come in and he's staring at himself in the mirror. I stand next to him, equally amazed at what we're looking at. I look twenty five tops and my hair is now the same color as his dark burgundy color.

"We truly are twins." He wraps his arms around me.

"I'm kind of scared to face them. We're freaks, right? Half vampire/half angel."

He turns to look at me. "We have power?"

"Well, so far just parlor tricks. Apparently you're supposed to teach me to fight and control the power."

We walk out of the bedroom. I look over and see Riley asleep on the couch.

"Riley," I say as I gently shake him.

He stretches and then rubs his eyes. When he finally looks up at us, his face drops and he just stares.

"Uh….so, yeah. Crazy night, huh?" I say.

"Trevor, your eyes," Riley gasps.

"My sister has healed me as I have her."

Riley shakes his head. "You look different, Luv, younger?"

"Is that a bad thing?" I smile.

"No, you're still the most beautiful female I've ever seen, and you're mine." He yanks me on to him and holds me tightly. "I missed you this morning."

"I missed you too. I think we should see who's up."

Riley nods.

We get up and then the three of us head out into the hall. Riley walks ahead of us. I have my arms wrapped around my brother's arm as we go down the hall.

"You're all sitting down so…." Riley steps aside.

"What's up?" Justin asks, then he stops and stares when he sees Trevor and me.

Mouths hit the floor as Trevor and I come farther into the room.

"Yeah, I would say they are definitely twins," Michael says.

"Shit, that's so crazy," Brandon says.

"The council asked me if she had found her brother yet. I think it's going to be pretty obvious now," Justin says.

"I'm starving, does somebody cook around here?" I ask. I can also feel how uncomfortable Trevor is with all the staring.

Me: You can take off. I'll find you later and bring you something to eat.

He kisses my head, and then goes back down the hall.

"Brian and I will go pick something up," Cash says.

"Breakfast burritos?" I raise my brow.

"I could do that," Cash says.

Michael comes and stands next to me. He leans in and quietly says in my ear, "I know one of your powers."

"Oh yeah, what's that?"

"You heal souls." He looks over at his brother and smiles.

I feel Michael at ease, something it seems he isn't used to feeling.

Chaz is standing near us. "And apparently she makes kings."

Cash comes back with a ton of food.

I take an extra burrito and look at Riley. "I'm going to bring my brother one. Can you show me where his room is?"

"Across from ours," Riley says.

I walk down the hall and see Trevor open the door before I can knock. "You sensed me?"

Trevor smiles. "Yeah, but I heard you counting doors on the way down."

"Here, I know you're hungry. I know I'm already a pain in the butt, but I feel so much from you. It worries me."

Sighing, he steps forward, takes the food from me, and then puts his forehead to mine. "I think I'm older, so it's me that gets to boss you around." He hugs me. "Thank you, I've never had anyone worry for me before."

"Yes you have, you just don't remember me loving you before." I put my hand on his chest. "I'm going to check on you later so you better eat it."

Back in the great room, I head over to the empty seat next to Riley. Before I can sit down, he scoots his chair out and pulls me onto his lap. Then he leans in and kisses me.

I lean to his ear. "I'm glad that so far you still want to be as close to me as I want to be to you."

"Always." Riley smiles.

"Did you get him to eat?" Derek asks.

"Yeah, why?"

"Trevor hardly ever eats, and he never sleeps," Derek says.

"Well we slept for about eight hours this morning and never moved. It's probably the best sleep I've ever had."

"Good he needs it," Cash says. "He's been pretty lost ever since he came to us twenty years ago."

"Something happened to him, I feel it. He's hiding something in his mind from me. I think it's really bad," I say quietly to Riley.

"We all have shit from our past Sky. It's just the way it is," Riley says.

I narrow my gaze. "I know."

He looks at me but makes no further comment.

We finish eating and then end up back in Riley's room.

"Riley, I need to check in at home. I left my cell phone at the condo. Danielle may end up calling me in as a missing person."

"Not tonight Luv. I have to go out, and tonight we are to be mated."

"If you're going out, just leave me at the condo and get me when you're finished doing whatever."

"No."

I'm not used to being told what to do. "Are you telling me what I can and can't do now?" I feel the anger inside of me growing.

He takes a breath. "No." He reaches out and tries to grab me.

I pull away from him and cross my arms over my chest.

"Luv, I need to know you're here safe. If I'm worried about you out there, I'll be distracted and that could end badly."

I hang my head. I know exactly what he's trying to tell me. He could be hurt or killed. "Who's going tonight?"

"Mike, Cash, Brian, Derek, and myself."

"Five of you, that's good." I look up at him. "Be careful and come back to me."

He grabs my hands and kisses them, then pulls me into his chest. "I will always come back to you."

"I think you need to have a talk with them. They act differently around you now. It's their job to protect you above everything else, even themselves. Nobody needs to worry about you, you can protect yourself. You've always been able to right? They need to concentrate on what's in front of them."

He nods. "This king shit changes the game a bit."

Which is probably why Justin is sending more of them out now. Which also makes me feel a little better. But I've seen how he is, and Riley can take care of himself.

"I have a bad feeling about tonight, just please be careful."

"You'll be here, right?"

"Of course." I kiss him.

"Then I'll be fine. Do you need anything?"

"Cable?"

Laughing, he kisses me one more time before he gets dressed to leave. Once all his weapons are on his demeanor changes. He becomes cold, hard, and looks like he could bring the world down around him. I draw on his strength, just like I feel he draws on my love.

I sigh as he goes to walk out the door.

He opens it and pauses to look back at me.

I jump up, run over to him, and hug him tightly. "I really do hate this part."

He runs his hands through my hair. "Tonight Luv, tonight." He touches my face and then leaves.

I sit on the couch staring at the clock. I wait thirty minutes before I head across the hall to Trevor's door. He opens the door for me before I even close Riley's door. It's still weird to have somebody else that can hear my thoughts, feel my emotions, and love me as unconditionally as I do him.

"No," he says.

"What?" I raise my brow.

"Don't ask this of me."

"How do you know what I was going to ask you?"

"You've been rambling about it for the last thirty minutes."

"Fine. I'll go ask somebody else to take me and protect me from the Moartea. I told you before, nobody's going to tell me what to do." I walk down the hallway to the great room and start looking for Brandon.

Trevor: You're a brat, and dangerous.

I ignore him. Once I'm in the great room, I spot Brandon over at the bar. "Hey Brandon, I need a favor."

"Sure, what do you need?" He smiles.

"I...."

"It's nothing, I have it," Trevor says coldly.

Brandon backs away from me slowly with his hands up.

The blackness in Trevor baring down on the nape of my neck. I shudder as I turn to look up at him. "Damn you're scary." I glare right back at him. "For them, and don't think you can stop me because I'll just walk until I can jump in the first car I see."

"Pain in the ass," he snarls at me with black eyes.

"So what's it going to be Trevor?" I cross my hands over my chest. "Are you taking me, or am I asking somebody else to?"

Trevor: You are asking me to disobey him.
Me: He never told you that you couldn't take me
*   somewhere. And I'm not his to command.*

Trevor: I am.
Me: We will be back before he is. He'll never know.
Trevor: This is dangerous. I have no idea if the area
*   is safe.*
Me: I've walked those streets at night for months.
*   The area is full of vampires, but I've only ever*
*   seen five Moartea. Please Trevor. I need to*
*   check in at home.*

"Fuck, fine." He starts towards the stairs.

"What the hell was all that?" Chris blurts out.

"Twins, I hear they can talk to each other in their minds or some shit," Brandon answers.

"You know they're going to be sitting there talking shit about us and we won't even know it." Chris says.

Trevor: I talk shit about them all the time in my head.
*   Only nobody else could hear it before.*
Me: You've been pretty terrible to be around haven't
*   you?*
Trevor: Let's see how long you go before you start
*   thinking crazy shit in your head listening to*
*   them all night.*

I bust up laughing as we walk up the stairs. "Why can't I do the disappear thing?"

"Not sure if you can or can't. Have you tried?"

"No."

"Half-breeds can't materialize, but I guess I'm a half-breed and I can, so you should be able to as well."

"How do you do it?"

"See that rock over there?" He points about thirty feet away.

"Yeah."

"Close your eyes and see yourself next to the rock."

I close my eyes and will myself to the rock. Nothing.

Trevor: Just breathe and concentrate. Relax your

whole body.

I take a deep breath, shake out my hands, and relax. I feel nausea wash over me. I'm so dizzy I almost fall down, but Trevor's there to catch me. He's smiling down at me as I open my eyes. My head feels like I have swimmers ear.

"It will pass," he says almost laughing.

"You like seeing me miserable don't you?" I try to get up. He laughs. "No, look."

I'm next to the rock. "I did it?"

"Yes." He smiles wide.

"How can you stand the nausea?" I grip my stomach.

"It's like working a muscle. It goes away the more you do it, and you can be anywhere you want as long as you know where you're going."

"I feel better. Take me to my house. I live a few blocks down from Distortion on Fifth Avenue."

I hold him tightly and we're in an alley near my building. I grab his arm trying to get my bearings. I hope the nausea stops soon, I feel disgusting materializing.

We walk down the street and are finally to my building. Trevor's very tense as he scans the streets, hand on his blade. Reminds me of the night Riley walked home with me from the club.

"This is it." I take his hand and pull him towards the building. "Hey Jake," I say to the door man.

"Good evening, Ms. Coppola," he says as he stares at Trevor. I can only imagine the glare he's getting back from him. Apparently, nobody can come near me or talk to me.

"This is my twin brother Trevor, he can come here anytime he wants alright?"

"Sure, no problem."

"You have money? You live well?" Trevor asks.

"None of this is mine. I had a horrible husband whom I recently divorced. My friend knew a doctor at her work who needed somebody to watch over this place. I just got really lucky, because I didn't have anywhere to go, or any family."

He stops me and pulls me into him. "You will always have somebody to look after you now." He hugs me.

"It's nice to finally have family. I don't think I could ever be away from you now. You're kind of stuck with me I think." I smile.

He shrugs. "And you're stuck with me."

We go up the elevator to the sixth floor. I open the door and get one foot inside when Danielle flies up and grabs me to hug the crap out of me. Trevor goes for his blade.

> *Me: This is Danielle my roommate. She was very*
> *worried about me because I always come home.*

She pulls back to looks me over. "I thought Riley kidnapped you or something. You look different."

> *Me: If I tell her the truth and she can't handle it,*
> *you can wipe her memory correct?*
> *Trevor: Yes.*

"I'm fine, a lot has happened. I need to talk to you about some things."

Danielle finally notices Trevor behind me. I come in past her dragging him inside. I close the door and as Danielle looks at Trevor I feel fear from her. I look up at his face and sigh. I will take that look away from him permanently if it kills me. I step in front of him.

> *Me: This is my best friend. She's the one that helped*
> *me when I had no one look out for me. I care for*
> *her. She was the only family I had.*
> *Trevor: She was good to you?*
> *Me: Yes.*

Trevor's face softens a bit and Danielle relaxes. She looks from his face to mine a little confused. I can tell she's trying to figure out why he looks so familiar to her.

"D, this is my brother Trevor."

"Hi," he musters up and looks everywhere but her.

"Wow. You didn't have to tell me, I can see it." She stares at him.

"Come on. Let's sit. I want to tell you what happened to me over the last couple of days."

She comes over and then sits in the chair. Trevor and I take the couch.

"Now where to start? So you know there's weird shit in the city, right? We've seen unexplainable stuff since we moved in that maybe was just dismissed as something else."

"Yeah, sort of." She narrows her gaze.

"Like at night there are people with yellow eyes. Especially in the clubs."

"I guess so, like Riley."

"Exactly." I smile. Here goes, "If I told you they were not human, Riley's not human, what would you say?"

"I would think you were losing your grip, but I would ask you what you think they are."

I can't read her emotions at all. I wonder if it's a human thing, or if she's actually all locked up without even knowing it. "Vampires."

She laughs.

We don't.

"You're being serious aren't you?"

"Yes. They're vampires. My brother….is a vampire."

She glares at Trevor. "Are you like part of some Goth Cult or something that has brainwashed her?"

He growls.

I grab his hand. "Can I show you?"

"Sure, whatever. The sooner you prove me right, the sooner we can admit you into psych."

He's glaring at her.

"Show her."

He looks over at me as I hold up my wrist. "No," he recoils.

*Me: It's the only way to show her, and I know you
need more. If she sees and accepts the truth I
can ask her what I need to.*

Trevor sighs rubbing his face. Glaring over at her, he takes my wrist in his hands. He's angry at me for making him do it in front of her, and he resents her for making him take from me at all, making me weaker. Maybe knowing exactly what someone is thinking all the time is not as fun as it sounds.

Me: I'm fine, I know you can feel how strong I am.

His mouth opens as his fangs elongate. Then he bites into me slowly.

Danielle gasps and gets up. Shaking her head, she begins to pace.

Me: Don't seal it.

He leans back and closes his eyes.

I bring my wrist to my mouth, then I show her the wound is gone.

"What the hell?"

"See I told you, and look I'm fine."

She comes back to the chair and sits down. "Are you?"

I take a deep breath. Then I open my mouth and let my fangs elongate.

She sits back and looks at me, wide-eyed.

"Yes, I am. A couple of nights back I went out to get us some food. I was attacked. I took a knife in my side through my lung. Riley found me dying, and his only option was to try and turn me."

Her hand comes to her mouth as she begins slowly shaking her head.

"My brother was living with Riley and others. I found him." I smile and lace my fingers through his. "I believe I was meant to be as I am now. I'm going to marry Riley tonight, and I wanted you to come. That's part of why I came here."

Trevor pulls his hand out of mine and looks at me.

Trevor: What!

Me: You can always take her memories right?
Trevor: Yes, but she's human.
Me: So?
Trevor: Humans can't be in our world, Sky. It's
      forbidden and dangerous for us all.
Me: I don't care, she's family. She was all I had
    for a long time.

I put my hand on his.

Her eyes narrow as she looks at us. "Are you two talking to each other?"

"Oh, yeah sorry. It's a vampire twin thing."

"Weird."

"Such is my life now. If all this is too much, I understand. I'm not supposed to tell you or show you any of the things I have. I guess it's forbidden. My brother can wipe your memories as if I came here, moved out, and that was it."

"You're leaving, aren't you?" she asks.

"Yes, I can't be in this world any longer. I don't belong here. The whole sun thing makes for an interesting challenge as well." I smile.

"This really sucks, Sky." Tears well up in her eyes.

"If there was a place for you with us, could you leave everything and everyone else behind?" I ask.

"I don't know."

"You love to cook, and you hate the hospital."

"Yes, but cooking is not in the cards for me."

"What if it could be different?" I grab her hand. "Come with me tonight and see what their world is like."

"Okay." She pauses. "Sky? Are we talking about an entire room full of vampires?"

"Yes. All of them are huge warriors."

"Like how many?"

"Eleven, but you already know Riley and now Trevor." I flip my hand back against his chest.

"Are they all as crazy scary as him?"

He glares.

She laughs. "I rest my case."

"No, he's pretty much the only broody tortured one." I elbow him. "I hear Riley was worse than Trevor, and you like him." I look over at him. "Be nice already."

"Is that and order my Queen?" He glares.

"Shut up." I grab his face, kiss his lips, and then rest my forehead on his. "You are so lucky I love you."

"Ditto," he growls.

"Can you ask Brandon to come here?"

He gets up, takes a deep breath, and then dials his phone. "Hey, can you meet me at my current location?...Yes now." He hangs up.

"Your brother is a douche isn't he?" she whispers.

I laugh as he turns to glare at her.

"Sorry, no offense. But what's the point of walking around being such a jerk all the time?" Danielle asks.

"Serves me best," he says coldly.

Brandon appears in the living room right next to Danielle.

"What's up?" Brandon asks.

Danielle screams and Trevor smiles.

"Oh, now you smile." She shakes her head. "By the way, you're pretty cute when you aren't trying to be such an asshole."

"I like her. Who is she besides a human I just materialized in front of?" Brandon raises his brow.

"My friend Danielle. We're bringing her with us--well actually I need you to bring her with us."

"I'm not a cosmic taxi you know."

"Brandon, please." I walk up in front of him as he looks down at me. "I know it's not allowed but I need her." I take his hands in mine and I feel him relax. "What if I demand she be brought back with us? I will suffer any consequences."

He sighs and looks over at Trevor. "This not being able to say no to her thing really sucks." He looks at Danielle. "If you come with us, you may never be able to come back."

"I understand, but she's like my sister. I go wherever she goes," Danielle says.

"She's my sister not yours, and this could get her into trouble, just so you know what you are agreeing to," Trevor barks.

Danielle steps right up into Trevor's face. "Look, I've had enough of you and your stare downs. You don't like me, I get it, but she's all I have and I'm not leaving her….got it?" she stabs her finger into his chest as she rants.

I step in between them. "Can you two just please try and get along for me?"

Both glare at each other.

"I need some of my things. D, you should call in sick for the next couple of days, and pack a bag. Are you sure about all of this? It's not too late to change your mind."

She hugs me. "I go where you go." She heads off to her room.

Looking around my room, I start thinking about everything Danielle and I have been through this last year. The plans to get away from our ex's, and everything that fell into place to bring us where we are today. Then there's always my stupid mistake.

The night I was attacked begins to play out in my mind. I trusted the wrong person, Randy. He worked hard to get me to trust him. Then he drugged me, and waited until I was almost out of it to rape me.

I can still feel the heaviness of him on me as his tongue forced its way into my mouth. I struggled as much as I could under the weight of him—until he punched me. Then I found myself in a daze and no longer had the strength to fight him off.

Danielle came home and cracked him over the head with a bat knocking him out. Then she called a couple of the neighbors to help throw him out of the building. She sat with me until I came out of it, and then even longer just holding me as I cried.

Nausea boils up inside of my stomach as I remember him on top of me, not being able to fight him off. I take a deep breath and try to relax.

Suddenly I feel pure fury behind me. As I turn around I see Trevor in my doorway with black eyes.

Oh crap. He saw my thoughts. "It was six months ago, nothing can be done about it now."

Narrowing his eyes, he says, "I know the face of this male, and he will die by my hands. This I vow to you." He walks over and pulls me into him. "No one will ever hurt you again."

"Please don't tell Riley or anyone else." I cry—mostly ashamed at myself for being stupid.

He takes my face in his hands. "Don't give him power over you by feeling ashamed. The shame is his, not yours. I will find him, and I will kill him." He hugs me tightly.

I know he means it, but I doubt he'd even be able to find him. I finish packing. We meet back in the living room.

"Brandon will bring you. He's one of the nicest ones I've met. If I'm not around, find him or Trevor? And materializing sucks. Just breathe and hold on tight."

"To him?" she looks up at Brandon.

Brandon looks like a GQ surfer boy. He's definitely the guy women swoon over. "Yeah, unless you want to hitch a ride with Trevor and I'll go with Brandon?"

Trevor tenses up and squeezes me to him.

Brandon smiles.

She looks over at Trevor. "Nah, I'm good here."

I hold Trevor tightly as she awkwardly grabs onto Brandon. We're in the apartment one minute, then in the woods outside the bunker the next. I hear Danielle on the ground throwing up.

"Yep, the first time is pretty bad," Brandon says. "Just take deep breaths."

"Oh my God, that's horrible," Danielle chokes out.

I laugh and look up at Trevor. "I'm fine now. I have the three people I love most in the world with me."

Trevor's thumb brushes across the spot where Randy hit me. "Sky, he's already dead. He just doesn't know it yet." He stalks off.

I sigh. "Brandon can you take our things to Riley's room? And thank you for this." I hug him.

Brandon brings his arms around me. "Anything your grace," he says as he hugs me.

"It's Sky, remember, just Sky," I rant.

He laughs. "Okay, Sky." Then he turns, grabs our stuff, and heads inside still laughing.

Danielle and I go inside. Now to try and figure out what I'm supposed to say about Danielle. Justin's going to freak out and

I know it's who I need to talk to first. We come into the great room and nobody notices at first, then Chris looks up.

"What the?" Chris says.

"A human, Sky?" Markus chokes out.

"Sky," Justin says firmly.

"Alright, quick intros. That's Chris, Markus, Chaz, you know Trevor and Brandon, and this very angry huge guy coming over here….is Justin.

She raises her brow.

Yeah I know, he looks like Thor, and by the look on his face….I need to talk to him right now." I look up and see Brandon coming back into the great room. "Brandon, can you show Danielle the kitchen?"

"Sure, come on," he motions.

She looks over at me.

"He's fine, just remember what I told you earlier."

*Me: I know you're mad at me, but please watch out
     for her.*
*Trevor: I wouldn't let anything happen to her. I told
     you, I'd never let anyone hurt you.*

Justin drags me into his office. Trevor's right outside the door and still looking in the direction Danielle is.

"Humans don't belong here Sky." Justin crosses his arms over his chest. "What were you thinking?"

Man, all these males have broody down pat don't they? "I've read the laws Justin, and I understand the reasons why humans don't belong in our world. Danielle would never hurt us. I believe she'll choose to stay here with me, rather than go back to her life."

"You know this for sure?"

"No, I'm sorry I don't. She was my only family before all of this. I had to try. I hope you understand and know I would never do anything to hurt anyone here."

He sighs. "You command me, I do not command you."

"You can advise me as you did. I appreciate it. Always tell me how you feel no matter what, okay?"

He pauses. "As your council?"

Ah that's right. The Queen appoints a trusted friend as council to her. They become her trusted advisor. "I can't think of anyone better than you." I smile.

"Thank you." He nods.

He looks like he's going to kneel or something. "I know this is not very royal or whatever, but if you bow, kneel, call me queen or your grace, I will kick your ass and we will no longer be friends. Got it?"

"Got it." He laughs.

"She cooks, and really good by the way."

He shakes his head. His phone rings. I leave him to it and go into the great room. I'm on my way to the kitchen when Justin flies out of the office.

"Trevor, Markus, Chris," Justin barks out. "They're in trouble."

The three of them are suited up and gone within minutes.

"Justin, how bad is it? Riley?"

"Riley's fine, Cash is bad. Stay put."

I find myself taking a deep breath. I didn't realize I had stopped breathing when I thought it might be Riley.

****

"I called for re-enforcements," Riley calls out.

Cash lost focus when a Moartea briefly overpowered Riley. The Moartea Cash was facing off with took the opportunity to run him through. It's bad and Riley knows it.

Trevor, Markus and Chris appear before him. Time to go back to work. This group is bigger than originally expected. There are at least twenty-four left inside. As the fighting begins to rage on, the six of them take the last ones down. Michael stayed back with Cash in case any got by them.

After Riley finishes the last one he heads back out to Cash. He can feel him fading. Having somebody sacrifice their life for his isn't sitting well with him at all. He's not worth another's life, king bullshit or not.

Everyone comes back, all accounted for.

Riley looks up. "Fuck. Trevor your arm."

Trevor just shrugs with one shoulder, holding his hurt arm to his body.

"All clear," Markus calls out.

Trevor looks down at Cash. Riley knows Cash is the one that found Trevor and brought him into the Ninth. He's been the closest thing to family Trevor has had before Sky.

Chapter 10

"Oh God," I groan as I hit the floor. My chest is caving in on me and my arms on fire. It like someone's torn it from my body. "Trevor," I yell out and scramble up the stairs.

Justin sees me come out before he leaves and tries to grab me. I think of Trevor. I see him, feel him, and then will myself to his side. The nausea hits hard as I'm thrown to the ground. I look up right into Riley's wide eyes.

"Trevor," I call out half hysterical.

"I'm right here." Trevor comes into view.

I finally take a breath. "You're hurt?"

"I'm healing." He shows me his arm.

Riley looks over shaking his head. "Holy shit, you're almost healed."

Trevor turns away and I feel sadness creep over him. Somebody's hurt….and badly.

Cash.

I get up, barely able to stand. I stumble over and then fall at Cash's side. "Damn." I take a deep breath.

Cash looks like he's been gutted. He's coughing up blood and not healing fast enough for the blood he's losing. I can actually feel him fading. I take his face in my hands.

"At least I get to look into your beautiful face before I die instead of these ugly mugs." He laughs and coughs up more blood. His breathing is becoming shallower.

I score my wrist and put it to his lips. "Drink now. Nobody's dying tonight if I can help it."

As he takes my blood in he's beginning to slowly heal, but he's still losing blood too fast. I put my hand against the gaping wound on his stomach.

"Trevor, help me stop the bleeding."

Trevor kneels down beside me.

"Here, put pressure here." I lay my hand on his, when suddenly there's light beneath mine. Trevor's hand begins to glow.

Cash takes a deep breath into clear lungs. When we pull our hands away his stomach wound has sealed.

Nobody says a word.

Justin kneels down and takes Cash into his arms. Then they disappear. I look at Trevor who's still staring at his hand.

Me: Is that your power? To heal?
Trevor: No, I didn't feel it until you laid your hand
*   on mine.*
Me: So together we can heal just as we did each other.
Trevor: The power is strong. I can still feel it through
*   my whole body.*
Me: I have a hard time channeling it. I just wanted
*   the wound to stop bleeding so he could heal,*
*   and through you it did.*

"Are you two going share what all that was or just keep talking amongst yourselves?" Chris asks.

I look up and realize everyone but Riley, Michael, Markus, and Chris are gone. "We don't know, we think it's me but only through him. Maybe only together." I shrug. I have no idea what that was exactly.

Riley comes next to me and swoops me up in his arms. "I missed you."

"And I you. I long for you." I look up at him. I can feel him hardening against me. I narrow my gaze and lick my lips.

He growls and kisses me deeply.

All of this with him in only three weeks. It still baffles me. Everything for a vampire is heightened. Love, lust, desire, anger, pretty much all of your emotions. Plus, they tell me it's even worse for a young vampire or newly bonded pair, and I'm both.

Me: We have an audience don't we?
Trevor: Yep.

"Will you make me yours tonight?" I whisper in Riley's ear.

"I can't wait." He kisses my neck, then he pulls away. "Let's get back." He looks back down at me. "I can't believe you materialized here by yourself. I wasn't sure if you'd be able to at all."

"Trevor showed me how." I smile.

Riley holds onto me tightly and we're back at the bunker. Everyone else is on our heels and begin to go inside.

"Wait till you get a load of our new houseguest," Markus says on his way down.

Danielle. I stop him. "Don't be mad at me, but I made Trevor and Brandon take me to the condo to get some stuff….and Danielle." I cringe waiting for the anger and yelling.

"She's here now?" he asks.

"Yes."

"Hmmm, how did that go over with Justin?"

"Not great, but he understands why I did it. You're not mad at me?"

"That you want to have someone here you're close to at the ceremony? No." He hugs me and draws me in. "I can't wait to take you as my mate. I hunger for you, Luv." He runs his fangs along my neck.

My whole chest warms and I feel the waves running across my body. I want him now. I look around for some place private. He brings us around to the side of the bunker slightly hidden from the back road. He shoves me up against the bunker and comes down hard on my lips.

The kissing gets intense. My sweats come down fast and then I unbutton his jeans to release him. He comes back down on my lips kissing me deeply.

He enters me all at once as he bites into me. To feel his power and strength as he thrust in and withdraws is insane. My body tightens up as the waves of pleasure run from his fangs to my core.

Sealing me up, he finds my mouth again. He comes right after me and wraps his arms around me as he pants in my ear. "I love you."

"And I you, my male."

We pull ourselves together.

Smiling as he looks over at me, he walks into me and begins kissing me softly. Hands make their way down my sides and pull me into him tightly.

To feel his passion for me is driving me crazy. I already want him again. It's probably a good idea to go inside now. I pull him inside and laugh as he continues to grab for me. As we hit the bottom of the stairs, I see Cash on the couch in the great room.

Cash looks up, sees me, and then stumbles towards me. He hugs me so tightly I can't breathe. These males need to learn their strength I swear.

"Thank you, I wasn't ready leave this realm. My life belongs to you." He pulls back to look into my eyes. "You may not like it, but you are special and very deserving of being Queen."

I'll let that slide from him just this once. I too wasn't ready to lose one of these males I've just gotten to know. I smell something yummy filling the entire bunker. I walk over to the kitchen.

"What is all this?" I ask Danielle.

"So you're getting married right? We need to celebrate. I'm making your favorite. Italian." She smiles.

"I got this bro, go relax," Chris says to Brandon.

"Thanks, she's trying to turn me into Suzy Homemaker," Brandon says. "No offense, you got some mad skills in here and everything."

"None taken, thanks for the help." She looks over at Chris. "Chris right?"

"Yeah."

They start talking about cooking and what she's preparing. I head back to my room with Trevor to get ready. He starts explaining everything to me. Not sure much of it's sinking in.

"So you will score my flesh, then what?"

"I'll fill a goblet with your blood so each warrior may take you in. Then they will kneel before you, pledging themselves to you as you take them in."

"Take them in how?" I'm freaking out at this point. I'm already coming to the conclusion if they're kneeling before me it's not going to be their wrist.

"You will kneel in front of each one. As Queen you must take from the neck. They submit completely to you, showing you their trust, love, and devotion. It's different now that you're the Queen."

"That's huge. I had a hard time even taking from Michael's wrist. I can't imagine taking from their necks. How is it different?"

"It would have been from the wrist before all the other stuff. For most of them, you'll be the first female to ever take from them."

"This is going to be so awkward," I groan. "What about you?"

"I'll be the first you take from, and your mate will be your last. From your family to your love."

"Alright, nice and scary."

"You'll be fine. It's how you become connected to the entire ranks." He sighs. "I'm sorry I didn't find you sooner."

Everything with Randy is still stuck in his head. "You blame yourself for my idiocy?"

"I knew you were real, but I told myself I must have dreamed you. Your blood has always been with me, a part of me. I should have tried. Through our blood I would have been able to find you."

"I could never blame you for anything that's happened to me. I'm just glad I have you now. Especially today. I love you, Trevor." I hug him tightly and feel the tears threatening to start. "Okay, enough of this tears crap, I need to get ready."

"As do I."

"What will you all wear?"

"Suited up, but only one blade worn across our bare backs."

"All of you?"

"Yes, a white shirt will be worn after."

I take a deep breath and try to relax. "Alright, meet me back here. I'm going to need you with me all the way."

Trevor: Always.

I plug my curling iron in and put my make-up on while it warms up. I don't wear much make-up anymore, but eye make-up is a must. I curl my hair in long spiral curls. I bring the dress box over to the bed and lift the lid. On top of the dress is a note and a large jewelry box. I read the note first.

Luv,

I bought this for you a few days ago. I was waiting for the perfect time to give it to you. I thought today would be the perfect day for something as beautiful as you are.

Yours Always,
Riley

Inside the box is the beautiful diamond necklace from the shop in Seaport Village. This was expensive and I'm going to have to kill him later, but as I put it on I can't help but smile.

I step into the dress and pull it up. Way too pretty for me that's for sure. I struggle to zip it. Ah, it has a long white cord on the zipper. I zip it up and turn to look at myself in the mirror. I actually feel pretty.

I sense Trevor behind me.

"You look beautiful."

He stands next to me and smiles as he looks in the mirror. "Ready?"

"Yes." I nod.

"I'm with you all the way, and I'll be telling you what to do. You'll be fine. This is my duty and honor as your family."

As we come down the hall and enter the great room, I see candles everywhere. As soon as we walk into the room, everything stops. These males make me feel beautiful, something that's really foreign to me. I look over and see Justin and Brandon go back to lighting the candles.

"Watch," I whisper to Trevor.

I take his hand in mine and wave it across the room lighting all the candles at once. I turn out the lights and then I light the fireplace Riley's standing next to.

"Whoa," Brandon says.

"Well that makes it easier," Justin says.

They form a line from Trevor and me to Riley. He's dressed in black slacks and a white dress shirt. Even though he doesn't have any weapons on him, he still looks like he could take on the world. To watch him take control and become such a strong confident leader, makes me so proud to be with him.

"Are you ready?" Trevor asks.

I look over and smile at Danielle who is standing off to Riley's right. Then I look back to Trevor and nod.

Trevor takes my arm in his hands and gently bites into my wrist. He takes from me, then he opens me up deep to bleed me into the goblet. It fills quickly then he seals my wrist. I feel a little woozy and he pauses to watch me for a moment.

I nod for him to continue.

He walks to each warrior and asks for a pledge. "Warrior, I stand before you asking you to protect my family and our King's mate above all others. Do you pledge your loyalty to your Queen?"

"I do," Brandon says. He takes from the goblet first.

Trevor moves down the line asking each the same pledge, all pledge themselves to me and take from the goblet. These males are being asked to put my life before their own. I don't feel I've earned that honor, but I'll work very hard to be something more than I am.

He gets to the end of the line, then he walks back and kneels down next to Brandon.

Trevor: Now come before me, and say....warrior
I take you unto me so I may always keep
you close to my heart.

I come before him, recite the pledge, and then bite into him. I seal him up and hug him tightly. Then I move to Brandon, and now I'm scared to death. It's one thing to take from Riley and my brother, but from Brandon's neck? Brandon holds out his hand and pulls me down in front of him. He smiles.

"Warrior, I take you unto me so I may always keep you close to my heart," I barely get the words out.

Brandon turns his head and I lean into him. I pause with my lips at his neck. He grabs my hand and squeezes. I bite into him as slowly and gently as I can. His blood is different than anything I have tasted. Not that I'm an expert, but I want more.

Man, is it going to be like this the whole way down the line?

I slowly pull away from him and stop next to his ear. "Thank you for helping me."

I move down the line kneeling before each one and taking from them. It's intimate, but easier each time. I'm so glad I have no idea which ones have never had a female take from them. I laugh quietly when I get to Markus.

"First the kiss, now blood," I whisper in his ear.

"Are you trying to get me killed, female?" he whispers.

Then I get to Derek and his eyes are intense. I say the pledge and then have the same nervousness come over me. He holds out his hand as Brandon did and slowly pulls me to him. I feel a connection like I do with Trevor and Riley. He makes me feel at ease.

I lean in to take from him. As soon as I pierce his skin and his blood floods my tongue, I have to stuff down the moan that's hanging off of my lips. I come up and my eyes meet his, he squeezes my hand and nods. I tear myself away from him and go to Justin next.

Trevor: Now go before your mate.

Standing before Riley, a smile begins to spread across my face.

Riley speaks first. "I take thee unto me, forsaking all others. I will protect and serve you for as long as I live. I will always put you before all others and sacrifice my life for yours. This is my pledge to you, now and forever."

He pulls me into him, caresses my face, then he slowly leans in and takes from me. Aw man, my body has responded to him and I want him badly. He seals me up and smiles.

Trevor: I take you unto me, pledging my love and
devotion to you, forsaking all others.

As Trevor continues to recite the pledge in my head, I add my own words. "I take thee unto me, pledging my love and devotion to you, forsaking all others. I, too, would sacrifice my life for yours, my King. I will serve, protect, and love you for as long as I live." I look into his eyes and then bite into him deeply. He wraps me up in his arms.

I hear swords being drawn. I look up and they have come in front of us, heads bowed on bended knee.

"Thank you. We accept your pledge of honor and devotion," Riley says.

They get up, put the white shirt on, and then the swords go on their backs.

Riley turns to me and kisses me deeply.

"You are mine now and I can kiss you whenever I want," I say on his lips.

"I've always been yours, Luv, even before we were together. I too was born to love you."

Danielle's huge feast is laid out before us. Lasagna, garlic bread, antipasti, spaghetti, fruit salad, and there are desserts from our favorite restaurants.

We eat dinner, drink, and laugh. I'm a little embarrassed that I can't keep my hands off of Riley. I want him like I've never wanted him before. He's my husband now, and somehow it makes him even more desirable.

I get up and slide up on Riley's leg while he's talking to Derek. He turns to look at me and kisses me deeply. He puts his arm around my waist and then continues to talk to Derek.

My eyes find Justin at the end of the table. "Justin, is there a room Danielle could use?"

"Yes. I'll make sure she gets there safe, don't worry." He smiles. "And you we're right, she is a good cook."

"Thank you."

I lean against Riley and slyly run my hand down his chest until I land in between his legs. As soon as I grip him, he stops talking and turns to me.

I bring my lips to his. "I want you to take me back to your room now, my mate."

"Our room, Luv." He softly kisses me.

The table has gotten quiet and we probably have an audience.

Riley pulls back and looks in my eyes. "Well brothers, I think we will be retiring for the rest of the morning."

He gets up, picks me up in his arms, and we go back to our room. I slide down out of his arms and walk into the bedroom. He stands in the doorway gazing at me.

"What?" I shrug.

"You're so beautiful. I almost wept at the first sight of you, I still don't know what I did to ever deserve you. I love you more than I ever thought possible to love someone else."

I smile. "Thank you for this." I lay my hand on the necklace.

"I was wrong about the necklace."

"Wrong?"

"It's still not as beautiful as you are." He smiles and starts towards me.

"Stop." I put my hand up, then I pull the cord down on the dress and let it fall to the floor.

He's clenching his jaw and his body is tense as he holds himself back from me. I smile as I remove the rest of my clothes. I slowly walk towards him.

I pull his shirt off and run my hands all over his chest. As I come behind him, I wrap my arms around him and kiss his back as I unbutton his pants. They drop and he steps out of them. I come back to face him and lean into him.

"You're so strong, and you have the most beautiful heart I've ever felt. I never thought I'd have somebody love me the way that you do, my husband. And I, too, love you more than I ever thought possible to love somebody. I'm yours, forever."

He picks me up around the waist and lays me on the bed gently. He kisses me softly as he slowly slides into me, holding himself back.

As I take him in, I look into his eyes and smile as a tear falls from my eyes. He wipes it from my face and kisses me again.

We slowly begin moving together, making love so passionately. There's so much love and emotion bouncing between our bodies that I feel our bond strengthening.

He runs his arm around and holds me to him as he continues to kiss me. In this moment I explode along with him. He slows his rhythm and relaxes on me.

"I'll love you forever," I say on his lips.

"And I you, Luv." He slides off and pulls me into him.

****

Riley is sound asleep next to me. I look down only to find that he's hard and it makes me ache to have him again, even though we ended up waking up several times during the morning to have each other.

I slowly slide up on top of him. I smile when he doesn't wake up. I take him in slowly and close my eyes as I come down on him.

Riley takes a deep breath, as his eyes shoot open. He arches up and grabs a hold of my thighs. He smiles as I begin to move my hips.

I'm there quickly and continue to move on him as waves of pleasure run through my whole body. I come down and bite into him.

He moans, and his whole body tenses up underneath me as he lets loose. As his body begins to relax, his arms come around me. He pulls me into him tightly.

I seal him up and squeeze myself to him. I still can't believe he's mine. It isn't long before I feel him hardening again. He turns us over and we go for round two.

Panting and absolutely sated he slides off.

"What a way to wake up." I laugh.

He pulls me into him. "Making love to my mate in our bed, I would say a perfect way to wake up."

We lie here for a while just kissing.

I feel myself melting into him as reality fades away. That's what he does to me, he makes everything else around us cease to exist. "I told you I could kiss you forever."

"I'm still not complaining," he says.

"I'm supposed to meet Trevor at six in the gym. There's a gym?"

"To train?"

"Yes. He wants me to be able to protect myself. He says no way you can keep me locked up here. He says I'm a brat." I frown. "He also says as my family it's his right to allow me to train or not."

"I don't want you fighting." Riley grimaces.

"I should be there when you fight. If I hadn't come for Cash when I did, he would have died. His wound was mortal. I felt him passing as I knelt before him. If that were you....I would have died with you." I run my hand across his cheek. "Those prophecies speak of us fighting together."

"Prophecies are not truths, only ramblings," Riley grumbles.

"You mean the ones foretelling of you finding me? How about the one that lead me to my brother? Or how about the fact you and Michael are heirs to the throne?"

He sighs and rubs his face.

"Look, I know you love me and want to keep me safe. But if you try to control me or tell me what to do, you'll lose me. When I'm out there in the real world, don't you think I should know how to protect myself if I need to?"

"Yes, and he's right, you are a brat and can't be controlled."

"Ah, I win yes? Say, 'yes, my mate, you win.'"

"Yes, my beautiful mate, you may train with your brother."

I go to get up but he pulls me back to him. I laugh as he takes me again.

Me: Trevor where are you. I can't find the gym,
   I think I've been in everyone's room.
Trevor: Look up goof.

"Goof?" I look up and see him leaning out of a doorway.

I walk in and holy crap. It's not a home gym kind of gym, it's the real thing. There's a fight cage like UFC, all kinds of workout equipment, a large section of mats, and every weapon you can think of.

"Ready?" he asks.

He comes at me and throws me down on my ass.

"What the hell was that?"

"You not protecting yourself." He shrugs.

"So I came in here for you to kick my ass all day?"

He laughs and helps me up. "Pretty much, until you can learn to fight back. Come on, I'll show you how to keep your balance and avoid contact."

Trevor works with me for three hours. "You're exhausted. Let's get lunch." He opens the gym door.

I will the door closed. "What about you working on your powers?"

"I don't have powers, you do."

"Try, like you told me to do with materializing. Just breathe and concentrate on that knife, then throw it at that dummy. Use your hand as an extension of your power." I choose a knife with my eyes and use my hand to move it where I want it. "See, now you try."

He does and the knife comes off the wall and into the mat a foot away from the dummy. He raises his brow.

"Takes practice and it becomes easier to do."

He looks perplexed. "Move me."

"What?"

"Move me like you do the knife, as if I was Moartea coming at you."

I bite my lip and concentrate. I can't do it. He gets a weird look then goes for the phone on the wall.

"Hey, send Brandon to the gym….thanks."

"Why are you asking for Brandon?"

"Just a theory I want to try."

"Okay?"

"What's going on? You two like to get me into trouble. Why do you always ask me for shit anyways?" Brandon whines.

"Because besides Cash, you're the only other one my brother actually likes." I smile.

I feel Trevor glaring at me. I'm finding it easier and easier to read his mind, and I sense that scares the shit out of him.

"Hmmm, interesting." He looks at Trevor. "So what is it you need?"

Trevor looks over at me. "Move him."

I concentrate and put my hand up. Brandon is knocked back a few steps. "Whoa."

Trevor steps next to me and grabs my left hand. "Try again."

I try again.

Brandon is knocked back ten feet and slammed face first into the wall. "Shit." He puts his hand to his face.

"Crap." I run to him and drop to my knees. "I'm so sorry. Let me see your face." I take his face in my hands and seal the cut. He caught the corner of the wall and it caused a huge gash across his jawline.

Of course it's this moment Riley chooses to walk into the gym. I feel rage run through me and I know it's not mine. I look up and Riley's eyes are red.

Riley comes over growling and rips me up by the arm.

I talk really fast and try to ignore the pain in my arm. "It's my fault. I threw him into the wall and he was cut open. I just wanted to fix it."

Trevor gets to us quickly and goes nose to nose with Riley. "You will take your hands off my sister or I will take you down," he growls. His eyes are completely black.

I have no doubt Riley would protect me, but Trevor would kill to keep me safe, including from Riley.

Riley drops my arm.

Trevor pulls me to him and gently takes my arm in his hands. He moves it around and looks up at me.

I'm pretty sure there's something going on in there that's not good. But with as mad as I feel Trevor right now, I'm closing off all my emotions to hide the fact I'm screaming inside as he moves it around. Well bright side, at least I'm getting better at turning off my emotions.

Riley turns to Brandon and growls.

Brandon throws his hands up. "Don't look at me. They called me in here to kick my ass."

Riley pulls me back into him gently. "I'm sorry, Luv, I didn't mean to do that." He looks up at Trevor who's still glaring at him. "Justin wants to see you two. We're going out tonight."

Trevor and Brandon leave. As soon as my brother is out the door I pull away from Riley and drop to my knees in pain. I rub my arm trying not to cry as everything I was holding back washes over me at once. Blocking emotions gets easier the more I do it. But having to get all of them rushing back in at once when I let them go is another story entirely.

In any other world this would be considered abuse. In my world now, it's a male vampire trying to control his bond. I still have a hard time controlling my own emotions good or bad, and I know Riley would never deliberately hurt me.

"You are hurt." Riley narrows his gaze.

"Well yeah, duh." The bruises are starting to show. Good thing I heal quickly. "My brother wanted to run you through. His hand was on the handle of his blade. If you would have made one more move to hurt me…."

"Now he thinks I've gone so soft that he can take me, huh?" Riley turns to glare towards the door.

"His only thoughts were that you were hurting me, and he would rather kill you than it escalate. My brother feels like he needs to protect me from the world."

He sighs as he looks back down at me. "I'm sorry. When I saw you with Brandon I lost control. It won't happen again."

"I hurt him. I felt it was my responsibility to heal him, got it?" I glare.

"Yes, my Queen." He smiles.

I reach up and punch him in the stomach.

He groans and laughs. "I will apologize to them both later."

I sigh. "Come here." I point in front of me and he kneels. "It's only you Riley."

"It's still hard to believe that, Luv. I'm waiting for you to finally see how unworthy I am."

I shake my head. "Says the King. I've never felt good enough for you, just so you know."

He drops his brow and shakes his head. He takes my face in his hands. "You are so good, so pure of heart, I promise you that it's you that's too good for me."

"Shut up and kiss me."

He does, then he kisses down my arm. "Danielle cooked again," he says between kisses.

"Why didn't you say so earlier?" I jump up.

He gets up. "Because I walked in on my mate running her tongue down another male's face."

"I see how that probably didn't look so good. I'm sorry."

"Never apologize to me for helping another. It's my problem, not yours. Our bond is so strong. I fight the urge every day to just lock you up in our room and never let you out near anyone. Let alone other males."

"It doesn't matter how many males I'm around, in my world, only you exist."

"Damn, female, you always know what I need to hear." He grabs a hold of me again. We leave the gym and walk arm and arm into the great room to eat.

After we finish I walk into the kitchen where Danielle is. "Hey D. How are you doing here with everything?"

"Everybody's really nice. Even though I feel like lunch in a room full of vampires. How is it possible that they are all so damn good looking?"

I laugh. "That's what I say. Can you give up your life for a life here with me?"

She looks over at Chris. "I'm thinking….yes. They are all so great, and I can do my thing here. But I think I should maybe get paid to do it. That way I'll have my own money, not just money from them."

"How much?" Riley comes up behind me and wraps his arms across my chest.

"Well, three meals a day, plus food allowance, maybe like $500 a week," she says.

"Done."

"I still need to think about everything, you guys."

"I understand. I had to try D, you're my family."

"I feel the same way about you. You're an angel?"

I shrug. "My mother actually was an angel."

"Crazy. Why do they keep calling you Queen, mostly when you're not around?"

Riley smiles, "Because that's what she is, the Queen." He kisses my cheek and heads to Justin's office.

I sigh. "Riley is the King. And they know if they say it to my face, I will punch them in theirs."

"Wow, that's crazy," she says. "And also….so very you."

"I know."

"Vampires have pretty strong emotions right?"

"Yes. It seems like everything gets magnified, good or bad. I have a hard time controlling my emotions. So does Riley."

"I'll remember that. Your brother's expressions change as soon as you leave the room. He's like the others when you're here, but goes very dark when you leave."

I frown and look over at Trevor. He smiles back at me. "I know. He's hiding something from me that happened in his past."

"Something happened to him?"

"Yeah, I think so." I nod.

"I need to finish up in here." She goes back to breakfast.

I walk over to Trevor and hold out my hand. He takes it and yanks me into his lap. I hug him tightly.

> *Trevor: Are you alright?*
> *Me: I am now. I just needed my brother.*
> *Trevor: Don't worry for me, I'm better now.*
> *Me: Except for the things you hide from me that*
> *you don't think I know about, still terrified*
> *I'll see something and leave you.*

I get a picture of a little boy around ten years old crying and terrified. Then it cuts off abruptly. He tries to pull away from me but I hold him tighter.

> *Me: I love you, and I would never leave you.*
> *Promise you'll never leave me.*
> *Trevor: I promise.*

He kisses my forehead refusing to meet my eyes as he pushes me off of him, then he stalks off to his room. I take a deep breath and slump over in the chair. I know it means he won't eat again tonight.

"He wasn't well when I met him, Sky. Give him time," Cash says as he sits in the chair next to me.

"I just worry about him."

"He's already better with you here."

I nod.

After we eat, Riley and a few others get ready to go out. Maybe if I work really hard I can eventually go out too.

"Hey Sky, you want to play pool with us? You and me against Chris and Markus," Brandon says.

"Sure." I walk over to them.

We're laughing and joking around as Riley comes out suited up. He looks over and comes towards us. His eyes are locked on mine. He grabs me up so fast I drop the stick. He lays into my neck hard with a deep growl, then seals me up. Then he comes down on my mouth and kisses me hard.

I'm confused by the very intimate PDA. Maybe annoyed and a little turned on at the same time. As he pulls back slightly to look at me he seems apologetic.

He sighs. "I'll see you soon. I love you."

"And I you." I'm having a hard time dropping the 'what the hell' face I'm currently sporting.

Riley walks off.

All three males have put the pool table between themselves and Riley. "What the hell was all that?" I frown.

Brandon picks up the cue and hands it to me. "He wants to make sure we know exactly who you belong to."

I narrow my gaze and look over at the stairs leading out.

"Don't give him a hard time. It's more instinctual than anything else. I hear when a male finds his mate, he holds her above anything else. And that male loves the shit out of you," Markus says.

Chapter 11

It has been a month since I was turned and Riley and I were mated. Riley is getting more involved with the council and spends a lot of time there looking over things. The council has him going through old laws and prophecies. He has a lot of really good ideas, but he's having a hard time getting things changed. He wants to get the local legions to start working together. Moartea are spreading faster and training their recruits better.

"Today D and I want to go to the mall and do a little shopping, is that alright?"

"I can't go today, Luv, I have a meeting."

"I can get Michael and Cash to take us."

"Michael's coming with me and Cash is on tonight."

"I'll figure it out."

"Make sure you have them stay with you." He looks up with a narrowed gaze.

"Don't worry, I will. We look like we have body guards though, and people stare at us thinking we're somebody special," I sigh.

He gets up and wraps me up in his arms. "You are special Luv. You're an angel born on earth and the Queen."

"When are you leaving?"

"Right now, I won't be too long. I may even be back before you are." He kisses me quick, turns to gathers his things up, and heads for the door.

"Hey." I walk over to him.

His feet stop in their tracks and he looks back at me.

I smile, take the papers from him, and set them on the table next to the door. "I know you can do better than that."

He laughs and grabs me up in his arms. He kisses me deeply and pulls me into his body. I run my hands down to his ass and feel him hardening against me.

"It's hard enough to leave you without all of this."

I shrug. "Have a good night, I'll see you when you get back."

"You're all that's going to be on my mind tonight." He gathers his stuff back up, adjusts himself, and then leaves.

A few minutes later I hear a knock at the door.

"Come in," I call out.

"Hey, are we going?" Danielle comes in.

"Yeah, but he wants whoever takes us to stay with us. I'm sure he's already out there choosing two of them to babysit us as we speak." I flop on the couch.

"He just worries about you Sky." She comes over and sits in the chair.

"I know, but sometimes this is all a little too much for me."

"Yes, I do know. You're not the kind of girl that likes to be the center of attention. Maybe you shouldn't have fallen in love with a king." She smiles at me.

"In my defense he wasn't a king when I fell in love with him. The thing is, I didn't really have a choice about falling in love with Riley. Even now, everything that surrounds him makes me want to run away. But I can't, because I love him too much."

"Sounds like you've been regretting some of your decisions."

"Not regretting exactly. I couldn't give Riley up, not now. I love him too much." I get up. "Ugh. I'm done thinking about all this crap. That's what the shopping is for."

She gets up. "Let's go see who he's picked to take us."

We come into the great room and I see Brandon and Markus suited up. Brandon's smiling, but Markus looks positively annoyed. Yep, must be them.

I walk up to Markus. "You're taking us?"

"Yeah," he says coldly.

"Sorry Markus, I told him we'd be fine."

"Sky, it's fine," he says trying to smile. "I was off tonight anyways."

Great, so his night off is wasted babysitting me. I hang my head and sigh. "You two can leave when we get there, I won't say anything to him."

"You know I can't do that. It's what he ordered me to do."

Throwing my hands up and not going at all seems like the best option here. Well, maybe when we get there we can figure out a way to ditch them. Then they can have some fun trying to track us or something. Man I'm losing it.

We head out. I go to Brandon and Danielle goes to Markus. They leave and I step away from Brandon.

"Markus really doesn't want to go. Maybe you guys can go do something he would like, and then we can meet back up before we come home."

He smiles. "We will stay with you while you shop."

Damn it, I knew that's where all that would go. I bet my orders don't supersede Riley's. "Can you at least tell me something Markus likes to do?"

He thinks for a minute. "He likes to play video games. He has a whole game system thing in his room. I'm not sure what else he likes, guns?" He shrugs.

"I can work with that. Let's go." I go into his arms.

"Pretty soon you won't need me to take you places anymore."

We appear in the back parking lot of the mall. I walk over to Danielle. The guys will stay just behind us, watching everything and everyone that gets too close.

"When we get near the game store I'm going to take Markus in. I know you hate them, so take Brandon into whatever store is next to it."

"You're funny. You always worry about everyone around you."

"You want to hear something funny?" I say as we come into the mall.

"What?"

"Markus was the first vampire I ever kissed, and wow does he know what he's doing there."

She whips her head around. "What? When?"

I laugh. "It happened before I met Riley. He was in an alley and I caught him in the middle of killing a Moartea."

She turns around to look at Markus.

I turn back and look at him, then smile.

"What?" he asks.

"Nothing. Just telling D about the first time you and I met."

He smiles and shakes his head. "Thought that was going to stay between you and me?"

"I'm the best friend, I get to know everything." She laughs.

We go into almost every store trying to pass the time. The mall is moderately busy. Markus looks miserable, but Brandon seems like he really doesn't mind. I think he may have been a girl in another life.

Finally, we come to the front of the game store. I look over at Danielle and she nods.

"Hey Brandon, will you come with me over to the Coach store?" She takes Brandon by the hand and drags him with her.

"Alright, I guess we'll be back," Brandon says.

I grab Markus's arm and drag him into the game store. I act like I'm interested in whatever the hell I'm looking at. Why are all these game stores so stuffy, and smell like sweaty boys?

He isn't paying attention to me at first, all business. He's intensely analyzing the crowd around us. Like Moartea are going to come into the mall and attack us in front of everyone.

"Hey,"—I pull on his arm—"what do you think about this game?" I act like I'm studying it.

He looks at me, brow lowered. He stops and takes a second to actually look around at the store we're in, then he looks back at me and smiles. "What are you doing?"

I give him the most innocent face I have. "What? I'm just looking at games. I used to have an Xbox 360 and I was thinking about getting another system. I thought I would look at games first to see which ones I want."

He narrows his gaze. "Really?"

"Nah." I laugh. "I just thought since you like games, maybe you would want to look around in here. And now that I know you have them, maybe I'll come bug you to play when I'm bored. I get all crazy in the head cooped up in the bunker."

He smiles and starts telling me about a bunch of games. He buys four and seems really happy. It makes me feel good to do something for somebody else. Why shouldn't they get to have some fun?

"Here." I hold my hands out. "I'll carry them so you can feel less guilty that you have them."

He hands them to me. "You're too smart for your own good."

"As soon as I took you all in, I could feel each of your emotions. It's how I knew you didn't want to come here with us, and you were angry that you had to. You resented me." I take a deep breath. "I get it though, I'm not judging you or anything. No male of any race likes to go shopping."

Markus stares at me for a moment. "I'm sorry. I didn't mean it, not really. I love you as much as the next male, and I want you to always be safe. And what you did here for me today, I appreciate it more than you know. You really do care for others."

"I may have a little bit of a soft spot for you Markus. You are the first vampire I ever kissed." I laugh.

He smiles.

I throw my arms around his waist and hug him.

He hugs me back tightly and kisses my cheek. "Since we're on the subject, why did you stop me?" he asks quietly.

I'm still tightly in his arms. "With everything I've seen and felt up to this point, I know you could sense that I was attracted to you, that I desired to have all of you."

He nods.

"You were a vampire, and we we're in an alley. As great and exciting as that sounds, I'm not a whore."

"But you wanted me?"

"Yes. You're very handsome, Markus, a lot of girls would want you."

He nods. "I can live with that."

"You just don't want to be stuck babysitting me, I get it."

"You're just going to have to get used to the fact you're like family to us, and even though we love you, sometimes we won't like doing everything with you."

"Fair enough. I love you too, Markus."

"Are you finished here?"

"Yes. Mostly I just come here to clear my head, shopping has never really been my thing. I struggle with everything and I feel trapped." I shrug. "Really, I could go almost anywhere. We used to go to Distortion and dance everything away. I miss that. Even sparing with Trevor helps, but he had to go out tonight."

"Well shit, why didn't you say something? I have a dozen places I could take you to blow off steam and have fun."

"Next time then, it's all yours to plan."

"And anytime you want to spar, I'm game."

I smile wide, "Really? Only if you go all out though."

"You are crazy, aren't you?" He laughs.

"If I don't go all out, how will I know if I can really handle myself out here? I need to go out, Markus. I want to kill Moartea, to feel useful and have a purpose. Right now I feel like a helpless human girl, not like a vampire angel with powers."

"Have you talked to Riley about all of this? Or Justin?"

"Yeah both, and both just want to keep me safe. But it's not up to anyone but me. If I want to go out, I'll go out. It's up to them to help train me or I'll learn in the field myself."

He smiles. "You will just go out on your own won't you?"

"Yep." I nod. "And now that Trevor has taught me to materialize, it will be sooner rather than later."

"I'll help train you, and if they won't take you out, I will. Maybe we can hunt for Moartea out by themselves. That's what I do when I need to blow off steam. Like the night I met you."

"I'd really like that." I squeeze him tighter.

"Tomorrow I'll train you to shoot. I'll let you know what time to meet me in the range."

"We have a gun range?"

He laughs. "Do you look around at all? Have you see all the cars in the garage yet?"

"We have a garage?" My eyes are huge.

"Maybe your mate could show you something other than his bedroom for a change." He narrows his gaze.

I laugh. "Thank you."

"A male could get used to being in your arms." He smiles as I look up at him. He touches my face and leans in, kissing me softly.

Brandon and Danielle are on their way back.

I still have an arm around Markus's waist and he has his arm across my shoulders. Brandon's gaze is narrowed and his emotions are closed off. I wonder what that's all about. Maybe he likes Danielle.

"You guys ready to go?" I ask.

"Yes, I'm beat," Danielle answers.

"I'm ready," Brandon says coldly.

We head out to the parking lot. Markus and Danielle leave.

"So you want to try and go yourself?" Brandon asks.

"I guess. It's a little different seeing a rock or feeling Trevor and wishing to be there. I have to just want to be at the bunker?"

"It's sort of the same. Just think of where you want to be and see yourself there."

I close my eyes and try to clear my mind of everything but the bunker. I open my eyes and look around. It's windy, and I have no idea where I am. My eyes adjust to the darkness. Luckily the moon is full. I'm starting to be able to make out where I am.

What the hell. Really? Arizona.

Damn, I thought of the Grand Canyon right before I materialized. I look around and just sit on my ass. What am I supposed to do now? Try again or call somebody? I pull out my phone and start to text Riley when I remember he's busy with the council. Great. Trevor's out tonight on a recon. *Brandon.* I start the text.

"Arizona huh? Maybe we should have had a discussion about where it is you actually want to be." Brandon sits next to me and knocks his shoulder into mine.

"Sorry, it just popped in my head at the last second."

"Why?"

"I guess my head's a little screwed up right now. I needed some clarity. I remember in the daytime, just looking out at the vastness of the canyon put my mind at ease. It's a beautiful picture of colors during the day. The canyon looks like the sunrise has been permanently painted into its cliffs."

"Sounds beautiful."

"It is." I look at him and narrow my gaze. "Are you okay?"

"Yeah, fine. Why?" He looks away from me.

"I don't know, you just seem off."

He shrugs.

"Alright then, I'm ready for you to take me home."

"Aw, you don't want to try again?" He smiles.

I get up. "Nope, I'm fine with you taking me for now."

He smiles and pulls me into his arms tightly.

"Brandon, do you like Danielle?"

"Yeah, she's cool." He shrugs.

"Not like that, are you interested in her?"

He pulls back with his brow all scrunched up. "No, I don't feel for her like that."

"Alright, I was just asking. You probably have all kinds of girls all the time anyways."

"Why do you think that?" He smirks.

"Uh, because look at you."

"What about me?" He tilts his head and smiles.

"You want me to say it, don't you?"

"I just want to know why you think I have so many females."

I sigh. "Because you're totally hot, duh."

He laughs

I punch him in the stomach. "I can't believe you made me say it."

He has us back in front of the bunker. "Materializing gets easier the more you do it. Maybe we should start around here and you can practice. Building jumping is fun."

"Building jumping?"

We start to walk inside.

"Yeah, you appear from one building to another. Helps you see where you want to go. It's good practice."

"That would be fun. I need to get out of here more. Will you spar with me tomorrow?"

"Yeah."

"Cool, thanks again, Brandon."

"Anytime."

I look up and see Riley walking into the great room. I smile and he smiles back at me. We meet each other in the center. He grabs me and kisses me hard.

"Are you busy right now?"

"Not unless you want me to be," he growls.

"Huh, you must read minds now."

"I spent all night in that meeting thinking about all the things I'm going to do to you."

We head off to our room.

****

I've been training with my brother for the last four weeks. I can hardly believe I've been here for two months already. I'm feeling more and more cooped up every day. Sparing with Trevor helps a little bit. Our powers have grown and we're using them to help during hand to hand combat.

Sparing with Trevor is one of my favorite pastimes these days, but the more time I spend with him, the more I notice the block in his mind faltering. He's so afraid I'll get through and see something that could change how I feel about him. There's nothing on this Earth he could have done that I wouldn't be able to get over.

He still doesn't let anyone but me touch him. I've noticed him watching Danielle. He seems enthralled with her. But when she comes too close to him, he less than gracefully gets away from her.

They would be good for each other. Riley thinks I'm crazy. He says I'm lucky Trevor is the way he is with me, like it goes against his very nature. Which I refuse to believe is true. My brother has so much love and kindness inside of him. I see it and feel it all the time.

Danielle's grown more comfortable here, and has decided to stay. We quit our jobs and moved out of the apartment. She is the legion's chef and the crazy girl loves it. Chris really likes her but he hasn't made any moves towards her that I know of. I see the way she looks at Trevor, and I'm not the only one. My brother is the only one that's too dumb to see it.

Brandon works out with me a couple times a week. I still drag him along to the mall with Danielle and me, but we make Chaz come with us now. Markus has been sparring with me and training me to shoot. He's a great kickboxer, and I'm learning so many more moves.

Markus and I have gone out a couple of times that nobody knows about. We've also snuck out to play paintball which was awesome. He and I kick everyone's ass on the course.

Tonight he's taking me out to hunt. I've been lying here in bed going crazy thinking about it. Plus, the whole sneaking out thing is stressful.

Riley pulls me to him. "Evening, Luv."

I look up and smile. "Hi."

"What are your plans this evening?"

"Training with Trevor."

He sighs.

"I've been training hard and I'm getting really good. I want to go out."

"We'll see," he says dryly.

I shake my head and try to get up.

He holds me tighter and comes over on top of me. "Can't you understand I love you, and that I don't want you getting hurt?"

"So you think of me as this stupid weak little girl that can't handle herself. You've never even seen me fight."

"Trevor says you're good."

"Yeah, so then why can't I go out?"

"Good, is not great, Luv. You're not ready."

"You're never going to think I'm ready." I narrow my gaze and then turn away from him.

He kisses down my cheek and then runs his fangs across my neck.

"Get….off….me….now," I growl.

He lifts his head up and rolls to his side taking a deep breath.

I get up and grab my shirt. "You will not tell me what I can and cannot do. I will go out when I think I'm ready, and you will not stop me," I bark as I get my shirt on.

He gets up fast and steps in front of me. "I am your King and your mate, I decide when you fight. You will fight when I say you're ready to and not before."

I glare. I push past him and grab my pants. He grabs me up in his arms and I can't struggle out of his grasp. I sigh.

"I don't want to fight with you today," he says calmly.

"Then why are you?" I narrow my gaze.

He sighs. "If I say I'll think about it and talk it over with Justin, will you quit looking at me like that?"

I drop my head. "It's what I want, and I feel like you're always going to tell me no. You want me locked up in here, and it's driving me mad."

He takes my face in his hands. "I promise you it's only because I love you. It's not because I think you're weak. I think you're one of the strongest people I know, and you're very important to me. If you continue to work hard, and when you're ready, I will let you go."

"Promise me."

"I promise, Luv." He holds me tightly. "I don't like fighting with you."

"Pffft. That was not a fight. We haven't really had one yet. But with as stubborn as you are, I see many in our future." I shake my head. "Do you know how hard it is to be angry when your God like mate is standing before you bare?"

He smiles. He takes my hand and puts it on himself as he kisses me. "Do you want me as much as I want you?"

I grip him tightly and he moans on my lips. "I told you, I always want you."

He rips my shirt off and throws me on the bed. He comes at me fast and I'm barely able to catch my breath as he drives into me.

We finally get up and dress. It must be ridiculous that everyone else gets up around four in the evening, and we don't make it out of our room until sometimes after eight.

Riley groans.

"What's wrong?"

"I don't want to sit in those meetings all evening." He grabs me up in his arms. "All I will be thinking about all night is all of that, and when I can be back inside you again."

I smile. "You are crazy, vampire."

He kisses me deeply, then tears himself away.

"I love you, Riley, no matter what. I just want you to know that."

"I love you, too. Is everything alright?" He lowers his brow.

Nope, I'm going out hunting tonight and might get myself killed. "Yep, great actually."

"Tonight Luv, tonight."

I wait for an hour to make sure Riley and Michael are gone. I pull out the weapons Markus got for me. I suit up and then head down the hall to Markus's room.

I knock.

He opens the door and comes into the hall.

"Ready?" I ask.

"Been ready. He gone?"

"Yeah, he left an hour ago."

"Where's Trevor?"

"In the gym."

"Alright, I guess it's time."

We go out the garage exit.

"We'll start out near the club and work our way north towards the docks. If we get lucky, we'll smell them," he says.

We have been walking in circles around the docks for three hours. Finally, I think I sense one. I stop and look around. I move in the direction my brain is telling me to run away from. Markus is right behind me.

"I sense one."

He smiles. "Do you?"

I come around a corner and see a Moartea. He turns and looks at me. Those damn creepy black eye holes stare back at me. As soon as I see him pull a gun, I run at him as fast as I can.

"Sky," Markus yells out.

I hear the gun go off right before I hit him in the face as hard as I can. He falls to his ass and loses his gun. Two more come around the corner.

"Fuck." Markus draws his blade and goes to work.

I pull the knife from my side pocket and stab mine in the chest. I run the blade across his throat and he's ash.

I jump up ready for more, but I'm left with only me and Markus smiling ear to ear covered in blood and ash.

"You did well." He looks down and sighs, "Let me see your side."

"My side?" I look down as he pulls my shirt up.

"It's just a flesh wound. Usually when they pull a gun, you take cover and pull yours." He smiles shaking his head, "I didn't sense any fear from you."

"Did you think you would?"

"I wasn't sure. But you were damn good. I'm going to seal this up."

I nod.

He kneels down and seals my side. "Let's get back before your brother comes looking for you."

"Can we do this again Markus?"

"Yes, most definitely."

"So you think I'm ready?" I raise my brow.

"I do, but it's not anything I can tell them Sky."

"I know."

****

Going out hunting with Markus and finally facing off with a Moartea was awesome. Dusting it was one of the most exhilarating things I've ever done. Now it's all I think about doing, but I still can't talk them into letting me go. Too bad Markus couldn't just tell them how good I am without suffering Riley's wrath.

Riley's been very busy with council stuff as usual. I feel like all we do is meet up before bed, make love for a couple of hours, and sleep. Then we wake up and eat together before he goes off and running again.

He's visiting more legions around us now, so he's gone most of the night into the early morning.

I'm headed to the gym now to work out with Trevor. He's off today. Well, more off than usual anyways. I come inside and he stops to look over at me. "How are you today?"

"Fine." He goes back to punching the bag.

I walk up and get in his way.

He sighs. "Sky, I said I'm fine."

"You know I'll never believe you until you tell me what you're hiding from me."

"Are we starting this again?" He glares.

"Nope." I shake my head. "Hey Trevor?"

"What," he barks.

"I love you." I smile.

Before he can say anything, I throw my arms around his waist and hug the crap out of him. I feel him shaking his head as he hugs me back.

"When do you think I can go out?"

"You know he may never let you on a raid."

"Shouldn't be up to him."

"Well, he's your mate, and the King, so you go tell him that." He smiles and goes back to punching the bag.

I take a deep breath. "What if I tell you I've already gone out, and that I've killed a Moartea?"

He stops and his face drops. I see a combination of anger and panic.

"Yep."

"By yourself," he yells.

"Nope, I had back up."

He glares. "You will tell me right now who took you out."

"No….I won't, and you won't make demands of me, brother." I glare as step away from him. I start wrapping my hands.

"It was Brandon wasn't it? I'll kill him." He starts pacing.

"Nope, not Brandon. You can stop now because I'll never tell you who it is." I cross my arms over my chest.

Markus and I keep our distance from each other in front of everybody else. Well, other than training.

He shakes his head. "Looks like I'll be glued to your side from now on doesn't it."

"Trevor, I want to fight. I told you, if you won't help me I'll go out on my own. At least this warrior realizes that. He's helped me instead of trying to lock me up here. I know you can feel me going crazy inside. Just please help me."

He takes a deep breath. "I have an idea." He walks over and grabs the phone. "Can you meet me in the gym?" He hangs it up and then looks back at me. "I want you to go one on one with Brandon using dummy swords."

"Seriously? Because that's his thing you know."

"Yes, Brandon's one of the best with swords."

"Great, because I suck."

"You suck, until you practice to get better."

"If I would have known you were going to test me, I would have had him show me how to use the swords instead of going hand to hand with him all the time."

Brandon comes in and looks from me to Trevor. "Oh no. I'm not getting my ass kicked this evening."

He turns to leave and Trevor moves his hand closing the door and locking it. Trevor's powers have grown and he can do everything I can do now.

"Come on." Brandon throws his hands up.

"No powers." He tosses Brandon one of the dummy swords. "She wants to go out on raids, so let's see how she does with you."

"Yeah, because he's ever going to let you go out." Brandon laughs.

I glare and start circling him.

"Apparently, somebody has already been taking her out. She killed a Moartea." Trevor glares at him.

Brandon shoots a crazy look over at me. "What," he growls. "Who the hell is taking you out?"

I roll my eyes. "Like I told Trevor, I'm not going to tell anybody that so back off."

"Looks like I'm going to be watching you a lot closer." He glares.

"Whatever. You two are ridiculous. Just so you both know, neither one of you can watch me all the time. Are we doing this or what?"

We go back and forth with the dummy swords and are surprisingly evenly matched. If you don't count that he's killed me twice, to me cutting his balls off once. But I feel like I'm getting it. I really like using a sword.

Now I see why it's their weapon of choice. The way it feels in your hands as you slice through the air, and coming against your opponent's blade is like a surge of energy. I want to see what it feels like to slice through a Moartea's flesh with a broad sword.

"Damn, she's gotten really good," Brandon says shaking his head.

"From you, I'll take that as a compliment."

"Now let's see you two go hand to hand all out," Trevor says.

"He's bigger than me and he always wins."

"You want to go out? Then you better be able to take out Moartea bigger and stronger than you are," he says dryly.

"Fine, let's go," I groan. Every time we square off, Brandon sweeps me and ends up on top. "I think my ass is broken."

"You know, if Riley walks in here right now I'm going to get my ass beat," Brandon says as he straddles me.

"Yeah, it would probably be better if you were ugly." I laugh as I shove him off me.

He laughs and gets up.

"I have to go. Can you work with her on hand to hand and balance training?" Trevor asks

"Sure."

Me: Be careful.
Trevor: I will, you worry too much.
Me: You're all I have. Don't you know that?

I hug him tightly. There's been more injuries coming back lately. Justin has been sending them out to tear down any training center they can find. Moartea are also getting pickier on the recruits they get as well.

"I'll be fine." He kisses my forehead before he leaves.

"Seeing him with you still blows my mind. You know he's only like that with you. Whereas, Riley is completely different."

I'm still staring at the door Trevor left out of.

"Come on let's go. I'm going to show you a few tricks." Brandon motions me over.

After an hour he goes to the phone. "Cash, hand to hand, meet me in the gym." He looks back at me. "You pick things up so damn quickly. It's like you mimic exactly what we do, and you do it perfectly. I want to see you do against Cash."

"Sure." I shrug.

Cash saunters in.

"Come on, you and Sky, hand to hand." Brandon motions him over.

"No way am I hitting a female. Especially this one," he says as he walks over.

That comment gets him punched in the face. Then I watch as he flies back on his ass. "Well then this female is going to use you like a punching bag." I smile.

"Ah, that's why I love her." Brandon laughs.

"Ooookay." Cash wipes the blood from his lip. "Let's go, little girl." He beckons me to him.

"Don't hold back. Remember, I heal too. I have to be better or he'll never let me go out."

Once again it's pretty evenly matched, but we're tied at two deaths each. We square off again and he comes at me. I sweep him and then get on top of him stabbing him with my fake sword.

I run it across his neck. "You're toast and that makes three against two, I win." I throw my hands up in the air like I just made a field goal.

Riley comes in, looks at Cash, then at me, and then starts towards Cash like a freight train.

I'm pretty bloody and so is Cash. I jump up and use all my strength to hold him back.

"Riley, we were just training," Brandon yells out.

Cash gets up and moves closer to Brandon but stands bracing for the impact. "Fuck me, this is going to suck." He cringes.

Using Riley's forward momentum against him, I flip him onto his back. Then I jump on top of him and do the same stabbing motion to his chest I did to Cash.

His eyes are huge as he stares up at me.

"Holy shit," Brandon chokes out.

"Uh, yeah." Cash shakes his head. "I can't believe she was able to take him down."

"See, they're helping me," I plead. "You think a Moartea would go easy on me?"

"Your face, Luv, you're black and blue." He shoots a look over to Cash and Brandon.

I pull his face back to mine. "I told them to go all out so I know what I can handle. I ordered them to."

He looks up at me and touches my face.

"Riley, she's really good and learns fast," Brandon says.

"I'm fine, and I just killed you by the way." I smile.

"Leave us, now," Riley growls.

They head for the door quickly.

I lock the door behind them because he doesn't look angry anymore. I actually feel desire beginning to burn through me. He pulls my face down to him. He kisses every bruise and seals every cut he comes to. Then he kisses me deeply and flips us over so he's on top of me.

"I'm all gross and sweaty."

He sits up on his knees and pulls his shirt off, next he goes for my sweats. He's smiles down at me and then takes me right here on the mats. It's rough and intense, and overall pretty spectacular.

When we finish, I sigh.

"What's wrong?"

"I'm supposed to work out in here. Now all I'm going to think about is you and me on these mats." I pull myself together.

He laughs. "Good, think about that the next time your legs are wrapped around one of them."

"Seriously? It's called training, you big jerk. Besides, you saw them just now--they're all too scared of you to ever make a move on me. Are you going out tonight?"

"No, you have me all evening."

"Good." I hug him and then get up. "I need a shower." I start for the door.

"Is that an invitation?"

I laugh. "No, because you never need one. I'm yours. But there's maybe something I would like to do with you in there." I lick my lips and look him up and down.

He growls, picks me up, and then heads to our room. The shower was fun, but we moved to the bed afterwards. We eventually make it out of the bedroom and head into the great room.

"I'm going to have Michael take me on a quick errand." I look over at him. "You know I'm not asking you right?"

"I can take you."

"No, I want to do this myself, trust me."

"Alright, but take Mike and Brandon."

"Don't you think Brandon's getting tired of always having to babysit me?"

"Sky, I like hanging out with you," Brandon says as he walks over.

"She has an errand. Get Michael and you two go with her fully suited," he says.

"Understood." Brandon heads off to change.

Chapter 12

Watching Riley become more comfortable being in charge is inspiring.

"I want a knife." I hold my hand out.

He stares at me.

I leave my hand out in front of him.

He finally hands over his.

I slide it in my thigh pocket of my cargo pants. I throw my arms around him. "Now it's you that sits here and waits for me to come back." I arch my brow and smile.

He takes my face in his hands. "Luv, I just want you to always be safe. I almost lost you once. I won't ever let that happen again."

"I can't imagine something ever happening to you either."

"Are we going?" Brandon says.

"Where exactly are we going?" Michael asks.

"I'll tell you outside, and sorry ahead of time, it's shopping," I say.

They hang their heads and Riley laughs. We head up stairs and come out into the cool night air.

I go to Michael and put my arms around him. "Can you take me to a jewelry store?"

He looks down and smiles. He holds me tightly to him then looks over at Brandon. "I guess follow me."

We end up in an alley. As we walk down towards the street Brandon appears. We come around the corner to the front of the building. I look up and see Tiffany & Co. Maybe I should have been more specific of how poor I am, now that I no longer have a job.

"Uh Michael, I should of specified I need a cheap jewelry store. I don't have a lot of money left in my savings and this one is really nice, but really expensive. Even a pawn shop would work."

"Come on," he says impatiently and drags me inside.

Everyone inside freezes as we come inside.

Michael's dragging me by the hand as Brandon stands to the left of the door. I can only imagine what the three of us must look like. Michael has tan skin, dark brown hair, very handsome, dressed in black jeans, combat boots, and black button up shirt with a leather jacket to conceal his weapons. Brandon has black short wavy hair, really hot, blue jeans, black docs, white button up shirt, also in a black leather jacket concealing his weapons. Then there's just plain ol' average me with these two hot guys that look more like body guards than anything else.

"What are you looking for?" Michael asks.

"Bands, but I can't pay for them from here," I say under my breath.

"Here." He brings me in front of the wedding band section. "You have money." He hands me a card that has my name on it.

I look over all the bands. Riley's a pretty simple guy and I'm not looking for anything fancy. I look at all of the price tags and put them back.

Michael leans over to my ear. "You can get whatever you want. Money doesn't matter."

A huge smile appears across the salesgirl's face. "Well aren't you lucky to have scored him."

I glare at her, but she's too busy drooling as she looks Michael up and down.

"So," I blurt out. "I need the plain 6mm platinum band and the 3mm one. I need the 3mm in a size 8 and here." I hand her a string, "I need the 6 in whatever size this is."

"I could just measure his finger." She smiles and gazes at Michael.

"Well, I don't know how much good it will do to measure my brother-in-law's finger." I glare.

"Oh, he's not with you?" Her smile widens.

"Look, we're kind of in a hurry." I sigh.

"Sorry. I'll get those for you right away, miss." She hurries over to get the measurement from the string, then disappears to get the bands. She pops back out with a bag. "That will be $4150."

Holy crap. I look back at Michael.

He takes the card from my hand and hands it to the salesgirl. "Our family has money. She isn't used to it yet."

That makes her lean over closer to talk to him, and I feel the lust. It makes me want to reach over and slap her, but he leans in and entertains her.

It wouldn't surprise me if he came here after her shift and took her right out back in the alley. Michael doesn't seem to be much for the club girls or whores. But I also notice he doesn't feed as often as the others do either.

The girl finishes up and we head out. I slide the ring box into my pocket.

We go back towards the alley, and as soon as we round the corner I sense them. Death, and there are five of them.

They see us.

Brandon steps in front of me and pushes me back. They pull their swords and it all happens very fast.

I had asked Markus what happens when were on the street and people see us fighting with Moartea. He said they don't see. Somehow Moartea and anything around them are masked from humans unless they want to be seen.

One gets by them and comes right at me. I move my hand and use my power to slam him against the building. He's confused for a second but then he flies back up. He's already to me as I pull the knife from my pocket. He punches me in the face hard, busting my lip open. I fall on my ass about ten feet from him.

Damn. They're really strong, Trevor wasn't kidding.

The demon comes at me again, but this time I'm ready for him. Just like with Riley in the gym I use the Moartea's weight and forward momentum against him. I flip him to the ground, get on top of him, and then stab him in the heart. I run the blade across his throat and he turns to black ash under me. Then just like that I'm on the ground.

I jump up. "Wow. That was crazy. I want to do it again."

Michael and Brandon are staring at me, then they look at each other.

Brandon walks up to me. "He's going to kick our asses for this." He brushes his thumb across my bottom lip. "But you were fucking beautiful."

"She fights just like Trevor," Michael says.

"Yeah." Brandon nods. "She's really good."

The stare he's giving me is pretty intense and I feel like…..Next thing I know, I'm knocked to the ground with pain so intense I can't breathe. "Trevor," I gasp as I grab at my chest.

Something's wrong. I scramble up and will myself to him. There's a Moartea standing over him ready to finish him off. Brian has two on him with more coming towards us. Thank God Michael and Brandon are right on my ass.

Completely enraged, I throw my hands out and watch as all three Moartea standing over Trevor and Brian fly fifteen feet back into the wall. I grab Trevor's sword and face off with the Moartea that was going to kill him. I swing the sword and he dodges it.

I need more practice with these damn swords. It's awkward to handle and I feel off balance. It's heavier than the dummy swords we use.

The Moartea pulls a gun from his side. No time to think, running as fast as I can. I catch him off guard and drive the sword straight into his chest. As his black eyes burn into mine, I yank the sword out and then spin around taking his head off.

There's one more coming at me. Tossing the sword aside, I grab him, flip him over, and with the blade from my pocket I dust him just like I did the one in the alley. I look around and the rest have already been dusted.

I kneel down and feel my brother fading. I score my wrist and then force blood down his throat. He's getting stronger and then eventually bites into me.

"Are they all gone?" I ask.

"Yeah," I hear Derek answer from behind me.

I turn and look up him. "Can you take him back?" I'm shaking uncontrollably. I don't know what I would have done if I lost him, he was so close.

Derek grabs my arms and pulls me up. He turns me around, takes my wrist in his hands, and seals it. "I got him." He squeezes my arms and nods.

I take a deep breath as his calm washes over me.

He gathers Trevor up and is gone. I will myself back home to the bunker. I see Derek as he takes him inside. As we come in everyone scrambles towards us.

"What happened?" Justin asks.

"We were ambushed." Derek goes towards the hall.

"Can you take him to his room, Derek? He needs more blood," I say.

I feel Riley's eyes on me. I turn and meet his gaze. I know I'm covered in blood and black ash and he's internally freaking out.

He starts towards me.

I put my hand up. "Not now. Yell at me later, I need to get to my brother," I barely choke out.

I hear a very intense conversation with yelling starting behind me. Brandon and Michael are on their own. They handled him before me, so they will have to handle him now. I need to get to Trevor.

I come into Trevor's room and go to the bedroom.

Derek lays him down, removes his weapons, and then begins to help seal off his wounds.

I put my wrist back to his lips and he begins taking it in again. He's slowly healing. I take a deep breath and touch his face. "I can't lose you ever, do you understand me."

"Sky?" Derek says.

I look up at him.

He touches my face. "You did really good out there."

I feel his warmth wash through me like I did at the mating ceremony. "Thank you."

He finishes helping me seal the wounds.

I put my hand on the large wound on Trevor's chest near his heart. Somewhere between praying and willing it healed, the wound seals. I feel him finally healing faster. I keep forcing him to drink, but I feel myself becoming weaker. I almost pass out.

Derek pulls my wrist away and seals me up. He pulls me up into his arms and holds me tightly. "He's better now, and healing. You can't give him anymore."

I look down and see that Derek has a large cut across his chest. "Let me see that."

"I'm fine."

I glare. "Sit down and take off your shirt."

He sighs and sits in the chair by the bed. He pulls his shirt up.

I place my hand on his chest and close my eyes. I'm so drained already, and it takes a lot to heal him.

He catches me as I almost pass out. "I should go get Riley." He picks me up and lays me in bed next to Trevor.

"No. Just leave. I don't care about me. I don't want anyone else in here. I just want to be with my brother." I curl up around Trevor.

Derek takes a deep breath, then he put his wrist to my lips and nods. He's right, I need it, and I need to stay strong in case Trevor needs more. My eyes meet his as I bite into him.

When his blood meets my tongue, I close my eyes and can't hold back the moan this time. His blood is Heaven. I seal him up.

He brushes the hair from my face and smiles. As he runs his hand across my cheek I grab his hand in mine before he pulls away. He looks at our hands then back to me. His stare is intense and he's running his fingers around mine.

"Thank you Derek."

He nods and then leaves.

Exhausted, I finally go out.

At some point something happened and I'm thrown from the bed. Trevor's baring his fangs, his eyes black, and he's slowly coming towards me. There's hate spilling from him. I freeze when I see he has a blade in his hand and is stalking me.

I get a flash of a young boy around ten or eleven being touched by a man. *Oh God. It's Trevor.* It's a movie playing in my head of different times he's been abused. My stomach wrenches up on me. This is what he has hidden from me. This is why he won't let anyone touch him. He begins to growl.

Me: Trevor, it's me, it's Sky.

He's still coming towards me growling.

Me: Brother, please stop.

I barely get the words out as he moves forward ready to plunge the blade into my chest. "I'll love you always." I brace for the blade.

He stops. His eyes clear, he drops to his knees, and then grabs a hold of my waist. He begins to sob into me.

I close my eyes and run my fingers through his hair as I feel all of his emotions wash over me. Disgust, shame, unwanted, and alone. The sorrow and hate consume me. I slide down to my knees and wrap my arms around him.

Trevor: You must think I'm disgusting.
Me: No, I love you.

He holds me even tighter to him. I feel rage boiling up inside of myself. I want to kill this man. I want to rip him into a million pieces for what he's done to my brother.

Trevor: He's already dead. I killed him.

He holds me tighter. I'm so angry, I clench my fists so tightly that my nails bite into my palms. He sits back from me, then lifts my palms to his mouth and seals them up. I can feel that he's still weak, and needs rest. I take a deep breath.

I pull him up, supporting some of his weight. I put him on the bed and lie with him until he falls back to sleep. I realize it's why he doesn't like to sleep. He relives his past through his dreams.

My chest hurts so bad I can't breathe. I come into the hall and slide down the wall to the floor. I pull my knees into my chest and just cry.

Riley sees me and comes to me. I'm still shaking as he pulls me into his arms. He's so strong, it makes me feel safe. He tucks me under his arm as he takes me back to our room.

He leads me to the bathroom where I catch a glimpse of myself in the mirror. I have black ash streaks on my face where the tears have run through it. My lip is busted open and my jaw is bruised. Most of the blood on me is not mine, it's Moartea and Trevor's. I have one gash on my arm mostly healed. I must have given so much to Trevor that it's causing me to heal slower. I also feel my power drained.

The shower is turned on and then begins undressing me. Once he sheds his own clothes, he pulls me into the shower. As I stand under the water he washes the blood and ash from me. He's so loving and gentle. I wrap my arms around him and begin to cry again. He pulls me into him and holds me tightly.

"I love you," I say mid sob.

"And I you, Luv. How is he?"

"His body is healing," I whisper. "But that's all. After what I saw tonight, I'm not sure if my brother will ever completely heal."

"You saw his past?"

I nod and cry more. "He's broken and I don't know if I can help him. I can't think about this anymore tonight. Just kiss me and make it all go away." I look up at him.

His mouth comes down on mine softly.

I turn the water off, open the door, and then hand him a towel. We dry off, then I take his hand and lead him into the bedroom.

For the next hour, I let myself be completely consumed with Riley. After we make love, I tuck myself against him and he pulls me in as tightly as he can to his body. I finally relax and allow myself to drift off to sleep.

Sometime during the morning hours my mind is flooded with rambling stirring me awake.

> *Trevor: She wasn't supposed to ever see me like*
> *that. It's disgusting.*

I fly out of bed. "Trevor." I throw my clothes on fast.

"Should I come?" Riley asks.

"No, it's bad. He won't be able to handle anyone else around him right now."

As I come into his room I see he's fallen down. He's weak and yet still trying to get dressed. I kneel down to help him and he shoves me away from him. I end up on my ass.

"No. Don't touch me. I'm disgusting," he yells.

I get up and drop to my knees in front of him. I grab a hold of him tightly as he fights against me. He finally drops his arms to his side and cries into me.

"How can you stand to touch me after what you saw?"

"I love you. I will always love you. Nothing will ever change that." I whisper into his ear, "Please don't leave me. You promised me you'd never leave me. When I thought you were going to die, I wanted to die. I can't be without you, ever." I start to cry.

He holds me tightly. "I'm sorry. I won't leave you."

"Swear to me. Everybody always leaves me."

"I swear, sister, I will never leave you."

> *Me: You have no idea, but I'm as messed up as you*
> *are on the inside. I can't do any of this without*
> *you.*
> *Trevor: I feel the same way.*

I pull back and take his face in my hands. I wipe his tears with my thumbs. "You listen to me now. What happened to you was horrible and not your fault. You didn't ask for any of it and you didn't deserve it. That man is lucky he's dead, because what I would have done to him would have been for the record books of hell."

He shakes his head.

"You are not unworthy brother. You are beautiful and courageous. You have so much love inside of you. You just need to open your heart.

"I fear you see more than I am." He hangs his head.

"I see all of you. I feel all of you. We are one. Each half of a whole. I know your soul and I know you're hurting, but isn't it you who says you can't give him power over you?"

*Me: Our past lies with each other and that's where
it will always stay.*

Relief wash over him. I stand up and reach for his hand to pull him up. "Please come back to bed. You need to rest. Do you want me to stay here with you?"

"Just until I fall asleep."

As I press my forehead to his, I softly caress his face. Eventually his mind relaxes and goes quiet, I will myself to take away half of the evil and pain he carries within him.

Holding my breath, not quite sure what's happening, he exhales a retched black smoke. Trevor's whole body relaxes. Then the black smoke suddenly shoots down my nose straight into my heart. I close my eyes and breathe through the pain. I'm so sick to my stomach, and I need to get out of here now.

I sit up, and quietly but quickly leave. I run to my room and barely make it into the bathroom. Riley runs to me as I begin throwing up the most disgusting black vial liquid. It has the consistency of oil and coats my throat and mouth as it's expelled. Hate, shame, horror, evil, and disgust. This is what my brother's been holding inside of him.

Riley holds my hair back with one hand while he rubs my back with the other.

"Water," I choke out.

He fills a glass with water and then hands it to me. I rinse my mouth out, and he grabs a wash rag to wipe my face off. I'm so sick and dizzy.

"Are you all right? What should I do? What was that?"

"Not a human thing, love. I think it was a fucked up angel thing. I would like to get off of the bathroom floor now." I smile.

He picks me up and lays me in bed. "Tell me what happened."

"Well, after I finally got Trevor calmed down and back in bed, I wished to take half of the pain and evil he's been holding inside of himself." I wave my hand over myself. "Then all this happened."

"Take his pain?"

"I felt hate, shame, and pure evil that's been growing inside of him. That's what I took in. As you can see, my body didn't agree with it." I sigh. "Tonight was supposed to be special for us."

He smiles. "Every night I have you with me is special, don't you know that?"

"I went to get you something. Well, for both of us actually. They're in the pocket of my pants." I point to the floor by the bathroom.

Riley gets up, cringing at my clothes. He pulls out the box from the jewelry store.

"Open it."

He opens it. He looks at the bands and then back to me.

"I grew up with these being the symbol of your bond to your mate for all to see. I wanted us to have them, if that's okay?"

"Of course it's okay."

He takes the smaller ring out and puts it on my finger, then I take his out and put it on his finger. He kisses me softly. I don't blame him for the quick kiss. Especially after what he just saw come out of my mouth. He slides back in bed and we fall back to sleep.

I wake up a while later to Riley staring at me.

"I'm glad you're all healed." He narrows his gaze. "You fought last night."

"Yes, sorry. It was definitely not planned."

"I heard you took out three Moartea," he says glaring and smiling.

"It must be really hard to be angry and proud all at the same time." I laugh.

"Very." He kisses me. "I just don't want anything to happen to you."

"Will you demand I still stay here?"

"I want to, but I won't. It's up to you now."

I hug him tightly. "Thank you. It was so much fun to kill them."

"Are you feeling better after this morning?"

"I feel gross and I'm still a little nauseated. I also really need to see my brother." I sit up. "Hey.'

Large arms come around me and a male burning with desire slides on top of me. Riley runs his hand down my body until it rests between my legs.

I laugh. "Is there something I can help you with?"

He nods as he kisses me deeply.

We finally get up thirty minutes later. We come into the great room and I see Trevor over in the corner with a book as usual. He looks up as I come in and smiles.

Me: You look much better.

He studies my face and then scrunches his brow.

Trevor: What's wrong? Are you ill?
Me: I'm fine.

I wave him off.

"I know. They're talking to each other right now in their heads," Brandon says.

I roll my eyes at Cash and Brandon. I think I've missed an entire conversation about Trevor and me.

Me: You need to come eat.
Trevor: I'm not hungry.
Me: I wasn't asking.
Trevor: I'M-NOT-HUNGRY.
Me: You will come sit at this table and eat, or I
*   will feed you like a two year old in front of*
*   all these males.*

I glare.

He glares equally as fierce. He slams the book closed, slams it on the table next to the chair, walks over, yanks the chair away from the table, and then flops in it.

I smile very pleased with myself.

He's glaring at me arms crossed over his chest.

"Yep, whole conversation we don't even get to hear," Cash adds.

"Maybe because the world doesn't revolve around the two of you like you both think it does." I raise my brow.

Danielle's been worried about Trevor. Usually she's good about keeping her distance. She comes to him with juice in her hand and touches his shoulder. He tenses up and grabs her wrist. She's wincing and almost drops the juice.

I lace my fingers in his other hand.

*Me: She was worried about you. She didn't mean
    to touch you without asking. You need to let
    go of her, you're hurting her.*

He looks at me, then drops her wrist.

*Me: It's fine. Just take the juice and thank her. I'll
    talk to her later.*

"Sorry….Thank you." He grabs the juice from her and sets it in front of him.

"So D, what did you make?"

She looks down at Trevor then back to me. She mouths sorry. "I made eggs benedict." She walks away.

Trevor drops his head.

Trevor: I'm broken. I shouldn't have done that to her.

*Me: If you were broken, brother, you wouldn't feel
    that way, and she feels the same about you as
    you do her.*

He looks up at me, and then over at her.

*Me: Yes, I know how you feel about her. But only
because I feel you longing for her. Please eat,
you're still healing.*

I still feel sick to my stomach. I know it's better if I eat something, but I just can't bring myself to take a bite. I feel Riley and Trevor staring at me.

"Why aren't you eating?" Riley narrows his gaze.

Looking over at Trevor's plate, I smile. He hasn't touched what's in front of him either. "I will as soon as he does. If he doesn't eat, I'll starve right along with him."

Trevor growls as he picks up his fork and shovels a huge bite into his mouth. Then he glares at me.

After breakfast, Justin sets up two teams to go into what he believes is another Moartea safe house. Trevor's pissed because they're keeping him off for a week.

"We working out today?" Brandon asks.

"Yeah, I'll meet you in there." I smile at him.

I see Trevor in the chair by the fireplace reading. I go to him and push the book aside. I sit on his lap and wrap my arms around his neck.

He winces.

"Sorry." I try to get up but he holds me to him. "I just want to make sure you're not mad at me."

"I'm not mad at you. But I still think you're a brat."

"So are you." I laugh. I kiss his cheek and lay my head on his shoulder.

He hugs me tightly. "Why are you so nauseas?' he asks.

"Meh, just everything that's happened I guess. Nerves and all. No big deal, don't worry so much."

"Like you do for me?" He raises his brow.

I smile.

*Me: Why is it so easy for you to let me hold you
like this? I can touch you anytime I want,*

> *but nobody else can?*
> *Trevor: Because you're a part of me. I feel whole*
> *when we're close. I feel your love as well.*

I kiss him again, and then slowly get up so I don't hurt him. I head off to the gym to work out with Brandon. He smiles as I come in. I look around and today he has actual swords out.

"What's all this?" I ask.

"I realized when I saw you with the sword last night that it's not practical to teach you with the dummy swords. You need to get a feel for the weight of the sword."

He works with me for an hour. I try a couple of different swords. I like the feel of the short sword the best, and it will fit better across my back.

"Here let me show you something."

Brandon comes behind me and positions my hands on the blade. Then he puts his hands on mine. He slowly swings the blade in front of me as he moves my legs with his.

He steps away and grabs his sword. "See, like this."

Each step forward he makes, the sword moves with him. I'm so mesmerized by watching how gracefully he moves, that I'm not really paying attention to what he's trying to show me.

"Okay, now you try." He looks over at me.

Crap. I try to move like he did, but I feel awkward. I don't have that fluid motion like he does. "I suck." I sigh.

He laughs. "Like everything else, it takes practice." He walks back to me. "Here, move with me."

Coming up behind me again, he puts his hands on mine. His body is pressed against mine as he moves with me slowly. His fluid motion flows through me. It feels awesome, and I have more control over the blade. It's like you need to become one with it, and it becomes an extension of your arm.

He comes to my ear. "That's really good."

"It's all you." I lean my head back against his chest

As he pulls away from me, he runs his hands up my arms and I get goose bumps. *Stop being all flirty with the hot guy. He's just here to train you, and I'm sure he has way hotter girls than you. Not to mention you're mated, remember?*

"No, it was all you. I felt it," he says.

I hadn't notice Trevor come in, but he's watching me. I suddenly feel I have to be ten times better. It's Trevor that has the power to help me with Riley and Justin.

We work out a little while longer. I'm definitely more comfortable with the sword. A little more practice and I'll be good to go.

"Thanks Brandon. I'm going to go take a shower and see what D is up to."

"Anytime."

I hug him. Then I walk over to Trevor. "I'm getting better. Just let me go out next time with you."

"We'll see."

I sigh, kiss his cheek, and then take off.

****

Trevor glares at Brandon.

"What's going on? You can't work out right now," Brandon says. He wipes his face with a towel.

"I'm just trying to figure out what it is you think you're doing here."

"Sorry?" Brandon drops his brow.

"With my sister."

He throws his hands up. "Training her."

"Are going to play stupid, or is it that you think I'm stupid?" he says dryly.

Brandon stares at him.

"I guess I'd prefer you say nothing, than try to lie to me. You're playing a dangerous game here, and I think it's in both of your best interest to stay away from her for a while."

Brandon takes a deep breath. "I'm just training her. I care about her, and I want her to be ready for when they say she can fight."

"So you are going to lie to me about your feelings for her?" He raises his brow.

"I'm not stupid either. I know she belongs to him."

"Yet you still fell in love with her, you still covet her. You take every opportunity to be near her no matter the task. She may not have noticed it yet, but I feel your desire for her."

Trevor leaves him standing there to think about what he's said. Brandon must be out of his mind. What if that had been Riley who came in and saw the way he was looking at Sky. When Brandon ran his hands up her arms, he felt their desire for each other. Not good.

He knows Sky has been lonely lately. Riley's been gone a lot and it's a strain on their bond. But when they're together, the whole house can feel it. Brandon has to feel it. Riley is all over her. She belongs to him.

Chapter 13

Trevor's been going crazy. He finally gets to go out tonight. They're stopping off at the club for sex and blood. He hasn't ever felt the need for sex, and with his sister feeding him he doesn't need blood from the whores. But a drink and music sound great before they hit the new training center.

He still can't stand anyone but Sky to touch him. Her touch is calming and puts him at ease. Loving somebody as much as he does Sky is scary as hell. If anything happened to her, he'd kill everyone responsible and then follow her into the darkness. Thinking about her going out into the field to fight is giving him serious anxiety issues.

Like I don't already have enough of my own fucking shit going on. Now I have to worry about her.

Riley's lucky he didn't meet his sister first. If he had his way, he would have never let that male near his sister. Anytime he's seen Riley with a female, he was brutal. It makes him angry to even think about it. He just always tried to stay away from him when he feeds, or rather hunts.

But man, that male with his sister is a completely different male all together. Kind and loving. He knows Riley would kill anyone that wronged her as he would.

He can still remember the feel of Danielle's skin against his. It wasn't terrible, she just caught him off guard. Being close to anyone but Sky is suffocating. When he fed from the whores, he never let them touch him. He didn't even want to touch them at all, only doing what was minimal and out of necessity. He can't ever bring himself to have sex with them, not after what was done to him. The fact that they won't remember the sex is way too close to using them against their will.

Danielle catches him looking at her like some stalker. He knows he's unworthy to have her. But his sister's right, he longs to touch her again. He hates watching her with Chris.

Sky and Danielle are going with them to the club tonight. Riley's uneasy because he prefers to keep her locked up here safe. He, too, would like to keep his sister locked up here, but he can feel how restless she is.

If he finds the male that's been taking his sister out hunting, there's going to be hell to pay. He believes it's Markus, but he's not completely sure yet.

He looks up and sees Danielle coming towards him. He tenses up. *Relax stupid.*

She stops four feet from him. "Trevor?"

He gets a little shifty and like a dumbass just stares at her.

Danielle sighs. "Never mind." She walks off.

Trevor looks up and Sky is staring right at him. He hates to disappoint her and feel her worry for him. Damn, he needs to be better.

Sky: She wants you to be the one to take her tonight.
Trevor: No way, I can't do that.
Sky: You can if you try.
Trevor: What if I freak out? No way.
Sky: Then you will have to watch as Chris wraps his
*   arms around her and takes her with him.*

Chris walks over to Danielle and they begin laughing together. What the hell did he say that's so funny? He knows Chris and he isn't that funny. He glares in their direction. Not that anybody is paying attention to him. Well, other than Sky. But no way can he have her that close to him. *No way.* As they all head up top. Danielle comes out right behind him.

He turns around and can't stop the words from falling out of his mouth. "I can take you," he rambles out fast.

Holy shit. Did I really just do that?

That smile of hers drives him to want to grab her right here and kiss her. He doesn't even know how to kiss somebody, other than you put your lips on theirs and whatever.

I'm so pathetic. The only female I've ever kissed is my sister. Damn, that's sad.

As everyone else begins to leave only Riley, Sky, and Danielle are left.

*Sky: She still gets a little sick. She will need you to
help her. You'll be fine just breath.*

Trevor nods then Sky and Riley leave. He's left with Danielle staring at him. They've never even had a real conversation in all the time she has been here.

"It's fine if you don't want to. I can just stay here or go get one of the others to take me." She's standing about six feet from him.

She always keeps her distance. She really would let him off of the hook wouldn't she? She turns to go back inside. She seems disappointed.

He steps to her and grabs her wrist gently. He cringes when he sees the bruises that are almost healed. He rubs his thumb across her wrist. "Sorry for this," he barely gets out.

"Don't be. I shouldn't have touched you without your permission." She stares at his hand on hers.

He drops her wrist and begins to pace like an idiot. His mind is racing. *Damn. I need to get my shit together.*

****

Being at the hospital Danielle has seen cases of sexual abuse. Patients are distrustful of even the slightest touch. Trevor's seems pretty severe. But she sees how he is with Sky and longs for him to put his arms around her. She's seen him watching her, and swears she feels he wants her. But the current pacing he's doing like a caged animal waiting to make his escape, makes her curse herself.

Maybe she'll just find one of the others and ask them if they can take her to the club. She starts to walk towards the door.

"Why me?" he says from behind her.

Startled she turns around and he's barely a foot away from her. "What do you mean?"

"Why do you want me?" His eyes burn into hers.

"I can't explain why. I just like you. When I'm around you, I want to be in your arms. I'm sorry I push you. It's not fair for me to force myself on you when you clearly don't want me that way."

She goes to turn away but he grabs her by the waist and pulls her into him. She keeps her arms at her sides, so afraid if she puts them on him he'll run away.

"You have to hold on tightly if we are going to go," he says.

She looks him in eyes and slowly brings her arms around his waist. She feels him tense up even more. "Trevor?"

"Yeah?"

"You can tell me to go away anytime alright, no pressure. I guess I just keep wishing for more." She lays her head on his chest. She'd like to freeze time and stay like this for a little while. Who knows if he will ever let her do this again.

****

Trevor's trying to relax himself. But that last confession from her has his mind spinning again. Maybe he could do this whole thing. It feels right being with her. She's pretty, tall, thin, has a beautiful face, and brown eyes. He realizes he's just staring at her in his arms and not answering her.

"Can I kiss you?" He thinks the words, but realizes he just said them out loud.

"I'd like that." She looks up at him.

He pulls her face to his and slowly presses his lips to hers. She parts her lips and he can smell the sweetness of her breath.

When her tongue brushes across his lips, he parts them as she pushes it inside to stroke his softly. It's a strange feeling but he wants to taste more of her. He follows her lead and begins to kiss her more deeply. He pulls her into his body as close as he can get her.

She pauses and looks up at him.

He realizes she's smiling and that he's hard—pressed against her. He steps away quickly.

"Are you alright?"

"Uh yeah, sorry." He tries to adjust himself.

"Trevor, may I come to you?" Danielle asks.

"I don't know if that's a good idea right now."

"Please."

He realizes he wants to take her right here, right now, and just be inside of her. That in itself scares the ever living shit out of him. "We should go or they will come looking for us," he says bluntly.

She comes to him and wraps her arms around him tightly. "No pressure at all, but so you know, I want you as well."

Crap. He needs to hurry up and get away from her. Once there he walks away from her fast like a total asshole. He knows she would be better off with one of the other males, but damn it. He wants to feel her lips against his again and would probably kill any of them if they got near her.

****

I see Trevor and Danielle come in. Danielle's facial expression is off and Trevor walks away from her towards us. I'm getting crazy emotions coming off of him. I feel his past forcing itself into his head again. I pull Riley's face to me and kiss him before I head off to Danielle.

"Luv,"--Riley pulls me back into his arms--"if you wish to keep that bartender breathing, I suggest you make sure he keeps his hands to himself tonight."

I laugh. "Oh stop. Besides that's what these are for." I point to our bands. "It tells him I belong to somebody. But it's not going to stop these lot lizards." I point to the prostitutes cruising the tables.

"They have nothing I want or need." He kisses me again.

Trevor sits down at the table. "I need a drink."

"You guys okay?" I touch his hand.

He flinches and rips his hand away from me. He sighs. "Sorry."

I slide into the booth next to him and hug him.

Me: Never apologize to me for things you can't control.

He holds me tightly.

I get up and go to Danielle at the bar.

"Hey, it's my Jack and Guinness girl. Where you been?" Bret asks me as he gets my drinks.

"You know, around." I smile.

He sets my drinks down and leans over to me.

"Thanks." I hand him my money with my left hand.

He grabs my hand. "Married, too bad," he frowns.

I laugh.

He smiles, then helps the next person at the bar. I feel Riley's eyes on me. I turn around to shake my head and roll my eyes at him. I turn back to Danielle. "So what happened?" I ask.

"He kissed me."

I know my eyes are huge, but this is big. I smile.

"I don't think he's ever kissed anyone before."

I laugh. "Yeah, Riley either. But he had it down pretty quickly."

She laughs and takes a drink. "I know something happened to him. I know you know what it is, but I would never ask you to betray him. It's important he has you and is able to trust you. I can be patient."

"You care for him?"

"Fuck Sky, I think I'm actually falling for him." She shakes her head.

"Uh hello,"--I hold my hand up--"I married mine after three weeks remember."

"I know I have to be patient and let him come to me."

"Thank you."

"For what?"

"For caring for my brother."

"Come on. I need to let off some serious sexual frustration."

I laugh.

We dance for about an hour. I need to hit the bathroom and I want to catch them before they leave. As I come out of the bathroom I'm shoved out the back door fast.

"Hey, what the hell." I turn and I'm instantly paralyzed when I see him.

Randy grabs a hold of me and slams me up against the wall so hard my head splits open. It's all I can do to keep from passing out. I can't get my body to do anything but stand here.

He has me by the throat and goes nose to nose with me. "How does that feel bitch? Not very good does it?" He rips my underwear off, and then he slides his hand up my skirt. "You and I have a little unfinished business to take care of. Mmmm, you're already nice and wet for me."

Me: TREVOR.

But my brother is already here.

"You will take your hands off of my sister," he yells.

Randy lets go and turns to face him.

I fall to the ground.

"This slut is your family? Man do I feel sorry for you," he laughs.

As Trevor looks at him I see his thoughts, and he knows this is the human that raped me. He punches him so hard that Randy is knocked into the middle of the alley, then draws his sword and begins to growl.

"What the fuck?" Randy turns to get away.

Riley comes out the back door just as Trevor runs the blade up Randy's chest and rips his throat out.

"Trevor," Riley yells.

Trevor leans over into Randy's face as he lay choking on his own blood. "Know that it's her brother that avenged her."

Riley's on him fast pulling him away. "What are you doing? Killing a human at the club we come to? What were you thinking?"

Trevor points towards me.

Riley spins around and sees me. I feel his rage as his eyes go red. "He did this?"

"Yes," Trevor answers.

*Trevor: You should tell him everything, but it's up to
        you. That human can never hurt you again.*
Me: Thank you.

Trevor heads back inside.

Riley picks me up. "I need to get you out of here."

He cringes as he grabs my underwear, then he has us back at the bunker. We come inside and go to our room. He brings me to the bathroom so he can clean the back of my head.

"It's sealed. What the hell was he thinking?" He grabs a towel and dries my hair.

"He was just protecting me."

"Are you alright?"

"No, there's something I should tell you, but not now. I'll tell you when you come back. I don't want to hide things from you, but I also don't want to upset you before you go out."

"That male tried to take you?" He glares.

"Yes. I will tell you the rest later."

"Then when I get back, you and I will talk about all of this, right?"

"I promise."

He kisses me and leaves. Danielle comes in right after him.

"What happened? Brandon said Trevor killed somebody."

"Randy."

"What?" she yells.

"He grabbed me and had me out back. He was going to rape me again, D. I became that weak pathetic girl again. I could have killed him but I froze." I shake my head. "I called for Trevor in my mind. But I think he already sensed me in trouble, because he was there quick. When he saw Randy, he recognized him and got enraged. He went so dark he ended up shredding him."

"Holy shit. How did he know who he was?"

"I accidently thought of it when we were getting you from the condo. We can see each other's thoughts like a movie in our heads."

She hugs me. "I'm glad he killed him. That excuse for a human doesn't deserve to still be breathing."

We talked for a long time.

I hear a knock at the door.

"Hey, it's Trevor. He needs to see me."

She gets up to leave and lets him in. I hear her start talking.

"She's in the bedroom." There's a pause. "Trevor."

There's another pause. "I'm glad that guy's dead. I've wanted to kill him for a long time for what he did to her."

I hear the door open and close. I come out of the bedroom and see Trevor still in his fighting gear covered in blood and ash. He's staring at the door Danielle just left out of.

"What's going on?" I ask.

He whips around and comes to me. He grabs me up and hugs me tightly. "I just needed to see you." He starts feeling around on the back of my head.

"Hey, I'm fine. What's up with you?"

He holds me tighter. "I can't lose you. You're all I have."

"I told you. I'm fine." I pull back, look him over and laugh. "You're getting blood and ash all over me."

"I saw your face in the alley. You were scared of me."

"Not scared of you, for you. Nothing you do could ever change the way I feel about you. You're my family, my blood." I grab his arm and bring him over to the couch. I lay my wrist across his lap. "You need to feed."

He nods.

Me: Please go talk to D. She feels she pushed you
and is beating herself up about it.
Trevor: Alright.
Me: She's good for you. Her last male was not good
to her.

He finishes and seals me up. He narrows his gaze. "How?"

"He beat her up a few times. She finally left him. That's how we came to live with each other."

"I hurt her." He hangs his head.

"She understands why."

"Doesn't excuse it or make it right."

"No it doesn't, but Trevor, she knows more than you realize about you."

His face drops.

"I promised you I would never speak of what I saw. I would die before the words ever passed my lips."

He takes a breath. "What does she know?"

I feel him getting sick to his stomach. "She worked in the hospital and saw a lot of things. But she only guesses. No one ever needs to know the horrible things done to that beautiful little boy. He didn't ask for them to happen, nor should he carry the burden of them any longer."

I will myself to take away the rest of the pain and evil from him. I lie back and just wait for it. He gasps and chokes. I look up as the black cloud begins to come out of him. I feel relief from him just before it comes straight into my nose and mouth and throws me to the ground.

"Oh God," I cry out in pain.

He rushes to my side. "What did you do?" he says frantically.

"Took the pain of the past from you, for me to carry," I choke out as I hold my stomach. "I need the trash can." I point to the one by Riley's computer.

Trevor grabs it, dumps out the trash, and hands it to me.

That horrible black sludge starts coming up like before. Evil. It's pure evil that he's let flood his soul, because of all the hate he felt. All that's left is dry heaves. I flop back on the floor.

Riley comes in. He assesses the scene and goes for a glass of water and a wash cloth. He holds my head up as he gives me the water. I rinse my mouth out and he begins to wash around my face. Then he holds me tightly. He's glaring at Trevor and he's angry with him.

"It's not his fault. It's mine. I just want him to be well and happy." I cough.

Riley sighs.

Trevor grabs my hand. "Don't ever hurt yourself for me again, do you hear me?"

"I can't promise that. You two are my family. I would do anything for you. Even die to protect you."

Trevor: Thank you. But it's me that's supposed to
protect you.
Me: And you did that tonight. But I will always
protect you as well. Shower before you go talk
to her.

Riley grabs his shoulder and squeezes. He doesn't flinch at the touch. "Be well brother, if not for any other reason, do it for her."

Trevor nods and smiles at me. Then he leaves.

"You're not everyone's savior. You need to take care of yourself," Riley says.

"You're hurt, love." I point to his arm.

"I'll be fine. I need a shower."

"Me too. I feel disgusting."

We shower and then curl up in bed together.

He looks down at me and caresses my cheek. "The human Trevor killed, did you know him before tonight?"

"Yes, he's someone from my past that hurt me. Then he came after me again tonight."

"How did he hurt you?" His anger is beginning to surface as he narrows his gaze.

"I'm afraid to tell you. I don't want it to change the way you look at me. He made me feel like that weak helpless girl again."

"I love you. I could never feel any different than I do now. Please just tell me what happened."

Tears spill from my eyes. Talking about it throws me right back into that night. Every feeling, every emotion and it makes me angry and sick to my stomach. "He raped me," I finally choke out.

He's furious, but all he does is pull me into his arms tightly and rock me. "I love you, Sky. I just wish I would have found you sooner so that I could have kept you safe."

"It's not your and Trevor's job to protect me from the world. I am working hard to be stronger inside and out."

"Until then, Luv, and even after, it will always be my job to protect you, because I love you."

I hold him tighter and fall asleep.

****

Trevor steps out of the shower. He'd like to go back to the alley and rip apart that human's body a little more for what he did to his sister. If he'd remembered he had a sister, he would have tried to find her. No one will ever hurt her again.

He comes out of the bathroom and there's a knock at the door. Probably someone wanting to give him shit for the human he filet in the alley.

"What," he barks as he opens the door. "Oh, sorry."

"I didn't mean to barge in on you. I just wanted to talk to you about something," Danielle says.

"It's cool. What about?" *It's so not cool.* He's assessing how long it would take to get her clothes off and into his bed. Yeah right, so he could lie there next to her and not let her touch him.

"Can I come in?" she asks.

Uh hell no. "Yeah, sure." He steps back and she comes inside. He debates on leaving the door open, but ends up closing it.

"What is it?"

"Can you train me like you did Sky, so I can protect myself?"

He narrows his gaze as she avoids eye contact. Definitely not why he thought she came here. "I can, but why?" He's interested to know why she wants to protect herself when she lives in a house full of warriors who would die to protect her.

"For two reasons. First off, I don't like that I'm the weak one here and everyone has to look out for me all the time. The second reason may make you say you don't want to do it, but then maybe you can have one of the others teach me."

"What's the second reason?"

Danielle walks over to him, slowly places her hand on his bare chest. "So I have an excuse to be close to you." She looks him dead in the eyes. "If that's in no way what you want, can you have another teach me?"

He puts his hand over hers. "You would never need to worry about being safe, I'd never let anyone hurt you."

"So you won't train me?" She sighs and drops her eyes.

"I can train you. I just don't know about all of this other shit," he blurts out.

"Like what?"

Trevor rubs his face and steps away from her. He's hard again. He wishes he would have thought to maybe throw some pants on or something before answering the door. "You have eyes, you can see I want you. I just don't know if I can go there."

"You think too much. You need to learn to live in the moment. You want me, I want you, so take me."

He gets to her fast. He brings her face to his and kisses her hard. He walks them towards the bedroom. She pulls her shirt off and she's bare.

As they kiss, he runs his hands across her back feeling every inch of her smooth skin. He slowly moves his hands up her sides. He longs to feel her breasts.

She takes his hand and places it on her breast. He grasps it gently. He would love to bring his mouth down on them. Her nipple is tight as he takes it between his fingers. She responds by a small moan on his lips. He wants so much more of her. He wants to be inside of her.

The towel loosens and drops to the floor. When she moves her hand around and takes a hold of him. He pulls away abruptly and grabs the towel back up.

Shit.

She crosses her arms over her chest and comes towards him. "It's just you and me here. Nobody else." She comes into him and wraps her arms around his waist. She lays her head on his chest. "It doesn't have to be tonight."

Damn this female is patient, and his fucked up head is screwing everything up. She takes him by the hand and leads him to the bed.

"Get in," she says. "Is it alright if I stay with you this morning, in your arms?" She smiles.

He figures he could lie with her, and he definitely could do more of the kissing. He climbs into bed and then like a dumbass just nods at her. He watches as she slowly undresses and stands before him completely bare. He pulls back the blankets and she lies next to him.

They lie there for a good hour not speaking. He goes to his side and looks at her. "Can I kiss you again?"

She smiles. "Yes, whenever you want."

He leans down and softly kisses her. As they kiss he feels his way around her body. He longs to feel every inch of her. As he moves lower her kisses become deeper and harder.

She longs to have him, he feels it. He moves his hand down to her core and she arches up at the touch. She's so warm and slick. He lets his finger slide inside of her.

"I want all of you," she moans.

He slides in between her legs. He's so close he can feel the heat radiating off of her core. She pulls him up and he begins to enter her.

He pauses.

Taking his face in her hands, she begins speaking to him softly, "I care for you deeply, and remember….it's only you and me here."

Danielle pulls him back down to her mouth and he penetrates her with his tongue. He's here with her, and he isn't going to let anybody else inside of his head. He looks into her eyes as he moves all the way up inside of her. Her flesh is gripping every inch of his.

She cries out.

He stops and looks down at her.

"I'm fine." She nods.

Trevor touches her face and kisses her again. He moves in and out of her slowly then begins to go faster. She digs into him with her nails and cries out again. He's about to stop when she moans his name, and he realizes it's in pleasure not pain. She pulls him down to kiss her again.

He begins to drive into her hard and fast. He moans in ecstasy as he feels a wave of pleasure run through him. As the spasms stop he slows his movement. He looks down and sees her beautiful smiling face.

Sliding off of her, he settles and pulls her into him. They kiss and he's ready for her again. As it hits her in the stomach she smiles on his lips.

"Again?"

He looks down and smiles at her.

She pushes him to his back and slides on top of him. "Is this okay?"

He looks up at her body. *Oh yeah, I can take her all in like this.* As she leans in and kisses him she goes for his arousal. He tenses up at the initial touch. *Fucking head.*

On his lips she says, "I would never hurt you."

She takes a hold of him gently and guides him inside of her. She sits back up and begins to move her hips.

He moans.

She feels amazing on him. He moves his hips under her and watches her moan in ecstasy. As he watches her breasts sway to his rhythm he comes along with her. She collapses on top of him.

"Wow, I don't think I've ever been so tired in my life," she pants.

"Come here." He pulls her next to him and into his arms. *She could be mine, for as long as she lives.*

Chapter 14

When I wake up, Riley's still holding me tightly in his arms. As I turn in his grasp to face him, his eyes come open. "I feel safe with you, like you will always protect me."

"I will kill anyone that tries to hurt you." He softly kisses me.

He moves on top of me and slowly enters me. He looks into my eyes as he begins to swing his hips. I run my hands slowly down his back until I reach his ass—pulling him in deeper.

After we make love, we lie in each other's arms for a little while.

"I could wake up like this for an eternity," I say.

"We need to be careful in the upcoming days."

"What do you mean?"

"You're nearing your fertile time," he mutters.

"Why do I feel like you're leaving something out?"

He smiles and looks flushed. "I would have never thought I'd have to have this discussion with a female."

"Well you're all I have, so spill. This is not a conversation I want to have with my brother."

He sighs. "When it's time, you'll want to be with me. You will want to, badly."

"Hmmm…..not much difference from now." I shrug.

"Luv, it's different. And I will want to be inside of you to get you pregnant. It will be instinct to take you over and over again until we can no longer move. If you don't want to take a chance of becoming with young, I should leave when it starts."

"Leave for three days because of me….no." I shake my head.

"If I'm here we will be together, and I will try to get you pregnant. It's just the way it is."

"You said it's rare to get pregnant right?"

"Yes, that's why the instinct is there to try the whole time." He smiles.

"Like three days of constant sex?" I raise my brow.

"Yes." He laughs. "Eat, sleep, and sex."

"I'm not sure."

"I will do whatever you ask of me." He brushes my cheek with the back of his hand. "But I want you with my young."

"Let me think about it."

He pulls me to him and kisses me.

"So next subject. How are you with tonight?"

"Worried," he answers.

I know he wishes I wouldn't have pushed him to go out. "But you won't worry about me over doing your job, right?"

"No more than I do Michael."

"Good. You staying safe helps me stay safe."

He takes a deep breath.

"Come on, let's get ready." I bounce up. I'm excited to finally be going out with them. I've killed four Moartea and it felt good to end them. Like I make a difference.

I have tight black jeans, blue docs, a tight black shirt and a black Dickies jacket. I'll have a short sword across my back, a Glock 19 at my side, and a large knife.

I meet Riley's intense gaze. "Do you like what you see?" I spin for him.

He narrows his gaze. "Any male says one word and I'll make him see double."

I slink up to him. As always he looks strong and powerful like he could level an army.

He grabs me by the waist and kisses me hard. "Tonight Luv, tonight," he growls.

I laugh. "Come on."

****

Danielle wakes up to fingers running over her face. She looks up and Trevor's smiling at her.

"Good morning," she says.

He laughs. "I think in your world it would be good evening."

That's the first time she's ever heard him laugh. He was so good last night, she couldn't believe it was his first time.

"I have to get ready."

"I know."

"We'll talk when I get back."

That makes her a little scared, but hopeful. She's afraid if he gets up and starts thinking about everything they'll never make it back to this place again. He starts to get up and she grabs his wrist to pulls him back to her.

"Kiss me?"

His eyes look hungry for her as he comes at her and kisses her. She urges his body between her thighs. He's hard and so big. She urges him further and he enters her so fast it takes her a minute to catch her breath.

He smiles on her lips.

They make love again. Afterwards, he groans and gets up to go.

That makes her feel a little more on the hopeful side. As she watches him get dressed she wants to know where his head is.

"I'm worried when you come back, everything will go back to the way it was before."

He turns and comes back to her. "Everything is different. I want to be with you for as long as you live." He kisses her softly and finishes getting ready.

She realizes everything is different, and that her own mortality is now screaming at her. How long do they live? She has, what, maybe fifty plus years at best. She needs to talk to Sky. Then she remembers that tonight Sky is finally going out with them.

"I will see you when I get back right?" he asks.

"Of course. I'll be in my room waiting." She smiles.
He leaves.

****

As we come into the hallway my brother comes out of his room. He looks different, happy. He looks up and smiles at me.
"Hey Riley, can I have a minute with my brother?"
"Sure. Hurry up though." He heads off to the great room.
"You look different."
"Thanks to you." He wraps me up in a hug.

Me: What's this?
Trevor: Thanks to you I've found peace.
Me: Danielle?
Trevor: Yes, she's in my bed at this moment.

I pull away and smile. "I'm so happy for you both."
"I love to see you smile. Stop worrying about me. When you found me I came alive." He hugs me tighter.
"Let's go. I don't want to be late my first time out. Plus, I really want to kill something."
He laughs hard. I turn and look at him and smile bigger. That's the first real laugh I have heard come out of him.
Club first of course, so the boys can feed and let loose before we attack a new recruit center. As Trevor and I come out of the hallway a few jaws hit the floor, and there's a lot of staring going on.

Trevor: That's so not for me.
Me: Aw man, Riley's going to do that thing.

Riley comes at me and wraps me up in his arms and kisses me. Then he bites into me hard. I hold him tighter. This is definitely not one of my favorite parts. The whole cave-man-she's-mine thing, but whatever. I hear a few coughs and when he seals me up he looks at me and sighs.

I smile and pull his lips back to mine, kissing him deeply. "Tonight love, tonight." I run my tongue across his lips.

He growls.

When I look up there's a lot of boys trying to look anywhere but me. I laugh. "Well I'm ready, what's everybody waiting for?" I run upstairs. Even though I can materialize just fine now, I still prefer to go with Riley.

He holds me tightly and we appear down from the club.

We will be in two teams of four. Derek, Brandon, Trevor, and I in team one. Team two will be Riley, Michael, Cash, and Brian. No surprise he has me on a team with three of the top four fighters. Justin feels it's better if Riley and I don't fight together. We could distract each other if one was hurt.

We were in the club for about an hour. I only had one drink to take the edge off. I want to stay sharp. I get up to go to the bathroom and realize I have a shadow. I turn and glare at Trevor.

"Don't bother," he says.

I glare harder, then drop my shoulders and sigh. After what happened yesterday, there's no way I'm going to talk him into leaving my side. I go in. When I come back out he's leaning against the wall.

"See, all in one piece." I throw my hands up.

"Yep, and that's how we're going to keep it."

I see two prostitutes heading over to the table. I glare and walk faster. We come back to the table just as one slides in next to Riley.

"Hey daddy. You haven't come to see me in a while."

He never has a chance to react. I'm there fast and rip her away from him by the hair.

She screams.

I kick and scream as arms grab me up, pulling me off of her. Yep, I may kill her for even touching him. *Ha. This is how he feels with me.*

"You will get up and leave us," Riley says.

She tries to stand up.

Riley grabs her by the arm and pulls her up. "You came and everyone refused you. So you moved on."

She nods and stumbles away.

I'm so angry. I still want to get at her as I glare at the back of her head. "Markus, get off of me," I yell as I struggle out of his grasp.

Riley takes me from him. "Luv, look at me." He takes my face in his hands and looks into my eyes.

I slowly begin to focus of his face.

"There's my beautiful blue eyed girl." He kisses me.

Turning my face away from him, I say, "Are we done here? Because I really need to kill something." I shove him away from.

He barely catches himself before he takes out the table next to us.

She must have been one of his regular whores before me. He had to have the blood, but that doesn't make me any less angry or sick to my stomach. I wish I could get a handle on all of these emotions. Controlling the anger is harder than any other emotion. Trevor says it takes time.

Riley's feelings starting to invade mine. I look back at him. "I'll be fine. I'll get over it." I wave him off.

These are some of the things he'd prefer to keep from me. But thanks to the angel part of me, I got to see the whole little show she played in her head of them together.

If somebody is picturing something when I touch them, I get to see everything they're thinking. I've also noticed that I don't always have to be touching somebody to see what they're picturing in their mind.

Me: I need to get out of here. I can't breathe.

"Derek, we're ready. We're first right?" Trevor nods.
"Yeah, let's go." Derek motion us up.

Me: I can't focus, can you take me?
Trevor: No, it will look weak. You have to relax.

He smiles and narrows his gaze.

Trevor: I'll try and leave you at least one Moartea.

I glare, and then I take a deep breath and concentrate on where we're meeting up. I'm being tested. None of them believe a female should be fighting.

Team one appears at the meeting point.

"Trevor, Sky, you two go around back and enter the second floor. Brandon and I have the front," Derek says.

We split up and go towards the warehouse. Trevor and I climb up the fire escape to a second story window. I can see two Moartea in the room on the left and three more down the hall.

He turns and nods to me, then slides inside.

We're headed towards the three down the hall first, when there's a bang and a huge commotion down below.

I look over the railing. "I count twelve."

Too late, the five on this level have spotted us. Trevor takes out his three and I easily take out both of mine. Trevor jumps down to the next floor.

"Jump," he yells up.

"Seriously?" I take a deep breath and then jump.

Trevor's already running towards the pack of them. He begins to slice his way through them. I see one on Brandon. I throw my hand out and use the power to throw the Moartea across the room. This gets the attention of five of them.

All five are coming at me fast. My power is not infinite, and I was only able to stop two of them coming at me. I get in a fighting stance as the other three get closer.

"It's the one," a grotesque one with his hair falling out says.

I wonder if after the human's soul leaves their body, the body begins to slowly die. Either that, or they don't take care of themselves at all. I guess when you smell disgusting, why bother.

Trevor: Run!

Not going to happen. I can do this. I duck away from one while I tear through another with my short sword. The one that ran past me grabs me around the throat. Grabbing onto his arms, I use it as leverage to kick the one coming towards me in the chest—

just like Markus showed me. Then I take out my knife and sink it deep into the side of the Moartea that's holding me.

While he stumbles backwards, I stab the one in front of me in the heart. I spin around and his head goes flying—nothing but ash. I turn to the one behind me and look him in the eyes. I plunge my blade in deep and let the last few beats of his heart vibrate up the blade. He drops to his knees before me, looking into my eyes with huge black soulless eyes, then his head is next. I turn and find fourteen pairs of eyes staring at me.

"Aren't we supposed to be looking for stragglers and intel?" I throw my hands up.

They finally start moving. Riley comes over and wipes what I assume is ash off of my face. "You were beautiful, and strong. I was wrong." He steps closer.

I put my hands on his chest to stop him. "I know this isn't your fault, and that I'm not being fair to you right now. But all I see when I look at you, is you with her. I need to be away from you right now. I know you can't change any of it, and I don't blame you for what I know you needed." I shake my head and swallow hard as tears run down my face. "All I see is her," I quietly choke out.

I run my hands down his face and turn away from him. As I walk away, I look back and see so much pain in his eyes. The ache in his heart is breaking mine. I rub my face and keep going. I run upstairs where Trevor is. I start searching through the desk in front of me.

Trevor stands and looks over at me. "You know he can't change his past. There may be a lot of things there you don't like there."

"I know. I swear I don't blame him, but when I touched her, I saw her being taken by him. He hurts them when he takes them. Did you know how brutal he was? He's been with her so many times she remembers him."

Trevor takes a deep breath. "I've seen Riley with others before."

I shake my head. "It's not good….he's not good. I've been reading the texts, we are to protect them."

"So this changes how you feel about him?" He raises his brow.

"No. Of course not. It kills me that I'm hurting him right now. I know he's not that male anymore."

"Is it not you, sister, that tells me to not look at the past, only to look to the future in front of me?"

I sigh and nod.

"Your mate's heart bleeds at the pain he knows he's caused you, and you just walked away from him."

I close my eyes as tears begin to fall again.

"You love him, right?" He takes my face in his hands and wipes my tears.

"With everything I am," I choke out.

He smiles. "Then Sky, why are you here with me, and not in the arms of your mate who's hurting?"

I grab him and hug him tightly. "I love you."

"And I you. Now go."

I walk downstairs looking around as I come down. I don't see Riley anywhere. "Derek, where's Riley?"

"He went outside I think." He rubs the back of his neck. "Sky?"

"Yeah?"

"That was some damn good skills tonight." He smiles.

"Thanks, Derek. Coming from you that means a lot." I go outside and I don't see him anywhere.

He steps out of the shadows when he sees me.

I run to him and throw my arms around his neck. I hit him so hard it knocks us back into the building. "I'm so sorry I'm such a brat."

He holds me tightly. "I'm the one that's sorry. I thought you would wish me away."

"Never." I shake my head. "I could never leave you."

"If you did, I don't think I'd survive it," he whispers in my ear.

"I'm so sorry for hurting you." I kiss his cheek and squeeze him tighter. "Let's finish up here so we can go home."

We go back in and I head back upstairs to Trevor.

"So?"

"Thank you, you were right."

"A male could get used to hearing that." A goofy smile spreads across his face.

"Well don't get used to it. I'm normally always right." I punch him in the arm. I turn around and see Brandon in the doorway.

"Can I talk to you?"

"Sure." I come out into the hall.

"Thank you for what you did down there," he says.

I smile and put my arms around his waist. "I had a couple of really good teachers"

He holds me back tightly and laughs. "I think it's a little more than that. It's just who you are…..amazing and beautiful."

"He's right, you are amazing and more than I deserve," Riley says as he leans against the wall.

I go back into Riley's arms. "I love you. Tired of hearing that yet?"

"Never."

As we come downstairs Derek comes out of one of the offices. "Looks like we have three more targets. They seem to be spreading faster." He looks over at me. "And Sky, good job tonight. You're going to be a great asset."

"She was fucking incredible," Brian says.

"Yeah, crazy good," Cash says.

"Like Trevor," Michael adds.

"See, Luv, more than I deserve." Riley squeezes me into him. "Let's go home."

****

As they come into the bunker Riley doesn't want to let Sky go. Seeing and feeling her hurt and angry as she rejected him had really scared him. There's no way he could live without this female--she owns a part of his soul. He draws from her strength and love to be this male he's become. He never wants her to see any of the terrible things he's done in his life.

"We need to talk," Derek says dryly.

Derek motions for him as he heads towards Justin's office.

"Luv, I'll be right back." He kisses her neck.

"I'll be here listening to them talk about me like I'm not even here." She rolls her eyes.

Riley heads to Justin's office. As he comes in he catches Derek finishing up with tonight's events.

"Then from now on Sky will fight with the Ninth," Justin says.

"What? No," he yells. "I don't want her in the middle of this war that's only escalating."

"Brother, you saw what I saw. How can she not fight with us?" Derek says.

"I don't want her involved in all of this."

"Riley, if you were to rank your top five warriors, with the strongest being number one, who would you choose?" Justin asks.

Riley shakes his head and sighs.

"I would rank them as Trevor, Sky, Riley, myself, and Brandon." Derek Says. "In that order with Trevor and Sky being damn near equals. Both are ruthless and deadly. She saved Brandon, then took on five Moartea coming at her without hesitation, and without a scratch."

"Riley, how would you rank your warriors?" Justin presses.

He takes a deep breath and exhales sharply, "The same."

"We will need all capable hands to fight. The Moartea in the area are growing and becoming more organized," Derek says.

"She's my mate. What if she's killed?"

"It's a risk we all take. But Riley, she's really good. Like she was born to be a warrior. I'm not sure I could take her at this point. Hands down one on one she has us all beat," Derek says.

"Yes, but when she's with a young, she would no longer fight," Riley says.

"Agreed," Justin says.

"Yes, I agree," Derek follows up.

"Know that it's always your call brother. We serve you. If you say the Queen doesn't fight, then that's the way it is." Justin pats his shoulder.

"Because what I demand has any bearing over what that female does," Riley mutters to himself.

Derek laughs. "It's your female, brother. But yeah, that one is definitely a handful."

Riley comes out of the office and as he comes through the great room, Markus and Chris sit there listening to the others run through what happened. Sky is the hero in all of it, and Riley knows what he saw her do was something amazing. Any one of them other than Trevor would have been hard pressed to come out of that without a mark. But she did. She was flawless and fluid in her movement.

She moves like Brandon. Each step, each blow was smooth and in sync as if she moved along with a symphony. She has taken the best aspects of each warrior that has worked with her. Brandon's blade skills, Trevor's hand to hand, Cash's knife skills, and he could swear when she kicked that Moartea away from her while she took the other one, it was a move Markus has pulled. He had no idea Markus was even working with her.

He takes a deep breath. She should work with Derek and even himself as well. He looks around and she's no longer in the great room. He can't wait to get back to her. His body is amped up and he's going to take her now.

He opens the door. His cock is instantly hard and the angle is all wrong in these pants. The air is thick with hormones.

Damn, this is it.

She comes out of the bedroom in only a robe. He growls and narrows his gaze. He can feel the desire building up inside of him.

"This is it isn't it?" She's holding herself against the bedroom door frame.

He's gripping the molding around the door frame into their room. He fears he may rip it right off the wall. It's all he can do to hold himself back from taking her right there on the floor. Doesn't help that he's already picturing exactly what he's going to do to her. Door wide open and all. Clear thoughts are leaving his head quickly as he continues to think of all the ways he's going to pleasure his female.

"Do you want me to leave?" he says through gritted teeth.

"No, I need to have you now," she pleads.

"You may get pregnant." His whole body is tense and screaming at him to take her. He sees her straining as well, and he also sees she's trying to think straight. He knows he should leave, but it's already too late for that.

She drops her robe. "I don't care anymore. I want you now."

He barely gets the door shut before he takes her right there on the floor. Pants halfway down, fully suited, weapons and all. She's so swollen and tight. As he drives into her she instantly climaxes and moans his name. As her orgasm runs the length of his shaft he gives her everything he has inside of him.

He stands up, strips down, and picks her up. As they move into the bedroom he's already back inside of her before they even get to the bed.

****

For three days all we did was make love. We barely slept. It was all about taking from each other, and the need to have him inside of me.

Holy crap. Did I really just have sex for three days straight? So much for not wanting to get pregnant. All I can do now is hope I didn't my first time out. But if I am, it will be Riley's so....yeah it will be fine.

"I've never been so tired in all my life."

"Nor I," Riley groans. "I'm sorry I couldn't leave. I know you don't want my young."

I look up at him. "If I'm pregnant, I'll be happy because I love you."

"Really?"

"Of course. Besides I wouldn't trade the last three days for anything."

He holds me tightly.

"I'll get us something to eat."

He stops me from getting up. "No, I will feed you, my mate."

After we eat, we pass out for what seems like an entire day.

"When will we know if I'm pregnant?"

"If you bleed in the first week, you're not with young."

"We shall see my mate, we shall see. Besides there's always next time." I smile.

He growls and smiles devilishly.

I get up and get ready to train.

Me: You hear me?
Trevor: Yes. How are you feeling? I've been worried.
Me: Good, meet me in ten?
Trevor: I'll be in the gym.

"I have to meet with the council today," Riley sighs. "I'm taking Michael."

"That sounds fun....not."

"Take it easy training today until you know," he pleads.

"I will. Relax, remember it's rare and my first time."

He kisses me, then starts to get ready.

"I've been thinking. If you aren't with young, you should train with Derek, me, and Michael. I've noticed that you seem to pick up all of the good points of each fighter you train with. I think it will make you even better." His gaze narrows. "Have you trained with Markus?"

"Yeah, he spars with me a couple times a week."

"I could tell."

"Are you really going to be okay with all of this?" I raise my brow.

"You will do it, because you feel it's your duty. So it's my responsibility to help you become the strongest warrior you can be." He takes a deep breath. "Something is bothering me but I'm not sure I want to bring it up right now."

"What is it?" I walk over to him.

"When the incident at the club happened, you said all you could see was her. What did you mean?" He touches my face.

Aww crap. I take a deep breath. "Turns out, Trevor's thoughts aren't the only thoughts I can see. I saw in her mind a time you had her."

He drops his head and tries to pull away from me.

I grab him and hold him tightly. "I know things were different before me. I don't care, alright?"

"I told you I was not a good male. I've done terrible things and hurt a lot of people. Not just Moartea, Sky. Michael stopped me from killing that same girl the night before I met you."

Wow, I really didn't need to know that. Maybe select honesty is better where his past is concerned. I rub my face and try to focus. "Do you love me?"

"Always."

"That's all I need to know."

He kisses me again before he leaves. My brother has gone four days without feeding I'm sure. He doesn't take from Danielle--he thinks he'll hurt her.

As I come in, I go to him immediately and hug him. "I've missed you." Four days is too long away from my brother.

"And I you." He squeezes me tighter.

I hug him for a long time. Then I pull him towards the bench. "Come here."

"I'm fine." He glares.

"Listen, when are you and Riley going to realize I always win. All of this is just wasted energy." I smile.

He kneels before me and takes my wrist. I lay my head back against the wall and my mind is going crazy.

I just got them to finally let me fight, I'm not ready to be pregnant. Maybe next year I'll be in a better place, maybe. I may start praying to somebody wishing to not be pregnant. Okay, so I may be completely freaking out here.

"You aren't with a young." Trevor seals me up and drops his brow.

"How do you know?"

"I would have sensed it in your blood. I would have stopped if you were."

Complete and utter relief sweeps through me. I may cry some happy tears.

He looks at me even more puzzled. "You don't want Riley's young?"

"It's just too soon with everything that's happened." I take Trevor's hand in mine tightly. "You said that you've seen how Riley is with females. What did you mean?"

Trevor can't pull away from me quick enough as him mind replays times he's seen Riley with females tearing them up and killing them, to him killing Moartea, and human recruits. But that's not all I see. I groan.

He rips his hand away from mine and growls.

I look up, wide-eyed. I shouldn't have done that to him, I know better. And damn, I shouldn't have seen all of that.

"If you want to know something, ask me. Don't ever just take it from me," he yells.

"Would you have shown me if I asked you to?" I say calmly.

"No."

Tears begin to fall. "I can't trust you either then. You too will lie to me or keep things from me because you feel I'm too weak to handle it?"

He begins to calm. Then he sits back down and wraps his arms around me, laying his head against mine. "I'm sorry. I didn't mean it." He pulls my face up. "If you ask me, I'll always tell you the truth, or show you anything you want to see okay?"

I nod. "I need to always be able to count on you. I have this feeling that in the end, you will be all I have left. I feel it Trevor, something terrible is coming. This house is going to fall."

"You'll always have me. But I have felt it as well. There's something, or someone that's trying to tear everything apart."

"He didn't just take females did he?"

Trevor looks in my eyes and slightly shakes his head.

I take a deep breath and then stand up. "I don't want to think about all this crap anymore. What will be, will be. All we can do is prepare for the things to come."

"So you and me, all out?" He narrows his gaze and smiles.

I laugh. I think my brother likes beating me up a little too much. "Yeah, but first how are you and D?"

"Fine, I think. She's worried about something and wants to talk to you."

"I'll talk to her after we train. Who's going out tonight?

"Riley, Cash, Derek, and Brian. Just reconnaissance."

"Riley wants me to work with Derek next. He says I pick up all the good traits of each warrior."

Trevor nods. "That sounds like a good idea. Looks like he's really all in."

"So it seems. Let's go already," I egg him on.

He starts out slow until I catch him with a blow to the mouth. When it comes to my brother, he doesn't hold back and most of the time has the upper hand. After hand to hand we start with the dummy blades. I've been wanting to use the bõ, so I grab them off of the wall just as Derek walks in.

"Riley wants me to work with Sky."

"Perfect timing, brother, she wants to move on to the bõs."

"Cool, I could do that." He walks over.

"Alright, I'm out. Sky don't forget to meet up with Danielle later," Trevor says.

"I won't. Have a good night and try to relax."

He leaves.

"Have you used the bõ before?" Derek asks.

"No, and you're huge and a little intimidating."

He laughs.

I don't see Derek laugh and joke around much, if ever. He looks like he'd be way more laid back then he actually is. He's a rules, by the book, all serious, no bullshit kind of guy. But standing in front of me with his black spiked hair, lip ring, Suicidal Tendencies t-shirt, and sweats smiling at me, he looks like a really cute punk rock guy. But he's huge. Derek and Justin are the biggest males in the house, and he's going to kick my ass.

"Come on, I'll show you a few things then we will trade blows."

"Alright, I've been dying to use these things. I feel like if you're in a warehouse, it could be any sort of broom or mop handle or if you're lucky a pipe or scrap metal bar."

"Exactly, you're pretty smart."

After two hours we're pretty beaten up and both smiling ear to ear. Derek's stronger than Cash and Brandon, so I was able to actually go all out with him.

"Maybe next time we can go hand to hand and you can teach me a few things. You're really strong and you learn fast."

I walk up in front of him smiling. "So why are you such a hard ass all the time? Because this male in front of me now, I've never seen him before, and I really like him."

This closeness seems to be making him tense. His smile drops and his gaze intensifies.

I put my hand on his chest and I think he's stopped breathing. These males are so funny around females. "I'm just making an observation Derek."

He lays his hand over mine and whoa….what the hell is that that just hit the center of my chest?

Derek pulls my hand down slowly. "Nah, it's fine. I can be more relaxed in here because it's not life or death you know. Out there, I feel I'm always at work."

I nod.

With my hand still in his, he squeezes it lightly, and then he slowly pulls it out of mine. I hear the door open and close. I'm still staring at my hand. It happened again and it's the strangest feeling, like how it was the first time with Trevor. I'm connected to Derek somehow.

I shake it off and head to breakfast. As I come into the great room I feel eyes on me. I look towards the office and I meet Derek's eyes for a second before he looks away. I feel a pull to go to him.

****

"What is that?" Justin asks coldly.

Derek finishes gathering up the maps for the next three targets they're going to check out tonight. He doesn't meet Justin's eyes. He already knows what he's asking him about. What he felt when she took from him, then again in the training room, is shit that's not going to go anywhere. But he felt her enter the room just now, and when his eyes met hers, he wanted to go to her.

"What is what?" He's still leaning over the printer.

Justin doesn't say anything else.

He turns around and sees him standing with his arms crossed over his chest and glaring. He raises his brow trying to prompt more of a question, almost daring him to say what it is he's thinking.

"I'm asking you, what is going on with you and your best friend's female. I'm asking you what that was I just felt." Justin narrows his gaze.

He hangs his head. "I don't know."

"You feel for his female?"

He looks up. "You know I'm not a male that would ever go after another male's female. And that female belongs to Riley, you can feel it. Whatever this bullshit is with me, I promise you is nothing."

"What I just felt….is not nothing."

"Can we just deal with this shit here?" He rubs his hand across his face.

"Yes, for now. But there is more here than you are admitting."

He knows he needs to get his head straight about all of this shit going on. Especially before somebody else notices what Justin just did.

Chapter 15

After breakfast I help Danielle clean up the kitchen. "How are things?"

"Fine with Trevor and me, I guess."

"What's going on in your head?"

"How long do vampires live?" she blurts out.

Ah, I see where this is going. I had the same thoughts after the second night with Riley. "We are immortal, but we're not immune to severe damage and bleeding out."

Danielle hangs her head. "Can I be turned?"

"No," I snap, shaking my head.

She turns to face me. "What, I'm not good enough?"

"It's nothing like that, D. Not all humans can be turned. I hear most die. I can't lose you, and neither can Trevor."

"So you would prefer he love me, possibly bond to me, and then lose me after say fifty years when I'm old and grey?"

I never thought past them both just being happy right now. Where could all of this possibly lead? "Have you talked to Trevor about this?"

"No, I came to you first. Will you deny me if it's what I want? To at least try."

I swallow the lump in my throat. I can't even think about her trying and not making it through the change. "If it's what you both want, I won't stop it."

She hugs me tightly.

"Just know that it will break my heart, as well as his, if we lose you to this."

"I have to try. I love you both too much for such little time with you."

I come out of the kitchen and look to my right. Trevor's reading in his usual spot. I feel my fang piercing my lip. I walk up in front of him.

Trevor: What's wrong?
Me: She wants to be turned.
Trevor: No.
Me: Relax, listen to her and just talk it out. Let
    me know what you decide.
Trevor: I say no, she could die.
Me: In fifty years or so she will die, Trevor. Maybe
    sooner if she were to get sick.

I see in his face that he, too, hasn't considered the future with her. He's still just trying to let go of his past and take one day at a time. Dread begins to pour out of him. He pulls me down into his lap and wraps me up in his arms.

Me: Our blood is strong. Maybe it could make a
    difference if we did it together.
Trevor: I'll talk to her.

****

Riley comes in exhausted. He had meetings all night and then went out on reconnaissance to scout a new target. He strips down and heads towards the shower.

He turns back and looks at me. "You coming?"

"You looked very pre-occupied and tired. I figured I'd just let you do your thing. Do you want to talk about it?"

"No."

I start getting undressed. I smile when I see his growing arousal as he licks his lips. He holds his hand out and we get into the shower. I soap him up and just let him stand there while the water beats down on him. He definitely needs to relax.

"How about some of my drama, or it can wait if you're too tired."

He brings his mouth to mine and kisses me. "I always want to hear about you."

"D wants to try and go through the change."

"She more than likely won't make it, Luv."

"I know, but I feel it's her decision to make not ours. She loves Trevor. Would you have denied me the request if I were still human?"

By his tense jaw and reluctance to answer, I can see he has no real response to that question. A bonded male would never put his female's life in danger purposely.

"Maybe our blood is strong enough to help her through it. Would you and Michael help if I asked you to? So she could have the best chance possible."

"Of course."

"Not sure what they're going to decide. Do we need permission to change her?"

"I just gave it to you. I order them now....remember?"

"Interesting." I take a hold of him. "I know you're exhausted but...."

He smiles and kisses me hard. He picks me up and I wrap my legs around him. "Like I would ever be too tired to have all of you." He takes me right up against the shower wall. He comes to my ear as he drives into me. "I'm going to take you again in our bed."

The water is shut off. There is no drying off, he wasn't kidding about not being too tired to have me again.

****

Trevor comes in dreading the conversation that he's going to be faced with. Danielle comes out of the bedroom and walks to him. He wraps his arms around her, and holds her tightly.

"I know she's already probably told you what I'm going to ask you."

"Yes."

"Will you consider it?"

"No."

She pulls away from him. "Then I want to leave. I want my memories wiped clean and to return to my life."

"What?" He feels a sudden heaviness in his chest.

"I won't love you for fifty years and let you watch me age as you stay young. I'd rather die trying to stay with you, or I want to leave and forget about you. Then I'll demand that you both stay away from me."

He has no idea what to say. This was no discussion. Her mind is already made up, and he's being given an ultimatum. He sits on the couch rubbing his face not knowing what to say or do. All he wants is Sky. She's better than him with all this kind of shit.

"I don't want to lose you," he says.

"Then you need to agree to try. I want to stay with you and Sky forever." She sits next to him.

He pulls her to his chest. "If you want, we'll try. You need to talk to Sky and hear what she went through. The likelihood of you coming through it is slim, and either way it's very painful."

"So you'll do it?" she says, eyes wide as a grin spreads across her face.

"I'll do whatever you ask of me." *Like she's giving me a choice.* He would choose fifty years over nothing at all, but that wasn't one of his choices. "Let's go to bed." He pulls her up.

****

I open my eyes and look up to watch Riley sleeping, then I pull the covers down slowly. *I'm so terrible.* I really can't look at him without desiring him. Even something as simple as watching his chest move as he breathes drives me crazy.

I get up on my side and run my hand across his chest. He growls as I move my hand to the base of the sheet, just below his belly button. I smile and look back at his face.

"Yes, Luv, I'm awake. Hard to sleep when your mate's desires sweep over your whole body." He smiles as he kicks the covers the rest of the way off. "As you can see, I want you as well." He pushes me over and gets on top of me.

I laugh. "It's just so hard not to want you when I can see all of you before me." I narrow my gaze. "Not really looking for it to be one of those nice kind of ways either."

Riley's smile drops and a growl vibrates through his whole chest. He gets up on his knees and looks down at me.

I run my hands down his thighs and dig my nails in.

He tenses up and takes a deep breath. He grabs me up and takes me fast. It's painful, but I don't care. He drives into me hard, then he comes down and bites into my breast.

What the…I moan as he takes from me. As my body tenses up, he takes my wrists and holds them over my head with one hand. With his other hand he comes under my hips so he can drive even deeper into me.

He comes in a roar with me right along with him. As he slows his rhythm I can see his eyes turning back to their beautiful citrine color. He moves off of me quickly to look me over.

I laugh. "I'm fine, stop already," I say, trying to pull him back to me.

"Sky. Your wrists, your legs." He shakes his head. He runs his hand across my chest. "I bit you here?" he chokes out.

I finally sit up so I can grab him and pull him back on top of me. "Kiss me now, vampire," I growl.

He's wide eyed.

"You will kiss me now or I will not speak to you for a week. I will also withhold all sex."

He kisses me softly.

I take his face in my hands and pull him into me, I kiss him hard and then shove him next to me. I get on top of him and growl again.

He just stares up at me unmoving.

"I want you so badly. I want you inside of me even now. Do you want me?"

He licks his lips and nods.

I take him in and come down on him hard. He grabs my thighs and moans. I ride him hard.

I slow my rhythm and come down to his face. "I love you, my mate. And I also love you to take me in every way possible. That last time, was one of my favorites."

He finally relaxes. He shakes his head and kisses me deeply. Afterwards he lays next to me running his hands across my chest.

"Did it hurt?"

"Actually, it was pretty hot. I didn't know you could take from there."

He gaze intensifies. "That's not the only place I can take from."

"Hmmm, now I'm intrigued. Where else could you take from?"

"I have heard males say you can take from here." He move his hand to the inside of my thigh.

I smile and shake my head. "Are you trying to drive me mad today, love? Because all I want is to have sex with you all evening."

He laughs and pulls me into him. "Sounds good to me." He runs his hand down my cheek. "You would tell me if I ever hurt you?"

I sit up and hold my hand just over his chest. I concentrate and use my power to push him against the bed. "Can you get up love?"

He tries to move, then he shakes his head.

"If you ever really hurt me, I could get you away from me if I needed to." I release him.

"I'm still worried I could hurt you when I'm like that. You are a crazy female, you know that?"

"Yeah, says the crazy vampire. But I'm your crazy female."

"That you are."

Speaking of being worried, I'm worried. I feel I'm about to get really bad news. I know that it's my brother's worry that's actually seeping into my head. He doesn't keep his mind as tight as he used to. Ever since I found out everything about his past, he seems more relaxed. Either that, or he isn't able to block me the way he used to, and he just hasn't admitted it to me yet. He's kind of a pain in the ass that way, always trying to one up me.

> *Trevor: She wants to try.*
> *Me: And you?*
> *Trevor: She isn't giving me a choice. She says she'll leave us if I say no. She will return to her old life and for us to have contact with her.*
> *Me: I'll talk to Riley. Everyone has to agree, that part hasn't changed.*
> *Trevor: I understand. And the council?*
> *Me: Riley said yes, and the council no longer matters.*

I plop down on the edge of the bed and sigh.

"Trevor?" he asks.

"Yes, they want to try. What if she doesn't make it?"

"If she doesn't make it, he will need you. But I know when it was you, if you hadn't made it, I would have lost myself." He grimaces.

I go to him and put my arms around him.

"Let's talk to everybody. They must agree with the decision," Riley says.

We come into the great room. "I need everyone at the table for a vote," Riley says formally.

Everybody sits.

"Do you want me to get Trevor?" Cash says.

"Not yet," Riley answer. "There is a matter for the table to vote on, and in this matter it must be unanimous."

> *Me: Bring Danielle.*

"Danielle would like to talk to you all on a matter of great importance to her. Please just listen to her," I say.

Danielle stands before everyone. Trevor stands behind her looking utterly defeated.

"I love all of you guys. You have always treated me like I belong here. It's because of that, I feel you have become my family. I can't bear the thought of losing any of you. I want to be changed. I understand I may not make it, but I'll only live fifty or so years as a human if I'm lucky enough to make it that long."

She pauses and takes a deep breath. "It's not enough time for me. I understand that if even one of you says no, it's binding. If that happens, I will choose to be returned to my world, instead of sitting on the sidelines of this one."

"You are asking us to allow you to die? Very few make it through the change," Justin says.

"Maybe with Trevor and Sky's blood it will help. I would like to be given the chance to try," Danielle says.

"Sky, where are you on all of this?" Derek asks.

I sigh. "I want her to be happy, and I choose to allow her to make her own decisions." A tear runs down my face, I brush it away. "It's her path to walk, not mine."

"Trevor, where are you on all of this?" Justin asks.

"My stance is as my sister's."

"Let's vote," Justin says.

The house vote is unanimous.

"I say yay reluctantly. I also feel it's one's choice to choose the path they walk, but this choice you're making must not be taken lightly. There is a male that loves you, so you see it's not only your path,"--Riley pulls me to him--"it's the path you're choosing for him as well."

"I understand. Thank you, all of you."

Me: Let me know her final decision.

Trevor nods and they head back to his room.

I look up at Riley and put my hand on his cheek. "You were thinking of me dying weren't you?"

"Yes."

"You would not have chosen this for me? You would have refused me."

"I think I would have....yes, but then I would have missed this life with you now. So I don't know the right choice here."

"What are we doing tonight?" I ask.

He smiles and shakes his head. "Five members are coming from another legion to observe and help if needed to take down another training center."

"And….who's up?"

"Derek, Brandon, Trevor, and you." He touches my face. "Derek and Brandon need to hit the club first, feel me?"

"Yeah, so we'll meet you all there. What was the surveillance count?"

"Twelve to eighteen varying. They want to see our tactics and potentially come here to train. I need my best warriors, and I need them out numbered. Please be careful, Luv."

"They know about me?"

"No, figured I'd let you show them. Can you and Trevor try to tone it down some?"

"Deviation from the norm and what's comfortable leads to people getting hurt. Are you asking me not….to use my powers?" I smile.

"Yes, unless you have to, to stay safe."

"Fine, but you will let those males say whatever they want to me and about me. You won't tell them who I am either. I'm Trevor's sister and that's it. Let me earn their respect."

He growls.

"If you have to protect me in front of them, it will make me look weak already. I can handle this." I nod.

"Fine," he snarls.

I go to get ready. I love going to the club beforehand. I totally get it now. They feed, may or may not have sex, drink, take in the music, and overall just loosen up and get their head in the game.

As I come into the great room his eyes are locked on mine. His gaze stalks me all the way to him.

"You like?" I smile.

"No, I love." He yanks me to him.

"Say it, I love when you say it."

He laughs and then pulls my lips to his. "Tonight Luv, tonight."

We come up in the alley and head to Distortion. As we sit at the table Brandon's already back up. He's let himself go too long in between feedings. My brother is finally using Danielle, and Derek seems closed off from me.

I go up to the VIP bar. "Can I get a Guinness?" I ask the bartender.

"Here you go." He hands it to me.

I pay him and start towards the table. I sit down and Derek is still off, and he needs to feed. "What's going on with you?" I ask.

"Nothing," he says coldly.

"You need to feed, I feel it."

He narrows his gaze.

I love when he looks annoyed with me. "Not feeding makes you weak. I feel your emotions all over the place as well. Tonight is important." I slide around in the booth to sit next to him. I put my wrist across his lap.

He gets up and walks away.

Great, I just told him he was weak. That's always a great way to keep a conversation going with a warrior. I put the beer down and go in the direction I saw him walk. He's leaning against the wall in the back.

I come and stand next to him.

"Sky, I said I'm fine." He starts to walk away.

I grab his hand. "I don't understand. You're the smart one, the one that takes all this shit so seriously. I know you've been to the club at least twice this past week, but it feels you haven't fed for at least a week and a half."

He tries to pull his hand out of mine, but I tighten my grip. He looks back down at me and sighs. "What do you want from me?"

"For you to tell me I'm wrong."

"I told you I was fine."

"Really?" I narrow my gaze. "I thought you a better male than one that would lie to my face."

His face drops.

I pull my hair back, take my blade out, and cut down my neck. His gaze intensifies. His hands lock tightly on my waist and he's trying hard to hold himself back.

I draw him in closer and bare my neck. "Feed, damn you."

He strikes fast and moans the second his fangs pierce my flesh.

I feel calm and completely at ease. He's holding me tightly in his arms. I run my hands up his shirt to feel his bare skin along with the crazy fluid connection we have.

He growls.

My hands find their way back down to his waist. Gotta watch the desire when sharing blood.

Derek seals me up and stays in the crook of my neck. "You shouldn't have done this. I shouldn't have done this." His hands come to my hips.

I hold him tighter. "I feel how much stronger you are now. You're important to me Derek, and for me can you please take care of yourself? If something is bugging you, you can talk to me you know."

He pulls back, takes my face in his hands, and puts his forehead to mine. "You belong to him. When you let another male take from you, he will be able to sense you all over that male."

"Oh shit. So not so good?"

"No, but I'll talk to him. It's my fault, you were right. I let myself go too long. It won't happen again."

I hear the back door and Brandon's walking in. I see him before he sees us and I'm sure this doesn't look good at all. I pull Derek back tightly into my body and tuck my head into him. He turns and sees Brandon.

"Derek," Brandon mutters.

"Get Trevor, we need to go." He looks down at me and sighs. "Let's go, I think you're trying to get me killed."

"Shut up. I was trying to do a good thing. Not my fault you guys don't tell me shit."

He laughs and shakes his head. "Problem is, I know better."

Finally, we take off and appear at the meeting place. Riley's there with four other large males. All equally as huge as our house. When the four of us appear I see a few narrowed gazes. Luckily for them, they're keeping their mouths shut for now.

"This is Matt, Daniel, Jason, and Joe," Riley says. "This is Derek, Brandon, Trevor, and Sky."

"Derek, you know where you're going in?" Riley asks.

"Yeah, as usual Brandon and I are hitting the front with Sky and Trevor going in the back."

"So you let the female fight, are you insane?" Matt barks out.

"You will hold your tongue, warrior," Riley growls.

Matt looks to Riley and nods. "Yes, sire."

Me: You will stay put no matter what happens, and stay close to Riley. We don't need him killing anyone.

Trevor shakes his head.

I go nose to nose with Matt. "You don't look like much. I know I could take you." I smirk.

He's actually a pretty large male. About as big as Derek.

He laughs and shoves me back from him. "You need to learn your place, female."

Derek takes a step forward.

I make eye contact with him, glare, and shake my head. He stops. I pull off my guns and drop them on the ground. "Let's go asshole, you think you're better than me? Hardly." I beckon him to me.

Matt pulls his guns off and drops his swords.

Trevor and Derek move next to Riley just in case he tries to step in. I catch Matt in the face, then he catches me and busts my lip open. I smile and lick the blood off. As he comes at me again, I overpower him and flip him onto the ground. I mount him and have my blade at his throat.

I lean into his face, smiling. "Told you I could take you. You're dead, asshole."

"Now this female I like." He growls and runs his hands up my thighs landing on my ass.

Trevor grabs Riley. I see him saying something to him as they turn around. His eyes are blazing red.

I jump up. "Sorry, I'm already mated."

"Enough of this bullshit. Let's go," Derek barks.

I look up as Riley grabs Derek's arm.

Derek looks at him and nods. "We will talk about all of this later, you and I."

Riley looks over at me.

I rub my face and look away. It's their fault, they should tell me all this shit. I get my weapons back on and we head off. I hear one last comment before we're too far out of range.

"Yeah, but let's see how she fairs with the Moartea."

Once inside Trevor turns to me and glares. "They are best friends."

"Yeah, so?"

He narrows his gaze.

"Ugh. I could tell he hadn't fed and he was weak. I made him take from me. How was I supposed to know that's not a good thing? I give to you all the time and nobody has ever told me anything. My thoughts were to make sure he was strong for tonight, that's it."

Trevor sighs. "It's my fault I should have told you, but he knew better than to take from you."

"He was really trying not to. I yelled at him to do it, then I cut my neck. His blood lust took over and he was pretty much screwed."

"He took from your neck?" Trevor chokes out then he takes a deep breath. "I guess we'll let them work that shit out. In the future, your mate and your family would be the only ones you can take from or give to. It's different when we're healing."

"Thanks, but that little speech there maybe would have been useful oh….I don't know, maybe an hour ago."

He throws his hands up.

We get back to the job at hand. The count is twenty. Trevor and I end up with six each. We tear through them in about five minutes. Both of us are covered in blood and ash.

"I finished first," I yell out to him.

"No way, I did." He throws his hands up and looks at Brandon. "Brother, help me out here."

"You finished first, but you're stabbed and she only has a flesh wound." He sighs, shaking his head.

"Ha. I win." I throw my hands up.

Now he and Derek are both shaking their heads. Just then a Moartea comes out from behind Derek ready to swing and take his head off with a broad sword. I throw my hand out and throw it against the wall.

Derek spins around and dusts him. He looks back over at me and slowly nods.

I notice Riley and the warriors from the Twelfth have all come in the back. They've been watching everything that happened. They saw me use my powers.

Me: Crap. He said no powers.
Trevor: He will get over it. That was a clean shot
on Derek and you know it, so do they. He
was dead, Sky.

"She's incredible. I understand it now," Jason says.

"They're twins right? They fight exactly the same," Daniel says.

"Yeah. Brutal, merciless, and fucking beautiful," Matt says.

The dark looking one nods as the others talk. He's staring right at me, like he's looking right through me.

Joe, huh? He looks like he'd be a lot of fun to spar with. I can't wait.

I look over at Riley as he watches and listens to them describe what they've just seen. I know it's coming as soon as his gaze meets mine. He's trying to hold it back, but there it goes, and here he comes.

He pulls my face to his and kisses me hard, then he bites into my neck. He softly growls.

Damn, he can sense Derek. I get close to his ear. "I'm sorry, I didn't know I wasn't supposed to, and he was weak. I was just trying to make sure he was strong for tonight."

"She's the Queen," one gasps.

They fall on bended knee.

"I'm sorry for my actions sire, I didn't realize," Matt chokes out.

"Oh relax boys, I'm not that kind of queen. If you decide to train with my brother and me, just know we don't take it easy on anyone." I motion for them to get up. "And in the future, my name is Sky, so that's what you will call me. No more of this kneeling shit or 'your grace' either--it will get your ass kicked."

Derek and Brandon both nod.

I hug Riley tightly. "I love you."

He touches my face and kisses me deeply. "And I you Luv."

Riley's going back to their place to talk with the rest of their warriors. The four of us are headed back home. Trevor and Brandon go inside. I'm right behind them when Derek grabs my arm.

I take a deep breath when I feel that crazy current go through my entire body. I turn and look up at him.

"Can you hold up for a second so I can talk to you?" he asks.

"Sure, what's going on Derek?"

He starts to pace.

I walk in front of him to block his path. I smile up at him and run my hands around his waist and hug him tightly to me.

He sighs and squeezes me tightly. "Thank you for everything you did for me tonight."

I pull away slightly to look at him. "Of course. I'm not going to let anything happen to you Derek."

He pulls me back into him tightly.

I let him hold me for a few minutes. "Are you feeling better?"

"Yeah. Don't worry about me so much."

I pull away and head towards the door. I turn back around. "Sorry Derek, I can't promise that. I care about you too much."

Chapter 16

Riley watches as his mate materializes home. Watching her fight is a thing of beauty. He had second guessed himself about letting them see her fight, but now he's glad he did. She has more than earned her place among them. He knows females fighting will never be a thing, but she's unique and an asset. She saved Derek's life tonight and they all know it. But he and that male have some unfinished business later this morning.

"Sire, forgive me for my forwardness with the Queen. If I would have known, I never would have put my hands on her," Matt says as he shakes his head.

"Let's just say you get a pass this time because you didn't know who she was, and I know exactly how you feel. But brothers, if any of you look at my mate that way again, there will be hell to pay."

Back at their bunker, the night's events are relayed to the rest of the legion. Minus the fact that one of the warriors that went was a female, and the Queen.

"We're going to have a vote on training sessions with the Ninth and forming an alliance between the two legions," Matt says.

The vote goes around the table and Riley hears all in agreement.

"Vote is unanimous," Daniel confirms.

"Excellent, I'll let them know to expect you," Riley says.

"We will send our top six to start with," Daniel says.

They continue to talk to him and ask him questions about his plans for the future. After an hour he gets up. "It's time for me to get back. Have a good night, and be well." Riley heads up top.

Once outside he sees the one named Joe sitting up on a wall smoking. That male's eyes never left Sky the entire time they were with them. Even looking at him now makes him want to rip his throat out.

"You let your mate fight?" he asks.

"Yes, I do."

"You aren't afraid that our Queen could be killed?"

"She's strong, and one of the top warriors in the house. She wants to serve our race by protecting our own on the front lines. You think she should stay home and be with young?"

"No sire, I find her amazing and you courageous for allowing her to fight. There's much to learn from your rule." He snuffs out his cigarette and heads back inside.

Riley appears home. He comes in and goes to the office where Derek and Justin are. He fills them in on all the details.

"They will have six come to train with Sky and Trevor."

"So it begins. A fusing of the legions," Justin says.

"It's better to have larger pools to reach out to and help each other. It's a good idea," Derek meets his gaze.

Justin looks from one to the other. "Is everything alright between the two of you?" he asks.

"I need you to give me a minute with Derek." Riley says.

"Alright, I'll leave you to this." Justin gets up and looks between them once more before he leaves.

Riley closes the door behind him. Derek just stands there as he comes right up into his face. "You took from my mate this evening. You think it's okay to use her like you use the whores at the club?"

"No, I'd never use her like that." Derek tries to step back.

He grabs his jacket and goes nose to nose with him. "So you're going to lie to me when I can sense her all over you?" he growls.

"Riley, I did take from her yes, but that's it." Derek throws his hands up.

"That's it, you think that makes it better?" he yells.

"No, I know it doesn't. She didn't know what she was doing. It was my fault, I knew better. My head's been all fucked up lately. I had gone almost ten days without feeding. She cut her neck and bared it to me. The blood lust took over. I'm sorry, it will never happen again."

His friend was hurting. His mate saw it and tried to help. Now here he is trying to beat him up. He lets Derek go and sighs. "If something's bothering you, why didn't you come to me about it?"

"You have enough shit to deal with then to have to listen to my bullshit. I'm not even sure what my problem is, but I can promise you I'll take better care of myself. Your female is pretty pushy."

"That she is brother. I'm sorry for this shit here."

"Don't be. You have every right to come at me. I can't believe I let that shit happen. I'm better than this."

"You are the best male I know, Derek, and we all have shit now and then. We're good." Riley pats his shoulder. "Have a good night."

He comes in and Sky's not in the living room. Then suddenly there she is in the bedroom doorway in nothing but a towel. She smiles at him and drops the cloth.

Damn, she's beautiful.

He could stare at her for hours, but….not this morning. He gets to her quick. He's thought of nothing all night but her, and he's finally going to take what belongs to him.

****

Trevor comes in and Danielle is on the couch. He finds it hard to even look at her. "I need a shower."

He gets in the shower and lets the hot water run down him. He already knows what she's going to tell him, she wants to try to go through the change and nobody's going to change her mind about it. But he's beat and he just wants her in bed and in his arms. He comes out into the bedroom and she's already in bed turned away from him.

Trevor rubs his face. "We'll talk tomorrow, alright?" He slides into bed. "Right now, I just want to hold you." He pulls her to him and wraps his arms around her.

Danielle holds his arms to her tightly. "I love you," she whispers.

He leans to her ear. "I love you too."

Later that evening he wakes her up by kissing her all over her face softly and moving his body in between her legs. She wakes up smiling and pulls him up inside of her. As he begins to make love to her he realizes this may be the last time they're together.

They get up and dressed. His feet want to take him as far away from the conversation they're about to have as possible.

"Can you just come sit next to me?" she tries to coax him back to bed.

He shakes his head. He needs Sky. He's starting to lose it. He needs to hit shit.

"I want it done tonight. Both of you are off tonight, so yeah it's tonight."

Still trying to get his shit together he stops moving, but doesn't make eye contact with her. "I'll be back." He knows he's an asshole for leaving.

"Trevor," she yells out after him. But he's already gone, and she doesn't follow him.

> *Trevor: I need you now, gym.*
> *Sky: Alright, give me a minute.*
> *Trevor: Send Riley to talk to her about the change*
> *   please.*
> *Sky: Sure.*

****

I come out in sweats and find Riley at the table looking over some papers.

"Evening love, Trevor's upset. He wants me to meet him in the gym."

"Can you tell that brother of yours to go easy on you? I'm tired of looking at my mate's beautiful face all black and blue."

"First of all, I don't do anything easy. Secondly, with as upset as I feel him right now, I don't think it's got any chance of going down that way." I sit on his lap and wrap my arms around his neck.

He sighs.

"Trevor wants you to talk to D about the change. He wants her to know exactly what you went through watching me."

"Pain, agony, and complete helplessness to change the outcome that would be whatever it would be. My life was slipping away with yours." He caresses my cheek.

"I'm sorry you have to think about all of this again, and I'm sorry I'm such a trouble maker." I frown. "Are you and Derek okay?"

"We talked last night. I understand why you did what you did, and I'm angry at myself because my friend was hurting and I didn't see it. But you did and you helped him, so thank you. In the future, can you please come to me and not let anyone take from you unless absolutely necessary?"

"Yes." I kiss him quick and get up.

"Go to your brother." He slaps my ass.

I growl and look back at him. He's about to get up, I can see it in his eyes and his pants. "No." I point to where he's sitting. "I have to go to him and we have all night for all of this here." I laugh.

He glares and licks his lips.

I leave quickly while I have the chance. As I come inside the gym I see Trevor going to town on a punching bag. I come around and hold it for him. Yeah, that's so not going to be my face tonight.

"She wants it done tonight," he says between breaths.

I don't feel any emotion from him. He keeps punching the bag, and his eyes are completely black. He's in a bad place right now.

"I hate when you do that to me." I glare.

"Do what?" He keeps punching the bag.

"Close your mind off from me so that I can't read any of your thoughts or feelings."

"I have them completely off." He throws his gloves down and heads to the treadmill.

"If it were me, would you let me try to go through the change?" I cross my arms over my chest and stand in front of the treadmill.

"No."

I narrow my gaze. "To only have fifty, maybe sixty years with me would be enough for you? Because it wouldn't be enough for me."

Trevor stops, still holding onto the sides of the treadmill. "Sky, I have no answers for you here. I'm lucky I get to have you and never had to make that decision. But I can't think of any of this right now."

He looks down at me and his eyes are still black and he's full of rage. That's the only emotion I feel from him.

"Well no way I'm going one on one with you right now-- you're way out of control. Best case scenario, I'd just get my ass kicked."

Brow about pops off his forehead. "You think I'd seriously injure you?" He comes towards me inches from my face. "I love you, and right now just being with you is the only way I'm even holding my shit together this much." He snatches me up in his arms.

"Trevor....can't....breathe," I choke out as I pat his back.

He slightly loosens his grip. "Will you prepare her so she knows what to expect?"

"Yes, I love her too." Before I can stop the memory of my transition it begins to wash over me. The pain, burning, and sheer feeling of terror like I was being slowly tortured for an eternity. Then there was only the blackness when I died. I shudder in his arms.

"I wish she wouldn't do this," he groans.

"Together we can be strong enough for her. I want Riley to be the first one to give to her since he's a pureblood. We will give her the best chance possible."

"You died?"

"Yes, that's the way it happens. Then you either fight your way back through the pain to breathe again as vampire, or you fall deeper into the calm of the blackness," I say quietly.

After about another half hour watching Trevor abuse the punching bag, he seems a little more relaxed.

"Come on. I need you and Riley to do something for me." I pull him out of the gym and towards our room.

"What's this about?"

"Just come on."

"Hi love, how did it go with D?" I ask.

Riley frowns shaking his head as he looks at Trevor. "Sorry brother. She's dead set on going through with it."

Trevor's shoulders drop and he stares at the ground with a sigh.

"I need you two to go to the club tonight and feed."

Riley's eyes are huge as he studies my face. "What?"

"You have to be strong for tonight. But you have sex with any of those women, and I give my brother permission to kick your ass, king shit aside." I glare.

He gets up and wraps his arms around me. "Luv, you're asking me to do something I can see in your eyes you don't want me to do."

"Yes, because she needs the best chance possible. I will ask Justin if I can feed from him."

"No," Riley barks. He pulls away from me.

"Trevor, can you go get ready to take Riley to the club. I need a moment with my mate."

Trevor leaves.

"He's also of the strongest bloodlines right? I can ask Michael, but he hasn't fed in a week, and I know Justin just went out last night."

"Justin is a pureblood," he answers reluctantly.

I stand in front of him as tears well up in my eyes. "We need to do everything we can to make this work. It's the only way I'll be able to live with myself if she doesn't make it."

He pulls me into his arms. "I will need to be gone when you do it, or I will take you after."

"I know, I'm sorry I even have to ask this of you."

"You're asking me?" He drops his brow.

"Of course. I'm yours. If you say no, it's no. I just want to make sure all three of us as strong as possible. I don't know what else I can do."

He drops his head to my shoulder and groans. "I want to say no, but I won't."

"Would you prefer Michael go with you to feed, and then I can take from him when you guys get back?"

"No, you need to do it while I'm gone." He grabs my face in his hands. "Luv, your eyes are red."

"Because I'm angry. I'm about to throw up thinking about you at someone's neck. All I ask is that you please don't use the red-haired prostitute."

He squeezes me to him, and then we go out to the great room. As I head towards Justin's office, Riley looks over at me and then runs up the stairs.

"Hey Justin, I need a favor. You may absolutely say no."

He turns around in his chair. "Alright, what is it you need from me?"

"Danielle wants to do it tonight. I've sent Riley and Trevor to feed at the club."

His eyes are huge. "You're going to be alright with that?" he says tucking his blond hair behind his left ear.

"Not really, but we all need to be strong tonight to help her get through it."

"What does all of this have to do with me?" He starts rocking back and forth in the chair.

"Will you let me take from you?"

He stops rocking, and the office chair comes up quickly and slams his chest into the desk. "Does Riley know you're asking me?" he chokes out as he rubs his chest.

"Of course. I wouldn't have come to you unless he said it was alright."

He rubs his face. "If that's what you need, I will give you what you ask of me."

"You can absolutely tell me no. You are under no obligation to allow me to do this."

He stands up. "Here or in my room?"

"Are you sure about this?"

"Here or in my room?" he repeats calmly.

"Here's fine." I sigh and close the door.

He sits on the office couch and I kneel down before him. "You're sure?"

He touches my arm. "Sky, I want to help. It's fine."

My fangs elongate as I take his wrist in my hand. I look up at him as I sink into his flesh.

Justin lays his head back and takes a deep breath.

As I take him in, I sense something familiar. Like Riley and Michael. His blood is strong. It's not like Trevor's, but it's still strong. I seal him up and turn my back to the couch. I lay my head back as his blood runs through my system.

The only way I can describe taking in another, is it's like choosing to have grape, cherry, strawberry, or orange. Not one is bad, you just have a personal preference. But the desire that follows is there with anyone you take in. Thank God it doesn't work that way with my brother.

"You'll need to be careful. You will each be able to sense the blood of another, and you will want to take each other and claim what is yours," he warns.

I turn and look up at him. "You are their family, aren't you?"

He just looks at me.

"Your blood is the same as theirs. Are you brothers?"

"Cousins actually." He rubs his face.

"How long have you known about this?"

"As soon as we learned who they really are."

"Why haven't you told them?"

"It never seemed like the right time." He shrugs.

"You know parts of their past and family that they don't. You need to talk to them both."

"I know." He lets out a breath. "Now who's advising who?"

I smile. "I need to go talk to Danielle. Thank you for letting me do this."

"You're very welcome." He smiles.

****

Derek see's Sky coming out of Justin's office. He almost runs into her she's moving so fast.

"Hi Derek." She smiles as she walks by.

He walks into the office and closes the door. Justin relaxing on the couch is filling him with rage. He wants to tear this male apart. "What is all of this?"

Justin looks up. "What are you talking about?"

"I can smell you all over Sky. You let her take from you," he growls.

"I was asked if I would, and I agreed. She has sent Riley and Trevor to the club to feed as well. They all want to be as strong as possible, Danielle has asked to be turned tonight."

"Whatever."

He walks out of the office and goes upstairs. He has no right to be jealous. This thing with her is wrong in so many ways, and he needs to get a handle on his emotions.

He heads out to the club. He will take the first female he finds. He orders a beer and see's Riley sitting in the VIP section. That male isn't even looking for a female.

A blonde walks up to him. "Hi handsome, you looking to party?"

He figures she'll do. She looks nothing like Sky. "Yeah."

"I'm Candy, what's your name?"

"Derek."

"Do you have a girlfriend, Derek?"

"Not really."

"Interesting answer." She smiles then takes his hand and leads him to the bathroom.

They start kissing.

He runs his hand up her skirt and finds she has no underwear on. Well that makes this easier. He pulls back and looks deep into her eyes. "There will be no pain only pleasure, we're going to have a good time."

She nods.

He comes back down on her mouth kissing her hard and then goes to her neck. He takes her in and has a hard time even swallowing her blood. Even the smell of her is wrong.

As soon as she unbuttons his pants and takes a hold of him, he knows it's game over. There's no way he's getting it up for her. She's not who he wants. He seals her up.

I'm so fucked. He takes her face in his hands. "Everything was great, go have a good time."

She stumbles off.

Derek rubs his face. He's bonding to Sky, and no other female is going to erase that. All he wants with everything inside of him….is her.

He must have been absent the day his brain decided that he was in love with her. Maybe he could have had a conversation with it and told it that she completely belongs to another male. He's going to have to watch himself around that female from now on. He will need to keep his distance.

****

Trevor and Riley walk into Distortion.

"You go ahead, I'm fine here," Riley says.

"You aren't going to feed?" Trevor raises his brow.

"I took from Sky last night, I'm fine."

"Are you sure?" He narrows his gaze.

"Her blood is strong. And brother, I can't take from another female, especially now. I'd kill her. Sky is it for me, and you saw her face earlier. This would only hurt her."

Trevor smiles. "I appreciate that, but I have to."

"Do what you need to do, I'll be here when you're finished."

Trevor stalks off.

He would kill for a drink right now, but it's probably not a good idea. Thinking of Sky at Justin's vein is driving him mad. He will have to keep his distance from her.

They will bleed Danielle out until she almost passes. He will be the one to feed her since he's a royal pureblood. Then Sky and Trevor will feed her, and hope their healing power is enough to get her through.

Riley has asked Michael to feed and be there as well. He will leave the room once Danielle takes from him. Then Michael, Sky, and Trevor will watch over her until she changes or passes.

The club is packed this evening. He's half tempted to take one out back and kill them just to release some of his frustration. But dealing with the council, and reading over the old teachings, makes him realize how messed up he really is.

His job is to protect his race, and with the powers he's been given, he has also charged with protecting the human race. Which is not something he's ever been very good at. But it's not something the council cares much about either. Even to them, humans are lesser beings. Things have become as twisted as he has over time.

Derek is coming out of the bathrooms with a blonde female. Well at least Derek is getting his shit together. One less male to worry about.

Trevor comes back over to the table. "Let's go."

They appear back in front of the bunker.

"Keep the feeding between us," Riley asks.

"For now."

They come downstairs and Riley heads to Justin's office. He closes the door. "Did you let Sky take from you?"

"Yes," Justin says.

"Thank you. I know that was a difficult position to put you in."

"I would do anything for the two of you. I'm also hoping for Danielle to make it through the change."

"I need to see Sky, where is she?"

"You know you need to keep your distance, or you will take each other."

Riley sighs and hangs his head.

"It was private so that nobody would know. There's also something I need to tell you. I should have come to you sooner with it." Justin leans back in the chair.

"What is it?" Riley looks up.

"Sky realized something in my blood when she fed."

He cringes.

"My mother was Richard Magnusson's sister. Sky knew instantly we shared the same blood."

"You're family?"

"Yes, cousins. With everything going on, it just never seemed like the right time to tell you." Justin laughs. "You're very busy, and you keep taking on more and more."

"There is much to talk about between you and me."

Justin nods.

Riley flops back on the couch. If he knew where Sky was, he'd know where he can't be. That way he could at least not have to be stuck here with Justin. He appreciates that Justin helped them out, but thinking about Sky at his wrist is killing him.

"First Derek takes from her neck, and now she takes from you. It's a lot to take, brother. I want to lock her up and never let anyone near her."

Justin looks up with narrowed eyes. "Derek took from Sky?"

"He hadn't fed in over a week, she realized he was weak and cut herself to get him to feed. Something's been bothering him. Have you noticed anything?"

"No, but I'll talk to him about it."

"Thank you." He gets up and goes to the kitchen.

****

I open Trevor's door.

"Hey, Sky," Danielle says.

"You okay?"

"Sure."

"Good, because I want to explain to you exactly what I went through, or at least what I remember."

"You won't be able to talk me out of it, so don't even bother." She walks away.

"D, I'm not going to try and do that. I just want to tell you how I felt, and what helped me come back. I need you to come back, D." Tears fall down my face as I watch her walking away from me.

She stops and comes back to hug me. "Sorry I'm so bitchy. But your male did a number on me earlier describing how he almost lost you."

"Come here and sit with me."

We sit down on the couch.

"When the vampire blood moves through your body, everything burns. You will think you're on fire. The pain is so intense, you can't wait for it to end. You'll beg for it to end, D. Your heart will barely beat, you'll draw your last breath as human, and then everything goes black. It's up to you to fight your way back through the pain or give up and sink into the calm of the blackness."

"It's that bad then?" She slowly nods as she stares off.

"The urge to give up and follow the calm is overwhelming. You'll have to become strong, and fight your way back through the pain. I heard voices, and it help draw me back out."

"I'm ready to try, Sky."

I explain how we are going to do it. "You need more than one can provide the first day." I try and give a reassuring smile.

Trevor and Michael walk in.

"Where's Riley?" I ask.

"It's better if he waits to come in. When he does, I'll have you go into the other room," Michael says. He hugs me tightly. "I know this is hard on you. He's a mess out there as well."

"I'll see you soon." I walk over and hug Danielle, then I head into the bedroom.

"Is everybody ready? Danielle?" Michael asks.

"I'm ready," Danielle answers.

"Trevor, go get Riley."

I hear the door and feel Riley close. I peek around the doorway and his eyes meet mine. I smile and then duck back into the bedroom. I sit on the bed with my head in my hands. It takes everything inside of me not to go to him right now.

"What's happening to her?" I hear and feel Trevor agitated.

"This is what happens, everything is fine so far," Michael says.

Me: Trevor, breathe. We will get her through this.

I hear the door after about thirty minutes. I come out and Riley's gone. Danielle looks so still and pale.

"Is she….." I start to ask.

"Too soon to tell. She hasn't started breathing yet," Michael says as he stares at her. He looks like he's trying to will her to breathe. He looks to be about as much of a mess as Riley.

Trevor has her hand and keeps talking to her. It seems like it's been hours.

"She's breathing." Michael takes a deep breath. "Now we need to wait for her to wake up. Her body's done the work, now her mind needs to come back."

I come behind my brother and wrap my arms around his neck. He lays his head against mine and holds my arms tightly to him. I take his hand in mine and place it on her chest. I close my eyes imagining myself finding her in the darkness and bringing her back.

"I know it hurts, D, just please come back to us. We need you. I know you can do it," I say quietly.

I hear a cough and a grunt come out of her.

"Sky, now." Michael grabs my wrist and scores it. Then he puts it to her mouth.

She bites down hard.

I grab onto Trevor and cry out. I take a deep breath and compose myself. "Sorry, I'm fine."

Michael smiles at me and raises his brow. "Newbies bite hard, don't they?"

"Shush, you," I glare with a half smirk. I feel her draining me. I'm falling into Trevor and becoming numb.

"It's too much," Trevor yells.

There's panic in Trevor's voice, but I'm too weak to reassure him that I'm fine. Michael replaces my wrist with his. I feel my brother pick me up and set me in the chair. He scores his wrist and puts it to my lips.

I seal him back up. "No. I'm fine. You have to stay strong for her," I barely get the words out as I feel myself fading.

"I need to take her to Riley," Trevor says frantic.

"Be with your female, brother. She will need to feed again soon. I have Sky," Michael says.

"I feel it, she's too weak, and she needs blood now."

Michael puts his hand on Trevor's shoulder. "I can't take her to Riley--he won't be able to fight the urge to take her. I'll take care of her. Relax, you need to take care of Danielle or she'll die."

Trevor nods. I look up and see him still staring down at me.

Me: Go.

Michael takes me in his arms and puts his wrist to my lips. He sits down with me in his lap. I feel worry coming from him. I take him in and pass out soon after. I feel myself being lifted, and then a door opens and closes. Then there's banging on another door. The door opens.

"What happened?" I hear Riley's voice.

"She gave too much, I had to give to her," Michael says.

Riley growls.

"I'm weak. I can't give her anymore. You must let her feed. If you take from her you could kill her. Do you understand? You will calm down or I won't leave her with you," Michael barks.

"Give her to me," Riley demands.

I'm being handed off and I feel Riley's arms come around me. He sits down and brings me to his neck.

My arms come around his neck and I bite into him. When I've had my fill, I seal him up and take his face in my hands. "I love you."

He kisses me softly.

I pull back and look at him. He's a wreck, somewhere between rage and tears inside of him. He's shaking and needs to take me.

"Thank you for everything you did, Michael, but I need to be with my mate now," I say as I stare into Riley's eyes.

Michael leaves.

"Do you feel the need to take me?"

"Yes," he says on a growl. "But I won't hurt you."

"Why don't I feel like that?"

He drops his head and refuses to look at me.

"You didn't feed at the club?" I barely choke out.

"I couldn't." He shakes his head. "I knew it would hurt you if I did. I couldn't think about doing it without getting sick."

"So I'm just a total blood whore who takes it from whoever."

"I'm glad you did. If you hadn't, you may have been killed from her feeding."

"Take me to bed." I nuzzle into him.

He picks me up and carries me the bedroom. He slowly undresses me, growing hungrier by the second.

I pull his shirt off and run my hands across his chest. Next, I go for the buttons on his pants. "I want you to take me and truly make me yours."

The words barely make it out of my mouth before he's inside of me and at my neck drawing me in. I'm weak, but I don't care. I want my mate satisfied and well. He seals me up quickly and looks down at me.

"I love you." I smile.

Chapter 17

Danielle wakes up with pain in her stomach. She feels Trevor pull her onto him and urge her to his neck. Her mouth feels weird. She puts her hand to her teeth and feels fangs. *It worked.* Then her stomach cramps up on her again.

Trevor pulls her back down to him and she bites into him. His blood is slowly making the pain go away.

She slides off. "It worked," she whispers.

"Yes," Trevor says.

She turns on her side, then leans in and kisses him. "Trevor?"

"Yeah?"

"Is it too soon to, you know? Because I really want you."

He comes on her quickly and plunges deep inside. The orgasm that follows is better than any she's ever had. The feel of him is intense, she can't get enough. She remembers Sky saying that for vampires everything is intensified, and boy howdy was she right.

She wakes up three times and feeds from him. So when she wakes up with her stomach cramping she remembers what Sky said about being careful. He won't have all she needs at first. Her stomach is starting again. She knows Michael's in the living room for her. She grabs a robe and gets up. She comes into the living room and sees Cash.

"Is Michael around?"

"No, he had to give to you and Sky so he's weak. I'm here to help. You look good, by the way. We hoped you would make it." He smiles.

She laughs. "Probably because you want to make sure you still have someone to cook for you."

Just then her stomach wrenches her to the floor. Cash picks her up and puts her on the couch. He comes next to her and lays his wrist across her lap. She brings it to her mouth and slowly bites into him. This is going to take some time getting used to. She seals him up and leans back next to him.

"Are you okay?" she asks.

"Oh yeah, totally fine. I just need a minute."

"Did I do too much?" She puts her hand over her mouth.

"Nah, it's fine. Males that only feed on human blood have a hard time feeding females. But I'll have to admit it's very satisfying, even though you're a half-breed."

"Half-breed, huh? You say it like it's of a lower class."

"Well, half-breeds are….I don't know, looked at differently. It's all about the purity of your blood, like Riley or Justin. But we all loved you as human, so this is definitely a step up." He laughs. "Sorry, your eyes are beautiful by the way."

"Yellow?"

"Golden. I feel better now. I'm going to cut out. If you need anything else just ask."

"Thank you."

Cash leaves and she goes back to bed.

****

I wake up and all I can think about is Danielle and Trevor. The new trainees from the Twelfth Legion are coming today. I get ready and head to the gym.

Me: How is she?
Trevor: Sleeping. How are you? You scared the crap
out of me. I told you to stop doing that shit to me.
Me: I'm fine, relax. Riley gave to me.
Trevor: That better be all he did.

Me: Shush. New trainees coming in remember.
Trevor: You need to rest.
Me: I'm healthy, strong, and already in the gym.

I'm warming up when Trevor comes in. He sits down and starts wrapping his hands. I come next to him and he lays his head on my shoulder.

"She still sleeping?"

"Yes."

I lay my wrist on his arm. He shoves it away. I put it back.

"Sky, stop."

"You need to feed and I know you feel how strong I am."

He sighs and takes my wrist.

Me: I always win. You're staying strong for her,
     remember that.
Trevor: When she drained you I thought I had to
         choose healing you or feeding her. I chose
         you--I will always choose you.
Me: I too would choose you above all others.

He seals me up and I hug him tightly. Then we get ready for the trainees.

"There's six today for basics. Then they're going to break up into two groups of three."

Derek comes in with six males. I smile at him. The connection we have is strong, and I'm still not sure what it all means. I also feel it growing. I still wonder if he feels the same thing I do.

"Boys, this is Trevor and Sky. Two of the best fighters in the house. This is Greg, Logan, Alec, and you already know Daniel, Jason, and Joe."

"Yep," Trevor says.

"Alright, we're going hand to hand with you guys to assess your strengths and weaknesses, then we'll move on to weapons," I say.

"I'm so not going hand to hand with a female. I'm supposed to be here to learn shit and actually get better, not worse," Alec says under his breath.

I smile.

Me: Ah, that one's mine, and the first little shit up.

"You, Alec, you're up first with Sky. Let's go, move your ass," Trevor barks.

"Seriously?" Alec mutters.

"Here's a tip, you hold back at all and you'll end up on your ass," I say.

"Well you asked for it, and apparently nobody's put you in your place yet. I guess I'll be the first one to do it," Alec sneers.

"Funny. I get that a lot, but it hasn't happened yet."

"Finally that big mouth of his is going to get his ass kicked." Daniel laughs under his breath.

Alec shoots him a dirty look.

He gets in position. We trade blocked blows. I drop my hands and let him knock me to my ass.

He laughs hard.

I get up, spit out the blood, and then smile wide. "So that was half strength, care to go all out?"

"Bring it," he beckons.

I come at him fast and hard. He's on the ground bruised, bloodied, moaning in pain, and grabbing at his two broken ribs. I lean down and make sure his ribs are back in place.

"Lose focus and you're dead. I think you boys need to learn something about all out. We heal, right? So what are you holding back for? You train hard so you can fight hard."

I turn to Trevor. "All out?"

"Let's show them how it's done." Trevor smiles.

"Sit down boys, this is going to take a while," Derek says.

We go at each other for thirty minutes.

"I win," I yell out.

"Not." Trevor laughs.

"Ah, broken leg says different."

He reaches down and sets his leg. "It's only a flesh wound sister dear."

"Pffft." I hug him tightly as I laugh.

One of my eyes is swollen shut and I can barely see, but it should be fine in a few minutes. I turn and look at the males across from me. Every one of their mouths are hanging open. I smile wide.

Me: Go check on Danielle and make sure she's okay. I got this for today.

"Derek, can you help me assess one on one today? Trevor needs to get back."

"Sure." He walks over to me and takes my face in his hands. He looks my eye over and shakes his head.

I hug him to me tightly. "You worry too much, I'm fine."

He squeezes me to him. "No you're crazy."

I turn to the trainees. "Does anyone else here have a problem going one on one with me?"

They shake their heads.

"Alright, then let's get started."

Three hours later Riley comes in. He looks at me and shakes his head. I'm pretty bloody, but damn I feel good. I walk over to him.

"That's the King," Logan chokes out.

"Yes it is," Derek says.

I throw my arms around him and he kisses me hard, then he comes to my neck and bites in. I run my hands up the back of his shirt and he growls. He seals me up, looks into my eyes and smiles.

"Sorry boys, but I'm stealing my mate back from you," Riley says.

We slip out into the hallway and his kiss deepens.

I pull his shirt off and pull him back into me. "I want you now," I growl.

He pushes me up against a door and pulls my leg up as he grinds into me.

Someone clears their throat next to us. "Can I get into my room, and then you two can carry on?" Markus says smiling.

We don't say anything. Riley just picks me up, still kissing me, and heads down the hall to our room.

****

They watch as the bonded male comes in and claims his female.

"You're a dick for not telling me who she was," Alec growls at Daniel.

He laughs. "Why would I do that? It was more fun watching you make an ass of yourself."

"Dude, you knocked the Queen on her ass," Logan says.

"You mean when she dropped her hands and let him, before she went all out on his ass?" Daniel says.

"Very observant," Derek says.

"Not really. I watched her do the same thing to Matt. Not to mention watching her take out six Moartea at once on her own."

"Watching a bonded pair is pretty crazy," Greg says.

"She is a thing of beauty to watch," Joe says staring at the door he watched Sky walk out of. He likes watching that female. If she wasn't already mated he would take her for himself.

Derek growls, "See something you like, warrior?"

"She's just amazing, that's all." He glares.

"Who's coming tomorrow and when?" Derek asks.

"Joe, Jason, and myself," Daniel says.

Joe's glad he's coming back tomorrow. He would like to work on that move she pulled on Matt. Coveting another male's mate could get you killed. He wonders how that would work with the Queen.

****

I lie in Riley's arms, thinking. My life seems to be moving at such a fast pace these days. But I'm really happy, and I'm dying to see Danielle.

Me: She up for company?
Trevor: Yes, she wants to see you.

"Come on, let's get up and go see D."

"Be careful around Joe from the Twelfth."

"Why?"

"I talked to him a couple nights back. He seems off and dangerous."

"Hmmm, you do realize that's how everybody described you and Trevor before me, right?"

"If he's anything like I was before you, I definitely want you to stay away from him."

I laugh. "You worry too much."

"Only for you." He kisses me.

We head across the hall and Trevor's there with the door open.

"I agree, he will train with me," Trevor says.

"I'm glad you know everything that goes on in my home, brother." Riley grimaces.

"Sorry." Trevor drops his head. "At least I agreed with you."

"Don't be sorry, I know it's your thing with her." Riley pats his shoulder.

Danielle comes out of the bedroom. Her eyes are a beautiful gold color.

"Thank you for everything, and sorry for hurting you." She hugs me.

"Don't be. It's just how it is. I'm so happy you have no idea." I hug her tighter. "I love your eyes and I'm totally jealous."

"It's all pretty interesting." She steps away and pulls up her top lip. "And these are crazy."

"It's all pretty crazy."

"Come on, I'm dying to see the others and I want to cook."

"Alright, but take it easy," I say. "Trevor, stay close to her--you remember when I overdid it the first day."

He nods.

We go back into the arms of our mates. Trevor takes Danielle's face and kisses her. He looks happy, but something's off.

"Must be nice to look into the beautiful non-bruised face of your mate." Riley grimaces.

"For now. I plan on training harder now, and with Sky," Danielle says.

"Uh, no," Trevor barks.

Riley laughs. "Good luck with that one, brother. You see how well it worked out for me."

"Hey." I punch him in the stomach. "You and I are going to be hitting the gym later, my friend, and I'm going to kick your ass."

He grabs me up. "I can think of a lot of things we can do in the gym."

****

The next day, Trevor and I meet in the gym. The three guys are already there before us warming up.

"I'll take one for hand to hand training and you take two for swords," I say.

"Sure, you take Daniel. I got Jason and Joe."

We worked with each of them, then it was time for me to work with Joe.

Trevor glares.

Trevor: Be careful with that male. He's dangerous.
Me: Shush. I got this. I could take him down and you
*   know it.*

"Where do you want to start?" I ask him.

"The shit you pulled on Matt. I want to learn how to do that."

"Alright, so you want to work on balance training?"

"Yes."

We go back and forth. He's really good--I can actually learn a few things from him.

"I see you don't need much work at all. You're really good. I would love to go all out with you sometime. Maybe next time you're here?"

"I could do that." He smiles.

Weird. I thought I caught something in the way he looked at me, but whatever. He's lucky he's good looking. Typical warrior build, short blond hair, chiseled jawline, perfect lips, movie star type. A girl could have a real good time with him. The violent and dangerous vibe he throws off makes him that more attractive.

We finish up with them and they head out.

I turn to Trevor. "You want to go a few rounds with the bõs?"

"Sure." Trevor takes them down and throws me one. "Do me a favor and watch out for that guy."

"Who?"

"Joe."

"Oh, he's fine. I don't know why you guys are so stressed about him. Maybe because he reminds you two of yourselves." I laugh.

"Sky, I'm being serious. I don't like the way he looks at you."

"He knows I'm mated. You really think he would challenge Riley?"

"He follows his own set of rules. I know you can feel he's off inside. Just watch yourself."

"Fine, now are we going to do this or what?"

****

Next Training session is Greg, Logan, and Alec. They are easier to work with. Less set in their ways and eager to learn new moves. We work with them for three hours. I finish up with Alec after everybody else has already left.

"Damn you learn quickly," I tell him.

"Yeah, because you're awesome." He smiles.

"Sorry about the other night."

"It's cool, got my attention. And I wasn't as good as I thought I was."

"Well I look forward to seeing how good you get, because you're learning faster than I did."

"Thanks. See you in a couple of days."

"Yeah, have a good night." I wave.

He takes off.

I hear the door open again.

"Forget something?" I look up and see Joe coming in. "Oh hey, what's up?"

"I've been thinking about the hand to hand all out thing, and I really need to blow off some steam."

"Hell yeah." I start rewrapping my hands.

He wraps his hands and comes over to me.

"All out, right? Means we're going to get pretty fucked up." I circle him and pound my fists together smiling.

"You're a pretty crazy female aren't you?" His gaze intensifies.

"You fight with the best and it only makes you better."

"True. Let's go."

He's obviously skilled, but he hits me everywhere but my face. His nose is broken and his mouth is cut. I have three broken ribs and my knee is twisted. He comes at me and I get the upper hand and drop him. He kicks my legs out from under me and I drop. He's on top of me fast, hand at my throat.

"I win, yeah? Because you're dead." His eyes burn into mine.

"Yes, this time." I laugh. "Next time I'll be ready."

He gets up and holds his hand out. I take it and he pulls me not just up, but into his body. His arm comes around my waist.

I bring my hands up on his chest to keep some distance between us.

"Too bad you're already mated." He steps away from me. "Thanks for this, I really needed it." Then just like that he's gone.

Wow. I guess there is something to what Trevor and Riley have seen. But I was right, he knows I'm mated so it's all good.

Riley comes in. "Was that Joe leaving?" He narrows his gaze.

I see a flash of anger as he looks at me. "Yeah, he wanted to go one on one like Trevor and I do. It was good practice. I learned a few areas I'm leaving myself open." I start unwrapping my hands.

He glares.

"Yes, we beat the crap out of each other, but that's all. I told you, they all know I'm mated. So stop all of this." I glare at him. "And those red eyes better not be for me." By this point I'm yelling. I take a deep breath.

He sighs and turns to leave.

"You're leaving?"

"You're not my favorite person right now." He opens the door.

I use my power to close the door and lock it.

Riley whips around with red eye and he growls at me. "You presume it fine to block my path? You will open this door and never do that to me again." He turns to leave.

I close my eyes to unlock the door. "Sorry love, I didn't mean to make you angry with me."

He storms out and slams the door.

Wondering what the hell just happened, I sit on the bench and finish unwrapping my hands. I think we just had our first real fight, even though I have no idea what it was about. I sit here for about ten minutes with my head against the wall. I hear the door open and look up to see Riley coming back in.

A calmer male walks over and pulls me up into his arms. "I'm sorry, I didn't mean to get so angry with you."

"I don't even know what I did."

"It's that male, he wants you. I want to kill him when he looks at you the way he does. I didn't mean to take it out on you."

"Tomorrow we're going out right?" I ask.

"Yes, but I won't be there so you need to be careful."

"Got it. Can we go to our room now?"

"Yes." He smiles.

****

For the past eight weeks Trevor and I have worked with the Twelfth. They've learned fast and are very good. I still go against Joe twice a week. Trevor hates it as much as Riley does. I've noticed the looks and holds that last entirely too long, but he's never pushed anything nor admitted his desires. Plus, he's helped sharpen my hand to hand.

Riley still meets with the council every day. He's talking about going to Europe and meeting formally with his father's council. I feel like we don't see each other at all. At least I still get to wake up in his arms.

Next week we'll start training with males from the Sixth. But on weekends Trevor and I will go to the Twelfth and check on their training techniques.

I'm in the gym waiting on Trevor. He wants to talk about something. He walks in and I can't read his face or his emotions. He starts wrapping his hands.

I put my hands on my hips and narrow my gaze. "You want to talk to me, but you're sealed up pretty tight."

"I told you, I'm broken."

I roll my eyes. "Alright?"

"I care about Danielle, but I'm not bonded to her. It's not the same as what you and Riley have."

"Does it have to be if you love her?"

"A male should want to bond to his female. I don't want to be bonded to her." He stands up.

"Oh….why?"

"I told you, I'm broken."

"Stop saying that. Do you love me?"

"Yes."

"You're not broken. I feel our bond. It's stronger than anything I've ever felt. You're a part of me. You could bond if you wanted to. Maybe you're just not ready to let yourself go."

"Enough talking." He catches me with a slap.

"Oh you really want me to kick your ass today, don't you?"

Afterwards, we both look pretty beaten up as usual. We sit on the bench. I turn to look at him.

Me: I know you sense things with me and Riley are

strained.
Trevor: Yes.
Me: Maybe we're both broken. He wants me to stay
*   here, and every time I go out he's distant.*
Trevor: He worries about you is all.
Me: He wants me with a young.
Trevor: And you don't?

"No I don't. I don't want to be the Queen. Sometimes, I just want to run away. I mostly feel numb. When I do this with you, Brandon, Derek, and Joe it's the only time I feel alive."

"You've been with Brandon a lot lately."

I laugh. "I'm sure he's tired of babysitting me as well. That poor male has done more shopping than any male should ever have to."

Just then Brandon comes in. "Hey, I'm ready for you to torture me tonight."

"See, you should feel sorry for him. He's always stuck with me."

"I do, brother, but better you than me." Trevor laughs.

"Yes, it's even more fun to go out with her after you've done this to her face." He takes my face in his hands and shakes his head. "I look like the abusive boyfriend."

"Okay, I'll go get ready. Sorry I'm running late." I run and get dressed.

Brandon loves Korn and I got tickets for the show tonight. It's not really his thing to go out into large crowds, but I want to do something for him. He sacrifices a lot of his time being stuck with me.

"Be careful tonight." Riley glowers at me.

"Yes, but in a huge crowd I don't think we need to worry much."

He pulls away from me.

"Is everything alright with you?"

"I feel I'm expected to be a certain way and follow tradition but you cannot be controlled."

"So now you wish to control me?" I narrow my gaze and step away from him.

"No, I want you to act like a queen."

"I don't want to fight with you right now. You've always known who I am and what I want, and none of that is it."

"I feel like I'm losing you." He sits down and pulls me onto his lap.

"I too feel the distance between us growing."

"We need to spend some time together." He kisses me.

I laugh on his lips as he runs his hand down between my legs. I struggle to get away from him. "Oh no. I have to go. I owe him one night that's just for him."

Riley growls. "You better be ready for me later."

Finally, I peel myself from that male's grasp and head up top.

"Where are we going?" Brandon asks.

Wrapping my arms around his waist, I look up and smile. "It's a surprise. I'm taking you this time."

Brandon holds me tightly and we're off to the concert. Riley made sure we had VIP privileges and backstage passes.

"What's this?" He looks around.

I take him by the hand and pull him towards the arena. He tugs me back and throws his hands up.

"I feel bad you're always stuck with me. You have become one of my best friends. I just wanted to do something for you and have some fun with my friend."

I hand him the tickets.

He looks them over and then back at me. "You did this for me?"

"Yes, now come on." I grab his hand and drag him along.

We dance, drink, and laugh. I feel like an old version of myself that I actually like. I feel free. The only thing missing is Danielle. I probably should have stopped four Jägers ago, but whatever.

As we head out I grab onto his arm with both of mine and lean into him.

He smiles down at me.

"Did you have fun?"

"Yeah, like I was free to be whatever. Thank you for this."

"No problem."

"And Sky, I don't think of you as just someone I have to protect. I think of you as my friend as well. I love being with you."

We come inside and I head to my room. It's two in the morning and Riley's still not back. Probably more council stuff. I have a great buzz going and nobody to have fun with. I pout then head to the shower.

Riley comes in at four. As I come out of our bedroom he's already set up at the table with papers and deep in thought. I never ask what he does with the council. I wish we could just leave it all, but I know he won't. He hates me fighting, and I hate him all wrapped up in that royal shit. We don't talk about anything anymore.

We're drifting apart.

"I would like to be with my mate this morning, is that going to be a problem?"

Looking over at me, then back to the pile of papers in front of him, and then back to me again—desire wins.

I walk to him and strip my clothes off along the way. When I get to him I'm bare.

He grabs me, shoves everything off of the table and takes me right on top of it. I look up at his magnificent body as he drives into me. He comes in a roar. He pulls out, strips off the rest of his clothes, then he lifts me up and we move to the bedroom. This time he slows down and takes his time.

Like this in his arms I finally feel connected to him again. "I've really missed you," I say.

"I have missed you as well."

"We're losing touch with each other and it makes me really sad."

"Sometimes I wonder if a king is meant to be bonded. All of this I do is important. I took this responsibility on, and I plan on changing things for the good of everyone. But when I care more for you, than I do my responsibilities, it makes things hard."

"I'll give you your space, especially since you put it that way. But when I want my mate, I'm going to take him." I run my hand down between his legs and grab him.

He growls and comes back over for a third round.

Chapter 18

Riley has finally made the trip to Europe to meet with the main council. They've been wanting to officially meet with him ever since they found out he and Michael were the lost sons of King Richard Magnusson. He had been putting it off, but they became very insistent that he go now.

We talked every day for the first week, but lately it's been weird. The conversations are all superficial and end very quickly. When I ask who he's been feeding from, he just dodges the subject. I feel sick to my stomach even thinking about it now. I hope they have females there that give their blood by wrist. I don't know why I'm even worried about it. When I gave him the opportunity to take a club girl he didn't.

I'll still demand the whole story when he comes back. Which is actually tonight. He flies into New York, then he'll have three jumps and be home. He has Chris and Chaz with him.

Michael is the one who told me that we can only materialize about a thousand miles out, and that we need to know exactly where we're going to end up. We need a picture in our mind of where we want to be, we just can't go 'poof' here I am.

Justin has us going out tonight. He tried to get me to stay home and wait for Riley to arrive. It took forever to convince him it would drive me crazy, or that I would drive him crazy if I sat here and waited for him.

We're taking out a basic warehouse manned with no more than five Moartea. Brandon and I are taking two guys from the Sixth Legion with us, Hunter and Brady. It should be cake, but you never know.

The raid starts like any other. The four of us go in met with five Moartea. Brandon and I hold back and let them go to work. Next thing I know, the shit starts to get out of control fast when over twenty Moartea pour into the room and take us down quickly.

I look over and see the two members of the Sixth have been killed. Then I see Brandon get taken down. He's been gutted and his throat has been cut.

"Brandon," I scream. I have four Moartea pining me down. I start screaming for Trevor hoping somehow he'll be able to sense me in trouble.

"We need to get her out of here fast," a Moartea yells.

"Get the van," another barks out.

I struggle and knock one of them off of me, when suddenly I'm hit hard in the back of the head. Everything goes black for a moment. I struggle to open my eyes. I know I need to get to Brandon now or he's dead.

They leave me lying here, probably thinking I'm out. I bolt to Brandon, tearing open my wrist. I drop onto my knees and slide across the floor to him. I put my wrist to his lips and ours eyes meet as he grips my arm and locks hands with me.

"Please be okay, I can't lose you. I love you Brandon. Tell Trevor and Riley that I love them." Tears run down my face.

They're on me fast. Brandon tries to hold on to me, but they yank me away from him and then my world goes black.

****

Trevor feels Sky in trouble. He suits up and goes running through the great room. He sees Riley coming in with Chris and Chaz.

"They've been hit," he yells as he bolts outside.

Riley's right on his ass. He gets to the warehouse and Riley appears behind him. Three warriors down and he can't sense Sky anywhere.

Brandon coughs up blood. "Took her, was ambush. White van, warded, license 3ZA65R," his voice trails off.

Trevor runs over to him and gives him his wrist. He puts his hand across his neck and tries to channel the power as Sky does. The wound seals. He puts his hand on Brandon's side and does the same thing, but it doesn't fully heal. He still needs more work back home.

Cash, Markus, Brian, Derek, and Justin appear.

"What happened?" Justin chokes out.

"It's not your fault, Brandon said they were set up," Trevor says.

"Why?" Cash asks.

"They took Sky, I can't sense her anywhere. They have wards around her."

"What?" Derek growls.

Trevor pauses for a moment and stares at Derek. He even feels him losing it inside, and that male is always calm.

Riley is furious and pacing. He begins to dig through desk drawers, throwing things around.

"We need to get him out of here," Trevor yells. "I have Riley. Justin, can you stay here and help me?"

"Yes." Justin turns to the others. "Get the other two back to their house. Let them know what happened."

Trevor feels their grief and anger at the loss of Sky. Not one male has moved. "Move your asses," Trevor growls.

"Can you feel her? I can't feel her anymore." Riley shakes his head.

"No." Trevor goes to the next office to start sifting through the papers. "There's nothing here. This whole place was set up."

"Grab the computer. We'll see what we can get off of it." Justin points. "Riley we have to go. They took her for a reason. She's still alive, we just need to find her."

Riley pounds his fists on one of the desks. "I'll rip them to pieces for this."

They come back to the bunker. As they come in, everyone is standing fully suited, ready for orders.

"Let me see what I can get off of here." Justin takes the computer into his office.

Trevor watches him take off and get to work. He closes his eyes and tries to sense her, but he's getting nothing. When he opens his eyes eager faces are looking back at him. He takes a deep breath and lays his head back and stares at the ceiling.

He's trying to calm himself. He knows he needs to stay strong because Riley is about to go off the deep end. One of them needs to keep their shit together if they're to get her back. Even though on the inside he feels lost without her.

"Anything?" Riley asks.

All he can do is shake his head. If he opens his mouth he may just sit here and scream.

Danielle comes out. "What's wrong?" Her eyes dart around the room. "Where's Sky?"

"Moartea took her during the raid," Trevor answers.

"What?" She chokes out and begins to shake.

Trevor gets up and holds her. *This is my flesh and blood that's gone. Why the fuck do I have to keep everyone else together?* At this moment he resents everyone in this house, including Danielle. He wants away from them all.

"I got two locations, let's go," Justin barks.

He's instantly relieved. He lets go of Danielle and is glad at the chance to take this shit out on something. He feels sorry for anything or anyone that gets in his path.

****

I wake up in pain, with more coming in waves. Blades are slicing into my flesh. I groan every time my flesh splits open. Soon after the cutting stops, the pounding starts. Some blows cause me to gasp. The pain is overwhelming, I lose the fight before I can even get my eyes open to see where I am.

The smell of death is everywhere. I'm slowly coming to again. Moartea is everywhere. I've never smelled them like this before. It's this putrefying smell of rotting flesh and wet earth. I must have been here for days. I remember going in and out of consciousness and seeing a few blurry images.

Listening to the dripping faucet is driving me mad. I've been beaten badly and lost so much blood that I'm no longer healing. I almost feel human again, except for the thirst. All I can see burned into the back of my mind is Brandon dying. Please let him have held on long enough for Trevor to get to him.

I look around but my eyes are still blurry. I'm strapped to a chair with my hands bound behind my back. The room looks like a shipping container. There are witches wards all over the walls and door. It means they won't be able to find me. I've read about witches, but witches working with Moartea? That's a new one. They practice with good magic and like to be in harmony with nature, not demons.

"She's coming to again," a demon with red hair says.

Another one, blond I think, comes up to me and slaps me across the face. I glare at him even though I can barely lift my head.

"Good job, it's her. The one with the angel's blood. He will be pleased." He giggles. "Call him."

This huge guy walks in. Dark hair, chiseled jawline, muscular build, black eyes, and overall he's beautiful. He grabs my chin in his hand and looks me over. He's not demon.

I narrow my gaze.

"No, I am not Moartea. I'm Cassius." He continues to look me over. "And you are the daughter of Lahash."

"I don't understand," I choke out. "Why do you have me?"

"In time, little girl, in time." He begins to pace.

"I have people that will find me, and you better pray I don't get loose from here."

He laughs. "You aren't going anywhere, and soon nobody will be looking for you either. Pictures," he turns and yells out. "Moartea are really good at torturing your kind."

He holds up pictures to my face and begins flipping through them. They are of vampires beaten and torn up. I turn away.

"Get her head and hold her eyes open," Cassius yells out.

I struggle but I'm too weak to fight it. He continues to flip through the pictures. The last one is me.

I gasp, "I look dead."

"Yes. Looks good doesn't it? The King will find these on his next raid. So you see, little one, there will be no one looking for you." He saunters out and closes the door.

Oh God. They will stop looking for me. But my brother will have to know I'm still alive. He will feel me and keep looking. I hope. I don't have any energy left. My head drops and I'm in darkness again.

****

It's been two weeks since Sky was taken. They've been through nineteen Moartea safe houses with no sign of her. Trevor knows he has to keep going. He can't bear to stop; stopping would mean she's dead.

Riley keeps going as well, but he's beginning to remind him of the old Riley. Lethal, dangerous, and ruthless. He kills Moartea and humans alike. It's a fucking mess.

"Alright, Justin has just given us another location," Derek says.

Joe, Matt, and Daniel have come along again tonight. Seems like everyone loves his sister. Trevor knows exactly why Joe is here, and he prays Riley hasn't figured it out.

They materialize in front of the building. There's five Moartea and two human recruits.

"Riley, we need to interrogate the humans," Trevor growls.

They get in and kill all the Moartea. It's useless to even bother to interrogate them. The demons will leave the host body once it's ended, and they don't feel shit.

They have the two humans separated. Derek and Joe take one to an office, Daniel and Matt take the other one. After a lot of bloodshed and laughing from the humans they were ended.

Trevor can see Derek and Joe looking through some papers. Joe begins to step away from them shaking his head and holding his chest. Derek drops his head and grabs at his chest as tears well up in his eyes. Then Derek makes eye contact with him.

He runs to the office. "What did you find?"

"You shouldn't look. Just know she's gone," Derek barely chokes out.

"What are you talking about? Show me what you've found," Trevor demands.

"No, Joe get him back," Derek yells.

Joe tackles him and holds him back, not allowing him to see what they're looking at.

Riley's in the doorway. "What have you found?" he growls.

"Please don't ask me for this, just know she's gone." Derek holds the paper in his hand.

Riley pushes past him and Joe and goes nose to nose with Derek. "You will show me what you've found or I'll pry it from your cold dead hands," his growl deepens.

Derek hands him the paper.

Trevor watches Riley's face. His eyes go black, and he's completely void of any emotion. He turns and is gone.

"Please Derek, I have to know what happened to my sister."

"Let him go." Derek shakes his head.

Trevor picks up the paper Riley dropped on the desk, but it's not paper, it's a photograph. It's Sky, cut open, beaten, drained, and lifeless. He collapses to his knees, shaking his head, and holding his chest.

"No, no she can't be dead. I don't believe it," Trevor chokes out. He feels eyes on him.

Derek goes out to the others.

Trevor gets up. *I need some fucking air.* Anger, panic, and abandonment are creeping in on him. As he steps outside, Joe is right on his ass.

Trevor turns to him. "What the fuck do you want from me?" he barks.

"Is she dead?" Joe narrows his gaze.

"You saw what I saw, why the fuck are you asking me that?" He gets in Joe's face.

"When my twin was killed, I knew the moment he was dead. Half my soul was ripped from my body. I became empty. Nobody had to tell me or show me of his death, I knew. Deep down, do you still feel like she is a part of you? Forget what you saw, and just tell me what you feel."

"I don't know what I feel. I feel fucking numb." He closes his eyes and concentrates on Sky. "She is still with me. I still feel her….here." Trevor puts his hand over his heart.

Joe walks away from him while he starts talking. "Then she's alive, and we will keep looking until you tell me different."

Trevor follows him and begins to gather whatever intel he can find. The picture could have been faked to get them to stop looking for her, and why would they still have her warded from them if she was dead? Then they could at least retrieve her body, but she's completely off the grid.

Witches, they will need to go after the witches, and they'll pay for their alliance with the Moartea. He will do whatever it takes. Even if that means killing them all until he has Sky by his side again.

****

"Ah, perfect timing," Cassius says.

These visits of his have been daily. Not that I have any real sense of time anymore, or how long I've been here. I know I'm dying; I feel it creeping in on me. It's all I can do to hold on.

All I want to do is see my brother again and be in his arms. I long to see Brandon's face. Hoping he lives, and seeing every possible scenario of how he could have survived until I can see him again, is how I fill my days, hours, minutes, seconds, whatever.

All there is around me is darkness with periods of dim light when they come in.

"Why do you have me? Just let me go," a graveled sounding voice I don't recognize comes out of me.

"Alas, I can't. You are my key," Cassius says.

"Key to what?" I cough.

"We are going to use your blood in a spell to open up the gates of Heaven."

"We?"

He steps up to me. "The Fallen have been searching for millennia to find the keys. There are many keys, but you are the only one I know of." He smiles down at me. "There is also more for you to see."

"Please,"—I shake my head and start to cry—"I don't want to see anymore. I can't."

Cassius places his finger on my forehead. My head is flooded with images of Riley taking females then snapping their necks, to ripping out human male's throats, and then he uses some kind of drug to go numb.

The faces that stare back at me in the visions are dangerous and pure evil. His black eyes pierce my soul making me ill and hollow inside. I no longer feel Riley. He's gone, and where he was is an emptiness and sorrow that's consuming me.

"Please stop," I whisper.

"I want you to know of the mate you've chosen. He is not worthy of you," he sneers.

"Ha. Because you care anything about me. Look at me,"— I try to look up and my head flops to my shoulder—"I'm dying."

He studies me for a moment and then leaves.

A little while later a human male is brought in by two Moartea. They cut his wrist as he struggles against them. His eyes are wide when he sees my fangs elongate. As his wrist is brought to my mouth, I bite into him and he screams. His screams become muffled through the hand of one of his captors.

The salty metallic taste of his blood makes me gag, but I need to feed. I wish this could give me enough strength to get out of here, but at this point, this human's blood barely gives me the strength I need to live.

I seal him up when I feel him fading. I've never fed from a human before. His blood is strange.

The man is stabbed in front of me, and then they leave.

"There is a lot of things I know about you my little Nephilim. I know you are about to be thrown from your destiny due to greed and unwarranted prejudice. You are going to give your heart to another, and you have found your mate making the others mean absolutely nothing. Yet, none of that matters since you will be bleed dry for the good of the Fallen."

"I don't want to hear your nonsense." I close my eyes and think about my brother and Brandon again.

"The race you fight for has lost their way, and the corruption of evil runs deep. Soon, very soon, child, all this will be over and you can return home." Cassius runs his hand through my hair before he leaves.

****

Trevor and Joe are headed out to find some witches. The wards that were put up belong to a particularly powerful coven. Trevor found out the hard way that witches can ward their houses against vampires. Entering a warded home gets you sunlight burns.

It would have been much easier for the witches if he could have just gone through their homes while they were gone, but looks like he's going to have to meet them head on. He sees now where all the myths have come into play about a vampire having to be invited into a home. That would only work for a witches' home.

When they went after the last coven, he waited until he could get a witch on her way in. Luckily for them, she knew which coven was responsible for the wards. Took a little bit to get it out of her, but she'll heal.

He gathers up the information he has so far. He knows where the coven is and plans on hitting them just after sunset. He's going to see if Brandon wants to come along with them. That male has been a mess without his sister. He hadn't realized that Brandon bonded to Sky, and he's sure his sister has no idea. Shit, she has two males bonded to her and he can't even bond to the one female he has in front of him.

"Trevor, are you even listening to me?" Danielle calls out.

Crap. Was she talking to me? He looks up. "What?"

"You need to stop all of this. It isn't healthy. We need to mourn and move on."

"Are you fucking kidding me right now?" He steps away from the table and walks closer to her. "I'm getting closer to finding her."

"I miss you, and I can't stand watching you work towards a never ending goal. Sky is dead, and you need to accept that." She crosses her arms over her chest.

He glares at her. "My sister is alive and I will find her."

"I can't watch this any longer. It hurts too much, and you act like I'm not even here."

He gets right in her face. "Sky is the only thing that matters to me in this entire fucking world. Without her, I'm dead already."

She shakes her head. "Do you care about me at all? Would you even care if I moved out of your room?"

"I would prefer you move out before I get back in the morning," he says coldly.

This was never going to work between them. His sister needs him and that's where his loyalties will always lie. He gathers up the papers and heads to Brandon's room. He's so angry at that female for giving up on Sky. She's strong, and she's waiting for him to find her, he knows it.

He knocks on Brandon's door.

"Come in," Brandon calls out.

Damn, he looks bad. "Hey I need your help. I have a lead on the coven that put up the wards."

Brandon gets up. "Give me a minute to suit up. I'll meet you up top."

"Alright." Trevor heads out. He gets to the stairs when Justin pops out of his office. "Don't want to hear it Justin," Trevor glares.

"Found anything new out?"

"Yep, headed out to deal with it right now." He runs up the stairs.

They have all tried to talk him into giving up. But he can't until he sees her body. Then he will follow his sister into the darkness. Until that time, he will search the ends of the Earth for her. He comes out and is met with Joe sitting on a rock smoking.

"There you are. I was about to come down and find you," Joe says as he snuffs out his cigarette.

"Got tied up. Brandon's coming with us."

"How's he doing? Any better."

"Nope."

Brandon comes out.

"Damn brother, you look like death," Joe blurts out.

Trevor has realized subtleness is not Joe's strong suit.

"I'm fine. We doing this or what?" Brandon barks.

"Yeah. We meet here, this is the location of the coven."

"Let's go," Joe says.

They appear behind the shed on the coven's property. Trevor walks up the driveway and motions them to follow. As they get near the house he picks up a newspaper near the door.

"Wait around the corner there. Three of us showing up after sunset will definitely tip them off," Trevor says. He walks up the steps and knocks on the door. A young female answers, she can't be more than fifteen or so.

"Hi." She smiles at him.

He takes a deep breath and smiles. "Hi. Is your mom around?"

"Yeah, hold on." She turns around. "Mama," she calls out.

"I picked this up for you." Trevor holds out the newspaper. He can hear her mother coming and he's not sure if this is going to work. The girl opens up the screen door. As Trevor holds the paper he makes her reach for it.

"Treeni, no," the woman calls out.

Too late. Trevor grabs her arm and pulls her outside. He has her around the throat as the woman grabs a shotgun.

"I could snap her neck before you ever got that shot off. You think you're a good enough shot to miss her?" Trevor growls.

"Let her go, vampire," she yells.

He bares his fangs and goes to her neck, never breaking eye contact with the woman. "You know what I am, so you know I can end her. Maybe I'll turn her instead."

"Please don't hurt her, I'll do anything." She lowers the gun.

"Your coven placed wards for Moartea. I want to know where the wards were placed."

Brandon steps out and holds up the pictures of the wards.

"Please, we can't say anything," she shakes her head.

"Then we start with this one and work our way through your entire coven. Up to you. Give me the locations." Trevor pierces the girl's neck.

She screams and tries to struggle more.

"Fine. Please don't hurt her. I have a map." The woman walks away. She comes back with a pile of papers. "Let her go and I will give these to you."

"That's not the way this is going to go down. You will step outside and hand those papers to my friend here. You have my word no harm will come to you and yours as long as my sister lives."

"Your sister?"

"You will give us the information now," Trevor glares.

She sighs and steps outside slowly. She hands everything to Joe.

Joe takes them from her. "Looks good. Remote locations. They planned on keeping tabs on this little experiment."

"We didn't want to work with them, but we weren't given a choice. We are working on a way to break the wards and get back our missing member." She holds her hands out. "Now please, I did what you asked of me. Please let my daughter go."

"You better pray my sister lives." Trevor lets her go.

They appear back outside the bunker.

"Seems we have six new targets," Joe says.

"You really think she could be there?" Brandon asks.

"Brother, if she was dead, why would they still be masking her under wards?" He sees hope in Brandon's eyes once again. He prays this is the answer or he isn't the only one that's going to head into the darkness to find her.

****

Michael comes in. He finally caught up with Riley again and has had the crap beaten out of him to prove it. They found out three weeks ago Sky was killed, and his brother has completely gone over the edge to a very dark place. Drugs and mass killings--it's worse than it's ever been.

"Damn. You must have found him." Derek shakes his head as he looks Michael over.

"Yep, let's just say he didn't want to talk about coming back."

Justin comes out of the office. "I can't keep the council in the dark much longer."

"I don't recognize him any longer, and it's harder to track him. Riley's gone and the monster left in his shell is dangerous for us all." Michael hangs his head.

"What do you want us to do?" Derek asks.

"Nothing. I'll do what needs done where my brother's concerned. Where's Trevor?"

"In his room I think," Justin answers.

Michael knows Trevor, Joe, and Brandon are still looking for Sky. He wants to know what they've found so far. He comes to Trevor's room and knocks.

Trevor answers, "Yeah?"

"Can we talk?"

"Come in. I don't want to hear any shit about how she's dead and I need to move on. So if that's why you're here, you can turn right back around. I'll move on when I have her body, not before."

Michael throw his hands up. "If you feel she lives, then she lives. What have you found so far?"

"We found a series of six underground bunkers. They're all warded. We hit four covens and finally found a witch that knew about it. She gave us these maps. We start here tonight."

"I'm coming with you," Michael says.

All four of them head out to start checking the bunkers one by one. They make it through four of the bunkers. All of them empty, like they were set up but not in use yet. Trevor destroys each one, making sure it could never be used. Dawn is coming.

"We will check the remaining two tomorrow," Trevor says.

They make plans to meet up again tomorrow then head out.

Chapter 19

There's talking, but can't hold my head up to see who it is. I'm too weak and beginning to fade again. My hair is brushed behind my ears, and I feel soft hands caressing my face. I feel love? I think I'm starting to lose it.

"Get her blood, if she's dead I can't use her."

It's Cassius. There's struggling, and then I hear someone scream. The smell of blood fills my lungs and my fangs elongate in anticipation. I can almost feel the blood already on my tongue. Somebody grabs a handful of my hair and yanks my head up.

"Careful with her, you idiot," Cassius hisses.

There's an arm at my lips, human. I bite into him and he screams again. I groan as I take in as much as I can. When I open my eyes, I realize it's a young teen and I've drained him dry. He crumples to the floor at my feet. I just killed a human boy. I shake my head as tears begin to fall. I bite my bottom lip as it begins to quiver.

Cassius kicks him aside. "Get this out of here."

"You're a monster," I scream.

"Ah, you're finally back with us. Good." He smiles.

"Untie me and I will show you how good I feel," I spit out at him.

He comes close to me and looks into my eyes. "You have your mother's eyes. You are very beautiful." He runs his hand across my cheek. "You remind me so much of her."

I turn my head quickly and bite into him.

He yanks his hand free and slaps me so hard it knocks me over. His blood is electric. I feel it making me stronger.

"You're not evil, you're an angel." I glare up at him.

"I'm a Fallen actually. I no longer feel our father's grace. I can no longer feel anything at all in this realm." He shrugs and looks at me.

Finally, a new position. I'm feeling stronger. When I lived a human life, I never believed in anything. Vampires, God, witches, demons, and angels. Now I live this shit, and look where it's gotten me. All for the love of a male that no longer cares about me.

"How can you work with Moartea?" I say in disgust.

"Serves my purpose." He walks off.

My hands have come loose, but I lie here just in case somebody comes in. I have no idea what time of day it is. Doesn't do much good to escape and end up out in the sun.

What seems like an hour has gone by, and nobody has come to check on me. I can't stand it any longer. I untie my legs and stand up. Bad idea—next thing I know I'm flat on my ass. *Damn it.* How long have I been strapped to that chair? I feel Cassius' blood slowly making me stronger.

I stretch and rub my legs. I try standing again, I'm a little wobbly but better. I go to the door and slowly open it. I don't see anyone, just a long hallway. I step out and almost puke at the smell of rotting flesh. I fall against the wall trying to relax and get my bearings. Again with the leaky faucet. I look around and then down next to me.

Fuck. I'm the leaky faucet.

As I start down the corridor, I come to a weapons room two doors up. I grab a sword and keep moving, though at this point the sword's more of a walking stick. I grimace. *This sucks.* I feel so weak, and I'm in a house full of Moartea. At least I can go out fighting instead of slowly dying tied to a chair.

Where the hell is everybody?

As I round the corner, it opens up into a large room and something's happening. Squinting my eyes, I try to focus. There's a warrior and at least twenty Moartea. I run into the room and kill as many as I can get through before my body has had enough. I collapse.

A Moartea is dragging me back to the corridor by my hair. I hear a loud roar and ash falls down around me. Then my body is lifted from the ground as I'm gathered up in someone's arms. Everything goes black again.

****

Joe can't believe Sky is actually in his arms and alive. He knew her brother would know if she was still alive. As he comes out of the bunker dawn is fast approaching. He can feel the burn of the sun on his skin. He puts his jacket over Sky, and takes the pain in and tries to relax. He materializes to his home in the city.

He lays her on his bed, scores his wrist, and puts it to her lips. She's so pale and weak. There are wounds all over her, but they're already starting to heal. When she finishes, he seals himself up.

Blood and ash cover her.

Pulling her clothes off, he leaves her underwear and bra on. He cringes when he sees the wounds covering her entire body. He strips down to his boxers, then picks her up and takes her into the shower. She can barely stand as she leans against him. He holds her up with one arm and washes her with the other. He gets her rinsed off, then grabs a towel.

Holding the towel up, he pulls off her bra and underwear, trying to hide her as much as possible. He lays her in bed and covers her up. He changes into shorts and grabs his phone.

> Joe: I found her, she's alive, took her to my place
> in city. Turning off phone, she's healing and
> needs sleep. Be well brother, your sister lives.

He turns his phone off and hears her shivering. He gets into bed and pulls her into his arms. She curls herself into him. He knows this will be the only time they can ever be like this. As soon as she wakes she will want her mate. He's exhausted and sleeps takes him quickly.

Fangs sink into his neck, he turns to give her more room. He holds her to him as she takes him in. Her bare breasts are pressed against his chest and he wants to take her right here, right now. But she belongs to the King.

She seals him up, nuzzles back into him and falls back asleep. All he can do is sigh and go back to sleep.

He wakes hours later to a strong feeling he's being watched. He feels soft female fingers run across his cheek then his lips. He opens his eyes and is met with her beautiful blue eyes.

"How do you feel?" he asks.

"Better….safe. You came for me?" she asks.

"Yes. I didn't believe you were dead. I couldn't."

****

I was in hell and now I'm in Joe's arms, because he fought to get to me back, he never gave up on me. Then he took care of me. I'm also completely bare, which is curious.

"Trevor?"

"We kept looking for you after the others refused to believe you were still alive. Trevor, Michael, Brandon, and I were hitting new targets we got intel on. We got through four of them this morning, but dawn was coming. They went back home, but I had to keep going. I felt I had to get to you. Then there you were." He shakes his head.

"Brandon's okay?"

"Yeah."

I take a deep breath. I see love in Joe's eyes. That's why he kept looking for me. I can still feel Trevor apart of me, but I no longer feel Riley. He gave up on me. My heart has nothing left in it.

"Why did you keep looking for me?"

He breaks eye contact. "Because I love you, I had to get you back."

Getting up on my elbow, I look down at him. "Thank you for coming for me, for never giving up on me."

As he turns and looks back into my eyes, I lean forward and press my lips to his. His kiss is soft, and filled with so much love.

I pull away and lie back down on the pillow next to him. "How long was I gone?"

"Five weeks." He rubs his face.

Nothing. I feel, nothing. Losing my connection to Riley has left me hollow inside. The only thing I know without a doubt is that I want my brother, but that's it. I have no other feelings. Except right now when I kissed Joe, it made me feel good, alive, and loved.

"You won't kiss me again will you?"

He gets up and hovers over me. "Not unless you ask me to," he says as his gaze burns into mine.

Taking his face in my hands, I pull him towards me and he kisses me deeply. I feel his desire to have me.

He breaks contact and rests his forehead on my chest, letting out a heavy sigh. "I should get up."

"I want you to stay."

"If I do, I won't be able to stop this."

"I want you," I whisper to him.

He pulls up, brow lowered, and looks at me.

I smile and run my hands down his back.

He closes his eyes and takes a deep breath. "I have wanted you for months."

"I need to feel all of you."

He pulls his shorts off. "Are you sure about this?" He says still holding himself back.

Pulling him to me and kissing him deeply is my answer. I have so much of his blood in me, and I know that it's part of the driving force to have all of him. But I also feel his love for me, and that helps fill this void I have inside that's threatening to consume me.

Joe slowly moves himself into me. I run my hands down his back as he comes all the way in. He's back on my lips as we start to make love. Afterwards, we just lie in each other's arms.

He takes a deep breath and sighs.

"What's wrong?"

"I know when you leave here, it will be as if none of this happened. I knew it was impossible as I felt myself falling in love with you months ago."

"I don't know what to say, or what's going to happen. I just know being with you makes me feel loved, and I desperately need my brother."

"Your brother grounds you. When you're not close you'll feel lost and like part of you is missing. It's the bond of twins."

"Yeah, how do you know that?"

"Moartea killed my twin five years ago," he touches my face. "Being with you before all of this, was the first time I have felt anything in a long time."

I turn over and stare at the ceiling. "I know I'm going to end up hurting you." I shake my head.

He pulls me back to him. "This is enough. I wouldn't change it for anything. Your heart belongs to another, but always remember that I love you, and you don't owe me anything"

"I owe you my life."

"No, I owe you mine." He smiles and kisses me again. He comes back on top of me, and when he begins to move inside of me again, everything else melds away.

We fall asleep in each other's arms.

I wake up just before five in the evening. He's looking at me smiling, but I feel and see the sadness behind his eyes.

"I don't suppose you have any female's clothes here?"

He grimaces. "Ah, actually I do." He gets up and sifts through a drawer. He comes up with black pants and a tank top.

I get up and dressed as he watches me. "My brother will be here soon. You should get dressed." I throw him his shorts.

"Afraid he'll know we were together?"

"I won't have to tell him, he'll know."

Joe stares at me.

"Twin thing remember? Besides, he will sense us all over each other." I sit on the edge of the bed and put my shoes on.

He rubs his face. "Shit. This isn't going to go well." He gets up and dressed.

"Could you talk to your twin in your head?" I ask.

He smiles. "Yeah. It's hard to live with the silence now. He used to drive me crazy--he never shut up."

He looks so sad. I couldn't imagine ever losing Trevor. I'm not sure how he did without me either. We go into his living room.

"Back to reality."

I go to him and hug him. "My heart no longer belongs to me to give away. But I've had feelings for you for a while."

He smiles and kisses me softly.

I pull away and turn around. I'm looking into my brother's eyes and tears begin to fall down my face. I run into his arms. He wraps me up in his arms tightly. I can't breathe, but I don't care. Now I'm starting to feel like myself again.

Trevor: God, I've missed you. Never do that to me again.
Me: I missed you terribly.

He pulls back slightly to grab my face in his hands and look me over.

Trevor: Are you okay, really?
Me: They almost killed me, but he saved me.
Trevor: I'm so sorry I didn't keep going.

He holds me tightly again. "I love you so much Sky. I can't ever be without you."

"I feel the same way."

He tucks me under his arm. "Thank you for everything you did. I owe you my life, brother. I need to get her home. Will you come with us?"

Joe looks into my eyes. "I can't do that. I need to get back to my life here."

"Be well."

Trevor brings us back home. "You laid with him?"

"I did."

"And your mate?"

"My mate gave up on me and left me to rot while he does drugs, has others, and kills. I can no longer sense Riley. I've lost him."

"How do you know all that? Did Joe tell you?"

"No, the angel that had me did." I let everything that happened to me flood my mind, along with the images of Riley. I feel Trevor's whole body tense up.

He growls as he pulls away and looks down at me.

"The Fallen Angel Cassius talked to me of how he wanted to use my blood to open the gates of Heaven. He wants to start a war. He's the one that told me, or rather showed me of Riley."

"Your mate saw a photo of what he believed to be you dead. He spent two weeks looking for you nonstop. But when he saw the photo...."--he shakes his head--"I believe he died in that moment, Sky. What's left is no longer Riley. He's lost to us all right now. He tore Michael up the last time he caught up to him. None of us can sense him anymore."

"But you never gave up, did you?" I look up at him. "Neither did Joe. But my mate found it so easy to believe what he saw and give up on me."

"I thought you were dead. I was spiraling into blackness when Joe came to me and told me of his twin. He said I'd know. I told him I still felt you, and in that moment I saw in his eyes he knew you were still alive, and together we kept searching."

"We were set up. They had weeks where only a few would be seen, but the whole time they were hiding and waiting for us to come in. Waiting for me. The two we lost are on my head," I barely choke out. I will carry Hunter and Brady's death with me for the rest of my life, along with the human boy I killed.

Trevor wipes my tears. "Brandon said you fought to save him. He feels he let you down. He was in his room when I came for you. He mourns you harder than anyone else. I tried to tell him that I felt you were still alive, but it didn't help. I think the only reason he helped me was because he couldn't bear to be here. He needs to see you."

I nod, and take a deep breath. "I'm ready to go home." I hug him one more time. "Never leave me. Being away from you was harder than anything else I endured."

"I told you, sister, never. You're all that matters to me. I would have torn apart the world searching for you." He opens the door and I run downstairs.

Danielle sees me first and runs to meet me. We hug and cry some, then laugh. "Don't ever do that to me again," she cries.

"I promise." I look over her shoulder and smile at the relieved faces around me.

I pull away. "Okay, who's first? Because you're all getting hugs."

"Me," a deep voice behind me says.

I whip around. "Justin." I wrap my arms around him. "I've missed you. It's good to be home."

"It's good to have you back where you belong." He hugs me tightly. "Seems we may be a little lost without you now."

Derek is coming down the hall from his room. He walks up to me and grabs my face. "I thought I sensed you home." He runs his thumbs across my cheeks. Then he pulls me into him tightly. "Damn, I've missed you, female. I'm so glad you're back."

My hands run up his back and I hold him to me tightly. It feels so good to be in his arms, I feel warmth and love fill my heart. "I missed you too."

"I'm not sure I'm ever going to let you out of my sight again."

"Good, because I can't wait to spar with you."

He laughs. "You're so crazy."

"Meh, maybe a little." I feel so calm in his arms. I don't want to let him go. I look up at him and smile, then I hug him to me again.

"Quit hogging her," Cash says.

There were hugs and tears all around. This is my family now. I belong here, and so does Riley. I look at Trevor and let him know I'm headed to Brandon. I head down the hallway to Brandon's room.

I try the door and it's unlocked. I step inside and close it behind me. He's sitting on the couch staring off.

I smile. "It's so good to finally see you. I was so worried about you."

"Sky?" he chokes out.

"You fought hard, and you were so brave. You gave me strength while I was being held, because I had to get free. I had to see you were okay. I prayed every day that you lived." I slowly walk towards him. He's sunk in and weak. Tears fill my eyes.

"Are you real?" he whispers.

I smile and kneel down in front of him. I run my hands into his.

Brandon looks down at our hands and grips them, then looks back at me. "He found you?"

"Yes, he did."

He comes down on the floor, grabs me up in his arms, and holds me tightly. "I'm sorry I let them take you. I tried to get to you," he says shaking his head.

"You did better than anyone else could have. It couldn't have been stopped. I'm so glad you're alright. But I need you to be strong right now, I need your help."

"I'll do whatever you ask. My life is yours."

"I love you Brandon."

That gets me squeezed so hard I can't breathe.

He pulls back slightly and comes to my ear. "And I love you."

I stand up and hold my hand out. "I need you to do something else for me first." I pull him down with me on the couch and lay my arm across his lap. "Feed."

He holds my arm and looks at it.

"It's the only thing that can help ease this pain I feel in my heart at seeing what you've done to yourself worrying about me."

Shaking his head, he doesn't move.

I climb onto his lap and take his face in my hands. "Please do this for me."

Pulling my hair aside, I bare my neck to him. One hand comes up my back, the other is on my thigh as he bites into me. I lay my hands on his chest and I can feel his heart racing.

He takes a lot from me. He seals me up then lays his head back and closes his eyes. I feel him getting stronger. I put my arms around him and lay my head on his shoulder.

Arms make their way around me and he holds me close to him.

It would have broken my heart if I had lost him. I sit up and look into his eyes. "I don't know how I would have handled it if I lost you." I take a deep breath. "Right now I need to go find Michael. Will you suit up and come with me to bring Riley home?"

"Yes." He runs his hand through my hair and down my back.

I get up and pull him up.

He leans in and kisses my lips softly as he brushes my cheek with his thumb. Then he turns and goes into his bedroom.

Confused, I pause for a moment and put my fingers to my lips. I shake my head and walk out, I don't have time to process all of that there right now. I head off to find Michael. I'm two doors away when he opens his door. I come and stand in front of him.

"I sensed you, but I didn't believe it was really you. You're home," he trails off.

"I am, and I need your help to find my mate. I can't sense him any longer."

Michael grabs me up in his arms. "There's things you need to know."

I'm going to end up with bruised ribs I just know it. "I already know everything, Michael." I bet I know even more than he does at this point, thanks to Cassius' home movies.

Michael pulls back and drops his brow. "Trevor told you?"

"No, an angel showed me of Riley." I look at the floor and swallow back the lump in my throat. I need to be strong right now.

His eyes are huge, just like Trevor's reaction. I wonder if it's that an angel told me of Riley's horror show, or that I know exactly what he's been doing in my absence.

"Told you what exactly?" His gaze narrows.

"He had the ability to show me." I take a deep breath. "Riley's lost and we need to get him back. I understand this has been your job for centuries, but you have me now. Together we will bring him home."

"He's not as you remember him."

I see worry across Michael's face.

"I know it's worse than it's ever been, and I know this,"-- I touch his face--"was done by him. He's dangerous right now, and he's angry with me for leaving him. It's me he curses as he kills them."

"It wasn't you're fault."

"It doesn't matter. All that matters to Riley is that I left him. He didn't want me fighting and I pushed him. The only reason he still lives is because of how angry he is with me." I take a deep breath. "Now suit up and let's bring him home."

"They will demand to come." He starts to pace.

"They will, but that's not the way it's going to happen. Riley's gone, so they will do as I command them. I'm still Queen, am I not?"

He smiles.

I go to my room and look around. There's papers everywhere, the dining table is turned over, the chairs are all over the room, and there's a bed made up on the sofa.

Me: Can you come to my room. I need to talk to you.
Trevor: On my way to you now.

I suit up, pick up the furniture, and wait for Trevor.

Trevor comes in. "What's going on?"

"There is a few things I want to ask you about."

"Alright." He pushes the blankets aside and sits down on the sofa.

"Cassius said some things to me when I was being held, and along with what I've read in the texts and prophecies I have a few questions I'd like answered."

"Like what?"

"Vampires were created to protect humans. I believe they do the opposite of that now. Riley pretty much shits all over that and he's the King."

"From what I understand, the council claimed humans were responsible for the death of the Royal Family. It was then they turned their back on the teachings."

I sit down in the chair and take a deep breath.

"What are you thinking?"

"I guess I'm wondering how humans were able to break into a heavily guarded castle and murder the entire Royal Family and their servants. There would have had to have been thousands, right?"

"One would think." Trevor narrows his gaze as he sits forward.

"I never learned of such a battle in school. The humans would have lost hundreds, maybe thousands of soldiers."

He lets out a breath and sits back.

"How many humans do you think you could take on at once?"

He begins shaking his head.

"You see it now too don't you?" I stand. "If it was other vampires would they try to cover that up with a false story?"

"This could be a dangerous trail to follow."

"I'm only seeking answers. It's written that the Royal Family's guard consisted of forty of the largest, strongest, and most skilled warriors. Maybe they weren't as good as everyone thought."

Trevor stands. "The Royal Guard was sent on a special mission by the King--at the request of his council."

"As in 'the' council?"

Trevor nods.

"Damn." I shake my head.

"This goes no further than this room, do you understand me?"

"Yeah. But I will no longer sit by and allow humans to fall at the hands of Moartea or vampire. Even if that means I have to do it on my own."

"You're never alone, sister."

I smile. "I want you to stay here while I go after Riley. This is my mess and I will be the one to clean it up."

He shakes his head.

I head out to the great room.

"I know you've all seen Michael's latest run in with Riley. I can tell you he's worse than he has ever been, and he's dangerous. I'm going to bring him home. I'm taking Brandon and Michael with me."

"Sky, I don't think...." Justin starts in.

I put my hand up to stop him. "Derek, Cash, Markus, suit up. You're coming with us."

All three nod.

"I want you close but out of sight. You're only there to protect each other, not me. I'll be the target of his anger and rage. I can handle him. No matter what he does to me, all five of you will stay out of it. That's an order, if I haven't made myself clear enough. This is between me and Riley. Suit up. We're out in five."

The three of them head back to their rooms.

"I'm not sure this is the best thing for you right now," Justin says.

"You're probably right, but we need him back. You can't tell me the council hasn't been after you about him."

He nods.

"That's what I thought. I know he's getting worse. I've seen it. He's cut off and I can't feel him, can you?"

"No, not for a couple of weeks." Justin rubs his face.

"Only Michael can sense him now and it's getting weaker. I feel his worry for Riley." I sigh. "I fear if we can't get him back soon, he will be lost forever."

Chapter 20

All five warriors are standing in front of me, waiting for me to give them orders. Somehow I have ended up right smack in the role I've been fighting so hard to stay away from, and for that….Riley's going to pay. "Let's go."

Trevor: I should go.
Me: You would kill him as soon as he touches me.
Trevor: I'm going.

I whip around. "No you're not. I will be fine."

Me: He won't kill me, but he's angry with me and
*   not thinking clearly.*

Trevor glares as he watches me leave.

Trevor: Please be careful tonight.
Me: I love you brother.
Trevor: And I you. Know that everything I do is to
*   protect you. I won't lose you again.*

Trevor heads into the hallway, I assume to his room. We come out and stand in a circle. I go to Michael.

"Not too close, alright?" I wrap my arms around his waist. "And I'm coming with you so you can't materialize out if it's too bad. No more hiding."

He sighs then wraps his arms around me. He closes his eyes and then we're standing on the edge of a shipping yard in a bad part of town. The rest appear around us.

"Where is he?" I ask.

Michael points to a bar about a block up. "Alley."

I turn to Michael and talk so only he can hear me. "Stay with Brandon. No matter what, nobody is to help me. He above everyone will want to protect me. The three of you stay out of sight."

I turn to walk away and Michael grabs my arm.

"He has killed." No emotion on his face.

"I told you I already know."

"No Sky, now, he has killed there." He points to the alley.

"Oh." I slump forward. "I'll be fine."

I walk away from them. *Hopefully I'll be fine, because the black soulless eyes I saw stare back at me in those visions were scary, and I didn't see any part of the Riley I knew behind them. Thoughts like that are why my brother couldn't be here.*

Trevor: Yeah, because I was going to let you tell me
what to do.

I turn around and look up. He's on the shipping yard building looking down on us. I was so preoccupied I didn't feel him here.

Me: Damn you. You will stay out of this.
Trevor: Till he lays a hand on you.
Me: You will stay out of this or I'll never forgive you.
Trevor: We shall see sister.

I look at Derek, then back up. He nods and appears next to Trevor.

Trevor: Ha. You think he could stop me?

I sigh and walk towards the alley. As I get closer, I smell death and blood. It's not Moartea, it's human blood. I come to the mouth of the alley and I'm able to see two males and one female torn up. I cover my mouth and try to stuff the nausea down.

A figure disappear around the side of the building. I run after it. As I round the corner I'm slammed up against the wall. He sinks his fangs deep into my neck.

It's Riley, but somehow not. I shove him away as hard as I can. He stumbles backwards, then I'm met with a blade at my heart. Those black soulless eyes are staring back at me and he's growling.

Holy shit. "Love, please put the sword down. You don't want to hurt anybody here."

Five swords are being drawn around us. Brandon and Trevor are right behind Riley, with Derek to his left closest to me. Riley's shaking his head as he stares at me.

Trevor: Sky!

I look over at Trevor.

*Me: You will stand there and do nothing. This is
    between me and my mate.*

I look back at Riley. Now I'm absolutely sure I do not like him with facial hair. It covers up his handsome face, and right now he looks like some mountain man or homeless person. I try to focus back on the task at hand.

"It's you and me against the world, remember?"

He licks the blood from his lips as his eyes focus in and out. "What are you? You were dead, I saw you."

"It was all a lie created to make you stop looking for me. I didn't die. I was being held by Moartea."

Stepping sideways, I bypass the sword. Then I step forward as he watches me lay my hand on his chest. He brings his hand up and places it on mine.

As soon as our flesh meets I feel our bond run through my entire body. By the look on his face he feels it too. Our connection is back. His eyes are going from black to yellow. My blood, he took my blood in and it's awakened him.

"I love you so much. I'm so sorry I left you."

He still hasn't moved.

I wrap my arms around his waist and lay my head on his chest. His body is so stiff. I just squeeze myself to him tighter.

"But you were dead," he whispers.

"I promise you it wasn't real, and I'm here with you now."

"Sky?"

"Yeah?"

He comes to my ear. "Is it really you?"

"Yes, and Riley…..I really fucking love you." I pull back and smile up at him. I wipe the tears from his eyes.

The sword drops and he grabs me up tightly. "It's you, I smell you, I feel you, and I've missed you."

"I missed you too."

"Sky?"

"What?"

"I really fucking love you." He squeezes me tighter if that's even possible at this point.

One minute we're in the alley, and the next we're in front of the bunker. All six warriors are right behind us. Michael has Riley's sword and a very relieved face.

Riley looks up at them. "I could never have hurt her, but thank you for always protecting her."

We enter the bunker and it's quiet as we walk through. I see relieved faces. We come into our room together for the first time in five weeks. In this moment it feels as if no time has passed.

I throw my hands up, "So what happened here? My mate is a neat freak. There's no way he lives here."

He looks at the floor. "I haven't been here in weeks."

"I know. There's so much to talk about between you and I. But right now, I need sleep. Can we talk tomorrow?"

"Yes. I need a shower." He looks down at himself.

He gets in the shower and I climb into bed. I have no idea what to do about Joe. I have feelings for him. It's nothing like what

I have with Riley, but I let him in, and I now have this longing inside of me to see him.

A heaviness settles on the bed and I'm pulled into Riley's side. I wrap my arm around him and hold him tightly. At least he is home and I'm in his arms. We will deal with everything else later.

I wake up before Riley. I look over at the clock and see it's six in the evening. We've slept for over fourteen hour's straight, unmoving. It's probably a good thing--we both needed it. He looks so much better all cleaned up and shaved.

His eyes slowly open and he smiles. "I thought I dreamed you, but you're here." He touches my face. "How are you here?"

"Trevor, Michael, Brandon, and Joe kept searching for me."

"They found you?"

"No, Joe found me and took care of me."

"By himself?" he says eyes narrowed.

"Apparently they narrowed the search down to six locations. They hit four before dawn. They were going to search the other two the next evening. But Joe decided he had to hit one more on his own. That's when he found me. He took on over twenty Moartea to get to me. He brought me to his place in the city and took care of me. We barely made it inside, I could feel the burn of the sun on my skin."

"How long have you been back?"

"One day."

"And you came for me?"

"Of course, to bring you home to me."

He leans in and kisses me softly. "I should go to him and formally thank him for what he's done."

I look away from his gaze. I feel sick to my stomach. "He can't come here, and you can't go to him."

"Why?" Riley pulls my chin up.

"He came for me because he loves me. You were right about him." I try hard not to cry, but a tear betrays me as it escapes down my cheek. "I let him make love to me."

He closes his eyes and lies back on his pillow.

I feel his hurt and anger. "I'm sorry it happened. I was numb and could no longer feel our bond. I felt like you gave up on me, and just left me. I was empty inside and I only wished to feel something, anything, and he made me feel safe and loved."

"I'm a weak male. I told you I wasn't as strong as you are. I should have been the one to find you. I should have kept looking. Instead I gave up hope, only wishing to die myself. I was so mad at you for leaving me. So another was able to take you from me then?"

"If it was you that was taken from me, I wouldn't have gone crazy….I would have died." I touch his arm. "Nobody could ever take me away from you. I love you. I only want to be with you. I couldn't bear it if you weren't able to forgive me."

"You don't want him?"

"No. I want to forget all of that happened and just be with you."

He moves to me quickly.

"I love you with my whole heart, Riley. It's only you for me."

The kissing deepens and we begin to make love. As we take each other in it only strengthens the bond. I collapse on top of him and try to slide off, but he wraps me up in his arms and holds me tightly.

"From now on we fight together," he says as he caresses my back.

I sigh. "There's still so much to talk about."

We get up and start getting dressed.

He stops and sits on the edge of the bed. "I've done terrible things. Things that will hurt you deeply, which I can't take back."

"I know. I saw last night." I shrug.

He looks up at me.

"I also know it was not the first time." I shake my head. "Nobody told me anything. A Fallen Angel showed me. He loved to torture me of images of you with others."

He growls and his eyes flash red.

"Yep, there are new players in the game. Angels and witches working with Moartea. To exactly what end, I have no idea."

"You were held by a Fallen Angel?"

"Yes. In the next few days I will need to make a trip to the archives. I'll bring Brandon and report to you and Justin when we return."

"You've taken Brandon as your first?"

I turn around. "What?"

"Your guard, you've chosen him as your guard?"

"Uh, I guess so. Well, he's sort of chosen me. But yes, I feel safe with him. He did everything he could to protect me, he even sacrificed himself."

"And who would you take as your second?"

"Trevor." I shrug. "I don't take Brandon to guard me you know. He's back up, and my friend."

"I know, Luv." He stands and comes to me. "But in the current times we find ourselves in, you will have them with you when you leave."

"Fine. Not like I could keep either of them from me after everything that's happened anyways." I pull him to me. "Shut up and kiss me. I've decided you talk way too much."

He laughs.

"Riley, I want you to be careful around the council."

"What makes you say that?"

"I'm not sure right now, I just don't trust them."

He grabs my chin. "I need you to never speak those words again, do you understand me?"

I nod. His whole body is tense. I know I'm not supposed to question things like this, it's treason. But hello, I am the Queen right? "Alright."

He takes a deep breath and smiles. "I don't want to talk about anything but you being okay and in my arms." He leans in and kisses me again.

"I like it like this, when it's just you and me."

He smiles and touches my face. "It's always going to be just you and me, Luv, Sempiternal."